GOD BLESS THE CHILD

KRISTIN HUNTER

God Bless the Child

Howard University Press
Washington, D.C.   1986

Printed in the United States of America

Library of Congress Cataloging-in-Publication Data

Hunter, Kristin.
  God bless the child.

(Howard University Press library of contemporary literature)
  Reprint. Originally published: New York: Scribner, 1964.
  I. Title. II. Series.
PS3558.U483G6   1986   813'.54   86–21138
ISBN 0–88258–154–6

TO *Flora*

The author wishes to acknowledge her
gratitude to the John Hay Whitney Foundation
for the assistance which helped
make it possible to complete this book.

INTRODUCTION

Kristin Hunter's *God Bless the Child* (1964) tells a story almost as tragic as that of the life of Billie Holiday, whose best-known song gives the novel its title. Deluded by her grandmother's imaginative idealization of the life-style of wealthy white Americans, Rosalie (Rosie) Fleming determines to fulfill her own vision of the American Dream. Defying the racial and sexual conditions that have chained many Black women to poverty, Rosie vows to elevate herself and her family to the world described by her grandmother. After ruining her health in her efforts, she finally understands that her dream world is as roach-infested as was the world of poverty she seeks to escape.

I

God Bless the Child, Hunter's first novel, appeared during a period sometimes identified as the "Second Reconstruction" because of the important social gains made by Black Americans. During the ten years preceding 1964, many Black Americans had become increasingly determined to gain equality and increasingly optimistic about gaining their rightful share of the American Dream. In 1954, the U.S. Supreme Court declared laws to be unconstitutional if they allowed race to be used as a basis for denying Black children admission to certain public schools. Beginning in 1955, Black citizens in the South employed boycotts and protest marches to attack practices of segregation in public transportation; one year later, the Supreme Court judged the laws of Alabama to be unconstitutional when they required racial segregation on buses. In 1957, the U.S. Congress passed the first civil rights act since Reconstruction and created

Introduction

the Civil Rights Commission and the Civil Rights Division of the Department of Justice. In 1960, sit-ins throughout the South attacked practices of segregation in public eating places and other public facilities. One year later, the Supreme Court ruled against segregation in interstate transportation; two years after that decision, the Supreme Court declared the segregation laws of Birmingham, Alabama, to be unconstitutional. In that same year, the massive, interracial "March on Washington" to demand new civil rights laws reached its emotional climax with Martin Luther King, Jr.'s famous "I Have a Dream" speech. In 1964, the year in which *God Bless the Child* was published, Congress passed a Civil Rights Act, affording Blacks equal access to public facilities; one year later, Congress passed the Voting Rights Act.

If the era from 1955 to 1970 can be called a Second Reconstruction because of the political and social ferment of the times, it is equally appropriate to identify the decade of the 1960s as a "Second Black Renaissance" because of the flowering of Black culture. During the earlier Harlem Renaissance of the 1920s, the interest of many Americans probably focused on Black music, song, and dance more than on literature. Although interest in Black music had not lessened in the 1960s, America provided greater visibility for Black literature than it ever had before in the twentieth century. Curious to learn more about these Black Americans whose civil rights demonstrations appeared in the daily newspapers and on the evening news broadcasts, Americans turned to works of nonfiction by Blacks. Examples of these works are James Baldwin's *Notes of a Native Son* (1955), *Nobody Knows My Name* (1961), and *The Fire Next Time* (1963); Martin Luther King, Jr.'s *Stride Toward Freedom* (1958), *Strength to Love* (1963), *Why We Can't Wait* (1964), and *Where Do We Go From Here: Chaos or Community* (1967); Alex Haley's *The Autobiography of Malcolm X* (1965); and Claude Brown's autobiography, *Manchild in the Promised Land* (1965). Encouraged by the commercial success of such works, publishers solicited and accepted other nonfiction by Black scholars and creative writers.

Introduction

Just as publishers solicited nonfiction, so they sought fiction, drama, and poetry by Black writers. Lorraine Hansberry's *A Raisin in the Sun* (1959), which has had the longest run on Broadway of any play written by a Black, and LeRoi Jones's *Dutchman* (1964) earned critics' awards early in the 1960s. In 1965, a group of critics and authors selected Ralph Ellison's *Invisible Man* (1952) as the most distinguished American novel since World War II. By the end of the decade, Lonne Elder's *Ceremonies in Dark Old Men* (1968) had been nominated for a Pulitzer Prize in drama, and Charles Gordone's *No Place to Be Somebody* (1969) had won one.

Possibly inspired by the political and social ferment or by the interest of publishers and the reading public, Black dramatists, poets, and fiction writers who are well known in the 1980s made their debuts in the 1960s. Johara Amini, Ed Bullins, Lonne Elder, Mari Evans, Sarah Fabio, Nikki Giovanni, Charles Gordone, LeRoi Jones (now Amiri Baraka), Audre Lorde, Etheridge Knight, Don L. Lee (now Haki R. Madhubuti), Marvin X, Larry Neal, Conrad Kent Rivers, Sonia Sanchez, and Douglas Turner Ward comprise a representative list of well-known Black poets and dramatists who published their first books in the 1960s.

Black fiction writers experience greater difficulty attaining visibility than do poets and dramatists. Blacks may produce their dramas through Black amateur, semiprofessional, or professional theatrical groups; many of these groups developed during the 1960s. If they compile small collections of poetry, Black writers may absorb the cost of publication themselves, or they may find outlets through underfinanced Black publishers such as Broadside Press or Third World Press. For a novel or a collection of short stories, however, a Black writer, more often than not, must depend on a large commecial publisher that has a budget adequate to cover the costs of publication and distribution. (This series of reprints by Howard University Press attempts to ease the problem.) Despite this economic restriction, a significant number of well-known Black writers published their first novels during the 1960s or shortly before.

Introduction

A few years before *God Bless the Child* was published, large, white-owned presses had published Julian Mayfield's *The Hit* (1957), *The Long Night* (1958), and *The Grand Parade* (1961); Paule Marshall's *Brown Girl, Brownstones* (1959) and *Soul Clap Hands and Sing* (1961); John A. Williams's *The Angry Ones* (1960), *Night Song* (1961), and *Sissie* (1963); William Melvin Kelley's *A Different Drummer* (1962); and Mary Elizabeth Vroman's *Esther* (1963). After 1964, the honor roll of newly published novelists of the 1960s continued with such names as Barry Beckham, Hal Bennett, Robert Boles, Junius Edwards, Ronald Fair, Rosa Guy, Clarence Major, Gordon Parks, Charles Perry, Carlene Hatcher Polite, Ishmael Reed, Henry Van Dyke, Melvin Van Peebles, Margaret Walker (published earlier as a poet), John Edgar Wideman, Charles Wright, and Sarah Wright. This abbreviated list of Black writers who published their first books of fiction during the 1960s contains approximately double the number of Black writers who published their first books of fiction during the highly acclaimed Renaissance of the 1920s.

If some scholars are correct when they insist that important art emerges only from eras in which political, intellectual, and cultural activities support it, the decade of the 1960s was a significant one for a Black writer. Even though Kristin Hunter does not seem to reflect the political activity of her era in *God Bless the Child* as much as she does in later novels, she develops themes and issues that are significant to other Black creative writers of the late 1950s and early 1960s.

Perhaps encouraged by political developments, writers of the 1950s and early 1960s focused less on the issue of a white-dominated society and more on human problems. Their focus contrasts with that of Richard Wright, Chester Himes, Frank Yerby (in some short stories), Ann Petry, Willard Motley, William Gardner Smith, and other Black fiction writers of the late 1930s and 1940s who had armed their earliest publications to attack American oppression of Blacks and other impoverished Americans. Even though they wrote about Black protagonists, such authors as Ralph Ellison, James Baldwin, Louis Peterson, and Lorraine Hansberry, who preceded Hunter in the 1950s, addressed national and universal questions. Following the exposé of dehumanization of Americans by American institutions, the Black narrator-protagonist of *Invisible Man* asks his white readers, "Who knows but that, on the lower frequencies, I speak for you?" Certainly, racial bigotry and oppression affect all of the Black adults in *Go Tell It on the Mountain* (1952), but Baldwin focuses on the question of what draws people into a Christian church. Even though major problems of the Black teen-aged protagonist in Louis Peterson's drama *Take a Giant Step* (1953) result from a white teacher's bigotry and are intensified by the bigotry of white neighbors, the drama emphasizes problems common to male youths seeking maturity. Although audiences responded to the sensational issue of white neighborhood opposition to Black residents, Hansberry's *A Raisin in the Sun* concentrates primarily on the aspirations of a woman and her two children.

Like these works, *God Bless the Child* transcends the immediate problems of race; instead, it questions and negates the American Dream—as Kristin Hunter has stated ("Kristin Hunter," *Black Women Writers at Work*, Claudia Tate, ed., New York: Continuum, 1983, p. 84). In questioning the values of the American Dream, Hunter follows a trail set by earlier Black novelists. Even though Frank Yerby, in the late 1940s and 1950s, seems to glamorize the American Dream in his novels about white protagonists who crawled from their positions as impoverished outcasts to luxurious stations as wealthy insiders in nineteenth-century societies of the American South, Yerby states his conviction that such success results not from good character but from a ruthless willingness to exploit others. Ann Petry, in *The Street* (1947), delineates a Black woman who fails in her quest for the Dream that she has patterned after the materialistic success of her immoral and unhappy white employers. Early in the 1960s, such Blacks as Baldwin and Malcolm X denounced

Introduction

the individualism, materialism, and greed of the American Dream in tones that are intensified later in the decade by writers of the Black Arts movement.

Despite a few notable exceptions, such as Zora Neale Hurston in *Their Eyes Were Watching God* (1937), most Black women authors who wrote about Black women protagonists before 1950 concentrated on their adult lives. Even in *The Street* (1946), Ann Petry sketches only enough of Lutie Johnson's early life to enable a reader to learn something about her values, their source, and her reason for an early marriage. In *Brown Girl, Brownstones* (1959), however, Paule Marshall sensitively delineates the maturing of a woman from her teen years into young adulthood. In *Esther* (1963), Mary Elizabeth Vroman reveals her protagonist's intellectual and emotional development from the age of thirteen into her adult life. In *God Bless the Child*, Hunter follows Rosie Fleming from the age of seven until her death as a young woman. In the 1980s, when readers familiar with Black literature automatically think of such novels as Toni Morrison's *Sula* (1974) or Alice Walker's *The Color Purple* (1982), a story exploring the maturing of a Black woman does not seem unusual. In 1964, however, Hunter was among the earliest to trace such development.

In summary, although *God Bless the Child* does not focus on the exciting political events of the late 1950s and early 1960s, it reveals ways in which Kristin Hunter, consciously or unconsciously, followed the literary traditions of Black writers of her time and blazed trails that others would follow.

II

Kristin Hunter (Lattany) was born in 1931 and began writing at the age of fourteen (*Black Women Writers at Work*, p. 74). From 1946 to 1952, she was a writer for the *Pittsburgh Courier* (James A. Page, *Selected Black American Authors*, Boston: G.K. Hall, 1977, p. 131). After earning a Bachelor of Science degree in Education

Introduction

from the University of Pennsylvania in 1951, she supported herself with jobs in teaching and writing. In 1972 she accepted a teaching position at the University of Pennsylvania, where she is at present an instructor of English.

At one point in her life Hunter planned to alternate between writing books for adults and writing books for young adults (*Black Women Writers at Work*, p. 86). She has maintained a balance between the two types: *God Bless the Child* (1964), *The Landlord* (1966), *The Survivors* (1975), and *The Lakestown Rebellion* (1978) are novels for adults; and *The Soul Brothers and Sister Lou* (1968), *Boss Cat* (1971), *Guests in the Promised Land* (1973), and *Lou in the Limelight* (1981) are works of fiction for younger readers. She has won critical acclaim for both types of work. *God Bless the Child* won the Philadelphia Athenaeum Literary Award. *The Soul Brothers and Sister Lou* received the National Conference of Christians and Jews Mass Media Award, the Lewis Carroll Shelf Award, the Council on Interracial Books for Children Award, and the Red Fist and Silver Slate Pencil awards from Holland. *Guests in the Promised Land* earned the Christopher Award and the *Chicago Tribune* Book World Award for the best book for older children; it was nominated for a National Book Award. In addition, Hunter has received a Fund for the Republic Prize for the best television documentary script for 1956 ("Minority of One").

Hunter describes herself as an optimistic, realistic writer:

> Up until now one of my motivating forces has been to recreate the world I know into a world I wish I could be in. Hence my optimism and happy endings. . . . I think I've always been a realistic writer, and I'm not just into the agony and happiness of black women. I'm interested in the enormous and varied adaptations of black people to the distorting, terrifying restrictions of society. Maybe that's why there's cheer and humor in my books. I marvel at the many ways we, as black people, bend but do not break. (*Black Women Writers at Work*, pp. 83–84.)

In these words, she has aptly described themes of the three adult novels that she has written since *God Bless the Child*.

Introduction

Told from the perspective of white Elgar Enders, *The Landlord* (1966) satirically addresses social, political, and economic issues of Black life in a society controlled by whites. Although Hunter has particularized these issues according to the ways in which they gained the most visibility during the 1960s, one readily perceives their significance to Blacks throughout the last half of the twentieth century. Some readers of the 1980s might describe the narrator, Elgar Enders, as an egotistical, liberal, immature, WASP wimp. Believing himself to be superior to women, Blacks, and others because he is white, physically attractive, and wealthy, Elgar assumes that he is liberal because he does not dislike such people. (He even dates a woman whom he suspects to be part Black.) He is dominated by his millionaire father and insecurely entrusts his support, his sanity, and his survival to a psychiatrist whom he visits Monday through Friday during office hours and whom he calls during after-hours times of panic. To prove his manliness in business to his father, Elgar purchases an apartment building, expecting to experience no difficulty with his Black tenants.

Elgar, however, has never experienced a relationship with Blacks who know how to use wile to survive. Exotic, coquettish Fanny Copee, who copes by supplementing her earnings as a hairdresser by suing people, uses sexual seduction to make him ignore her rent and purchase expensive gifts for her and her two children; then she blackmails him. Marge Perkins, former well-known entertainer, uses the lure of food and housekeeping to convince him to permit her to live rent free. The elderly Cumbersons avoid paying rent by staying out of sight. Neither other tenants nor rent-collectors have seen them during the twenty-five years that they have lived in the building; when they leave, they take the apartment refrigerator and stove. Professor P. Eldridge Du Bois, formerly a self-proclaimed preacher and now president of a college consisting of one faculty member, himself, refuses to admit Elgar to collect the rent. To complete the complications, Charlie Copee, Fanny's husband, vacillates between Choctaw, African, and Afro-American identities and always perceives Elgar as the white foe who must be destroyed. Trying to develop an appropriate relationship with his tenants, Elgar unconsciously imitates the ambivalence of American foreign policy. At one moment he is the love seeker who wonders why people do not shower him with gratitude for his efforts to mold them as he believes they should be molded. At another, he is a stern, aloof white ruler demanding obedience and payment from inferiors.

Finally, Elgar attains maturity when he learns how to use his wealth to help others define themselves. Having received Elgar's financial support to open a very successful beauty saloon [*sic*] where free martinis are served, Fanny sells the business to return to her role as wife and mother. Deluded into believing that he has become white, her husband Charlie, a parody of Black and Native American militancy of the 1960s, repents his former abuse of whites and is committed to a mental institution. After Marge Perkins uses Elgar's support to regain her fame as a singer, she abandons her career to marry again. After receiving the funds to purchase a building for his college, the radical intellectual P. Eldridge Du Bois—we are led to believe— will become a successful educator despite the contrasts between him and his namesakes. Unlike Black Panther leader Eldridge Cleaver, he is homosexual; and unlike W. E. B. Du Bois, he is a confidence man. Elgar's most important use of money is to block one of the popular renovation schemes of the 1960s that allowed cities to condemn buildings rented to the poor so that real estate agents could acquire the land and build apartment buildings for the more affluent. Elgar purchases the property and provides attractively designed, appealing, low-rent housing. Thus, Elgar is seen to have attained his maturity, and Blacks have survived once again.

Hunter's adult novels after 1970 continue to articulate her earlier themes. Even though Hunter creates strong, dominant, independent-minded women in her adult novels, those who survive develop sustaining relationships either with men or with their children. In *The Survivors* (1975), Lena Ricks, who has left her alcoholic husband twenty years earlier, believes that she can survive without human companionship. When street-smart, thirteen-year-old survivor B. J. invades her life, Lena resists the intimacy that he demands. Even after learning that he is the son of her former husband, Lena attempts to maintain the privacy she cherished before his appearance. Finally, she admits that she needs him just as he needs her. These two wise survivors learn that survival can bring happiness if one is not alone.

In *The Lakestown Rebellion* (1978), as in *The Landlord*, Hunter satirically addresses contemporary political issues affecting Blacks. In the later novel, white political leaders plan to build a super highway that will destroy a Black community by dividing it. With no assistance from Mayor Abe Lakes, who considers himself superior to other Blacks and who covets white support for his political aspirations, the Blacks of Lakestown—like Brer Rabbit—use their guile to prevent the construction of the highway. In this novel, as in others, Hunter creates a dominant Black woman, Bella Lakes. Bella is determined to remind her husband that he is Black, but she will not abandon him if she can save him.

Whereas Hunter has emphasized the importance of her themes when she has discussed her novels, most adult readers will remember her humor, her memorable plots, and her even more memorable characters. Whether they are considered strong or weak, Fanny Copee, Charlie Copee, Marge Perkins, P. Eldridge Du Bois, Elgar Enders, Lena Ricks, B. J. Ricks, Bella Lakes, and Abe Lakes are remembered. Even when they behave outlandishly, they remind us of people we have known.

Although Hunter has often used satire to express social criticism indirectly in her novels for adults, she has addressed problems more directly in her novels for young adults. *The Soul Brothers and Sister Lou* (1968) reveals the bitterness of some Black youths, their difficulty in finding places to play, and their harassment by some white police.

The message in *Lou in the Limelight* (1981) even more somberly discourages Black youths who hope to attain fame and fortune in the entertainment world. Seeking riches, Lou and the "Soul Brothers" nearly succumb to prostitution, drugs, gambling, and the divisiveness and exploitation by white gangsters in the musical world. Even when guided by a well-meaning Black promoter, they experience problems of racial discrimination, inadequate financial support, and incompetent management. Finally, Lou gives up a musical career to remain in a small southern town with her new-found relatives.

In short, although Hunter satirizes the problems of Black life in the novels that she writes for adults, she clearly identifies those problems in novels that she writes for younger readers. She takes no chances that they will miss the horror.

III

God Bless the Child may be remembered longer than Hunter's other works even though that novel has neither earned as many awards as *The Soul Brothers and Sister Lou* nor had as much visibility as *The Landlord*, which was adapted into a movie. In some ways, *God Bless the Child* contrasts with her later works of fiction. For example, it lacks the characteristic happy ending of Hunter's novels. *God Bless the Child* shows how delusions and false dreams can destroy the dreamer.

Unlike *The Landlord*, *The Lakestown Rebellion*, and even the novels and stories for young adults, *God Bless the Child* does not seem to examine current topical problems of Blacks in society. Although whites stage a small protest when the first Black family moves into Rosie's new neighborhood, Rosie experiences no difficulty.

Some characteristics of the novel that foreshadow Hunter's later work may fail to attract attention. For example, I believe that few readers would describe *God Bless the Child* as a humorous work. Overwhelmed by the novel's intensity and misdirected by Hunter's fusion of comedy with pathos, readers—even careful readers—miss or forget the moments, the traces of satire and

Introduction

humor. Yet I suspect that Hunter has never written a more comic scene than that at the beginning of Chapter 24, when Rosie's underworld friends, carefully tutored by Rosie, attempt to behave in a manner that will please Granny and her three companions:

> Rosie's cream cheese sandwiches were magnificent and inedible. They were tinted pastel pink and green and arranged on a three-tiered crystal tray in patterns that were obviously not meant to be disturbed. After they had been passed and refused, the bar that silently churned its rainbows into the room was used for the serving of pale pink lemonade and bright green Kool-Aid.
>
> As each couple arrived, Rosie led them to Granny's chair for elaborate introductions, then separated them into the seating arrangement she had designed. Soon an uncomfortable row of girls sat facing an uneasy row of men.
>
> Rosie darted restlessly from background to foreground, harvesting invisible bits of litter from the floor, feeding the hi-fi a steady diet of Nelson Eddy and Jeanette MacDonald, and urging liquids and sandwiches on her underworld friends, who all strove heroically to balance cut-glass cups and plates and lacy napkins on their knees with grace. The only topics permitted for general discussion were the state of your health and the weather. Men were also allowed to exchange low comments about sports with their neighbors, and women might engage, if they wished, in whispered discussions of clothes. Both sexes were supposed to cough discreetly, at regular intervals, into elegant handkerchiefs.
>
> The three old ladies who surrounded Granny, sipping daintily and sighing and rustling their fans, were the only ones who seemed to be enjoying themselves. Everyone else seemed afflicted by a terrible itch. They looked about desperately, but no opportunities for scratching were in sight. As the minutes creaked along, the old ladies' fans flew more and more furiously, whipping up the air like egg white until it was stiff with discomfort. The little smile on Granny's face grew broader and broader. Twenty people crossed and uncrossed their legs thirty times.
>
> Of all the young people, only Dolly seemed comfortable within the constraints Rosie had imposed. She sat with the calm propriety of a nun, hands resting quietly in her lap. On her right Ginger and Amber tugged nervously at identical tight satin dresses which kept doing exactly what they had been designed to do, ride high above the knee. On her left Bettina, the shapely stripper from The Cotton Club, suddenly ashamed of the endowment that

Introduction

earned her salary, seemed to be trying to wriggle down lower into her low-cut dress.

Even if it were her only work, *God Bless the Child* would signal Kristin Hunter's importance as a novelist, not merely because of the theme nor even because of the realistic dialogue but because of the characterizations. Certainly, the theme of *God Bless the Child* is important, but earlier writers, Black and white, have revealed how destruction can ensue from a deluded quest for a false American Dream. Similarly, even though her realistic dialogue differentiates her characters, other writers write dialogue just as realistic as hers.

The combination of theme and dialogue with characterization, however, elevates the novel. Each character seems to have a memorable personality, biography, and function. This memorable quality is seen even in the fringe characters, those wh' appear on only a few pages. One is the incompetent, alcoholic Miltie Newton, who chooses to die rather than to betray Rosie. Pockets Robinson, who preaches salvation of the race through business, pretends to be a powerful numbers man and real estate agent; but he is finally revealed to be little more than a "pet monkey" of the white man who controls him and tosses him crumbs. Shadow, the pimp, haunts Rosie from the age of seven, when she allows a white merchant to feel her legs, until her adult life, when, seeking an abortion, she comprehends that Shadow is Destruction and Death.

The minor characters in the novel are significant because of their great influence on Rosie. Benny, who seems to dominate the numbers racket, tries to teach Rosie that self-protection is the first law of life; finally, Bennie reveals that he is controlled by the Mafia just as firmly as he controls Pockets and other Blacks. Solomon Schwartz is a kindly Jewish merchant who, troubled by his own family, offers respect and paternal love that Rosie abuses and rejects.

The major characters of the novel, if portrayed in other works, might seem minor. In *God Bless the Child*, however, their stories and their relationships to Rosie make them memorable.

Introduction

Dolly Diaz, Rosie's closest friend, resents but needs her own sheltered middle-class life. To prove herself different from her snobbish, class-conscious mother, Dolly seeks companionship with Rosie and Rosie's mother. Dolly finally realizes, however, that her desire to rebel against her own class has caused her to romanticize Rosie and ignore the weaknesses in Rosie's lifestyle. Even though Dolly enjoys living vicariously through Rosie, she can never imitate Rosie's bold and reckless actions.

Orphaned at an early age, Tommy Tucker takes his name from a nursery rhyme that Rosie whispers to him in school. Reared as a "state child" and exploited by his foster parents, Tucker, who needs no one, unsentimentally exploits everyone he can as he strives for illegal or legal success. After he has betrayed Rosie while living illegally as a numbers man, he subsequently tries to marry Dolly to complete a facade of respectability for his new life outside of crime.

Larnie Bell is an ambitious, athletic, and musically talented Black man. The most promising person of Rosie's generation, Larnie loses his opportunity to earn a college degree because of his lack of self-confidence and his relationship with an aggressive white college girl who seduces him. Despite the hopes of Rosie's mother that Larnie can help Rosie, he weakens progressively, moves in with Rosie, and becomes another economic and emotional dependent whom she must support. Larnie finally reaches manhood but much too late to save Rosie.

Regina (Queenie) Fleming is Rosie's mother. Believing that sex is "eating . . . breathing . . . living," she married a man despised by her mother, who succeeds in forcing him to leave four years after Rosie's birth. Trying to compel Rosie to be strong and independent, Queenie drives her into the arms of Granny. Granny spoils Rosie and replaces Queenie's practical advice with her own romantic ideals. Ironically, however, whereas Rosie matures into a woman unwilling to depend upon anyone, Queenie cannot follow her own advice: "They [men like Tucker] the sweetest thing in life. Have a good time with

'em. But don't depend on 'em for nothin'. Colored women has
to shift for themselves."

The two most important characters are Lourinda (Granny)
Huggs, the unsuspected antagonist, and Rosie, the protagonist.
Granny spoils Rosie with gifts that the seven-year-old child
cannot perceive as trinkets, stolen from or discarded by Granny's
employers, who no longer value them. She creates for Rosie a
dream world of white people, who live luxuriously in palaces.
Unable to comprehend that Queenie and Rosie have spent their
lives in roach-infested rooms participating only vicariously in
her world of luxury, Granny demands that her daughter and
granddaughter marry Black Prince Charmings. Glorying in the
life that she cannot afford for Queenie and Rosie, unable to
admire the true worth of a Larnie above the glitter of a Tucker,
and blind to the fact that the economic and emotional failures
of the idealized whites portends possible failure for their
imitators, Granny is simultaneously pitiful and monstrous. She
would be pitiable if she injured only herself; but she becomes,
in Hunter's hands, a vain, selfish woman who infects Rosie with
her disease and then drains the life from her.

The protagonist is Rosie, who learns independence as a child.
Defending her friend Dolly against bullies, seven-year-old Rosie
proves to herself that she can endure pain. What she never
learns or believes, however, is that people can love her. As
Rosie ages (Queenie argues that she fails to mature), she endures
the pain—two full-time jobs as a salesclerk and a waitress, a
numbers racket on the side, and debts that cannot be paid—to
buy extravagant luxuries for herself, her family, and her friends,
possessions she hopes will soothe her and win their love:

> Rosie had bills at nearly every store, but she had just remembered
> one charge account that had been idle for months. Maybe she
> couldn't replace the money she had lost that day—but she could
> spend it, and that was the next best thing.
> Spending money was a need more ferocious than sex, more
> urgent than hunger, which came down on her with predictable
> regularity—about every two weeks—as well as whenever things

Introduction

went wrong. Buying necessities was no good. Lots of money had to be spent on things she didn't need, and some had to be lavishly wasted before she could breathe again.

When she swept past the doorman at the store's entrance she felt a surge of lust at the glittering counters, the racks hung with shadowy silken mysteries, the hushed alcoves where saleswomen tiptoed and beckoned. All the things were spread out, inviting her to possess them. Her eyes roved restlessly; her mouth tasted hot and salty. She hurried through the store as if pursued because she had so little time in which to touch and see everything.

When she swept out three hours later with two pairs of shoes, a cashmere sweater, a rayon slip for Mom, and a silk dress and a pint of cologne and six lace handkerchiefs for Granny, she felt purged and at peace. She was happy again, and her strength was restored. If necessary, she could now wait tables for six straight shifts at Benny's.

The gifts, however, do not help her; for Rosie, certain that no one can love her, distrusts anyone who professes love and offers help. Too late, the termites in her "palace" teach her the fallacy of her materialistic dream:

One thing was clear: she had fought and clawed her way to the place where she wanted to be, only to see it crumble into the same ruins she had left behind. . . . The question was: . . . Had it existed only in her imagination—this gay, glamorous world inhabited by beautiful, perfect people . . .? . . . The question was: *Did rich white people have roaches too?*

Thus Kristin Hunter added her voice to the voices of others in the 1960s who observed the need to replace the greed and materialism of the American Dream.

Darwin T. Turner
University of Iowa
March 1986

ONE

Crusts of Bread and Such

Seems like that bus just don't want to get here today, and me with my feet hurtin' to beat the band.

Mrs. Lourinda Baxter Huggs shifted her weight and squinted down Madison Drive toward the place the bus would come from if one were coming. A few sleek cars glided past her, making less disturbance than the fingers of the wind in the trees, but of a bus there was no sign.

And me with two shopping bags today instead of one.

Thinking of what was in that extra bag, Lourinda smiled. 'Course it wasn't as fine as those handmade, real-hair china dolls Miss Emilie's daddy used to get her from Germany, but it was good-sized. That pinafore outfit was right cute even if it was machine-made. It should give Rosalie a deal of pleasure, especially since she wouldn't have to know, say, exactly how her grandmother came by it.

That snippy little white child had too many dolls for her own good, anyway. Too many mothers, too—her mother Emilie, her grandmother Helen, both interfering with Lourinda's ways of raising her.

No wonder the child acted up like she'd done this morning. Throwing the doll in Lourinda's face and screaming, "Take that to Rosie! I don't care if she never comes!" All because Rosie wasn't coming to her birthday party.

"Next year, dear. I'm sure she'll come next year." That was Emilie, babbling to her child.

"Not next year or any other year. Facts are facts, Emilie." Miss Helen, the only one in the family with any sense it seemed besides Lourinda, had motioned Lourinda to follow her.

"Apparently you have talked so much about your granddaughter, Iris would rather be with Rosie than with anyone else in the world."

God Bless the Child

Lourinda had lost her temper then, an indulgence she rarely allowed herself around her white folks. No one knew better than Lourinda that the more white folks thought you belonged to them, the more they really belonged to you. But this time she forgot and spoke right up. "Well you tell me how I'm gonna stop talkin' about Rosie, when all that Iris asks me is 'How's Rosie?' and 'What's Rosie doin' today?' and 'What she do yesterday?' and 'When she comin' to see me?'"

"The next time she asks you about Rosie, you will change the subject. You may keep the doll, Lourinda. I hope your granddaughter enjoys it."

Well.

She'd never thought, in the old days Down Home, that it would come to this. Raised up with Miss Helen Livesey she'd been. Raised her child Emilie same way she'd raised her own child Queenie—strict by the book, no loving without grumbling, and both of them knowing the back of her hand.

And now both of them turning out to be fools. Emilie covering all the good stone floors and wooden cabinets in the pantry and kitchen with common congoleum, like she didn't have good sense. And proving it by her marriage. She didn't know the difference between a Virginia gentleman and a Louisiana gambler, any more than she could tell Venice many flower glass from five and dime ceramic.

Well, the Lord knew it wasn't Lourinda's fault. She'd certainly tried to bring the girl up right. She'd suffered and prayed and struggled right along with all the Liveseys, from Helen's marriage and her move North to Emilie's marriage and the birth of *her* child. For forty years she'd supported Hoover and hated Roosevelt; refused Heinz's and insisted on S.S. Pierce; snubbed the Italian help and bobbed her head to the English ones.

She felt she'd had a perfect right, this morning, to soothe her hurt by helping herself to that many flower bowl—though sometimes she wondered why she bothered, the way things always got smashed at Queenie's—and slipping it into her bag underneath the doll. Like everything in the house, it was as much hers as

4

theirs. She'd had a part in choosing every thread of fabric and every splinter of furniture; she'd measured for curtains, shopped for linens, and needlepointed the chairs and footstools in the upstairs sitting room herself.

Lourinda smiled as she thought of the doorman at the linen shop holding the door for her as she swept in.

"Good *afternoon,* Mrs. Huggs."

The man behind the counter, bowing low.

"Always a pleasure, Mrs. Huggs. What can we do for you today?"

"Afternoon. Need new sheets for the guest rooms. Blue room, green room, yellow room, monograms to match. No, don't show me that cheap stuff. Take that trash away."

"Yes, Mrs. Huggs. Whatever you say." Bowing again as he walked away backward.

Yes, at first the tradespeople had thought her an ignorant old colored woman. But they soon found out that she knew quality and would pay what it was worth and not one cent more. And that her signature was good for payment from one of the country's largest fortunes.

They would never find out that she did not know how to write anything but her name.

Lourinda glanced over her shoulder and saw the new assistant gardener, one of those greasy Eyetalians, setting in a row of burlapped shrubs. Those rambling roses were too close to the house; they would spread like the chicken pox and block the side entryway. She started off to tell him so, then thought better of it.

Time was, nothing was decided without asking Lourinda. "Lourinda, do you think this mirror will do in the upstairs hall?" "Lourinda, do you prefer the butter from Reynolds Dairies or from MacIntyre's?" "Lourinda, what do you think of this new young man Emilie's picked for herself?"

But now no one stopped to ask Lourinda's opinion. Once you got old, nobody had any use for you, and the whole world passed you by. Oh, it was hard, the ingratefulness of your own children. Especially with the heartbreak of them turning out wrong,

5

marrying wrong, marrying trash and turning common. Queenie letting Rosie grow up anyhow while she was laying around the apartment drinking or laying up in bed with men she'd picked up in bars. How had she gone bad? Born bad was all. Born to take up with all kinds of ragtag trash and go from coarse talk and painted lips to drink and the Devil.

But Rosie was different.

From the day she was born seven years ago, Lourinda's grandchild was a little fighter. Maybe she was a bit too dark, but she had Lourinda's own spirit and quality.

They say sometimes the Devil skips a generation. It was a consoling thought, and Lourinda began to sing in her sweet silvery voice—

> *"You must be*
> *Born again,*
> *O yes you must be*
> *Born again—"*

as she paced up and down past the bus stop. She broke off with a sigh, thinking, Someday I'm gonna take my hand to that little Iris's bottom like I took it to her mother's, and then—

But she stopped, not knowing when it had happened, knowing only that her position in the white family had changed. She had a vision of the way it would end—with her beating Rosie instead.

This thought was too much to endure for long, and Lourinda turned her eyes to the side yard again. An arc of water announced that Dudley the chauffeur was washing the Rolls. She squinted down the street again, this time carelessly, half hoping no bus would appear. She was not disappointed.

That Dudley, she thought contemptuously as she picked up her bags and started toward the garage, that Dudley got nothing to do all day but shine them cars. Time he earned his living before he gets too lazy for his own good.

The quick little gates of her mind snapped open and shut, sorting, examining, rejecting the excuses that would get her chauffeured to Queenie's. —Taking groceries to a poor colored

family for one of Miss Emilie's charities—no, she had used that
one last week. —Fell off a ladder while I was dusting the books in
the library this morning and twisted my ankle, and Miss Helen
said for you to—no, this would not do, he had already looked up
with his vacant poorwhite gaze and seen her not limping but
walking lightly, with her strong small precise step, toward him.

And then, indignantly: Why bother saying anything at all? He
may be white but he's just field help and he's got no business
knowing what goes on inside the house.

"Twelve-Oh-One Pearl Street," she said, flinging the bags and
the address at him together, as she would fling them at any paid
taxi driver.

And soon she was riding in the back of the limousine, flicking
the little blinds shut against the squalid sights of the neighborhood she could never call *home*.

2

"Queenie, you got my Number Two irons?"

A hissing cloud of steam pungent with burning hair rose from
each of the six four-foot-square cubicles in Sophie's Beauty
Salon.

A handsome, heavy bronze woman emerged from one of them,
wiping the sweat drops from her shining forehead and revealing
a large damp halfmoon under the arm of her white uniform.

"No, I ain't got your Number Twos, or your Number Ones
either, Lottie Mae. Can't you keep track of your own things?"

"I'm sorry, Queenie," the skinny young operator next door
said. "I just found 'em this second. Here, underneath my *True
Love* magazine."

"Well, next time look before you holler, Lottie Mae. That's
the third time you've called me out for somethin' in the last half
hour. While I'm looking for your things, my customer's hair is
curlin' up and chokin' her to death."

Queenie returned to her booth. Her hand poised above a gorgeous row of jars—pink, gold, blue, orange, green—she addressed the large fuzzy cloud that awaited her.

"Cream press or regular, Miss Delaney?"

"Oh, give me the cream, Queenie," a muffled voice answered. "And just press it light."

Queenie hesitated. This was a delicate matter. "Well, you know you got a fairly heavy suit of hair, Miss Delaney. Light pressing might not hold up so good."

The cloud tipped back suddenly, revealing an indignant cocoa-colored face. "You think I don't know what kind of hair's been growin' on my head for thirty years?"

"Yes ma'am." The customer was always right, even if it were closer to fifty years. "You're lucky to have such fine, healthy hair. Had a lady in here this morning, hair falling out in patches, would give anything to have hair like you."

The cloud grunted an acknowledgment, neither angry nor quite pacified, and Queenie went to work with subtle skill to give this woman what she needed rather than what she wanted, and keep her from knowing the difference. The customer was always right, even if she were the kind who would come back in three days complaining and demanding a free retrace—always right for four dollars, sixty cents out of each dollar, two dollars and forty cents for two hours' hot, hard work.

If only she could luck up on a nice man who worked steady. Or some rich white folks like the ones her mother worked for. Dreaming, Queenie let the hot comb rest in a patch of damp hair. Her customer squealed as the steam reached her scalp.

"Excuse me, Miss Delaney." Queenie was suddenly awake. Better dream about hitting the number than either of those things. The odds were better. In this fast town, she was old at thirty-five, and the only men she could get were trifling, lying ones like Roscoe. Men who worked steady were all for skinny little chippies. And rich white folks were all for themselves, leaving you nothing but their kind remembrances. She had only to think of her mother's wasted life of devotion to know *that*.

Crusts of Bread and Such

Anger flashed through her at the thought of her mother, living in a castle without being able to help Queenie pay the rent on the matchbox where she had to bring up her daughter. And having the nerve to put on airs when she came to see them.

The curd of resentment that always rested somewhere in Queenie's chest jiggled, expelling a sour bubble left over from lunch, the greasy hoagie gobbled standing up, between customers, with one hand kept busy plucking stray hairs from the food. Her working hand jerked.

"Ow!" her customer exclaimed. "You tryin' to kill me, fool?"

"Well, why don't you hold still, bitch?" Queenie heard herself growl.

"I'm getting out of here! I don't have to pay my good money to be scarred for life and insulted too! I'll take my business someplace where they got some manners and respect! Did you hear what she called me, Miss Sophie? Did you? Well, ask her! Just ask her!"

The door slammed. Miss Delaney went down the street, looking like an inverted turkey-feather duster with two skinny brown handles instead of one. Sophie succeeded only in retrieving the cotton cape which belonged to the linen-supply house, and that just as her customer passed out of her door forever.

The little woman who owned the shop stormed into Queenie's booth.

"Maybe you don't need a job here. Maybe with those real pearl earrings you wear, you can afford to stay home all day and give yourself airs. Well, if you don't need to work, I sure don't need you. I don't need anybody who can't treat my customers with respect."

The earrings weren't real, they were castoffs from her mother's white folks, but Queenie didn't mention that. She laughed. "Respect? For that black whore? You know who her old man is? A thief. A dealer in hot wrist watches."

Lottie Mae, wriggling with excitement, had come into Queenie's booth behind Sophie. "Yeah," she said. "I bought one of them watches off of him myself. It stopped runnin' in two

9

hours. Maybe that watch was hot once, but it was so old, it had plenty time to cool off."

"You get back to work," Sophie told the girl. "And *you*—don't be talking about the color of my customers, or their love life, neither. All I care about is the color of their money, and I don't care where they gets it."

That remark about color had been unfortunate. Sophie was so black she glowed purple in her white uniform. "I'm sorry, Sophie," Queenie said.

"Mrs. Sellems to you. I guess maybe you don't need to work. I guess maybe you don't have responsibilities like I do."

Queenie swallowed the curd. It always gagged her at times like these. "Mrs. Sellems, I do have responsibilities, you know I do. I have rent to pay and clothes to put on my little girl's back."

"Yeah? Well you sure don't think about her much. I got a little girl myself, and she says your child's out of school more'n she's in. She wasn't there Monday or Tuesday, and yesterday I saw her myself, running up the Avenue like some little barefoot urchin. My Cecily said last night Miss Jenkins is gonna send the truancy officer after Rosie Fleming if she doesn't come in by Monday."

Queenie was already half out of her uniform.

Sophie's little eyes burned crimson. "Now what, Miss Independent? You worked enough for one day? What about those clothes you got to put on your Rosie's back?"

"I got to go home and tan her hide first. Then I'll put some clothes on it," Queenie said, buttoning her blouse. "I ain't like some of these women who's so money-mad they neglect their children."

"Oh, so I'm money-mad!"

"I didn't say that, Mrs. Sellems."

"Well, I got a little girl who goes to school regular and looks nice and minds the teacher, too. And what's more, I got a husband. I may be money-mad, but I don't wear fancy real pearl earrings to work."

"If I was ugly as you, I wouldn't wear earrings either!"

Queenie got out of the shop fast, to keep from saying more.
But not fast enough to miss hearing Sophie say, "Did you hear
that? I swear, I hope I die before I hire another of these half-
white bitches!"

But she won't fire me, Queenie thought proudly. I'm a good
hairdresser. I got my own following. I bring twenty customers
into any shop where I work, and if I had my own shop, I'd have
forty.

In this world, it ain't an easy job, making black women think
they're beautiful. It's a real talent. Even if I do get too mad and
disgusted to work at it sometimes.

3

The cockroaches came crawling out of the cracks in the walls
and the ceiling and the moldings and the little crevices under
the edges of the linoleum. Three generations of cockroaches, all
sizes: long, skinny granddaddy cockroaches and fat mama cockroaches and baby cockroaches smaller than ants. They had fed
on the grease that glazed the kitchen walls and now they marched,
plump and stupefied, across the counter where Rosie was making
her breakfast.

The counter was three feet high and eighteen inches deep.
Rosie could just reach the back of it by standing on tiptoe. She
raised both hands and came down on the marching column of
baby cockroaches, killing four in one smash. Another quick smash
caught two more babies at the end of the rapidly retreating
column. From the corner of her eye she saw the giant granddaddy
of them all scurry from the ceiling and rush down the wall. She
rocked on tiptoe, waiting, gathering strength.

Now he was within reach. Her palm came down on him just as
he was about to dart inside the cupboard.

"Got the bastard," she said.

God Bless the Child

She opened a drawer, ignoring the sudden flurry of movement inside, and took out a pencil and the notebook that said:

"Rosalie Fleming.

My Book."

She wrote the date and, beside it, the number 10, then carefully put book and pencil away. Seven babies and a big one who was worth three points. Not a bad morning. Rosie decided to stay home from school and kill roaches all day.

That had really been a big bastard. Maybe he was worth four points. Debating, she looked at the counter where the legs were waving feebly, then at her palm where a large stain still trembled with cockroachy life. Not so big after all. She brushed the shell of the insect aside and looked into the pot to see what Mom had left.

Grits. She wrinkled her nose. Burned at the edges and stuck to the pot. She put a finger in, drew out a gob, tasted. Her stomach heaved up to her chest and dropped down again. She put the lid back hastily and reached for the box of Rice Krispies. Rosie disliked Rice Krispies because they reminded her of roach eggs but she liked burned grits even less.

She poured a big dish of cereal, dumped the entire contents of the sugar bowl on top, and went to the ice box to look for milk. There hadn't been any milk for a month, so why look for it now, like a damn fool? Rosie laughed out loud. There was the little tin of evaporated milk Mom used in coffee, though. Trickling it into a glass of water gave her a nice white liquid to pour over the cereal. She sat down at the table and ate, jumping up often with her mouth full to see whether any more roaches had ventured out of the walls. By the time the bowl was half empty she had killed four more. One was pretty big. She wrote a large 5 in her notebook before she ran to the bedroom to see if Mom had left any cigarettes lying around.

Mom's big rumpled bed had stockings in it, and a long lacy thing, and a man's sock, and droppings of ashes and lots of hairpins, but no cigarettes. Rosie leaped on it, delving everywhere with quick fingers, then scrambled away because she was sinking into the softness of it and suffocating in the overwhelming smell of Mom, a rich sweet blend of flesh and whiskey and perfume.

Over in the corner Rosie's cot stood the way she had left it the last time, the blanket drawn up stiffly over the pillow. That had been a week ago. Uncle Roscoe had been coming around regular the last few nights, and when that happened, Rosie slept on the day bed in Granny's room. As she had done before to make way for Uncle Nathaniel and Uncle Harrison and Uncle John. Ever since Rosie could remember, she had been displaced by a dim procession of uncles; mysterious creatures of the night, never seen in the daytime. Who, she had known almost from the beginning in spite of Granny's gentle deception, were not uncles at all.

Rosie shrugged and tossed her head so hard one of her wiry plaits came undone. She didn't like sleeping in here anyway, except that it gave her a chance to see where Mom put her cigarettes. She flung open a dresser drawer and immediately forgot what she had been looking for.

For here was a shiny red dress that hung to the floor; Rosie bunched it at her waist, secured it with a giant safety pin. And a pair of gunmetal shoes with pointed toes, and a green velvet bolero with gold fringes, and a lavender cloud to throw around her shoulders. And millions and millions of beads. Rosie put them all on, screwed dangling gold hoops into her ears, pinned a paper rose into one of her stiff pigtails. Mom hated for anyone to mess in her dresser drawer. Knowing it was forbidden only increased Rosie's excitement. Working fast, for Mom might get home any minute, she grabbed a deep purple lipstick and smeared it on. At last she dared to look.

The vision in the mirror was not Rosie Fleming. It was Missiris, Madam Queen in the house where Granny worked, Princess in all the fairy tales Rosie was just learning to read. Missiris wore long red skirts and lots of beads and bangles and silk scarves and clinking earrings. Missiris was spoiled rotten because she had a sweet mother named Missemilie and a beautiful grandmother called Misshelen. Missiris had her meals brought to her on silver trays, and she had a magic carpet that flew her out the window. Zoom! And when Madam Queen Princess Miss-iris walked down the street and swished her skirts everyone stepped out of her way. Swish! Rosie stamped her feet and the crowds made way for her. Crowds of frightened roaches, scurrying under the bedroom linoleum. Swish!

Crash! A splintering of glass, a spreading odor of perfume, a large white stain on Mom's dresser. Rosie mopped frantically with the hem of her skirt. Soon most of the damage was hidden. But when she looked at the dress it was bunched and wrinkled and stained. And reeking of perfume.

She struggled for five minutes to get the pin undone, her mouth stuffed with chiffon and velvet to keep them from hanging in her way. When the pin finally gave, Rosie gave with it. Sprawled on the floor, she heard the fumbling of a key in the lock down front and Mom's slow heavy tread on the stairs.

Clump. Clump. At the fifth clump the jewelry was off and in a heap at the bottom of the drawer. Clump. At the seventh the dress was stuffed in a ball beside it. Clump. At the tenth the shoes were back where they belonged. Clump. The bolero and the scarf were piled beside them. Clump. Slam the drawer. Clump. Rosie was glad they had the Third Floor Rear.

She looked up innocently as her mother entered the bedroom. Why was Mom advancing angrily toward her, seizing her by the hair, whirling her to face the mirror? She had hidden everything.

Except for the vivid smears of violet on a face that now undeniably belonged to Rosie Fleming. And the paper rose, bobbing insolently on a wiry stem.

"Spillin' my best perfume! Messin' up my new clothes!

"When you gonna learn my things don't belong to you? Do I have to lock this room? And why aren't you in school? What am I gonna do to make you mind?

"I work two months to pay for that dress and you mess it up before I get a chance to wear it! Standin' on my feet in that shop all day and then when I get home—"

Rosie shut her eyes tightly and waited for the blow. It did not come. Instead, the grip in her hair relaxed and Rosie slipped free.

"—when I get home I'm too tired to beat you." Harsh, strangled sobs came from Mom. She flung her heavy body on the bed.

For a moment Rosie felt sorry for Mom and wished she could feel more for the fleshy, exhausted woman on the bed. The word, "Mom," was a hard lump of coal in her throat. She moved toward the bed and tried to make it come out.

Mom's arm rose up, struck Rosie's cheek a glancing backhanded blow that did not hurt because it had defeated itself in mid-air. "Keep your greedy little fingers out of my things. Get your own." The arm dropped tiredly. "I don't know how to make you mind. Every time my back is turned you do the opposite of what I say. Now get out of here and leave me alone. Maybe your grandmother knows what to do with you. I don't no more."

Rosie tried to go on feeling sorry for Mom, but she was never able to feel sorry about anything very long. Especially when it was Thursday and Granny was coming home.

She ran to the window and looked down at the street. A long, shiny black car pulled up. A tall man in a blue uniform got out and opened the door.

And Granny, proud and dainty as a queen, stepped out.

Rosie ran down the three flights of stairs and almost collided with Granny, who stood in the vestibule as if she had never been there before and was just visiting. Her face was screwed up in the way that meant she smelled something bad, or disliked something enough to pretend it smelled bad.

The hallway did smell bad, now that Rosie noticed it. The Robinsons were cooking greens and the rank odor almost but not quite covered the stink of the Longs' toilet which had backed up again yesterday. The beauty shop in the basement contributed a pungency of burned hair. These smells were everywhere in the house. They seeped in through the walls and the floors and even the windows, for they were the smells of the neighborhood. They were not so bad in the apartment, but Rosie had heard Mom say they knocked you over in the hall.

Somehow it was all right for Rosie and Mom to smell these odors, but Granny was different. Granny did not live here; she lived across town in a white palace with marble stairs and crystal fountains, and when she came to be with them on her Thursdays and every-other-weekends, she was company. Rosie tried to hurry Granny upstairs. She took one of the shopping bags from her arms.

"What's in here, Granny?" she asked, skipping ahead up the stairs. "What'd you bring me?"

"Laros to catch meddlers," the old lady said behind her. "How many times I told you it's not polite to ask for presents?"

"I'm sorry," Rosie said.

Granny's shopping bag was a magic container better than Pandora's box. On top, always, were a rolled-up black uniform and a neatly folded white apron and a pair of low-heeled black shoes. And a black umbrella in case of rain. Under these things were hidden the surprises.

There was always something good to eat—a slice of cake starred with raisins, vanilla cookies frosted in snowdrifts, a bag of speckled rolls, the wings and legs of strange, sweet-fleshed fowl. Once there had been pickled beets and, another time, little salty sandwiches which Granny had said contained fish eggs. Rosie had not liked them, but she had eaten them all because they were wonderful.

Sometimes there were other surprises too. A paper fan painted with pale flowers and butterflies, from Japan. A faded blue silk sash with a huge black rose at one end. A tiny train made of real spools of colored thread with little buttons for wheels. A pile of magazines in which beautiful ladies and gentlemen with stiff backs paraded on pretty sidewalks or in meadows filled with horses. Twice a year there were Missiris's dresses, all colors, with stiff skirts and lace collars and tiny velvet bows.

But the last two times these had been too small for Rosie. Mom always put them away with a promise to fix them but somehow she never got around to it. Now Rosie made herself forget the dresses because she knew she would never wear them. She never looked at them. But sometimes when she got tired of everything else she would open Mom's closet and reach under the wrapper that kept off dust and run her hand quickly over lace and velvet and silk.

"Wait!" Granny commanded as soon as they were inside. Rosie stopped. "What you been doin' to your hair?" Granny's hand caught the offending pigtail, skewered it into place. "You look like somebody's orphan. You don't look like no grandchild of mine. If you don't learn how to comb that kitchen—"

Rosie turned a mischievous face, removing her nape from Granny's scrutiny. "What you gonna do, Granny?"

"I'm gonna tell Bo Ditley to come and get you."

Rosie giggled. Bo Ditley was the name of the neighborhood tramp, a ragged, hulking monster who slept in alleys, but by now she knew that every tramp was called Bo Ditley to frighten children.

Granny smiled. "Queenie," she called. "Queenie! Don't you think it's time you started touchin' up this child's head?"

Mom came in in her corset, a glass of whiskey in her hand. She was sulky and mean, and that meant she had only had Two or Three. In another hour she would be at Six or Seven. The day would be a blur in her memory, and she would be gay and full of fun.

Rosie liked Mom best when she'd had Six or Seven. But Granny liked her least of all then.

"You hear me, Queenie? What you gonna do about this child's head?"

"I might take them irons and split it open," Mom said calmly. "I like to died today when I came in and saw what she did to my new red dress."

She hadn't had time for more than One, Rosie decided.

"You don't have to make no curls," Granny went on, smoothing Rosie's hand. "Just a nice straight press all over."

"I'll straight-press her behind," Mom said. "And krokonol it, too."

"Regina, that's no way to talk in front of the child."

"I'll talk to her any way I please. You know that little monkey ain't been in school one day this week? If you don't whip her, I will."

Granny hated unpleasantness, so she changed the subject. "What do we have for dinner?"

"Chinese food on the table," Mom said, pointing, and pouring herself another drink. "Help yourself."

Granny touched the cardboard carton with one reluctant fingertip. "It's cold."

"Well, I ain't movin'," Mom said. "Let your precious grandchild do some work for a change."

"Rosalie," Granny chirped in her best peacemaking voice, "you run set the table while I heat this up a little bit. Get out the flowered tablecloth and put water in some glasses. And get the blue Chinese platter Miss Helen gave me," she added. "Nobody but field hands eat out of cardboard boxes."

After a long search, Rosie found three plates in the cupboard that weren't cracked. She killed two roaches when she went back for glasses.

"What's all that racket?" Granny called.

"I'm just setting the table, Granny," Rosie answered. She always hoped Granny didn't know about the roaches.

"That's a good grandchild. Now look in the top of my bag and see if you can find some little lemon dessert pies."

Rosie ran to the shopping bags which everyone else had forgotten but which glowed for her like forbidden fire.

"In the top of the bag, now," Granny called. "I didn't say you could look in the bottom."

"What's in the bottom, Granny?"

"Laros to catch meddlers."

"Oh, Granny!" Rosie stamped her foot. But she turned away and carried the pies to the table. She divided the chow mein among the three plates.

Mom did not come to the table right away. She had two more drinks before she lumbered over and sat down, her fat, creased legs drooping over the edge of the chair. She smiled vaguely, and Rosie knew she had reached the second stage.

"Rosie," Granny said, "Miss Iris's birthday party is tomorrow."

Rosie leaned forward eagerly. "Tell me, Granny."

"They brought in the cake today. It was big as me. Made in seven rings with a different kind of flower on each one."

Crunching the noodles of her chow mein, Rosie tasted candy violets and roses.

"It took three men to carry that cake. They had to bring out ten punch bowls for the lemonade."

"Gosh!"

"And they opened up the doors between the dining room and the drawing room. And hung it up with striped drapes like a real circus tent. And some man is comin' tomorrow what has trained animals, monkeys and dogs, to do tricks for the children."

"No foolin', Granny? Real live animals?"

"Yes, I said to Miss Helen, 'At least these cloth drapes are nicer than that trashy crepe paper we had last year.' And she said, 'Lourinda, it's a shame the way these labor unions are changing everything.' And I said, 'Miss Helen, you're right, it ain't like it used to be. I remember when your daddy hired a whole traveling carnival and had them set up a Ferris wheel on the front lawn.' "

"Great day in the morning!"

"Of course all the kids do get a costume. The costumes is real nice, Rosie. I helped press 'em myself. Little dance dresses with stars all over for the girls. And long-tail satin coats and high chimney-piece hats for the boys. There were fifty of them costumes. I hear tell they invited forty-nine."

Rosie nodded. "Because now she's seven years old. Just like I am. And seven times seven is forty-nine."

Mom grunted. "I shampooed seven times seven heads today. Now I need seven times seven drinks." She poured a sloppy tumblerful. "Rosie, honey, don't let her fool you. That fiftieth costume ain't for you."

Granny said nothing.

"Sometimes I get sick of hearin' how white folks live 'cause it makes me remember how I gotta live. Sometimes, just sometimes, I wish you'd stop. The more you talk about your white folks the blacker I feel."

"Regina, hush," Granny said.

Rosie stared at Mom, whose breasts were a dirty yellow pushing against the dirty gray of her corset. She looked at Granny, whose wrinkled skin was peanut colored. *Inside* peanut colored. And glanced down, now, at her own smooth arms which matched the ruddy maple wood of Mom's dresser.

"Granny," she said. "Granny, how come you're so light?"

"Down Home," Granny began, in a chanting voice that evoked, for Rosie, visions of beautiful white castles floating on clouds and the mingled scents of a thousand mysterious flowers, "Down Home, we were always the lightest. That's how come we were house servants, not field servants. My mother was mixed. She was a gypsy creole. Her name was Tamir, and she used to play on a funny kind of round-shaped guitar."

From the corner, where she had gone for a new bottle, Mom laughed.

"She had wavy black hair so long she could sit on it," Granny sing-songed. "She spoke three languages, French and Indian and Gypsy."

"And all she ever said in all them languages," Mom said, "was 'Yes, Boss' and 'Yes, Ma'am.' Same as you."

Usually Rosie wanted nothing more than for Granny to drift off into a misty reverie that carried her Down Home and took Rosie along. But not now. Now she wanted to find out something.

"Granny," she asked, "if you are so light then why am I so dark?"

"Because," Granny snapped, scowling at Mom, "that no 'count father of yours was black as coal tar. I tried to bring this girl up right, and then she ran off and got married without thinkin' about improvin' the race."

"You're a fine one to talk," Mom said. "I remember my father. He wasn't no lily of the valley."

"Your father James Huggs was part Indian," Granny said with great dignity, "may he rest in peace. He had thin features and hazel eyes."

Mom snorted. "Hazel eyes! Lot of good they did him." After a pause she added, "He left out of here good and alive, didn't he? What makes you so sure he's dead?"

Granny sniffed and did not bother to answer.

"Rosie," Mom said suddenly, "don't you let her set you against your father. He was a nice sweet man." She downed Five and shifted on the couch, lifting her haunches to let the breeze blow beneath them. "She drove him out of this house. Now many a night I wish Clevie Fleming was here to cool me off when I'm hot and warm me up when I'm cold."

"You hush," Granny said fiercely. "Hush that talk in front of the child."

"She gotta learn sometime," Mom said. She closed her eyes and shifted her legs again. "Ain't nothin' sweeter in life than trim. I can state you that for a fact. I can spell it, too. T.R.I.M."

"Will . . . you . . . hush?" Granny said in her loudest voice, which was only a hoarse whisper.

"And color ain't got no connection. I done tried both vanilla and chocolate, and they both taste good to me."

"Rosie," Granny said quickly, "I almost forgot. I brought you a little something for being a good girl."

Rosie ran to get the shopping bag.

"And caramel and licrish too. And butterscotch. And coffee and maple syrup and lemon cream," Queenie chanted, on the far shores of Six and about to sail out on the tides of Seven.

"I was cleaning Miss Emilie's room today," Granny chirped, holding something that glowed in her hands, "and I picked this up and held it to the light and I said, ' 'Pears like this might get broken here, Miss Emilie. It's cracked already. I'll just put it away.'

"And Miss Emilie, she said, 'It's not worth anything, Lourinda, it's just in the way. Why don't you take it on home?'

"And I said, 'Thank you, Miss Emilie, I will, 'cause my grandchild likes these kind of doodads.' "

Rosie took it wordlessly.

It was a rainbow caught in a thin glass bubble. A bowl of glass like clear water, with strips of pink and blue and orange and green. When she buried her face in it and raised her head Mom turned pink and green, Granny turned gold and purple, the whole room turned beautiful.

"I don't see no crack, Granny," Rosie said finally.

The old lady winked and smiled. "There ain't no crack, child."

Rosie felt it was grand to be old enough at last to be let in on Granny's secrets. "Ain't it really worth nothin', Granny?"

"Child, them people got so much money they forgets it as soon as they spends it. It might be worth a thousand million dollars." This time Granny chuckled, and Rosie permitted herself to smile.

"Bring it here," Mom called.

Rosie hung back, looking at her grandmother.

"I said bring it here!" Mom snatched the bowl from Rosie's hands, inspected it briefly and set it on the table. "Not bad for a hunk of junk. I think I'll keep it right here."

"Granny brought it for me," Rosie said.

"Well, I'm taking it for me," Mom said. She laughed. "Don't you want to pay me back for that dress you ruint?"

"No!" Rosie screamed. "It's mine!" She snatched the bowl from the table and held it close.

"Gimme back that, you little monkey!"

Rosie dodged her mother's reaching hand. "No!" she howled. "I don't want Uncle Roscoe putting his nasty old cigar ashes in it. Or Carmen and Cleo and your other friends breaking it up when they get drunk!"

Queenie was up and raging. "You must think you're talking to some child, not your mother. I'm sick of you showing off in front of her. Now you're gonna give me back that dish or I'll beat your tail till it sings." Her hand forced Rosie's wrist back. "Let go, you hear? This is your mother talking! Let go!"

Rosie held on grimly as long as she could. The pain was so blinding she did not hear the crash. When she opened her eyes two jagged halves of a rainbow lay on the floor. Slowly she knelt to pick them up. Through her tears she defied her mother's knees.

"When I grow up I'll have another one just like it. The biggest one in the world. And I won't let you touch it. You won't even see it, 'cause you'll be dead!"

Queenie looked at her mother. "You hear how she talks to me?"

Granny was grim.

"Come on, Miss Smarty. I'm gonna give you a whipping you won't forget so soon.

"Doin' this for your own good!" Granny said. Thwack! "Even if she does like a taste of whiskey now and then, she's your mother. Taste or no taste, she's your mother. Remember that!" Thwack! Rosie howled. "Even if that Roscoe and that Cleo and that Carmen are no good trash, they're your mother's friends. They're older than you are." The blows were getting lighter all the time, but Rosie howled suitably. "You gotta show some respect. Even if they are a bunch of no good trashy niggers." The last blow was almost a tender pat.

"Now here's something I almost forgot," Granny said. Finger to her lips, she put a big curly-haired doll in bed with Rosie. She smiled slightly, that new special smile that was just between the two of them, before she turned out the light. And did not take the pieces of the bowl away.

The lumpy day bed felt full of rocks. It was not as nice as Rosie's own stiff little cot but it was better than Mom's mattress where you sank until you drowned. There was no light for looking at the pieces of glass so she stroked them dangerously in the darkness, listening as the doorbell rang and the buzzer responded and the front room filled with Uncle Roscoe's hearty laughter and the high-pitched giggles of Carmen and Cleo and the acid chuckles of Slim. Night time was the bright time for Mom, the only bright time, because Eleven came after Seven. But for Rosie it was the darkest time, the time for lying alone in a black box while laughter floated in from another room.

The fragments of glass slipped from Rosie's fingers to somewhere in the covers. She remembered the cereal she had eaten that morning and thought: What if it really was roach eggs? Hatching now, in the moist dark places deep inside her. And through long hours of fitful sleep and brief periods of terrified wakefulness they hatched and laid more eggs and hatched and skittered and crawled around and around in her belly.

Until morning poured in at the window and shattered in a million multicolored splinters on the floor.

4

"Now, I'm staying home and going in to work late this morning," Mom said, "just to make sure your behind goes to school." She finished braiding Rosie's hair so tightly her eyes were pulled up at the corners.

"Owww!" Rosie complained, looking at herself in Mom's dresser mirror. "You made me look Chinky."

"Well, be glad of it. It's the only way you can look like somethin' else." But Mom relented and eased the braids. "There, I've loosened 'em up some. Now you're ready." She pushed Rosie off her lap and gave her a spank. "Be there on time. You got a whole half hour. And Rosie—"

Already halfway out of the door, Rosie turned. "Yes ma'am?"

"Don't make me have to stay home on your account again."

Rosie mumbled something vague and hurried out of the apartment, taking the steps three at a time, because she didn't want to promise. Out there was the Avenue, buzzing and humming with excitement and important knowledge. In school there was nothing but dusty silence and dull books. Fairy story books were good but the rest gave Rosie a pain. She didn't understand why she had to go to school, anyway. School was for kids, and she had been born grown up.

She took a zigzag route, crossing and recrossing the Avenue, that would get her to school eventually if nothing more interesting turned up. But first she would explore all the possibilities.

She hesitated in front of the candy store on the corner, debating whether a free licorice twist would be worth letting Mr. Connelly run his hands over her legs. She had always known he would exact this fee, long before he tried it, just from looking at his slippery eyes.

Not this time, she decided. She could always get a penny from one of the guys on the next corner, outside Benny's Bar. The hustlers and gamblers and loafers were all her friends, and none of them ever did anything more than run rough friendly hands over her hair.

"Hi," she called as she reached the corner and the open doorway through which good music blared. They were all there, B. J. and Pockets and Slew Foot and Clint and Bunky; they were always there, every day, standing around, waiting for It to happen. Rosie had no idea what It might be, but she knew Benny would have something to do with it. Benny owned the bar and everything else on the Avenue. He was The Man. Everyone knew that.

"Hi, Rosie. What's the number?" B. J. teased. He was a tall handsome gambler who made his living taking bets on the races and lost most of it on his own bets.

"Aw, you know the number don't come out till afternoon," Rosie answered.

All the guys laughed, and B. J. tossed Rosie a whole nickel. Why was it, she wondered, that people who had nothing could always afford to give some of it away? While rich people like Benny and Mr. Connelly always made you pay for everything? The juke box answered her:

"Well, I started at the bottom, and I'm stayin' right there
It don't seem like I'm ever gonna get nowhere
That's why I'm gonna take it easy
Gonna take it easy
Take it easy, baby, that's what I'm gonna do. . . ."

Much as she liked the music, Rosie stopped dancing and backed away when a small dark figure drifted out of Benny's and sidled toward the next doorway. Shadow ran the place over top of Benny's which was called a hotel. She could hear one of his whores up there now, crying in a high piercing wail. Rosie wondered which one it was and whether Shadow had beaten her. He moved like a black cat and spoke in whispers; he was more like a ghost than a man. He gave Rosie the shivers.

And so did Bo Ditley, who was stumbling up the Avenue toward her now, looking like he'd slept in a pile of leaves somewhere. He'd beg and she would be afraid to refuse him her nickel because it was bad luck. What with both of them closing in, Rosie decided it was time to get the hell out of there.

She skipped across the Avenue, forcing three cars to scream to a stop. Halfway down the block was a luncheonette she couldn't look into because it was so papered with signs advertising Ginger Ale and Hoagies and Fish Cakes and Pork Chop Sandwiches and Chocolate Beat-Up Drinks. She thought of spending her nickel for a hot sausage on a stick, but then she had a better idea.

She ran down the steps next door into the basement room that was Bud Lewis's Shoe Shine and Billiard Parlor. It was a dark, cool, damp, wonderful place. Big, easygoing, brownskin Bud, his hat over his eyes, was snoring in the shoe-shine chair. Rosie was in love with him whenever she wasn't in love with B. J.

"Hey Bud, wake up!" she hollered.

"Whoa! Whoa!" he cried, awakening in a fright. "Who's there?"

"It's me, Bud. Come on down from there. I'll shoot you a game."

"Oh, it's *you*, Rosie."

"Play me a game, Bud. I got a whole nickel."

He got down slowly, grumbling, "Okay, but not a whole game. Just a couple shots. First ball in a side-pocket wins."

They cued up and Bud broke the balls. Rosie was so excited she missed her first shot by several inches. Then Bud, aiming so coolly he didn't even seem to be looking, jammed her ball into a side pocket.

And pocketed her nickel, too, just as coolly. "I'm keeping this, to teach you not to gamble away your money."

Rosie stuck her tongue out at him. "Nyahhh. Next time I'll beat you."

"Ain't gonna be no next time. You ought to be in school like all the other children." He spanked her fanny to send her out the door. "Now get out of here. Git."

School again! Shoot. Dragging her feet on the way, she looked in the window of Schwartz's Department Store, and decided she didn't really mind losing the nickel. It wasn't real money anyway, not real money like she was going to have someday. A nickel would never buy one of those gorgeous Sunday school dresses that looked like candy in Schwartz's window, raspberry or lemon or lime fluffy stuff over shiny silk. Someday Rosie would have one in every color. One for every day of the week.

"Rosie! Rosie! Wait for me!"

Oh, Lord. Here came that silly little Dolly Diaz, that simple-minded thing that always followed Rosie around like a puppy dog. Now she would *really* have to go to school.

Looking like the doll baby Granny had tucked in with her last night, all pink and gold peach-face and long bobbing Shirley Temple curls, Dolly ran up breathlessly and put her arm through Rosie's. She smelled like a peach, too: sweet and fresh and clean. Nobody who lived in Rosie's neighborhood could ever smell like that.

27

"I'm so glad I saw you, Rosie. Now we can walk to school to-gether. Where've you been all week? I've missed you."

"I've been busy," Rosie said, reluctantly allowing herself to be steered toward school.

"Busy with what?"

Lord, it was a shame. This child was so foolish and trusting, Rosie could never resist fooling her.

"I got a job," she said.

"Oh, Rosie," Dolly said, "come on. You know the law doesn't allow children to work."

"I don't pay no mind to The Law when I got to make me some money."

"Oh, Rosie," Dolly said again. But she half believed her. She half believed all of Rosie's stories—that she was an Egyptian princess being brought up in secrecy in America, that she was also somehow related to the wealthy white people her Granny worked for, that she had a grown-up boy friend, and, now, that she had a job. Somehow, when Rosie told them, they were true. And after a whole week in which it seemed she had lost Rosie forever, Dolly was so glad to see her, she would accept anything. "We had fun yesterday, Rosie," she said as they entered the schoolyard. "Miss Jenkins let us paint the whole afternoon."

This, she knew immediately, was a grave error; Rosie's eyes, as they gazed through the schoolyard fence, had a remote look that said at home she had much better things to do than paint silly pictures, and yesterday she had done them. Dolly was left with no way of finding out what these things might be except to wait, which she did, while Rosie finished her minute analysis of the vacant lot next door.

"Want to see something?" Rosie asked suddenly.

Dolly moved close to the fence and stared eagerly through the holes in the wire. She saw nothing but weeds and rubbish and a few clumps of sunflowers attended by bees, but she continued to stare, patiently, waiting to learn which of these commonplace things would suddenly be raised to the level of the miraculous.

Behind her, Rosie laughed. "What you lookin' out there for,

stupid? Look here!" Rosie's hand withdrew a few inches from her pocket and halted in mid-revelation. "Unless you scared, that is."

" 'Course I ain't scared, Rosie." Dolly felt a warm flush of pride. She had succeeded in breaking the rigid pattern imposed at home; she had managed, with apparent ease, to say *ain't*. She heard herself say it again; she would remember forever how natural it had sounded and how easily it had rolled from her tongue. *'Course I ain't scared.* Savoring it for the third time, she watched Rosie's hand come all the way out of her skirt. Then, belatedly, she received the full shock of seeing Rosie's fingers covered with blood; a great deal of blood, all of it a stunning vivid red.

"Know what this is?" Rosie asked. She brought her hand so close to Dolly's eyes that a drop ran down from the little finger to Dolly's starched white collar. Fascinated, Dolly watched the stain spread until it reached the rick-rack at the edge.

She nodded. "It's blood."

Rosie rallied quickly. " 'Course it's blood, silly. I know you seen blood before. Blood ain't nothin'. But do you know what *this* blood is?"

Dolly shook her head.

Rosie leaned close and said in a thrilled whisper, "I got the *bleedin' disease.*"

"Come on, Rosie," Dolly said, touching the unwounded hand with her own smooth pink fingers, "we better go see Miss Banks right away."

Rosie jerked out of her reach. "What Miss Banks know about it? She just a nurse. Doctors don't even know what to do about this disease. I seen about a hundred doctors already, and they all say—" she raised her hand until the blood trickled down her wrist, then swiftly returned the mystery to her pocket "— when you got the bleedin' disease, you got to die."

She resumed staring through the fence at a point high in the air where Dolly thought she must see the angels descending to take her. After a long silence she turned back to Dolly and said somberly, "You better not tell nobody about this. You the only one I told, Dolly Diaz, and you got to promise not to tell nobody. Promise, now."

"I promise."

"You better not stand so close to me, neither. You might catch it too."

Dolly nodded calmly and stepped back, then lost control. "Oh Rosie," she cried, "I don't want you to die!"

"Hush," Rosie said fiercely. "Hush up that crying. Here comes Bessie Benson and a whole bunch of kids." Dolly stopped sobbing with a jerk that took more will than she had known she possessed. She looked up and saw Rosie's face screwed up in silent laughter which exploded and showered down around Dolly like the fragments of a bomb.

"Girl," Rosie said when she had stopped shaking, "you believe everything I tell you?"

There was a perfect moment which would have lasted no longer in any case because Rosie could not accept love for more than a second at a time and would soon have to fuss, or fidget, or tease Dolly or run away shouting, "You can't catch me!" But this time it was ended by Bessie Benson coming on them in a great rattling of heel-plates on cement, propelling three other girls before her like a bull shepherding cows. Bessie halted, and the three lined up dutifully against the fence.

"This is the Hair Inspection Patrol," Bessie announced. She was a tall heavy girl who already had breasts; the knowing grin that played around her lips revealed large front teeth that had come in crooked over baby teeth still in place. She patted the heads of the three in quick, routine succession. "Bad hair, bad hair, bad hair," she chanted. She reached next for Rosie's head but it was swiftly ducked out of her way. "Might cut my hand on that Brillo anyway," she said sourly. The trio laughed.

Bessie's hand touched Dolly's head next, lingered there, ran over it again in long, careless heavy strokes.

"This feels like good hair to me," she said. "Arlene, what it feel like to you?"

Crusts of Bread and Such

The chosen one stepped forward quickly and touched Dolly's hair. She nodded. "It don't feel like bad hair."

"Well, let's ask her," Bessie said, counterfeiting a smooth reasonable tone. "You think you got good hair, gal?"

Dolly knew she was the target of a long series of carefully planned moves around the playground; knew too, sickeningly, that in this particular test there was no answer she could give that would not fail.

"I don't know," she said softly.

"Gal don't know what kind of hair she's got!" Bessie shouted.

The three by the fence delivered laughter with the precision of a well-rehearsed chorus.

"Must be mighty stupid," Number One said.

"Sure must be," Bessie agreed. She cocked her head and regarded Dolly. "You think maybe you got bad hair, gal?"

"No, she ain't got bad hair," Number Two said.

"That hair ain't no more trouble than white on rice," Number Three concluded.

"I'll ask you again, since you didn't seem to hear me," Bessie said. "You think you got bad hair?"

"I don't know," Dolly said after a long pause.

The chorus laughed on cue.

"Well, look here," Bessie said, "what kind of hair your mother got?"

The three shrieked in positive frenzy and Bessie, needing no more encouragement, buried her fingers in Dolly's curls and twisted hard. "I think this is good hair," she said. "Bet you think so, too. Bet you think you're cute, too, don't you?"

Time slowed down while Dolly saw a dazzling light emerge from Rosie's pocket, saw the scabby, rust-colored fingers move to Bessie's throat, then felt the grip in her hair relax and fall away.

"I think she's cute," Rosie said. "You better think so, too." The fingers moved very slowly. A thin red line appeared on Bessie's neck and was joined by a drop of perspiration. The ter-

31

rible fingers hovered there, holding fire. "What you think? She cute or not?"

"She's real cute," Bessie said in a low voice.

"She's the cutest little thing we ever seen," Arlene shrilled, sidestepping quickly. Four pairs of heels flashed briefly; soon four specks disappeared in the crowd at the far end of the yard.

"Thank you," Dolly said. She wanted to say more, but for once her fear of Rosie was stronger than her fascination. Then she saw that Rosie was not listening. She was staring at the fiery weapon in the palm of her hand. Dolly looked: it was a harmless, pretty thing with bright colors sparkling in the sun, a broken bit of decoration from someone's Christmas tree.

"It's broke," Rosie said softly. From her pocket she withdrew and held out the dozen more pieces of glass that had been squeezed all morning by penitent fingers. "It's broke," she said again.

Now Dolly noticed something she had never seen before: Rosie's eyes about to spill over. She touched one of the pieces. "I'll help you fix it, Rosie."

"Ain't no way to fix it," Rosie said in a monotone.

"Yes, we can," Dolly said with growing conviction. "Miss Goings has some real strong glue in her office. She'll let us use it if we ask her nicely."

Rosie did not look convinced.

"It's the most marvelous glue you ever saw, Rosie," Dolly urged. "It'll stick anything."

Rosie came to a sudden decision. "All right. We'll go and steal it. You can help me."

Dolly hesitated. Stealing the glue from the principal's office was not what she had meant at all. But Rosie always chose the dangerous adventurous way of doing things.

"You comin' with me, Dolly? Or you scared?"

Dolly glanced down at her white collar and at the stain that was brighter and braver than the golden honor badge she had worn there last term.

" 'Course I ain't scared, I'm comin'!"

5

They got away from Miss Goings just in time. Rosie's chest was still heaving. At the desk beside her, Dolly sat tensely with her back straight and her hands primly folded.

She scared all right, even if she don't let on, Rosie thought. Little scaredy cat, why's she keep on followin' me around?

Rosie hunched down lower in her seat and raised her desk top another three inches while inside the desk her left hand squeezed the two pieces of glass together. A new trickle of blood started from her left thumb. She calmly watched it flow as she squeezed harder, then reached with her right hand for the glue which Dolly held out in answer to an imperative wave. Dolly had been too careful with that glue, painting it on like it belonged to her. Wasn't enough on there to stick two pieces of paper together. Rosie snatched the bottle and turned it upside down. No sense in her hangin' out with me if she's gonna be scared all the time.

Miss Jenkins began calling the roll. Rosie usually livened up this dull routine by answering, "Not Here!" when her name was called.

"Dolores Diaz?" the teacher called.

Dolly's hand shot up instantly. "Present!"

Rosie looked away in disgust.

The desk at her left had been empty last week, but now it was occupied by a new boy, taller, darker, older than any of the others. Intent on the book that was spread out on his desk, he did not see Rosie. His lips moved painfully, spelling out the words.

Rosie leaned over, took a quick look, contemptuously recognized the baby primer she had learned to read last year.

"Little Tommy Tucker sang for his supper," she rattled off in a whisper.

God Bless the Child

The boy jumped and looked up. For a long time he stared at Rosie in alarm. Suddenly a grateful smile spread over his face.

"Rosalie Fleming?" Miss Jenkins called.

"Here!" Rosie responded before she had a chance to think of anything. She added lamely, "Maybe."

"Never mind, Rosie," the teacher said tartly. "You. You new boy back there. Do I have your name?"

"Tucker," the new boy whispered. Then he repeated it louder, raising his head bravely. "Tucker."

"Tucker what?" Miss Jenkins asked crossly.

"*Tommy* Tucker."

"It's not down here," Miss Jenkins said with an annoyed glance at her list. "That ignorant girl in the office must have made a mistake again." She raised her voice. "All right, Thomas. You may keep that seat for the rest of the term."

Rosie giggled. This was the best joke yet. But when she looked at the new boy again, his eyes were enormous with fear.

She quickly put out her bloody hand and laid it on top of his, the way pirates and Indians made pacts. If she showed him she could be trusted with this great secret, he would trust her with others.

Her eyes roved the room again and came to a stop at the place where they rested most often, the seat in front of Bessie's. Larnie Bell. Rosie guessed she kind of liked Larnie. Some of the time, anyway—when he talked to her and she would say something bold and his eyes would drop shyly while a warm peach glow spread under his smooth tan skin; when he let her ride on his roller-skate scooter or play boys' games with him; when he stood at the end of the boys' line for assembly so Rosie, at the head of the girls, could sit beside him and sing from the same book. When she could watch him, like now, and admire his well-shaped head and the way it was set on his broad shoulders.

But not all the time, because Larnie was too good. Not goody-good, just not interested in being bad. There he sat, his hands folded, looking straight ahead and paying attention to no one but the teacher. He probably don't even know how to make a spitball, Rosie thought as she rolled one expertly and aimed it at the beautiful spot where the silky hair stopped on the back of his neck.

Larnie turned; his great, golden eyes looked quizzically at Rosie. She did not know whether to smile or frown so she did both by laughing softly. His slow answering smile was like the sun coming up on a summer morning.

As she was warmed by it she felt the pieces of glass fall apart in her fingers. Her gift from Granny was broken, and nothing would put it together again. She did not want to go home without it. Home was an ugly place now that she had looked at it through the rainbows of the bowl.

Her hands moved as if to toss the fragments in a wide sparkling arc out the window, then returned unopened to her pocket. She would keep them, even though they wounded her whenever she touched them.

6

Dolly could close her eyes against the sun that beat down on the high school stadium and still see Rosie toss that spitball, still feel the crawling at the back of her neck where she had imagined the principal's hand grabbing both of them by the collar. Rosie was a born outlaw; she enjoyed danger. And Dolly could never resist following her into its presence because Rosie was so different from anyone else she had ever known.

Now the desks had grown larger and they had grown to fill them, but Rosie's face had not changed. It was still an outlaw's face: old-young, determined, with a small, pointed, cinnamon nose and chin overbalanced by a large mouth and enormous hungry eyes. From the concrete schoolyard with swings and see-saws they had moved to a larger playground: a stadium with a quarter-mile track, and Larnie Bell a brown and white dot moving swiftly around it. Now they were all seventeen, but Rosie was still no particular age. She was simply both older and younger than everyone else.

"Know what I'm doing, Doll?" Rosie said, with a nudge in Dolly's ribs. "I'm writing my own class prophecy. We the three Most Likely to Succeed. Here's what it's gonna say in the newspapers: 'That world-famous educator, Doctor Dolly Diaz. That rich-bitch businesswoman, Miss Rosalie Elizabeth Fleming. And that human cannonball, Lightnin' Larnie Bell—'" She gestured elegantly with one hand. "'—Gathered at a soiree in Miss Fleming's mansion on Madison Drive.'" She jumped up and cheered. "Look at that boy move! Go, Larnie!"

"Rosie, I swear, I never know when you're serious," Dolly said when Rosie sat down again. "Sometimes I think the wildest things you say are the things you mean the most."

"What makes you think I'm not serious?" Rosie said indignantly. "I'm *always* serious."

Dolly laughed.

"Well, I am. And someday I'll be so rich I won't speak to you, except for old times' sake."

"And how are you going to get so rich?"

"I've started already, Doll. While you're sittin' around gettin' fat, drinkin' sodas at The Hangout, I'm working. Afternoons after school and Saturdays, at Schwartz's Store. I got me a job, and I've got plans."

"What kind of plans?"

"Never mind," Rosie said, half teasing, half angry, "since you don't think I'm serious. I'll just tell you this, Doll. There's Rockefeller and all them other people with all that money. And here's me wanting some of it. So why shouldn't I have it?"

"Because," Dolly said gently, "you can't always have things just because you want them."

"Why not?" Rosie asked. "Just tell me why not." Her face had that set expression that would not budge for Dolly or anyone else. By now Dolly knew better than to try. Even back in grade school, a face set as fiercely as Rosie's could never belong to someone like Dolly who missed only two or three days of school each year and always arrived early on the morning after each absence with a long, careful letter that told what the doctor had said and what her temperature had been and what schoolwork she had made up at home and what pills she was supposed to take three times a day and was signed, *Very truly yours, Mrs. Jules Diaz*. It could only belong to Rosie, who stayed out most of the time and brought—when she brought at all—illegible notes written by herself on the back of a brown paper bag or a sheet torn from someone else's tablet; notes which she deposited grandly on the teacher's desk with an air that defied her to read them.

Rosie sighed. "Oh, hell. No sense in talkin' to you. There was just one person in this school could understand me, and he's gone."

"Who do you mean?" Dolly asked.

"I mean Tucker," Rosie said. Her face became distant.

Dimly Dolly remembered a tall, dark boy who had seemed older than all the other kids and seemed always to possess some secret superior source of amusement. He rarely had anything serious to say, but when he did, it was impressive. When he clowned, his jokes were at the expense of others, and made everyone present feel uncomfortable. No one had seemed surprised when he disappeared from school last year, and no one seemed to miss him.

"Whatever happened to Tucker?" she asked.

"He was too smart for this school, that's all," Rosie said. "He had big plans, and I was in on 'em. Right now he's in the Army. But he's comin' back someday. And that'll be the day. Money 'n honey all rolled up in one, Doll."

Dimly Dolly also remembered seeing Rosie and Tucker whispering together in corners, then separating whenever someone approached. She was vaguely apprehensive. "I'll ask you once more. What kind of plans, Rosie?"

"Plans for a business, Doll. I won't tell you anything about it. Except that it ain't strictly legal—but it pays." Rosie tossed

37

her head and added, "When he was just sixteen, Tucker was makin' more money than most people ever see."

"He never talked to anyone, Rosie," Dolly said. "How do you know so much about him?"

"He was my lover," Rosie replied, and popped her gum to put an explosive period at the end of the sentence. She leaped to her feet as Larnie moved past them in a golden blur.

"Look at my lover man go! Just watch his dust! *Go*, Larnie!"

Rosie jumped up and down in the stands, cheering Larnie on. If their school had allowed colored girls to be cheerleaders, Dolly thought, Rosie would have been the best they'd ever had.

"Here, Doll," Rosie said, handing her the stop-watch. "Hold this thing before I break it. Great God Almighty! Look at that boy move!"

Rosie seemed scarcely to have grown any larger over the years. She was still nothing but skin and bones and energy. But Larnie, coming toward them on his last lap, had become a broad-shouldered beige giant.

He slowed to a walk after he crossed the finish line. "How'd I do?" he asked, squinting up at them with crinkly eyes.

Rosie took a flying leap from the stands and threw her arms around him, forcing him to stagger backward under her weight.

"Baby, you're the fastest-movin' nigger since Jesse Owens! You run like you're down South and some sheriff is chasin' you!"

Larnie recovered his balance and finally freed himself from her skinny embrace. "Yes, but how'd I do? Did you time me?"

"Four minutes, eighteen seconds," Dolly supplied.

"Yeee!" Rosie screamed. "You broke the state record!"

Larnie could not help grinning. "Now if I can only do it at the meet Saturday."

"You can't fail," Rosie said solemnly. "Dolly and I will both be there. Come on, sit down between your two most gorgeous fans."

She led him up to the stands and made a place for him between them. "Tell us what's new, lover," she said as he continued to smile down at them—that open vulnerable smile that always warmed Dolly and always, also, made her wonder what Rosie might do to someone who smiled like that.

"I don't know, Rosie," he said. "I'm taking college entrance exams next month, and between studying and track and my music I'm so busy I don't know what's going on."

"Pretty soon he'll be soundin' like Errol Garner," Rosie said to Dolly.

Larnie had the patience of an angel, but now it seemed exasperated. "No, Rosie, I mean serious music." He gestured with his large graceful hands. "You know I don't want to be no cocktail bar piano player. I'm going to the University to study."

"Yeah, I know." Rosie laughed. She rubbed the thumb of her left hand against the two middle fingers. "You just studyin' how to make that loot."

"No, Rosie." He frowned and looked at Dolly, as if asking for help with his explanation. "There isn't much money in serious music, unless you get to be so good they want you for concerts and recitals all the time. I expect to teach for a living."

"*Teach?* You gonna go to college just so you can come out and teach? Like *Dolly?*"

Dolly laughed. All year, Rosie had been telling her she was crazy to want to be a teacher, that she ought to go to work in a factory instead.

Rosie scowled at both of them. "Doll can go on and be a fool if she wants to. She's just a girl."

"So are you," Larnie said with amusement.

"What's that got to do with anything?" Rosie asked indignantly. "The point is, you're *not*. Larnie Bell, you gonna spend the rest of your life in school?"

Larnie tried to appease her. "There's things more important than money, Rosie."

"You just name me one." Her fierce stare defied him to try.

He dropped his eyes. "Guess I can't, Rosie, no way you'd understand."

"Where you gonna get the money for college?" Rosie demanded of him.

Larnie seemed unhappy. "I'm going to try for an athletic scholarship. If I can't get it, my folks are going to take out a loan on the house."

Rosie was too sophisticated to believe this. She probed it suspiciously until she found the weak place that seemed to give way. "You mean they gonna loan you the money and you gonna pay it back?"

"No," Larnie said. "I wouldn't be able to pay it back for a long time. Maybe never. Besides, they wouldn't want me to."

Dolly thought of Larnie's father, little stoop-shouldered Mr. Bell who was surely getting too old to go on sweeping and carrying—he had been janitor at the grammar school since it was built, some said—and whose eyes shone with such youthful brilliance whenever he talked of education.

Apparently Rosie was thinking of him, too. She was silent for a minute. Then she tossed her head defiantly. "Well, my Mom says nobody never put down no bed of roses for her to lay on. She says I've got to make my own, same way she made hers." She looked up proudly. "I will, too. I ain't takin' nothin' from nobody. I believe in 'Mama may have and Papa may have, but God bless the child that's got his own.' Bet you never even heard of that song, Larnie."

Larnie shook his head.

"Look," Rosie told him, "you don't have to go to college. Just come see me. I can show you how to make all kinds of loot. You take my family, for instance. Now my Granny don't like music much, except for hymns. She ain't sanctified or nothin', she just don't think music's very important. But she can't stop my Mom from buyin' them blues records. Them real low-down painful blues, you know the kind I mean? Now that's *really* serious music."

Larnie looked doubtful. Rosie grabbed his hand.

"Lover, you listen to Rosie, you'll be wearin' diamond rings big as lima beans. You'll be takin' me for rides in a Cadillac as long as from here—" she shut her eyes and saw the car; her hand described a wide ecstatic arc that broke off in mid-air because it could not travel far enough "—to my house." She grinned up at him. "Crazy?"

Larnie grinned too. "Crazy," he agreed. "But I've got to finish college first. Right, Dolly?"

"Right," Dolly said. "Don't let her talk you out of what's important."

Rosie, helpless with fury, looked from one of them to the other, then jumped up and ran to the grandstand rail. "All right," she said. "You fools can spend the rest of your lives in school if you want to. Go on, be scholars. Me, I'm gonna be rich." She threw one leg over the rail. "I'm quitting school right now."

"But Rosie!" Dolly protested. "You're only three months away from graduation."

"That's three months' salary I'll be missing out on," Rosie answered, "and a lot of other things, too. That poor old Mr. Schwartz doesn't know what to do without me, Doll. I'm practically running his store already. The sooner I go on full time, the sooner I can move up—and start branching out a little."

"But can't you wait just three more months?" Dolly cried.

"Don't bother, Dolly," Larnie said glumly. "It's no use talking to her. I've tried."

But Dolly persisted. "In June you'll have your diploma, Rosie."

"What good is it? It's just a piece of paper. Can I eat it? Can I put it in my bank account?"

Before either of them could stop her, Rosie leaped over the barrier and landed on the track on her hands and knees.

Dolly ran down to the rail and looked over. "Did you hurt yourself?"

"Are you kidding? I'm tough." Rosie scrambled to her feet and dusted off the gravel. "I got to go to work now. So long, scholars."

When she was gone, Dolly and Larnie looked at each other with something like shame.

The way she had said it, it sounded more like "suckers."

7

It was inventory time at Schwartz's. Rosie emerged from the stockroom with an armful of purple velvet jumpers just in time to hear Mr. Schwartz say,

"Vere is Rosalie? While you are creating such a *tsimmis* she would have it all figured out! Must I do everything myself? *Vere* is Rosalie?"

She walked toward Mr. Schwartz. He looked like a snowman: spherical body, round face, little coals of eyes, a mound of white hair.

"Ah, Rosalie." He beamed. "Come here. Explain something, please, to this idiot nephew of mine."

She took the black book from his trembling hands.

"Give us please the rundown on Vogue Vashions, Rosalie."

She ran a finger down the page. "We got seven dozen from Vogue the first of September. Three dozen 1540 and four 1680— you know, Mr. Schwartz, that princess corduroy?" He nodded. She checked the figures again. "Two dozen black, a dozen pink, one split dozen aqua 'n blue."

"So," he grunted in grudging approval. "Did it move, Rosalie?"

"Pink 'n aqua sold right out the first week, Mr. Schwartz. Black's movin' too. We're all out of size 12's." She checked the pages again and frowned. "I don't think Elaine's been enterin' them stubs though. I know I sold five this week and they ain't down here."

The old man's shoulders slumped; his arms fell heavily to his sides. "Must I do everything myself?" he wailed. "I give a thousand dollars to a bright young college boy to figure me out a system. Another thousand for a machine and tickets. We got tickets with three stubs, four stubs, *five* stubs, still they get lost. And nobody bothers to write them down! So what good is the system?" He whirled fiercely to face his nephew Aaron. "The style is in the window, it sells out in a week, customers are screaming for it, but you don't reorder!"

"I did so reorder, Uncle Sol," Aaron said. His heavy-jowled pink face resembled his uncle's, except that it perpetually wore an expression of bewilderment.

"So. You reordered? By the book the style isn't moving and you reordered? Explain, please, just how you knew to reorder. You have learned to read between lines? You have suddenly become—" he tapped his forehead "—clairvoyant?"

Aaron looked even more embarrassed. "Rosalie reminded me."

"Rosalie! Rosalie!" Mr. Schwartz stormed. "All I hear is Rosalie! How long can a store go on with all its records in the head of one small girl?" He made a gesture of supplication. "God deliver me from relatives. If you weren't my baby sister's son, I'd fire you and give Rosalie the job."

Mr. Schwartz turned to Rosalie and shrugged. "You see what comes of having relatives? With all the troubles I got already, I have to have an idiot of a sister with this for a son. If it weren't for relatives I would be rich. And you—you would be Better Dress Buyer for Schwartz's Store. And you yet may be." He whirled on Aaron. "Now," he said in a threatening tone, "where are those dresses you have so clairvoyantly reordered with the help of Rosalie's memory?"

"They didn't come in yet, Uncle Sol. I talked to Manowitz, he says he's short on help this month, he had a layoff six weeks ago on account of no orders and now he's behind, he's trying to re-hire—"

"Aaaah! You listen to Manowitz's sob stories, he'll have you paying double for every dress and making them yourself on top. Must I do everything myself? You get on the phone and tell him—"

Rosie interrupted quietly. "I already called him, Mr. Schwartz. He promised they'd be here Monday."

"And how did you extract this promise?" He shook a finger under Aaron's nose. "Listen, now. Listen. It is not impossible you might yet learn a little something. What did you tell him, Rosalie?"

"I told him Glamour Modes has the same number 'n they promised us delivery this week."

"And what did he say?" He looked beseechingly at Aaron. "Listen, now, please listen."

"He said they were a bunch of robbers 'n pirates. He said they copied his design 'n stole his designer away from him 'n besides it's a cheaper fabric 'n they don't know how to sew a seam at Glamour. 'N I said it makes no never mind to the customers, all they want is the style, 'n besides if Glamour uses a cheaper fabric they might give us a better price." Rosie smiled. " 'N that's when he said he'd lose a fortune on overtime, we were killing him, but we'd get 'em Monday."

"Ah." Mr. Schwartz joined the tips of his fingers and sighed as though he had just contemplated a rare work of art. "I am thankful you are a woman, Rosalie. Otherwise I would have to say you are as good a businessman as I am." He swung once more to face his nephew. "I have not yet heard you thank her for saving your job."

"No need for thankin' me, Mr. Schwartz," Rosie protested.

"I will thank you personally," he said. "With money, which speaks much louder than words. A ten-dollar raise. Tell Sammy he should start figuring your check this week."

"I just did it 'cause I knew I could sell them dresses," Rosie said modestly.

"Sure you can sell them," Mr. Schwartz agreed. "You're our best salesgirl. Aaaah—" His tongue found the scolding tone which fit it more comfortably than praise. "So what are you doing lugging stock? Are there no customers outside?" He shoved her gently. "From now on you touch no more stock. Go. Leave those things for Freddy. Get out on the floor."

When she was gone Mr. Schwartz bent once more over his nephew.

"You see how I am covered with shame?" he hissed. "That a *shvartse* should be smarter than the Schwartzes!"

Rosie's next customer was Ginger, one of Shadow's girls. As she was zipped into the tight black number, 1224, with net frou-frou at the hem, Ginger keened a sad, sad wail.

"Oh, that Shadow," she moaned. "That man has no heart at all. Held out all my money this week, and when I told him I just *got* to have this dress for the Blues' cabaret party this Sunday, he laughed. Then he gives me just enough for the dress and not one cent more. —Make those straps tighter, doll, I got to show my glamour. —Gave me a ten and a five and counted out ninety-nine cents and said, 'Here, I'll put it on your bill next week.' Honest to God, it almost makes me cry sometimes. I can't even buy myself a drink."

"You couldn't pay me to work for a man like that," Rosie, on her knees, said around a mouthful of pins.

"Oh, he ain't as bad as some," Ginger said. "Anything's better than makin' it on your own. That solo flyin' is somethin' rough. This way I get all the dates I want, and I get treated with respect."

"Shoot," Rosie said, and spat out the pins. "You can have it, girl."

Ginger seemed not to hear. "Besides," she went on, "this is only for a while. I'm bound to luck up and get married or hit the numbers or something." A childlike eagerness lit her face, erasing the hardness of her makeup. "You heard what's happenin'?"

"Too early," Rosie said. "First one don't come out till afternoon."

Ginger dug down into her bra and whispered, "Look, maybe you can bring me some luck. I been waitin' for a three to come out ever since last year. Take this and put it on a three and a six and a nine. They just gotta walk home today."

"Why me?" Rosie asked, taking the much-folded dollar bill.

"Shadow's waitin' for me outside. He don't know I been holdin' out a few bills. He don't like us to play."

"Who you play with?"

"Oh, Miltie Newton, mostly, but I give it to Pockets Robinson when I can catch him. That Miltie's a drunk, and I don't trust drunks with my hard-earned money. Or maybe you might happen to run into Tom Tucker."

Something dropped suddenly in Rosie's chest. It was her heart, but Ginger did not notice.

"Yeah," she went on. "I hear Tucker's back in town and playin' it jam up at the K.D. Club. He a smart cat. But ugly. So ugly it scares me to look at him sometimes."

"Okay, I'll make your play for you," Rosie said coolly, though her thoughts were spinning in several directions at once. Tucker back in town. He'd been gone so long, so long. Everybody playing the numbers. All that money there for the taking if you were strong enough to stand on your own two feet and not work to pay for somebody else's Cadillac.

One was parked at the curb, Rosie saw as she left the fitting room; a black, shiny one that was so long it looked like a hearse. The man behind the wheel was even blacker than the car, so inky he didn't look real.

Shadow was looking at her from behind those dark glasses, she was sure of it. He knew all about Ginger's play.

What was the matter with her, anyway? Shadow never did anything to her, never even threatened her. He was just able to scare her because he was there. That was pure foolishness.

Rosie turned her back on him abruptly, stumbled, and bumped into Aaron.

"Whyncha look where you're going?" he grumbled.

"Why don't *you?*" she defied him, though her knees were knocking with the fright Shadow always gave her.

"Look," Aaron said belligerently, "you better learn what's good for you around here. Where do you get off, acting like you own the place, anyway?"

Rosie was full of suspicion. "You been listenin' in on me?"

"No," he said. A thought seemed to cross his mind. "But maybe I will from now on. Yeah. If you're up to any funny business, Uncle Sol would want to know. I got to protect his interests."

"Maybe you got nothin' better to do," Rosie said, "but *I* got to ring up this dress. So out of my way!" She dug into his arm with one sharp elbow. "Make room!"

And as he stared open-mouthed, she added, "You don't scare me, fat boy. Know why? I got a boy friend twice as big as you and he's scared to death of me!"

8

The Avenue drowsed in the April sun like an enormous bee-hive able to awaken into angry buzzing if disturbed. In front of The Pork Store's windowful of ham hocks and bacon ends, two plump housewives were having a good time criticizing the scandalous love life of the new preacher at Mountolive Baptist. Next door, outside Benny's, the dudes lounged, their processed pompadours glistening in the sun, and called out elaborate compliments to passing girls.

"Hey baby, you can speak to me, I'm colored," one shouted as Rosie hurried by.

On the next corner, sweet, innocent music came through the open door of the Healing Water of Holiness Church. Three sisters robed in white raised their soprano voices and sang,

> *"Come with me to the river,*
> *Let Him wash you pure and clean. . . ."*

Outside, in the gutter flowing with a month's uncollected rubbish, three thin-legged girls did the latest step, the Bottom, to the rhythm of the sisters' tambourines.

Suddenly at one-thirty a wave of energy swept along the Avenue, stirring it into wakefulness, making the skin on Rosie's arms prickle with excitement. It began when Crip Nelson, the oldest client on the city relief rolls, pushed his wheelchair into the vestibule of his decayed house. The navy blue Welfare Lady with her black briefcase was only twenty yards from his doorway, and

47

his ninety-five-year-old muscles were too frozen for speech, but Crip managed to wave three of his gnarled fingers. Back across the street came the nod from Miltie Newton, the runner, lounging in front of Benny's, and Crip's mouth twisted in a silent, terrible paroxysm of joy.

Picking up the signal from Crip's wildly flagging fingers, Mrs. Lucia Luby switched herself angrily past Madame Esther's seance parlor.

"How you like that?" she complained to the first person she met, who happened to be Rosie. "That Esther swore a five would lead off today. I paid my good seventy-five cents for wrong information!" She paused, taken by a new thought. "Maybe I should've known, though. I gave her *three* quarters. —Lord, you just can't figure 'em all!"

"No you can't, Sister. Only the good Lord can do that," said a pious friend of Mrs. Luby's who had rushed up from the opposite direction. "I was counting on a seven today, but He just didn't see fit to send me one. Now you just come with me. We'll pray for better news tomorrow."

They went off in a flurry of white robes to the services. Moments later, the singers were silenced while the message was flashed through the congregation. Rosie shook off the strangeness of the encounter, and moved on.

It was her lunch hour, and she decided on a hot sausage at Sam's Short Ribs Stand, the most public restaurant on the Avenue because it was open on all three sides. Several people besides Ginger had asked her to make plays for them this morning. She was encouraged to do a little branching out. She flagged down Miltie Newton as he shuffled by.

"How's business?" she asked him.

He shrugged. "Pockets Robinson is doin' all right." He turned a small pile of change out of his baggy pants. "My pockets ain't doin' so hot, though. Price of sherry at the Blue Moon is up to a quarter, and this—" he spread a few coins on the counter"—is my percentage for the day."

"How'd you like a bigger percentage?"

His bleary eyes looked at her without hope. "Same way I'd like a big gallon jug of muscatel, only I don't see nobody givin' me none."

"Well, I am." She held out two dollars. "Here, buy yourself that jug. Only don't get so drunk you forget to steer some of the new business my way."

"Pockets wouldn't like it," Miltie said. But his shaky fingers closed around the lucky two-dollar bill.

"I'll do better by you than Pockets ever did. 'Stead of commissions, I'll put you on salary, soon's I see how you perform. Did you take care of that little thing I gave you this morning?"

"What little thing?"

"That dollar for Ginger Brown," Rosie said impatiently.

"Oh sure," he said, shaking the fog from his mind. "She's one third the way home already. You never know when your customers are gonna get lucky, that's why you got to have connections. You got connections, Rosie?"

"Maybe," Rosie said. "Pass the word around."

"Pockets wouldn't like it," Miltie repeated.

"Look, I ain't takin' nothin' away from Pockets," Rosie said angrily. "Let him keep his nickel and penny customers. Just send me all the new business that looks good. I ain't interested in penny ante."

"That's all seemed to come along this week," Miltie said. "Must be the world situation or something. People is scared."

"You scared, too?" she asked him sharply.

"Not when I can get my wine."

Rosie said, "You're getting it," and relaxed her grip on the bill.

"You workin' for Benny, Rosie?"

"Working for *myself*," Rosie emphasized.

"Ah, shoot," Miltie said, showing the spaces where some front teeth were missing. "Don't believe it, girl. Benny's The Man. Pockets hustles for Benny. Shadow hustles for Benny. Everybody hustles for Benny. Sooner or later, you hustle for him, too."

"Well, I gotta be going," Rosie said, feeling nervous at hearing this.

49

He put a grimy hand on her arm. "Wait. You did talk to Benny, didn't you?"

"No. What for?"

"What for? Damn, girl, you tired of livin'?" Miltie handed the money back to her. "You oughta know I can't do nothin' for you till you get the word from The Man."

Rosie did not accept fate, but she knew when she had to meet it halfway.

"All right, I'll talk to him today," she said. "Keep the deuce anyway. And meet me here noontime tomorrow."

"Sure, Rosie," Miltie said. "I wish you luck." He smiled wanly, the wine-o's lost, sweet, sad smile. "But sooner or later, Benny boss you like he bosses us all."

"Anybody tries to boss me got a job on their hands," Rosie said. "Meet me here noontime tomorrow. You hear?"

He nodded, touched his filthy cap, and shuffled off.

Damn Benny, Rosie thought as she paid for her lunch and hurried back across the Avenue. Did he have to own it all, the bar, the restaurant, the hotel, the whore house, and the whole numbers operation, too? Couldn't he leave anything for her?

Mr. Ahmed's disciple had moved in on Benny's corner. His eyes gleamed in his sweaty brown face as he harangued his amused listeners, "Black men and women! The time has come to cast out the white devils!

"—You," he said to Rosie. "Why are you entering that den of iniquity?"

"I got to see me a white devil," she replied, and pushed him aside.

After the glare of the street, it took a minute for her eyes to admit enough light. When they did, she saw that Benny's was divided into two dim rooms. The room in which she found herself, on the left, was a long, narrow restaurant; on the right was a long, narrow bar, with communicating doors.

The kitchen was at the back, and this was where she found Benny, a stocky, rosy-cheeked man with an abundance of stiff black and gray hair. Standing there, peeling onions, with tears

Crusts of Bread and Such

in his eyes, he didn't look at all like The Man in Charge of Everything. But he spoke like him.

"I'm Benny," he said. "You got something to say to me? Say it."

"I'm Rosie. Rosie Fleming," she said, and was suddenly, for the first time in her life, stuck for more words.

"Here," he said, thrusting an extra paring knife into her nervous hands. "Slice up some tomatoes while you talk. I'm short of help today. My sandwich boy got busted this morning. I try never to hire junkies, but he looked like anybody else, how was I to know? It's a hell of a thing, running a business."

"It's what I'd like to do," Rosie said boldly. But her hands, unable to refuse a voice so accustomed to command, were dutifully slicing tomatoes.

"Oh?" He gave her a penetrating look. "I thought you wanted to work for me."

"Not if I can help it," Rosie said, and put down the knife.

Benny laughed, an odd convulsion that began as a short braying sound, then trailed off into silence while his thick midsection continued to shake. "Why not?" he demanded when it was over. "Everybody else does."

"I'd rather work for myself," Rosie said.

"Doing what?" he asked with interest, and added, "Make up a couple hoagies while you're at it."

Rosie's courage had returned. "Writing and banking," she said, neatly shaking the oil over two opened Italian rolls. "Someday I might get big enough to run you out of business. But I won't if we can have us an understanding now."

"Look at you," Benny said. "You aren't big enough to lift that chicken on the stove over there. You're gonna run *me* out of business?"

"I ain't scared of you," Rosie said, swiftly assembling layers of meat, cheese, lettuce and tomatoes. "I only came to see you because everybody else is."

"Well, you came to see the wrong guy," Benny said. "I'm in the restaurant business."

51

"Everybody knows that ain't all you're in. Hand me them onions you just sliced."

He obliged, then pointed the blade of his knife at her. She did not flinch.

"You got money?"

"Some."

"You got an organization?"

"No."

He moved closer. "You must have. Who sent you here, anyway?"

Rosie was suddenly conscious that she had stepped into waters that were over her head. They were unexpectedly cold. But she did not panic. "Nobody sent me. I ain't got no organization but me."

"If you don't work for no corporation—why should I let you move in on my business?"

"Because there's plenty out here for both of us," Rosie said. She lifted her chin and looked straight into his onion-reddened eyes. "And if you don't say yes, I'll do it anyway."

Benny was rocked back on his heels again by his strange, silent laughter. But when it stopped he was serious. "Look, you don't know who you're talking to. I own most of this neighborhood. I probably own the house you live in."

Rosie said coolly, "I'm glad to know it. When you gonna fix the plumbing?"

Benny was not laughing any more. "Don't get too fresh," he said. "I could just say a word, and you'd never bother me again. I could get rid of you—just like that." He snapped his fingers.

The burly black counterman appeared in the doorway. "Yes, Benny?"

"Nothing, Jim. I don't want you. Go mind the store."

Benny turned back to Rosie, his face expressionless. "But I'm not gonna do that, because I like you. I don't trust you, but I like you."

He stuck out his hand. Rosie, after a moment's hesitation, shook it.

"You understand—I can't afford to trust anybody. I've got a hundred people working for me, and I pay fifty of them just to keep an eye on the other fifty. I can't even trust my own wife. I pay my brother-in-law to watch *her*. Cigarette?"

Rosie took one of his crumpled Camels. He lit it for her, then lit his own and squinted through the smoke. It effectively hid his face.

"I need a waitress on the night shift," he said finally. "Seven-thirty to two. You can start tonight."

Rosie picked up her big satchel-like pocketbook and closed it with a loud snap. "Mister, you must not have heard me right. I said I didn't want to work for you."

His arm barred her way.

Rosie looked at him in fury. "Excuse me. I already got a job. I'm late gettin' back from my lunch hour."

"Hold it," he said. "I'm gonna find out right now just how ambitious you really are. And later on, if you work for me, I'll find out who you really are and where you come from. I have to know who I'm dealing with before I say yes to anything."

Benny held up his hand as Rosie started to interrupt. He went on, "—Sure, I could say, 'Okay, go ahead, make your own contacts, write your own business, organize your own funeral.' If you're on your own like you say you are—all the business you could do around the clock wouldn't hurt me. But soon my organization would say, 'Who is this Rosie?' And if I didn't know, they'd begin to wonder about me. Then they'd say, 'Do something about her.' And if I didn't, they'd say to somebody else, 'Do something about Benny.' "

The idea that The Man might have a Man of his own was upsetting, like stumbling into a hall of mirrors.

"You mean you ain't really in business for yourself?" she asked plaintively.

"Everybody in this world has a role," Benny said enigmatically. "You want the secret of success? Find out what your role is and play it. You've got a lot to learn, Rosie or whatever your name is. You better do yourself a favor. Come to work for me. Keep your eyes and ears open and your mouth shut, and don't do anything but wait on the customers. I'll let you know when you're ready to do more."

The Man turned his back on Rosie in dismissal. "You make pretty good hoagies for an amateur," he said, biting into one. "But you forgot the peppers. Be here at seven."

"*Two* jobs?" Mom said. "You ain't even eighteen yet. Ain't you got enough to do now at that store?"

"She's young," Granny put in, "so it won't hurt her to work hard."

"She's young, so she ought to be enjoyin' herself, you mean," Mom retorted. "When's she gonna have time for a little fun? How's she gonna find herself a man?" She looked Rosie up and down. "And how come you wear such dikey clothes, anyway?"

Rosie looked down at her new man-tailored flannel suit and her crisp white-on-white oxford shirt. "Aw, Mom, this is the latest style. You just don't know what's happenin'."

"I know it makes you look like a little bull dagger," Mom said. "And you've cut your hair short, too. How you ever expect to get a husband?"

"Plenty of time for that," Granny said briskly. "She don't want none of the trash in this neighborhood anyway."

"Oh, everybody's trash to you," Queenie said irritably. "What you want her to do—wait till the rich white boys up in *your* neighborhood get around to her?"

"No," Granny said serenely. "I just don't want to see her married to something that'll run off and leave her, like yours did."

Mom pretended to ignore Granny's remark, but Rosie could see that it affected her. She came over unsteadily and took Rosie's chin in her work-roughened hand.

"Rosie," she said, "look at me straight, now, and answer me straight. Is that what's happenin'? Are the boys so worthless—the young girls don't want to be bothered with them any more? Is that why it's the style to dress ugly?"

"Style is just style," Rosie said uncomfortably, pulling away from her mother. "But—aw, Mom, you know most of the boys around here don't have no money and no ambition neither. They just want to lay around and let some woman take care of 'em."

"I know, I know," Queenie sighed. She went back to the sofa and stretched out on it. "All right," she said in her most tired and beaten voice. "Go on and try, if you think you can do better than I did. I shouldn't be the one to stop you. Lord knows I ain't made such a grand success of my life."

"I'm glad you realize it," Rosie said, then bit her tongue.

Mom sat up angrily. "Well you won't do any better, workin' in that cabaret. You'll do worse!" she cried. "I know what hangs out in there. A bunch of fast sportin' niggers and racketeers."

"I'm not takin' this job for the social life," Rosie said.

"Regina, you ought to encourage her," Granny said. "You ought to be glad she's ambitious."

"You don't know that place," Queenie said to her mother. "I don't know how you could reach your age and be so ignorant, but you don't know anything. She's too young for the kind of men that hang out in there. —Rosie, please listen to me," she urged softly. "Don't ruin your young life. First give yourself a chance."

"I told you, I ain't interested in meetin' men, I'm just interested in makin' money," Rosie said.

Mom got up to pour herself a drink. "That's what you say now. But the time will come when money won't make you happy. And you'll wish you'd snatched yourself a good man while you was young and had the chance. But you'll decide a no-good man is better than none at all."

"Like Roscoe, you mean?" Rosie said. "The hell with that. I'd rather go on takin' care of myself."

"Well, you're gonna have to, the way you look," Mom said. She half drained her glass. "Look at that handbag, it looks like a U.S. Mail Bag."

"At least it's nice real leather," Granny chirped. "I think she looks nice and neat and businesslike."

55

"Aaaaaah," Mom exploded in disgust. "She looks like somethin' a man would rather pick a fight with than go to bed with."

"So what?" Rosie yelled. "Where'd it ever get you?"

"It got me you," Mom said quietly. "But I'm beginnin' to think you wasn't so much of a bargain."

9

The phone rang at ten o'clock on a Saturday night.

Cursing, Queenie hauled herself out of the bathtub and padded into the front room leaving a trail of wet footprints on the linoleum. "Since Rosie had that thing put in, I ain't had a minute's peace," she muttered. "Can't even scrub my ass in private."

"No, she ain't home," she yelled into the phone. She was about to hang up when muffled buzzes somewhere near her mouth told her she was speaking into the wrong end.

"Excuse me, I had the thing ass-backwards," she said into the mouthpiece. "You want Rosie?"

"Yes, please," the voice said faintly.

"Well she ain't home. She ain't never home these days. You wouldn't know she has a home the way she's out all hours of the day and night runnin' the streets and lookin' for trouble." She paused, breathing hard, waiting for the voice at the other end to contradict her. But she had cowed it into silence. "Well," she said reluctantly, "you can look for her over at Benny's. That's where she's supposed to be workin'. But if I know anything about it she ain't there. She's hangin' out in one of them bars on the Avenue."

"Thank you. I'll try Benny's," the voice said, very small. It was followed by a faint click.

"Don't waste your time," Queenie said into the dead phone. She hung up. Behind her she heard another soft click, the sound of the door opening. She turned with her hands on her hips.

"Roscoe Gordon, why can't you ring my doorbell like everybody else? You keep on lettin' yourself in that way, you gonna get shot dead for a sneaky thief."

She tried to look murderously angry but was conscious of being naked, fat and ridiculous in the presence of this natty little man whose eyes sparkled with wickedness.

"If I waited for you to open the door I wouldn't see you like that. Now tell the truth, Queenie. Would I?"

He turned on his slow teasing smile. It was irresistible. Like all his ingratiating ways, it by turns delighted Queenie and infuriated her because she knew it was calculated to have the same effect on many others. She knew it most painfully at times like this, when she was perfectly sober. After a few drinks she was sometimes able to forget. But, drunk or sober, she had little resistance to Roscoe's charms.

"If my mother was home she would kill you," was all she could think of to say. "She ain't got no use for you, anyhow."

Roscoe pretended to be wounded. He took a step backward. But all the while he looked and looked at her until his eyes seemed full of looking.

"Well," she said at last, "you just let me dry myself. You can wait that long, can't you?"

After speaking to Rosie's mother Dolly knew instinctively that Benny's would be the sort of place she was not allowed to visit. When she looked it up in the phone book and found out that it was on the Avenue her instincts were confirmed. She was not even supposed to set foot on the Avenue.

She saw the big red *BAR* a block away. Then the blue letters flashed beside it: *Benny's BAR*. Finally the little green lights winked on and she read: *Benny's BAR-B-Que*. By turns the green and the blue snapped off, reappeared and vanished again, but the red hung constant in the black sky. When she shut her eyes for a moment, the word burned on her eyelids.

Suddenly she was less than twenty yards from Benny's. She slowed her steps. The corner was dense with men. Men always

God Bless the Child

noticed Dolly—though all she craved was to be inconspicuous—
and these were the kind who would notice her with noisy
originality. A blare of brazen music came to her on the wind;
she stopped and tried desperately to be interested in a window of
astonishing blue-black wigs. Dolly disliked her timidity, but by
protecting it she had learned to live with it comfortably.

Then why did she push her way into the heart of this section
which her mother called the Black Belt, and which seemed to
her as exotic, and as dangerous, as a marketplace in Marrakech?

Because she wanted to see Rosie before she went away to
teachers' college. And she had followed her into danger ever
since their escapades in second grade, so it seemed natural that
she should pursue her into the neon-light district tonight.

The wind changed; the reek of fish frying in rich fat blew full
in her face. Dolly's nostrils constricted. She breathed cautiously,
then deeply; it smelled good. She was suddenly hungry. Two girls
brushed past her with purposeful heel-clicking strides; the same
wind blew back high laughter and an even higher perfume. Dolly
found herself moving. She was swept into Benny's behind them.

The air was unbreathable; the temperature was at least eighty
degrees. The girls had disappeared. Dolly moved forward alone
in a lurid red light that made the forms and shadows of men
and women seem projections from the heart of an intense flame.
As she penetrated further into the murk she made out that it
was a sort of restaurant. The booths on the right were packed
with restless people who shouted to each other while music
shouted over them:

> *"You're beautiful baby but*
> *You gotta die someday . . . I said*
> *You're beautiful baby but*
> *You gotta die someday. . . ."*

At the left she saw the dim outline of a long counter with
stools. As she plunged toward it she heard one voice that could
only be meant for her:

"Yo, cowboy! Yo, Tex Ritter!"

58

In spite of herself Dolly smiled. When she sat down at the counter she pulled off her wide-brimmed hat and crushed it in her lap with her bag and her gloves. And, in the darkness, she began to laugh—whether because it was the funniest thing any-one had ever said to her, or because Benny's was so dark and noisy no one would notice her laughing anyway, she could not tell.

". . . Better give me some lovin'
Before you pass away."

"What'll you have, doll?"

The voice was automatic; brisk fingers flipped the pages of a pad, tapped a pencil on the counter.

"Well, doll?" A note of impatience. "You decide yet?"

"I'll have some of that fine filet of flounder."

"Yeah. So would I if—" Rosie's eyes flew open; they were sud-denly enormous. "Dolly!" She lunged across the counter to kiss Dolly, lost her balance, and succeeded only in banging her hand against a seltzer tap. "Damn," she said, sucking her hurt finger with a child's bewildered expression. "Doll, you big jerk, how come you didn't say somethin'?"

"I wanted to see how long it would take you to see me."

Rosie removed the finger from her mouth with a loud sucking noise. "Child, in here we don't see the customers. We just serve 'em."

"Hey, chippie. Where's that ketchup?" The voice came from one of the booths. It was a gravelled whisper that carried above the general noise with strange authority.

"Same place it always is, fool," Rosie muttered. She ducked from behind the counter. "Excuse me while I go see what this monkey wants."

He was a very small, very dark man dressed in black and wear-ing dark glasses, and he was completely eclipsed by the magnifi-cent pair of girls who had passed Dolly on the street and now glowed on either side of him. While she watched he seemed to melt into his background and become a mere shadow on the wall.

59

"I ain't no chippie," Rosie told him. "I got a big mouth and I'm big enough to back up anything it says."

The girls had a brilliant metallic luster set off by black taffeta dresses; winking rhinestones swung from their ears and their dyed hair matched their skins exactly—one copper, one bronze. They were looking at Dolly. She smiled. They quickly turned their splendid faces away.

The man gestured and Rosie leaned down to let him whisper in her ear. She straightened almost immediately. "No, man. Ain't no happenings like that."

He whispered something else.

"Yeah, yeah, okay," Rosie told him. She came back to the counter.

"Listen, Doll," she said, "you wait for me in that empty booth back there. Okay?"

"Can't I stay here?" Dolly asked. But Rosie had a firm hand on her elbow and was guiding her toward a far corner.

"You can but you better not," she said.

Before Dolly could think of a protest, she was seated in a booth where a partition joined the wall behind her and screened her on the right. Though others could scarcely see her, from this point she had the widest possible view of Benny's. She could see down the entire aisle and across to the adjoining bar that was slowly filling with customers.

"You'll be real comfy here," Rosie said. "I'll come 'n have coffee with you soon's I feed some more of these monkeys."

Feeling like a child chafing under some incomprehensible adult discipline, Dolly watched the pink apron bow bobbing on Rosie's skinny hips as she hurried back into the mainstream of the crowd. As she passed the booths, people called out to her from all sides. Stopping to take an order from a couple, she leaned over and dropped a casual arm around the man's shoulders while he scanned the menu. When she moved on, an elderly man reached out and smacked her playfully on the bow.

Rosie grinned, shook a warning finger. "Careful, Pops. It's fragile."

Laughter rang from all the booths.

They all love Rosie, Dolly thought, envying her easy responses to familiarity. If anyone ever slapped me like that I'd scream and run. But it's nothing to Rosie. It's as natural for people to touch her as it is for them to warm their hands at a fire.

She had not seen the middle-aged white man come from the booth near the door where he had been watching Rosie carefully for the past two hours. Suddenly he was swaying in front of her, blocking her path.

"Hey, girlie," he said thickly, "I'll give you ten dollars."

With an involuntary movement like a released spring Rosie stepped back.

"You can't afford it," she said. "Your mother only gets three."

The Negroes who had heard laughed heartily. The man flushed and backed toward the door. He stopped there and seemed to be trying to say something more. The last of the laughter had died; everyone in the room was watching him quietly. With a furious, frustrated gesture he opened the door and slammed it behind him, leaving an uneasy silence.

Through that silence Rosie moved like a spark of electricity between two wires, wisecracking and sweet-talking and joshing the customers to take their minds away from the ugly thing that had almost happened. The noise began to climb toward its previous level. Someone dropped a coin in the juke box and music blasted out. Clowning and singing, Rosie trucked up the aisle; when she reached Dolly's corner she did a two-step and a kick and collapsed laughing into the booth. And did not move.

"God, I'm beat," she said. "You're lookin' at a natural wreck, Doll. 'Rosie, get coffee. Rosie, get ketchup. Rosie, get a broom and sweep the damn floor,' " she mimicked. "When the boss gets on me like that, it really drags me."

"Who's the boss?" Dolly asked.

"Benny? He's right over there." Rosie pointed to a portly Italian, with cheeks so red they seemed painted, who was turning hamburgers on a grill behind the counter. "You can bet a man he ain't never very far from the scene." Out of his sight, she tilted back on her spine, swung her feet up and crossed her ankles on the table.

"Feet are naturally killin' me," she said. "Got to get 'em up. Start the blood jumpin' down there again."

"You ought to wear more comfortable shoes," Dolly said sensibly. She touched Rosie's sandals—white cobwebs on four-inch heels.

"You like my hussy shoes, Doll?" Rosie asked eagerly. "They some wicked shoes, ain't they, if I do say so myself? The tariff was wicked, too."

Dolly breathed a deep sigh and looked at Benny again. "I thought he'd be colored," she said.

"Who?" It was not a question. "Child, you know your people ain't got the money to put up for a place like this. If they did I wouldn't work for 'em."

"Why not?"

"They mess up."

"What do you mean?"

"They mess up, that's all. They leave Aunt Minnie to watch the store while they go on the church picnic. Or if it rains they invite everybody over'n have the picnic in the store. 'N you all have a ball, but when payday comes they say, 'Rosie, you're a great kid, we love you madly, but we're sorry.' Now Benny, he never leaves this place. He don't even sleep. He's too busy watchin' the money come in."

"You won't work for a colored man," Dolly said slowly, "but you won't let a white man get fresh with you."

"Benny's all right," Rosie said after a pause. "White customers is different." She frowned and stared at her fingernails. "That cat's been around here talkin' his trash before. Next time there won't be no next time." She dipped her fingers in Dolly's glass and flicked a drop on the table. "The boys'll just pour on a little water and wash him away."

"Who was that man, Rosie?" Dolly asked suddenly. She shivered a little at the thought of the fugitive stranger.

Rosie lit a cigarette with elaborate casualness. "What man, Doll? What man you mean?"

"The man you talked to. The one who made you bring me back here."

"He didn't do no such thing, Doll. I just thought you'd like a booth all to yourself so's you could feel like Madam Queen."

"I don't believe you."

"Long as you've known me, Dolly Diaz, did I ever lie to you?"

Dolly said nothing.

Rosie was silent for a long time. "You were cutting his chicks," she finally said.

"I was what?"

"You should be flattered, Doll. Shadow has the highest priced trim on the Avenue."

"You mean he thought I—"

"Sure. Why not? All he could see was the boys diggin' you instead of Ginger and Amber. 'Course when I told him you was my friend he was relieved. But he still wanted you off the scene."

"Why?"

"He didn't want you distracting customers from the merchandise, that's all. Distractions is bad for business."

"Rosie," Dolly asked, trying to sound calm, "suppose I hadn't been your friend? What would have happened if—"

"If you was meat? You'd be hamburger." Rosie stabbed out her cigarette. "I got a lot of respect for Shadow. He's a real businessman."

There was a long silence while they looked at each other across the space between two worlds.

Finally Rosie moved restlessly, shrugged, and said, "So what's new by you?"

"Nothing," Dolly said. As always after a few minutes with Rosie, she knew nothing interesting had happened to her. "Nothing at all," she repeated. Remembering Rosie's shrug and her intonation, she added, "You sounded like a Jew just then."

Rosie laughed. "I oughta, Doll. I'm around 'em all day."

"You mean you have another job?"

"Sure. I still work in the daytime at Schwartz's Store. I sell Better Dresses now. I don't know what they're better than, 'cept rags, but I sell 'em."

"Do you like it?"

"They're all right. They ain't exactly white people, you know what I mean? I mean they're white but they act like they don't know it. You take this saleslady I work with, Betty Perlman. She's real regular. She helps me buy stuff wholesale. Stockings, handbags, anything I want. I don't buy nothin' Gentile any more." And while Dolly laughed Rosie went on to say that Betty had a good heart, but she didn't know the score. Take the day Rosie had admired Betty's new hairdo. The other girl had immediately offered to let Rosie take her next appointment at her hairdresser's.

"Child," Rosie said, "I had a time gettin' out of that one. Believe me. 'N I could just see that poor fool takin' me out from under the dryer 'n droppin' dead from the shock. Can't you?"

"I don't know," Dolly said thoughtfully when she had stopped laughing. "I went to a white hairdresser once. He did a nice job."

"Well, that's different," Rosie said. "You're white anyway."

Dolly was angry. "That's not true."

"It is so. That stuff of yours is as straight as my Uncle Jump's razor."

"Rosie, you know perfectly well I'm colored. Why, my father's as brown as, as *chocolate!*"

"No, you're white, Doll," Rosie said. "You know it. But that's okay. I'm democratic. You can still be my friend."

Dolly knew her face was burning, but she didn't care. She was bitterly angry. "Rosie," she began, "you make me so mad I—"

Rosie doubled up in laughter so excruciating she choked on her cigarette; tears streamed from her eyes while smoke poured from her mouth and nostrils. "Doll," she said at last, coughing, "Doll, you still the same old fool. It's good to see you."

"It's good to see you, too," Dolly said primly. She fumbled in her purse for one of the reasons why she had come. "Here. For your birthday. No, don't open it now," she said, for Rosie's fingers were already tearing at the wrapping. "You'll embarrass me. Wait till you get home."

"Thanks, Doll," Rosie said. "You good to me." She covered her mouth with her hand; her giggles were threatening to erupt again. "What flavor'd you say your father was? Vanilla?"

Dolly refused to bite again, she waited calmly while Rosie subdued herself. She glanced at her watch and was shocked at the hour; nervously she began to rehearse the explanation she would give her mother. Then she noticed that Rosie's eyes were closed, her head drooping and nodding peacefully.

"You must not get much sleep these days," she said softly.

"Child, I can't even remember what it's like to sleep." Rosie yawned. "I guess it must be your bedtime, though."

"I wish you could get more rest, Rosie."

"You know something, Doll?" Rosie sat up alertly, her face animated again. "When I'm awake the only thing on my mind is sleeping. No lie. Every minute I'm not working that's what I think about. I plan on getting myself a room with a great big king-size bed and a lock and a chain on the door. The bed'll have curtains hanging around it like in olden times. And percale sheets and an eiderdown quilt and a foam rubber mattress. It'll be in a big old house way out in the country where it's so quiet you can hear the snow falling outside. 'N I won't tell anybody where I'm going. I'll just sneak in there and lock my door and flop down between my sheets and fall asleep listening to the snow. And—but you know something else?"

Dolly shook her head.

Rosie laughed. "If I had that room I wouldn't stay in it five minutes. I can't stand to be laying around in bed when there's all this loot out here to be made."

Her eyes were closed again; she was whispering, and the words were meant for no one but herself. "I want things. I want things so bad I'd kill myself to get 'em." Finally she blinked and shook her head as if to clear it. "Looks like it's time for me to start scufflin' again."

Dolly got to her feet. "I have to be at school Monday. Promise you'll write me."

Rosie stood too. She picked up the package and dropped it casually in her apron pocket. "Thanks, Doll. Someday I'll do the same for you."

"Happy birthday," Dolly said. You're eighteen now, she thought. You're eighteen and so am I but you've lived twice as long as me.

Outside Benny's she was surprised to find everything the same and herself intact. She had a miraculous feeling as if she had survived a hazardous ordeal. As she walked along with mounting pleasure because she, Dolly Diaz, was strolling fearlessly up the Avenue at one o'clock in the morning, she decided not to invent any explanations for her family. Though they would surely be waiting up for her, she would not lie. Borrowing courage from Rosie, she would say absolutely nothing and let them think whatever they wanted.

10

Most of the time Rosie had no objections to Uncle Roscoe, though she knew his slender graceful hands and his dapper little mustache and his deep appreciative laugh were good for only one thing: to delight women. She even respected him a little because he did this one thing so well it provided him with a living. He made Mom happy. So Mom wanted him around. It made sense. It was okay with Rosie.

Most of the time.

But when she got home nights from Benny's, she'd been on the go since eight in the morning and the last seven hours had been spent on her feet. After giving out warmth and charm for all sixteen of those hours she had none left for anyone.

So it was unfortunate that the first thing she saw when she

walked into the apartment was Uncle Roscoe pouring himself a drink of her private whiskey. It was expensive whiskey, and she kept it at her bedside for one necessary purpose — to knock her out. To make her sleep a solid drugged five hours before it was time to get up and start the whole routine over again.

"Well, if it isn't our little career girl," Roscoe said when she walked in.

That didn't improve matters.

Rosie felt tired, hot and dirty. The stink of Benny's—grease and smoke and alcohol fumes—was embedded in her hair and her clothes, but Roscoe was as new-looking and immaculate as if he had just stepped from a men's furnishings store. His neat little mustache was perfectly groomed; he smelled of barber's tonic and wore a red bow tie and a crisp tan sharkskin suit that Mom had bought him. He was stirring his drink with one of the sterling silver spoons Granny had brought home to Rosie to put away for her hope chest. Little bubbles sparkled to the surface of his glass and burst there. Something in her seemed to burst as she watched them.

"What's the news from the business world?" Roscoe asked pleasantly. Mom moved closer to him when he sat down beside her on the sofa and crossed his legs and carefully adjusted his trousers.

"You really want to know?" Rosie asked.

"Certainly," he said. "You know I'm always interested in progress."

"Well, I'll tell you." She walked to the couch and stood over him. "The news is one of your chicks was in Benny's lookin' for you tonight."

Roscoe raised his eyebrows. He looked at her steadily, trying to stare her down. "Little girl's got a great big imagination," he said. He patted Mom's knee; a rumble of laughter came from his chest. "A great big imagination."

"This chick," Rosie went on heedlessly, "claims her old man is lookin' for you too. On account of you took twenty dollars from his pants pocket the last time you was at her house."

67

Roscoe managed another easy laugh. "Does she always make up these tales, Queenie?"

"Maybe I made up her name," Rosie said, " 'cause anybody oughta have better sense than be named Wheatena Cartwright. But I didn't make up that straight-edge razor she was carryin' in her handbag."

Roscoe chuckled. "She's a cute little thing, Queenie. In fact she's gettin' to be almost as cute as her mother. But she's gettin' much too big to be tellin' fibs like that."

"Save your sweet talk for Wheatena," Rosie said. "You'll need it 'fore you get through explainin' where you been all this month. 'Course for a while you had her believin' that jive about a business trip out of town." She snatched up her bottle, tipped it and swallowed a generous mouthful, then capped it and dropped it in her handbag. "But I straightened her out on that score. I told her you been around here every night seein' my Mom and drinkin' my whiskey."

"Look at her," Queenie said with distaste. "She thinks she's a woman."

"I was eighteen today," Rosie said, "in case you didn't happen to remember."

"I'd like to forget the day you were born."

That hurt, but Rosie was good at pretending she didn't care. "I'll bet Granny remembers," she said. The thought comforted her. She waved her wrist; her new bracelet sparkled in the light. "Somebody else remembered, too."

"You a regular hustler, ain't you?" Mom said. "What racketeer did you sleep with to get that?"

Rosie's eyes were filling with pain and something else. She turned and walked quickly to the bedroom door. "My friend Dolly gave it to me!" she shouted. "Not that I care if you believe me or not."

"That little yellow girl sure must think a lot of you," Mom said. "Damn if I can see why."

"Try and be quiet in there," Rosie called from the bedroom. "If your rowdiness keeps me awake I won't be able to go to work and the rent won't get paid this week. 'N the landlord'll save me the trouble of throwin' you out."

In her room she took off the bracelet and held it to the light, studying the dainty gold links and the small white stones shot through with bright colors. Granny will like this, she thought, planning to give it to the old lady. Dolly probably paid plenty for it. But if it had been up to her, Rosie would have chosen something a little more flashy. Hell, you couldn't even see those little bitty stones unless you got right up on 'em in a bright light.

She stretched out on the bed. Her feet were so numb they might be lying on the floor beside her shoes. She could feel her legs though; they tingled with little flutters of pain. Eight dollars in tips tonight. She poured the change from one hand to the other, but the jingling did not drown out the rattle of dishes and the screams—"Double order Frenchfries!" "Slaw on them crabs!" "Bottle a beer!"—that rang in her ears. And Benny was still stalling her, holding up her bigger dreams. Over five months of working like a dog for him, and he was still watching, watching with that impassive face of his, and never saying a word. She was sick and weary to her soul.

"Sick and Weary to My Soul." That was a church song Granny knew. Granny wasn't really religious, but she sang spirituals with an artistic air. Rosie could almost hear the sweet crisp notes coming from the kitchen. With sudden excitement, she looked across the bedroom. Yes, a small hump was barely visible under the day-bed covers. Delicate snores came from it, and a long skein of silver hair was strung out on the pillow. Rosie turned out the light quickly. Soon it would be Sunday morning, and when she got up an elegant breakfast would be waiting. She was nearly asleep when she heard Roscoe's smooth, reasonable voice arguing in the front room.

"Queenie, you know I wouldn't be giving these chippies the time of day if you and I had a permanent arrangement. But the way things are, I just can't afford to lose all my contacts."

Rosie giggled into her pillow. She had not seen 'Tena Cartwright in months, and her tale had merely been an accurate invention.

"You telling me the truth, Roscoe Gordon?" Mom would be smiling, believing what she wanted to believe.

His voice throbbed with emotion. "You know I am, Queenie. If we got married it'd be different. You know you're all I could ever want in a woman."

There was a long silence before she heard her mother say, "Roscoe, I think you better go on home now."

"Queenie." He was whispering. "Queenie. You think maybe you could let me have that twenty you promised?"

Rosie screwed her eyes tight against the light that went on in the hall. She heard clumsy sounds as Mom shuffled into the other bedroom. A drawer was opened, then slammed. That would be Mom's share of the rent. Rosie would have to pay the whole bill again.

Footsteps trudged back to the front room.

"Queenie darlin'," he said, "I'll never be able to thank you."

Rosie burrowed under the covers. Her eyes were threatening to water, and she thought of tough dirty words to stop the shameful tears. She said them again and again into the pillow. Mom was generous to everyone. Except her own daughter. The grown-up daytime Rosie didn't give a damn, but the child in the lonely dark couldn't help caring. The child would never understand. It was just a moist secret between her and her pillow.

It was dry by morning, when Granny appeared at Rosie's bedside in a beautiful brocade housecoat.

"Breakfast is served, Miss Rosalie," she said, ducking her head in a graceful little bow.

"Who fixed it?" Rosie asked suspiciously. "You or Mom?"

Granny smiled. "I did, 'cause I know you've been cravin' some of my short biscuits. I hope you don't mind."

"Me mind biscuits? Does Rockefeller mind money?" Rosie jumped up and hugged Granny roughly, then drew back and looked at her with concern. "You're company though. You're supposed to lay around and take it easy. Why can't Mom get up off her butt and do the cooking for a change?"

Crusts of Bread and Such

"Now don't start a lot of argument first thing in the morning. If there's anything I hate, it's quarreling on the Lord's day," Granny said piously.

Rosie expelled a violent breath. She had been about to say much more about Mom's laziness and the rankling presence of Uncle Roscoe, but she never disobeyed Granny. "All right, Lady Katy." She put an arm around her grandmother's tiny waist. "Let's go taste this fabulous breakfast."

"I know you don't plan on coming to the table in that," Granny stated.

Rosie looked down at her bare feet and her cotton pajamas. "I'm sorry," she said meekly.

"Well, put on something respectable," Granny ordered. "And don't be fiddling around in front of that mirror neither. Just wash your face and comb that disgraceful head and come on."

"Right away, Granny," Rosie said. In one lightning movement she pulled down her pajama pants and kicked them onto a chair, froze for an instant to light a cigarette, then ran, naked from waist to heel, to the bathroom.

"You're bad as your mother," Granny called out. "I never know whether I'm raisin' girls or jaybirds." With an air of resignation she picked up the pajama trousers, folded them neatly and put them on the dresser.

Rosie took a "birdie" under the tub faucet, dabbing twice in certain places and once in most, then hopped out. She needed no towel. She moved so fast the friction of the air dried her body as she ran back to the bedroom to comb her hair.

The dress, a bright red rayon taffeta, was draped in intricate folds to create the illusion of the bosom she would never have. She wriggled into it with violent spasms of her shoulders, then studied herself in the mirror. The skirt stood stiffly away from her boyish body and was lined to make her hips seem curved. A price tag dangled from the zipper. She seized it in her teeth and pulled it free. Twenty-nine fifty; with the discount, twenty-five.

"Now this is what *I* call a Better Dress, Mr. Schwartz." She announced this in arch accents to the mirror with a condescending wave of her hand. Chin high, arms stiff, hands waving languidly as a ballerina's, she minced grandly across the room to the bed. She explored the floor beneath it with her bare toes until she found her new patent leather sandals and kicked them out. They were the most expensive shoes Rosie had ever owned; they had cost just six dollars less than the dress.

"And they worth it," Rosie told the room as she forced her feet into the tight straps, " 'cause this baby's hard on shoes." With the left shoe still flapping loosely she hobbled back to the mirror. There she worked her foot gradually into its prison while she smeared on brilliant lipstick, sprayed a halo of perfume and screwed golden teardrops into her ears.

"Rosalie, you knock me out," she said admiringly to the mirror. She gave herself several approving pats. Then she bent forward suddenly and kissed her image.

"I love you madly," she whispered, " 'cause you're so good to me."

She found the kitchen in darkness. No natural light ever entered this room because its only window looked out on the wall of the house next door. The lights that burned constantly had gone dead again. Rosie added electrical repairs to her long list —leaky plumbing, stained ceilings, rotted linoleum, heat that poured out in summer and hibernated in winter, insect life that honeycombed the walls—

"Damn that landlord's hide," she said, and wondered if he really were Benny. "All he knows how to do is raise the rent."

"Now don't start a fuss," Granny called sweetly from the closet. "We're gonna have something much nicer than 'lectric lamps."

When she brought the lighted candles to the table Rosie stared in amazement. It was magical.

Granny had transformed the table with a cloth of real white linen. It glowed in the warm circle of light cast by candles flanking a vase of pretty orange flowers. Across the table, Mom's face again had the brazen beauty Rosie could barely remember. She had sleepy, hazy memories of Saturday nights when Mom had still dressed up in the gay colors that set off her brilliant dark eyes, her bold red mouth and her bright gold skin. Granny had not yet come to live with them, and there was a large jolly man with a vague face who always tugged at Mom's arm and made her laugh at her fears of leaving Rosie alone, then took her away. People then had another reason why they called her Queenie: because of her arrogant way of walking down a street like she owned the world. Those Saturday nights had been long ago; by the time Rosie was seven she had forgotten that her mother had ever been anyone but a sullen, fat woman who shuffled tiredly around the house in a torn kimono. But now, by candlelight, her eyes snapped and sparkled again.

Why, Rosie thought, Mom's beautiful.

Granny was quick and gay, pouring Sunday morning coffee by evening candlelight, as if she was happiest when the world turned upside down.

"Now isn't this just like a party?" she said. "Flowers on the table and everything. Isn't this just grand?"

At that moment the lights came on. Mom instantly blew out the candles.

Rosie blinked as the cracked gray walls and the sink piled high with dishes came into view; as she heard again the familiar drip, drip, drip of the faucet that had needed repairing as long as she could remember.

Now she could see that Mom's first effort to fix herself up in years was a failure. Her straining bosom had burst the pin that fastened a large tear in her cheap print dress; a grayish edge of slip showed beneath. Pancake makeup had turned her skin a dirty tan, her orange lipstick was violently wrong, and her hair refused to stay tucked beneath the rat where she had pinned it. It stuck out in all directions.

"Lost my appetite," Rosie said. She pushed away the biscuits, which had chilled quickly in the damp, drafty room.

"Now you just eat those biscuits," Granny said. "I made 'em special for you."

"I can't stand the sound of that water," Rosie said irritably. She jumped up, ran to the sink and wrenched at the faucet with both hands. It refused to budge. When she let go the steady

73

dripping persisted as before. In fury she kicked the exposed pipes, dislodging a dozen frightened ants who scurried across the floor.

"We got a Sunday paper in this house?" she demanded.

"Look on top of the little buffet in our room," Granny said.

Rosie ran to the room she shared with Granny and whirled in circles until she saw the thick newspaper lying on the white tin cabinet that held sheets and towels. She ripped her way to the Real Estate pages and returned to the kitchen.

"I'm findin' us another place right now," she announced. She ran her finger down the page. After passing three columns of *White* apartments, it lighted on: *Colored—Room and toilet, $26 week.*

"Room and toilet!" Rosie balled the paper up and flung it on the floor.

"I think a nice coat of white paint would brighten up this kitchen considerable," Granny said mildly. "White or maybe cream. What you think, Rosie?"

"I'm sorry, Granny. I ain't paintin' no landlord's apartment so's he can go raise the rent on us."

"You should try and not notice it then," Granny said. "If they's things you don't like and you can't do nothin' about them, you just best pretend they ain't there."

"I can't do that, Granny," Rosie said. "I'm sorry." She shivered a little and hugged herself. "Pretendin' ain't gonna keep me from catchin' colds. This place is damp as Froggy Bottom."

"Wrap up and keep warm then," Granny said practically.

"I still got to look at them walls every day. And listen to that spigot. And hear them rowdy noises next door and smell this stinkin' air and eat garbage the roaches been runnin' over—"

"Now stop that," Granny said sharply. "Things could be worse. At least you got a home. You don't *have* to move, like my folks, with no place to go."

"Them poor miserable millionaires," Mom said. "It breaks my heart every time I read in the papers how somebody robbed them of some more of their diamonds. Pass me a biscuit."

Crusts of Bread and Such

"Everybody has their troubles," Granny said firmly, "rich *and* poor. 'Course the young ones don't care. Miss Emilie and her husband don't 'preciate that beautiful old house. They can't wait to chase after somethin' new and modern. But Miss Helen's lived there so long it'll be like cuttin' off an arm and a leg to leave."

"The poor old thing," Mom said. "She sure must be sufferin'.'"

Rosie shot her a disapproving look, then returned her attention to Granny. "Why do they have to move?"

Granny put on her most distasteful expression. "You know that old fortune teller woman named Esther? Black as the evil she is?"

"Yeah," Rosie said, her interest growing.

"Well, she's branched out lately. Wasn't satisfied just to be foolin' folks around here. Had to start workin' her tricks on the ladies up our way."

"You mean Miss Emilie and her friends believe in *spooks?*" Granny nodded.

"They can afford to," Mom said with her mouth full. "They can afford to believe in anything they want."

Rosie shook her head, as always respectful of a successful racket. "Esther sure must be makin' money up there."

"Oh, she charges something disgraceful," Granny deplored. "Fifty dollars for a reading, and five hundred for a service."

"Seance, Granny," Rosie corrected.

"I don't care what you call it, it's the Devil's work," Granny said. "Pretendin' to tell the future and call up spirits, and not lettin' the dead rest in their graves. Proof is the way she got them ladies under her control. 'Specially poor Miss Birdie."

"You mean Miss Birdie Rice? Miss Helen's best friend?" asked Rosie, who knew all the names of Granny's exalted circle and had followed their histories avidly since childhood.

"They ain't been friends for a long time. After her brother died, Miss Birdie got kind of simple. She wouldn't do nothin' without first askin' that witch-woman what *he* said about it.

75

And then last month Miss Birdie up and died—" Granny paused dramatically "—and left her house to Esther."

Rosie sucked in her breath.

Granny nodded. "That's the way everybody up our way took it at first. They just couldn't believe it. Folks was talkin' about tryin' to break the will, but wasn't nothin' they could do. Miss Birdie didn't have nobody else to leave her property to."

Mom had begun to shake with silent laughter when Granny's story reached its climax. Now it erupted in a full, free explosion. "Lord, I'll bet they're scared to death up there," she said when she could speak. "Every time they see us comin', they run. It always tickles me, how scared they are of us niggers."

Rosie was tempted to agree, but she was conscious of Granny's feelings of regret at leaving the place that was most her home. "Miss Birdie had a nice house, didn't she?" she asked.

"Even nicer than ours," Granny said, " 'cause she got there first and picked the best spot in the neighborhood."

An idea was taking hold in the recesses of Rosie's mind. She could feel it grow. She got up and turned her back to hide her excitement.

"Wonder how much it's worth?" she mused, looking out the cloudy gray glass at an identical kitchen window two feet away, and seeing wondrous visions.

"Oh, that house is worth plenty," Granny said calmly. "I spect it cost pret' near thirty thousand to build, and that was back in the old days. You couldn't replace it for twice that today."

Rosie turned a desperate face to Granny as she went on, " 'Course houses on Madison Drive are all coming down in price now. Nobody wants big houses any more. Everybody wants to live in a apartment. Or way out in the country, next to some pig farm." Granny's nose wrinkled at an imaginary bad smell. "I don't understand people today, Rosie. If they can't respect themselves, seems like they could at least respect something that's better than they are, like a fine old house. That beautiful big place across the street from us went for seventeen. To Jews, too. It's a crime and a shame. There's no telling what Birdie's place will bring."

76

Rosie stopped trying to hide her eagerness. "Wonder if Esther wants to sell it?" she asked.

"Sit down, child," Mom said quietly. "Sit down here and let me talk to you."

Rosie turned to her in surprise.

"Sit down," Mom said again.

Rosie approached the table warily. She could see Mom had something on her mind. Her broad, usually humorous mouth was drawn up in a tight line.

"Rosie," she began. Her tongue came out nervously and touched her upper lip. "Rosie, you know I ain't gettin' any younger."

Rosie noticed how the naked bulb showed up the heavy dark circles below her mother's eyes and the black scars, from years of handling hot curling irons, that disfigured her arms and hands. Then she hardened her thoughts and looked away. "Hurry up," she said. "I ain't got all afternoon."

Dull color came into Queenie's cheeks.

"Hush that sass and listen to your mother," Granny said.

Rosie darted a surprised look at Granny.

Mom's voice was carefully humble. "I been workin' ever since you was born. Eighteen years is a long time to work and have nothin' to show for it."

"You got me, ain't you?" Rosie retorted. "Ain't I somethin'?"

"Yes, I got you," her mother said with irony. "I only hope you remember what you owe me after all these years."

"What do I owe you?"

"All my life I been slavin' in other people's shops for commissions. Now you're pullin' down good wages, it's the least you could do to help your mother get her own business." Realizing she might have gone too far, she softened her voice. "I'll pay you back, hon. It wouldn't take much money. We could rent it cheap and just put in one booth and one dryer to start."

"I don't have that kind of money," Rosie said flatly.

Mom's voice was harsher now, more insistent. "I'd paint it and fix it up myself, Rosie. You wouldn't have to do a thing but sit back and watch me make money."

"Don't you want your mother to go in business?" Granny urged.

"I ain't got it," Rosie repeated.

"Don't you lie to me, you little bitch!" Queenie was almost screaming. "I know how much you got!"

She laid Rosie's bankbook on the table.

Rosie snatched it up. "I guess you know you messed up now," she said softly.

Mom dropped her eyes. "I ain't askin' you to give me nothin', Rosie. I just want a loan. I'd pay you back in no time."

Rosie turned away from her.

"I'm a good hairdresser," her mother pleaded. "I'd have plenty customers. You know it, Rosie."

"You been satisfied all these years," Rosie said. "How come you wanta go in business all of a sudden?"

The room was suddenly quiet. "I told you," Queenie said. "I ain't gettin' no younger."

"Naw. That ain't it." Rosie pretended to be baffled. "It must be somethin' else." She snapped her fingers. "I got it. Is it 'cause you wanta marry Uncle Roscoe?"

Granny did not say anything, but her face shriveled in a frown.

"Rosie," Mom said in a low voice, "it just ain't natural for three women to be keepin' house all by themselves. —But that ain't the only reason," she added quickly. "I want to be independent."

"How you gonna be independent if I'm payin' for it?" Rosie laughed raucously. "Naw. You went and promised that Roscoe you'd take care of him if he married you."

"Well, suppose I did?" Mom flushed. "I wouldn't be the first woman worked to help out her man. That's been goin' on since slavery."

"That don't make it no better," Granny grumbled. "It's a disgrace the way these young boys all want their wives strugglin' out to work. No matter how many babies they got draggin' around their necks."

78

"All the more reason," Queenie said practically. "Takes money to feed them babies."

"Well, how come the fathers ain't working? How come they're hangin' on the street corners all day? You answer me that." Granny looked at Rosie sharply. "I hope you ain't gonna let no good-looking trash mess up your life. If they can't provide for you, you're better off single."

She means Larnie, Rosie thought. She did not answer Granny, but fixed a hard stare on her mother. "How you gonna get married?" she said. "Ain't you still married to my father?"

"That don't matter," Mom said. "We can still get a license and go down City Hall and say the words."

"That's against the law," Rosie said.

"Rosie," Mom said wearily, "you oughta know the Law don't pay no mind to people like us. Divorces cost money. Cleo's had three husbands and she ain't studyin' no divorces."

"But you wouldn't be married in the sight of the Lord," Granny interposed.

"I'd be married in the sight of Roscoe Gordon," Queenie said. "That's the main thing."

"Well, I ain't stoppin' you," Rosie said. "Go on, get married."

"Rosie—" Mom's eyes were desperate. "You just got to understand. When you get my age, if you want a nice man, you got to offer him something."

"Well, offer him something else besides my money," Rosie said. "I work hard. I make good money. But it's for Rosie. I ain't workin' night 'n day to help you support no Roscoe Gordons. You just better make up your mind to that."

"I'd pay it back," Mom said dully. "I'd pay you right back, Rosie."

She looks awful, Rosie thought. Pity touched her for a moment, but she shoved it away. "Naw. You won't pay it back. You'll just give it to Roscoe first time he asks you, same way you gave him the rent money. So's he can take it and spend it on the first young chick he sees on the Avenue."

"That's a lie," Mom said.

"It's the truth and you know it. All you gotta do is look at yourself in the mirror. What man's gonna hang around just for that?"

Mom's hard backhand was on her cheek before Rosie finished. The blow brought tears to her eyes, but she managed to laugh. "That don't hurt," she said airily. "You even gettin' too old to hit worth a damn."

The grotesque tearing sounds of her mother's sobs followed her out of the room as she went to answer the phone.

"Sure, hon, sure," she said into the mouthpiece a moment later, "you know I always wanta see you, but right now I'm beat, you know what I mean?"

"What'd you say, Rosie?"

Rosie coughed to clear her throat. It hurt her chest when she coughed, but it was necessary. In the mornings her voice was so husky people could hardly understand her.

"I said you're sweet and I'm mean," she said in a strained, cracked whisper.

"Does that mean I can come over?"

"Okay," she said after a pause. "Later on. I got an errand now, but you can take me over to the club later."

"Rosie, it's a nice day. Can't we just go for a walk in the park or something?"

Her voice was coming back. "I get all the walking I need all week long, Larnie Bell. I got to walk someplace right now, and my feet will be cryin' when I get back. So you just go on and walk in the park without me, you hear?"

"No, Rosie." He sounded resigned. "I'll take you any place you want."

"Well, come on over in two, three hours. And I'm togged today —so wear your new blue, you hear?"

She hung up and saw that she was still clutching her bankbook. Where she was going, she didn't need anything else—except nerve, and if she waited, she might lose that.

The house was tiny and shabby, set back from the Avenue and sandwiched between large four-story commercial buildings. It seemed to be shrinking from view. A store-front window had been chopped out of most of its façade. The window had a sign:

What Is Troubling You ? ? ?
Bring Your Troubles to MADAME ESTHER ! ! !
Genuine Gifted Medium
She Sees All—Knows All!

A curious display of wares was arranged in the window against a backdrop of gaudy flowered cloth. Rosie gave them a quick once-over—Lucky Conqueror Incense, Money-Drawing Oil, African roots, Indian herbs, animal bones, a stuffed snake, a dirty skull. She shuddered and turned back to the door. Its shiny black paint and bronze knocker contrasted oddly with the decrepitude of the rest of the house.

Rosie rapped twice. Almost immediately, a light-skinned old man with terribly deep-set eyes opened the door and led her into a small, airless parlor crowded with straight chairs, dusty plants, and small tables draped with crocheted shawls. He indicated a table in one corner at which two chairs had been placed facing each other, and disappeared.

Rosie sat down and looked around her with interest. For a minute her eye was arrested by a photograph on one table; it was a boy wearing such an old, wise expression that it was difficult to tell his age. It was another minute before she recognized Tucker.

She spent the next quarter of an hour, with growing nervousness, studying the worn Oriental rug with its patterns of hexagons and circles divided into wedge-shaped areas inhabited by crude figures, fish and archers and mermaids and bulls. She wished she could read the strange script in its corners. Instead, she occupied herself reading the quaint little half-religious mottos —"Work, for the Night is Coming," "Faith is the Mover of Mountains," and "Search for Diamonds in Your Back Yard"— which were tacked here and there on the oatmeal-papered walls.

The flowered drapery in the window had suggested an exotic gypsy; but Esther, when she finally appeared, was a very short, very stout, very dark sybil. Without a word or glance she seated herself opposite Rosie and buried her head in her hands, keeping both index fingers pressed against her forehead.

Rosie sat rigidly, afraid to breathe or speak, checking her impulses to break the absolute silence.

After ten minutes of concentration the woman abruptly looked up.

And she had marvelous eyes, the color of Rhine wine, startling as stars in her dark face. They were great wells of pale yellow light that seemed to flood through Rosie and light up all the secrets she carried inside.

Rosie backed away and raised her hands in a defensive gesture. "Now wait a minute," she said fearfully. "You didn't give me a chance to explain. I didn't come here for a reading. I just wanted to talk over a little business."

"Then I won't charge you," Esther said calmly. "But I must warn you. You are going to be very sick. If you don't change your ways before it is too late, you will die while you are still young."

Rosie managed to laugh. "You ain't foolin' me. I don't believe in this mumble-jumble."

"Then go to church and pray," Esther said. "It's Sunday, go today. Pray to get rid of the bad influences in your life."

"What influences you mean?"

"A man and a woman. One young, one old. One is already with you, and one is coming back into your life soon. But the worst influence of all is right there inside you." Esther leaned across the table and pointed her finger at Rosie's chest. "You don't know what's good for you. You choose the wrong things and the wrong people. You are wise for your age, but you have a lot to learn."

Esther pushed her chair back from the table and lowered her luminous eyes. "That's all."

"You could've said those things to anybody and been right," Rosie said defiantly.

"That's so," Esther said, her face impassive.

"I was kinda surprised to find you still here," Rosie said, after a nervous pause. "I sorta thought you might've moved uptown."

Esther fixed her with a golden stare. "You want to buy the house," she said.

Rosie felt her bravado crumbling. "How did you know?"

"The way everybody could know things if most people didn't keep knowledge out. I let things in. Then I add them to the other things everybody knows." She smiled, displaying a gold tooth and dispelling some of her aura of mystery.

Her odd West Indian accent was what made her sound so scary, Rosie decided.

"Besides," Esther admitted, "you're not the first one to come askin' about the place." She named a half dozen prominent people: a lawyer, a preacher, several businessmen.

"I'll offer you a better price than any of 'em," Rosie said recklessly.

"You haven't seen the house."

"I don't need to."

"And you don't have enough cash."

"No," Rosie admitted. She looked up defiantly. "But I will."

Esther nodded. "All right. I believe you. The price is fifteen thousand dollars."

Rosie was incredulous and a little indignant. "But look here—" she began.

Esther's eyes took on a menacing light. "That's my bottom price. Take it or leave it. I can't go no lower."

Rosie's perverse anger at succeeding so easily finally found words. "You mean you gonna trust me, when I just walked in here off the street? After all those other people?"

"I'm not worried," Esther said. "You pay the bank. The bank pays me."

"But you ain't seen my bankbook. You don't even know my name. How you know I'll get the money?"

" 'Cause I know you want that house," Esther said. "I never saw anybody with a worse case of the wants. You got Want written all over you. So I know you'll find a way to pay." Then she explained, "You just think those other folks I mentioned got money 'cause you see their pictures all the time in the paper, at balls and parties. Truth is, all they got is high life and a whole lot of debts."

Esther's shrewd grin made her homely and human again. "I know who you are. You're little Rosie Fleming, and you have more money than they do."

Rosie was still unable to feel the relief that should be there. "It might take me a while to get the down payment together," she mumbled. "Maybe two, three years."

"I'm in no hurry," Esther said cheerfully. "I'll wait. I've got nothing but time. Nobody here but me and my old man, and we ain't going no place. My customers uptown wouldn't like it if I moved next door to them."

Rosie could see the logic of this, but she was still disturbed. "You say there's just the two of you?"

"Yes," Esther answered without hesitation. "No children."

Rosie felt a mysterious chill. Her eyes darted to the photograph on the table. "Well, thanks a lot," she said, rising. "I'll be in touch."

Esther detained her. "How about a little something for luck? I got some powerful roots here. Bring you anything you want."

Rosie shook her head, not wanting to see whatever it was that Esther was rummaging for in a drawer.

She turned with a tiny bottle. "Here. Have some of my Special Blessed Perfume. Free."

"No thanks," Rosie said. "Some other time." She made swiftly for the door, because she was about to scream at the stifling room, Let me out of here!

Outside, though her mission had been accomplished with amazing ease, she did not feel triumphant. She felt more like crying. First the fight with Mom, and now that conjure woman saying she was going to die. She felt an immense sorrow for herself, so young, so small, so still, lying in a chapel lit with candles. She began to walk dejectedly home, seeking something to lift her mood again. But on a Sunday afternoon, the deserted Avenue was particularly depressing.

Where did they go in the night? she wondered, walking by the blank buildings that yesterday were Edwards Cleaners and Jackson's Shoe Repair and Viola's Beauty Salon and Henderson's Hoagie Shop—all empty now, all dark, with signs down and doors padlocked and naked windows gaping like the faces of old women with mouths too shrunken for false teeth.

It would go on, of course. Tomorrow there would be other tense hands fussing over a window display of crepe paper draped over a jar of pressing oil or three cans of beans from the stock of twelve. Viola's Beauty Salon would have a freshly painted sign— now it would be Vivian's, or perhaps Vernon's Pool Parlor or simply Boot Black in the steady shrinking of aspiration that shriveled a neighborhood until all its buildings were gatherings of ghosts, rust heaps of hopes that when new had seemed bound to work because they were patterned on the best machinery, but now were as thickly encrusted, and as sad, as a billboard slashed to show six inches of forgotten messages.

Tomorrow there would be new faces, terribly eager faces, smiling with undue encouragement at the customer who only wanted the evening paper, carefully putting the three pennies in the drawer and saying Thank You Call Again with ringing conviction and closing the drawer with a flourish and rearranging the smile so it would be fresh for the next customer who never came. On the Avenue—the Avenue of Greens, Rosie called it, thinking of the grocers with their baskets lined to the curb, and of the song about the Avenue of Dreams—on the Avenue, few things stayed. Schwartz's Store stayed, though it did not grow, and Benny's, and the Friendly Loan Office, and the Forty-First

Precinct Police Station, and Wiggins & Meritt, Constables, and Skyros' Drug Store with its posters advertising roach killers and rat poisons. For of course the rats and the roaches stayed. They would be the last to leave. At the end the rats too would be ghosts, with milky bodies from the long years underground, and they would scurry from the unsettled dust of the loan company's foundations in a spectral dance down the Avenue that was a dream landscape at last.

Where did they go?

Rosie knew.

The smartest ones left first and went to better places. Those who first moved in after them were smart, too: the first to leave worse places. But sooner or later someone pulled the gear that reversed the direction and the long dreary march backward began, until the last arrivals met the rats leaving their new homes.

Rosie was smart.

She would leave soon, and she would go where rats and roaches could not follow, if it meant keeping on the move forever.

12

"Well, Molasses-in-January?" Rosie said as she opened the door for Larnie. "What took you so long?"

His eager expression faded; the golden lights in his eyes darkened. He stepped diffidently inside. "I'm sorry, Rosie," he said. "I stopped to watch some kids playing football."

She gave him a don't-tell-me look. "Oh, no. You didn't just stop and watch. You got in that game. Didn't you?"

"Well—" he confessed.

Staring at him, Rosie burst into raucous laughter.

"What's the matter?" Larnie asked resentfully. "Don't I look right?"

She scanned him rapidly. He was wearing a new blue suit, the one she had specified; his tie matched his socks; his black shoes were new, with a shine dust could not obscure—yet even in these clothes Larnie managed to look as if he had just come in from a long hike in the country. "I don't know," she admitted. "The pieces are all there. On you they just don't hang together."

"I'm sorry," he said stiffly. "I did the best I could."

She studied him thoughtfully. It was not a question of clothes. It had to do with his loose, relaxed walk and his swelling muscles that refused to be imprisoned; his rude physical presence that triumphed over all camouflage. She moved close to him and patted his cheek. "Never mind, honey. I still like what's inside the clothes."

"You mean that, Rosie?"

"Sure I mean it." She looked up teasingly through half-closed eyes. When he responded by pulling her against him she wriggled away. "You fixin' to spoil my new dress, Larnie Bell."

He scowled; it made his face even more handsome. "You just tease me all the time, Rosie. You treat me like a toy or something. You—"

She stood on tiptoe, touched his ear with the tip of her tongue, and whispered, "Your face gonna freeze like that if you ain't careful."

He laughed. Feeling safe now, she permitted a kiss. "You got breath like a baby," she said dreamily afterward. "Real sweet 'n clean."

"I take good care of my teeth. I guess that's why," he said.

Rosie's tongue ran over two gaps in her jaw, awakening memories of recent soreness. She broke away from him and sat down on the couch.

Larnie followed her. "Now what's the matter?"

"Oh, nothing." She pronounced it in a way that distinctly meant "something."

"What is it, Rosie?" He sat down beside her. "Please tell me."

Her voice was very small; she kept her face turned away from him. "My teeth don't happen to be perfect like yours. So I suppose I got bad breath."

"I never said that, Rosie," he pleaded. "It's not fair putting words in my mouth."

When she first saw the pain in his serious, sturdy face she was tempted to laugh. Then she was ashamed. She sighed impatiently. "Larnie, I ain't no good to you, am I?"

"Sure you are, Rosie."

"No." She patted his knee comfortingly. "Here I am draggin' you over to the club, and you don't even wanta go. What you wanta see a lot of phony people and drink a lot of whiskey for? I bet you even went to church this morning."

He nodded. "Sure, Rosie. You know I play the organ every Sunday."

"See? Now you wanta do something nice like take a walk or listen to music or—"

"I want to do what you do, Rosie."

She shook her head violently. "No. It ain't right. I make you do all kinds of things you shouldn't. I can't help it. I ain't like you, Larnie."

"Don't you think I know that?"

She looked at him in surprise. She met a steady, resolute gaze.

"I know you're different from me," he said. "I know you don't like any of the things I care about. You've told me enough times."

Her voice was hard. "What you keep on comin' around for then?"

He spoke haltingly. "I guess because—I never knew anybody like you before. You're so—exciting." He looked up eagerly. "You're like you're on fire. When I'm around you I'm on fire, too." He touched her hand delicately, pleadingly. "I just got to keep on seeing you, Rosie."

She shrugged. "Well, it's your funeral." She summoned a laugh from nowhere, jumped to her feet and shook herself like a wet puppy. "Come on, sourpuss. Don't take it so serious. You believe everything I say?"

She grabbed his arm and towed him toward the kitchen. "Come on. Let's show Granny how nice you look."

Larnie seemed embarrassed at being put on display. He hung behind her in the doorway.

"Look what I got for my birthday," Rosie said proudly. "Ain't he pretty?"

Mom looked up at Larnie. "You a nice boy. How come you waste your time on a mean little girl like her?"

"Now don't talk to the young man that way, Regina," Granny said. "He's a guest in our house." She sat up straight in her chair and inclined her head stiffly toward Larnie. "We always rather have Rosie bring her company home than meet 'em on the streets."

To break the frozen awkwardness of the moment Rosie stepped forward. She revolved like a model and struck an exaggerated pose. "Nobody's said nothin' about my new dress. Ain't it glamorous?"

"Why is it," Mom said, "the blackest ones always want to wear the brightest red?"

"Now, now," Granny soothed. "I thought you wanted her to wear pretty dresses. Maybe it is kind of gay, but she's a young girl."

"You ain't heard the news," Queenie said. "She's a woman now. She informed me yesterday."

Larnie backed toward the door, trying to become invisible.

"I didn't forget," Granny said. She smiled. "Rosie, hand me my handbag."

From the capacious purse of worn but good black leather she withdrew a neat little package wrapped in tissue paper. "You take good care of this, you hear?" she told Rosie. "This ain't none of your five-and-ten junk jewelry."

She unrolled the paper. A snake of fire slithered into her lap. Rosie caught her breath.

"Them's real hand-cut crystal beads," Granny said proudly. "Miss Helen wore 'em when she was a young girl. I been savin' 'em till you was old enough to wear 'em."

Rosie ducked her head so her grandmother could drop the

89

beads around her neck. "They're fabulous, Granny." She kissed the papery cheek. "Simply fabulous."

"Well, you better not lose 'em." Granny reluctantly let go of the beads. She seized Rosie's sleeve and rubbed it between her thumb and forefinger. "Thought that wasn't real silk," she said with mingled distaste and satisfaction. "Your old Granny's eyes ain't so bad after all. 'Course it's very nice material, but I knew right off it was one of them imitations."

"Thank you for my present, Granny," Rosie said softly. "I'll be real careful with it." She backed swiftly toward Larnie, seized his hand and squeezed it hard.

"Look what thinks it's a woman," Mom said, looking off into space. "And got no more legs'n a grasshopper."

Rosie dug her nails into Larnie's palm. "I guess we got to be going now."

"You oughta give me them beads," Queenie said to her mother. "She don't appreciate 'em."

Rosie's words came out hot and crackling as chicken in a frying pan. "What you got to complain about? Didn't I buy you a new dress this month? And stockings and gloves and a pair of shoes? Ain't you eatin' regular these days? What's your complaint? You're drinkin' good whiskey, ain't you?"

"What right she got to complain?" she repeated indignantly to Larnie as they hurried out of the apartment. "You tell me. What right?"

Larnie's instinct for self-preservation was still strong enough to back him away from all feuds among women. He put an arm around Rosie and said nothing.

The air was cool outside, with a faint scent of smoke that made Rosie think of Hallowe'en. "Wish I had some peanuts," she said.

Larnie smiled indulgently. "What for?"

"Them peanuts we used to get for coalpieces was the best I ever ate. You remember the year I dressed up like a boy and stuck a knife in my belt and Old Man Skyros chased me out of his drug store?" She laughed. "He was really scared of me. He thought I was gonna cut somebody." They laughed together, the happy, conspiratorial laughter of children.

"I wish we could go out this Mischief Night 'n ring doorbells again, Larnie," she said with sudden wistfulness. " 'N ask for coal-pieces on Hallowe'en." She bent her knees and hunched her shoulders. "You think we could get away with it? You think if I put on a mask and walked like this, people would think I was still a kid?"

"I don't think so," he said reluctantly. "You're too big, Rosie. You're grown up now."

"Aw, I know. Jerk. Didn't you know I was just foolin'?" She straightened, took his arm properly, and walked stiffly beside him, like a child imitating a lady.

Larnie let out a long breath. "It's the first real fall day. You feel it?"

She nodded.

"Why don't we take a nice walk someplace?"

"Told you I don't want to go for no walk, Larnie Bell." She kicked some leaves before her; they sprayed the air, fell, and mingled with the rubbish that choked the gutter. "I seen these streets before. I know what's out here."

She walked faster, trying to get ahead of him. Her heels struck the pavement like furious hammers.

"I'm goin' straight over the club, you hear? You don't have to come along 'less you want to."

The K.D. Club had wall-to-wall carpets, soft music, low lights and a solicitous staff who saw to it that everyone's drink was always fresh—and always paid for. It was rumored that Benny also owned this place, where the rowdiness of his regular Saturday night crowd was toned down to the decorous buzz of a Sunday afternoon church social. It made Larnie yearn for fresh air.

Feeling big and awkward and obviously underage, he followed Rosie across the thickly cushioned floor. Shouts greeted her from all sides, but they were dampened by the carpet and the sound-proof ceiling, and she responded with equal restraint, as if she were afraid to be herself in here and were playing at being some-body else. She walked regally beside him, looking straight ahead and acknowledging each greeting with a slight nod. When one stout woman, trailing white foxes, rushed forward and attempted to clasp Rosie to her bosom, she stepped aside and said in a frosty voice, "Mr. Bell, this is Mrs. Wiggins, a friend of my grandmother's." Then she turned away, cutting the woman dead.

"I can't stand people who lowrate you when you got an escort," she whispered as she took possession of Larnie's arm.

At the bar, Rosie denied her appetite for whiskey to order a champagne cocktail. She flirted with a cigarette holder and man-aged to look like a young girl smoking for the first time. As she blew a cloud of smoke and stared into it with her head tipped back, Larnie wondered what visions she saw there to make her eyes shine like that.

At last she came back to her surroundings and smiled at him. "You wanta make Rosie happy, lover," she said, "you got to make it like this for her all the time."

Flustered and happy, Larnie mumbled that he would if he could, though he suspected that "like this" meant something that was not like Rosie, nor like himself, nor like anything else that was real. He was about to say that he wished she could reconcile herself to living the way other folks did, because that was all he really wanted, a life like everybody else's with Rosie— when he heard a click and felt the cold embrace of metal on his wrist.

"At ease, man. It ain't The Law," a voice reassured him. "I just wanted to call your attention to this fabulous buy in a richwatch."

Larnie looked up at an elegant hipster dressed in dove gray from head to toe.

"Genuine Swiss works," the man recited. "Jooled movement. Twenty-four fabulous jools, and I *do* mean jools. This here watch is imported, man. Custom made. Now I want to tell you some-thing. If you was over there and had a million dollars you couldn't buy this watch. Nobody over there can buy it, 'cause they only sell it to *dukes* and people with *titles,* you dig? The *King of England* has a watch like this. Now, can you afford to pass this up for only ten dollars? Can you stand to let me take this fabulous thing away?"

"Ask him what pawnshop he robbed it from," Rosie said.

With a shrug the well-dressed pitchman moved on, making room for another who appealed to Rosie.

"This here is genuine imported tweed, baby," he said, unrolling a length of fabric on the bar. "English hand-woven. No other cloth on earth like it. Wouldn't you like to see him dressed up in a jacket made of this stuff? You could take and make yourself a fine suit to match—"

"How much?" Rosie asked.

"Dollar ninety a yard, sugar, but I'll knock off fifty cents for you just because you're so sweet."

"Will you take it out and show me in the daylight?"

"No, baby. Just between you and me, this stuff is hot. I got to be careful. If the man catches me—"

"Okay, okay. Move on," Rosie said impatiently. She played with her cocktail a moment longer, then drained it in one gulp to help her see visions again.

"This place reminds me of that movie with Rita Hayworth," she said.

Now Larnie knew who she was pretending to be tonight.

"You remember, lover. Her old man was a millionaire, and he owned a club like this. All the other millionaires hung out in there, and she was a singer, with all them fabulous clothes. . . ."

Rosie was happy, and when she was happy she immediately became restless. She slipped from her stool and began to dance, heeling-and-toeing in a small semicircle around Larnie. She put on a good show. He was entertained.

Until she suddenly stopped and leaned against him, shivering as if a door had just opened on winter.

Larnie looked up and saw a small, dark man watching them with speculative, colorless eyes.

"Looking mighty sharp today, doll," he said.

Rosie pressed herself against Larnie so hard she seemed to be trying to squeeze into his clothes.

"Thanks, Shadow," she said.

"You know, I hate to see a gorgeous gal like you working so hard all the time. She works like a dog," he confided to Larnie. "It ain't right."

"If I want to work it's my business," Rosie snapped.

"Yeah, but with your looks and your figure, you could do so much better, baby. You could be a model."

"I don't wanta be your kind of model, Shadow."

Shadow clucked deploringly. "Now, that don't sound nice at all. Maybe you never thought of yourself as the glamorous type, but you ain't the one to judge. I'm tellin' you, you got a certain kind of appeal. Ain't that right?" He winked. Larnie smiled back at him.

"See?" Shadow teased. "He knows. You listen to the young man. He won't steer you wrong."

"Shadow," Rosie said, "how come I don't never see your models in no magazines?"

"Oh, photography isn't the coming thing any more. The coming thing is personal appearances."

"Yeah." Rosie laughed. "I know all about them personal appearances."

Shadow smiled wryly. "What you gonna do with these young girls nowadays? They know it all. They won't let you tell them a thing."

"Rosie, how come you were so rude to him?" Larnie asked when Shadow had gone. "He sounded like he wanted to help you."

Rosie was clutching his arm. "Where did he go, Larnie? Did you see him walk out the room?"

"No, I didn't exactly see him," Larnie admitted. "But he must have. He's gone."

"Well, where did he go, then? Did he just disappear? Just sort of—float away?"

"Don't be crazy," Larnie said.

94

"He's after me," she said unreasonably. "Everybody has some-body after them and Shadow is after me. I got to keep running or he'll get me sure."

Larnie put an arm around her. She was still shivering.

"Don't you feel it, too?" she said in a barely audible whisper. "Like a cold wind blowin' down your neck when he comes around? You feel it too, Larnie? Or is it just me?"

"Hush," he said gently, not knowing how to cope with her small insanity except to distract her. "Stop scarin' yourself and listen to the music."

He nudged her toward her stool. With a sigh of impatience, she climbed back on it and listened dutifully.

The one thing Larnie liked about the K.D. Club was that good jazz was sometimes played here. And tonight four young men with goatees were saying very interesting things to each other on a piano, a bass, drums and a vibraharp.

"It sounds but it don't swing," Rosie complained after ten minutes of pretending rapt interest.

But Larnie was not pretending. His eyes were closed, and his hands wove imaginary keyboard patterns on the bar.

Rosie, made restless by the music, was about to begin her seri-ous drinking when Rabbit, the bartender, removed her empty glass. Rabbit was on old hand at discretion. He leaned over the bar to give it a wide swipe with his cloth and simultaneously brought his lips to Rosie's ear.

"What you drinking? Gentleman down there is paying."

Rosie swiveled on her stool and found herself staring at a broad-shouldered fellow who was winking at her and making a come-on with his finger. He shifted his gaze to Larnie and made an obscene gesture, then winked at her again. In the crowd, he had the three-dimensional quality of a man against a background of painted figures that might be real or might only be the way she always saw him. Standing out sharply because he was waiting for her.

"Double V.O.," she whispered, "I'll have it down there," and elbowed her way to the end of the bar.

He tipped his glass toward her in mock salute. "To Rosalie and the Avenue. They haven't changed."

She hadn't seen him in two years, but he hadn't changed either. Rosie did not think Tucker was ugly; she thought him handsome. He had a face like a broad, satirical African mask, all ebony planes and angles.

Anyway, it had nothing to do with looks or intelligence or even money. His power over her was generated by his smooth assurance and his delightful jive and his fantastic energy that kept wheels spinning, balls dancing, worlds revolving around him. It was contained in little things like the ease with which he signaled for and received service and the indifferent competence of his hands with the mechanism of a lighter. But most of all, it was expressed by the devilment in his constantly flickering eyes.

"Where's my kiss?" he demanded, thrusting out his lips like a Ubangi. "I've been a lonely soldier for two years. I want a big wet sloppy kiss right now."

"Oh, Tucker, stop," Rosie said, resisting as he pulled her toward him. "Not in here. It's Sunday."

He laughed. "Since when are you so proper? What are you, anyway, twenty or forty?"

Rosie sat primly on her bar stool. "I'm sweet sixteen and never been—"

"Now you know that's a damn lie," he said. "And you know I know it."

"Hush," she said in genuine alarm. "You ain't too cool, Tucker."

"You're unreasonable as ever, baby," he complained. "How can I be cool with you sitting next to me—wearing that dress that keeps everybody warm but you?"

Rosie laughed then, and relaxed, and permitted him her hand. It was as if they had last seen each other not two years, but two days ago. They smoked in silence for a minute, absorbing each other, while voices drifted in the rosy haze around them.

A mellow baritone: "Why waste your money in here, old

buddy? I got everything you could want up at my place. Shrimps, Scotch whisky, women. . . ."

A delicate birdsong: "Darlin', you just got to let me invest in this property for you, it's A-1 real estate. . . ."

A hearty bass: "Now you just stop worryin', sweetheart. I've cured a hundred backs like yours with this machine of mine."

"Everybody's workin'," Rosie said. "Everybody comes in here to hustle." She watched dispassionately as one of the girl hustlers, a trim blonde, moved in on Larnie and engaged him in conversation.

"Amateurs, Rosie mine," Tucker said. "They just have the props, the cars and the clothes and the scenery. They don't know what the play is all about." His left hand played casually with the crystal beads around her neck. "Nice," he said as his fingers tightened on her breast.

She slapped his hand away.

"Owww!" he said ruefully. "What did I ever do to make you treat me so mean?"

"Now you're home, Tucker," Rosie asked coolly, "what's *your* hustle?"

"Oh, I sell the main merchandise of the U.S.A.," he said with a rich resonant laugh. "Dreams. You can buy a penny dream, a nickel dream, a quarter dream, or a dollar. On the side I even put out the books that tell you what dream to buy."

"I know where you get that dream stuff from," Rosie said, giggling. "Your mother. I hear the spiritual business is pretty good these days."

He frowned. "She's not my mother." He was silent for a minute. Then he shook off the unnatural seriousness, laughed, and gestured at the decor around them. "How do you like my office? The setting is important. Helps everybody believe their dream will come true." He leaned forward and tipped her chin up with one finger. "What's your dream, little girl?"

She answered him with a probing look. "What's yours?"

"I'm not buying, I'm selling," he said with another easy laugh. And began to sing under his breath,

97

God Bless the Child

"Rosalie, I love you,
Rosalie, be true . . ."

She did not take her eyes away from him.
He put his hand on his heart.

"Since that night when stars shone above,
I'm oh, oh, so much in love. . . ."

She clucked her tongue impatiently. "Tucker, I asked you a question."

He stopped singing; the animation left his face. "The same as always, baby. To be top man in this town, Number One."

"All by yourself?"

"You can come along if you want."

"I do want," Rosie said with great seriousness. "You need me, Tucker. You've been away, been out of it. I've got lots of contacts you could use. My customers at Schwartz's, customers at Benny's—"

" —Your friends who drop by your house," he finished for her.

"Naw," she said, thinking of Granny. "Not at my house. I'll work for you any place else, though."

"Sure, Rosie," Tucker said. "I always said you and I could go places. You've got brains, you've got push, you've got what it takes." He paused significantly; there was a new thrilling vibrancy in his voice. "I mean you've got what it takes for me."

"Excuse me," he said before she could respond. The bartender slipped a note to him. He scribbled an answer and put it into Rabbit's hand with a folded dollar bill.

Rosie saw that the same respect was still accorded Tucker. People who had business with him approached the bartender first and waited for their instructions. Pockets Robinson's sending him a note impressed her more than anything Tucker could say. Pockets usually waited on no one; he was the only colored man on the Avenue with a numbers bank of his own.

Tucker turned back to her and explained with a chuckle, "Pockets decided to play along with me. I told him I didn't mind letting him work the whole Avenue while I was away, but now I'm back he's lucky to have the north end of it."

Rosie, though she had been all business a minute ago, thought suddenly, perversely, Who cares?, because now she was ready to be hearing other things.

As if he read her mind, he said, "But don't let me bore you with my dreams. Let me take care of yours."

He beckoned, and Trixie the flower girl came over with a gardenia for Rosie's shoulder. She buried her nose in its scent and did not dare to look up.

When she did, a jeweled wrist watch lay on the bar before her. She put it on.

He snapped his fingers, and Rabbit was pouring champagne for her.

Magic man, Rosie thought as the bubbles danced before her eyes. Too good to be true. Magic man. Now if he could only make her beautiful.

And then he did that too, with his steady eyes and his restless hands. "It's been a long time, little girl. Too long. Too, too long."

He was still able to turn her into water. There was no hesitation as she followed him to his car.

"Time to trade this in," he said of his last year's Cadillac. "Your people don't trust a man unless his car is a big piece of their dream right there in front of them."

"—As for where I live," he said as he led her into a particularly fly-specked and musty-smelling hallway, "that's nobody's business but mine."

She did not have time, anyway, for more than a quick look around his small, seedy apartment before his hands became black satin ribbons tying her into a package for him. They were all over her, and then he was too, like a great black bat covering her with its wings.

"Tucker," she said weakly as they lay idly together, yet separate again, "Tucker, don't you ever feel sorry for all the poor people who lose their money playing the numbers?"

99

He laughed at her innocence. "Look," he said. "I'm black. Only way I can make it in this country is be an outlaw. I could do worse things. I could push dope or rob people or beat them up or smething. All I do is make them happy.

"Besides," he said, moving away from her, "you shouldn't ask me to have feelings. I stopped having feelings when I was ten years old."

She did not have to ask why. Things happened to kids on the Avenue. Things that should never happen to small creatures with big eyes always happened to the ones with dirty faces and ragged clothes and untied shoes. No, his remark disturbed her for another reason.

"If you got no feelings, Tucker," she said softly, "what you want with me?"

He gripped her chin and forced it up and bent swiftly.

"I need a little capital and a smart woman. What do you say?"

The lines of a song, "Everybody's Somebody's Fool," ran through Rosie's mind as she reeled beneath his kiss. But her answer was, "Anything you say, Tucker."

She was still singing it softly as she came up the street at three in the morning. At the steps, rummaging in the jumble of her bag for the key, she did not at first notice the large shadow bulking in the doorway. When she did, she jumped back in alarm.

"What you sleepin' here for? This ain't no Salvation Army."

The form jerked awake. "Huh?" it said.

She peered closer. "Is that you, Larnie Bell?"

"I've been waiting for you, Rosie. I was worried you wasn't coming home."

His voice, at once sleepy and resentful, amused her. "Ain't you up kinda late? I thought you was supposed to be in training."

"Stop making fun of me, Rosie." Now she could see the yellow blaze of his eyes, like a cat's in the moonlight. He caught her arm roughly. "Where you been?"

She shrugged free of him and backed away. "I had to take care of a little business," she said pertly.

"What kind of business you got to take care of with Tucker till three in the morning?"

"None of your business. You ain't my father."

"Yeah? Well, I was talking to your Mom, Rosie. You know what she said? She said I'm crazy to worry about you. She says she gave up worrying long ago. She says you're nothing but a—"

"Don't you talk that way to me, Larnie Bell!" Her eyes were suddenly stinging. "If your friends believe anything anybody tells 'em, they ain't no friends at all. They just—" Her voice broke on a high note.

"I'm sorry, Rosie," Larnie said after a pause. "But you've been gone six hours."

"I ever give you permission to watch the clock on me?" she raged. "I don't punch no time card for nobody, Larnie Bell. You best find that out right now. I come when I please 'n I go when I please 'n all I want to hear from any man is 'Goodbye' when I leave and 'Hello' when I get back." She tossed her head. "I don't have to tell you this, but Tucker and me are going in business. I'm gonna be his partner. We made all the arrangements tonight."

"I believe you, Rosie," Larnie said finally. "But I don't want you fooling around with that Tucker. I don't trust him."

"You just mind your own business, Larnie Bell!" She climbed the steps until her head was on a level with his. "Ain't I big enough to take care of myself?"

"I worry about you, Rosie," he said miserably.

She was touched. "Look," she said, "I don't want you worryin' about me. You going to college and all now, you got enough to worry about. Don't worry about this mule. This mule's been to school." She leaned over and kissed his forehead. "Now go on home and get some sleep, you hear?"

"Can I call you up tomorrow, Rosie?"

"No," she said. "Ain't you got studyin' to do? And practicin'?" She held his arms and looked at him steadily. "You oughta be 'shamed of yourself, stayin' up this late, Larnie. I want to be proud of you. I want you to do perfect in school. I want you to be the greatest so's I can point to you and tell everybody, 'That's my Larnie!' "

"You mean that, Rosie?"

"Sure I mean it. Just 'cause I didn't get no education don't mean I don't want you to have none. There's gotta be somebody smart in the family!" She kissed him again, absent-mindedly. "Now you hurry on home, you hear?"

"Rosie," he said softly, "when you walked out on me tonight I was so mad I could've killed somebody. But I'm not mad any more. You're wonderful, you know it? You're wonderful."

Finally she managed to murmur good night and slip inside. She stiffened before she crossed the threshold of her bedroom, expecting a small high voice to call out, " 'Bout time you remembered where you live!" But the room was quiet. Granny had gone home to her other family. Moonlight flooded the room in an eerie bath of white light. While Rosie undressed and slipped into her cold bed the print of lipstick on her mirror seemed to curve in a faint, ironic smile.

TWO

Money, You Got Lots of Friends

13

Rosie was as fond of Mr. Schwartz as he was of her, but sometimes he was a pain, and on the Thursday that ended the month the old man was particularly like a fretful four-year-old at her hem. Complaining about his overhead and his sick wife and his incompetent help, especially Aaron. Fussing because Rosie had overstayed her lunch hour to do some shopping; then following her and drowning her in apologies until she nervously rang up two wrong totals on the cash register. Insisting that she stay to help him take inventory, because he couldn't depend on anyone else.

When she finally got home, sweating and swearing, Granny greeted her at the head of the stairs with a fingertip to her mouth.

"Hush that noise, child. You got a visitor."

"Who, Granny?"

"A real nice young man. Let me look at you, now. I swear, sometimes—" Granny's hands dove beneath Rosie's coat and busied themselves brushing and tugging at invisible lint and wrinkles. "Best I can do," she sighed with a final brisk pat. "Better run a comb through that head before you come in."

Rosie handed Granny her packages. "Here, look through this junk. You see anything you like, you keep it. But don't let Mom get in it, you hear? There's a nightgown in there for her but that's all she's gettin' this time." She dug in her purse, then snapped it shut impatiently. "Can't find no comb, Granny. Sorry. Who'd you say was here?"

He was already in the doorway, smiling and extending his arms for the packages.

Granny put the last hatbox in his arms. "You're a real gentleman, Mr. Tucker." She smiled up at him in a way that momentarily drew the veil of wrinkles from her face and gave Rosie a glimpse of the girl she must have been.

"Come on, Rosalie," Granny said, linking arms and leading her to a chair, "let's sit down and be sociable." She included Tucker in her smile. "Mr. Tucker and me were just havin' a little chat about wines. I asked him if he'd take some refreshment, and do you know what he said? He said he was sure a lady like me had a favorite wine she liked to serve when she entertained." Granny chuckled. "I gave Mr. Tucker some of Miss Helen's sauterne, Rosalie, and he knew what it was right off. Most of our folks think it's just some kind of sherry." She sniffed. " 'Course they ain't used to nice things like Mr. Tucker is."

Rosie looked at Tucker. He was beautifully dressed; his superbly cut brown suit and his creamy shirt made the living room seem unbearably shabby. Beneath his polite silence she sensed, and resented, a hum of suppressed amusement like the chattering of high-tension wires.

"You comfortable, Mr. Tucker?" Granny asked him solicitously. "Don't you think it's a little warm in here?"

"I'm fine, thanks, Mrs. Huggs." His hand darted to a table. "But let me offer you a fan."

"Much obliged, Mr. Tucker." Granny made several token passes in the air, then laid down the cardboard fan with its legend, *Strange Funeral Home.*

"Is this a social call, Tucker?" Rosie demanded, more sharply than she had intended.

He laughed. "Business first, huh? Oh, I know you, Rosie. I know you from way back." He winked at Granny. "She's a little go-getter. Always was."

Rosie felt whatever softness she had left drain out of her. —And yet, back in school, she had originally been drawn to Tucker because his passion for success was like the strongest thing she felt herself. That, and the need to keep moving.

"No," she said brusquely. "I told you I never talk business at home."

"Why not?" he said with an easy shrug. "We have nothing to hide."

Rosie looked in alarm at Granny, who sat nodding and fanning herself and smiling.

"—Besides," he said, "there aren't that many details. The main thing I wanted to say was—we have to build up our reserves before we can start filling orders."

Rosie stared at Tucker in appalled silence, trying to send the message, "Shut up your fool mouth!" with her eyes.

But he went on. "Of course, we can start *taking* orders right away—but we'll have to turn them over to the big investment brokers for a while."

"Folks I work for are in the investment business," Granny put in. "Stock breaking. High finance."

"Well, that's my line too, Mrs. Huggs," he said with a smile at Granny. "Rosie is thinking about going in partnership with me."

"Praise the Lord," Granny said. "Go on, young man. Rosie, you listen to every word he says."

"I'm almost through," Tucker said. "Now, Rosie—didn't you say you have some contacts? People who might be interested in, —er, investing with us?"

"That's right," she said numbly.

He raised his hand to cover up the beginning of a smile. "Do you have anybody to help you take orders?"

Rosie's tongue was dry from panic. "There's Miltie Newton," she managed.

"Fine, fine," Tucker said. "Milton's a good lad. You just tell him to bring all your orders to me. He'll find me at my club every day at lunchtime."

It was amazing how words could mislead. Tucker made that after-hours drinking joint sound like the sort of place where old men sat in deep leather chairs nodding over the financial pages.

"Why can't he just take them to Ben—I mean, the broker?" she asked suspiciously.

"Because," Tucker said smoothly, "he only knows one source to take the risk for us. I know several. You'll just have to trust me, Rosie. That's what partnership means." He smiled at Granny. "A business partnership is like a marriage."

"Praise the Lord," Granny said again. She sipped delicately from her glass. "How you find the wine, Mr. Tucker?"

"Perfect." He raised his glass and studied it. "Never tasted better. Not even while I was in Europe."

A smile of satisfaction stole across Granny's face. "Well, this here come from France. It says so on the label." She took another sip. "I got a wine cellar big's this room to pick 'n choose from— at the house where I work, I mean."

"I can tell you've had all the advantages, Mrs. Huggs," he said with a little bow of his head. "It shows up in Rosalie."

Granny smiled. "Down where I come from, Mr. Tucker, the white and the colored are a lot closer together." She closed her eyes. "Everybody know everybody else, and y'all go to each others' houses and talk, and everybody gets to be a lot more re- fined. I know of one family in V'ginia, the Godsons, the finest people you ever want to meet. Well there's the white Godsons and the colored Godsons, and they all got lovely homes and nice children, doctors and lawyers on both sides." Her voice was a rhythmic lullaby; for a moment Rosie closed her eyes. "Old Mr. Benjamin Godson, that's Colonel Henry Godson's nephew, he got him the biggest house in Charlottesville, and Reverend Billy Godson, he got him a big church all paid for and bought him a nice little farm. He wanted to marry me, Billy did, but I was too young . . ." Her voice trailed off into the mists of memory.

Tucker's eyes met Rosie's over the old lady's drooping head. "Didn't tell me your grandmother was such a remarkable woman. She must steal all your boy friends."

"Oh, shuh!" Granny waved her hand and released a silvery tide of laughter. She rose to leave and, seeing Tucker rise with her, nodded her approbation. "Guess I'll leave you young people have a little time to yourselves." She shot a meaningful glance at Rosie. "Shame Rosalie's got to rush out to work before her mother gets home."

Tucker put a hand on Rosie's shoulder, implying protective concern. "You think she works too hard?"

Granny laughed again. "Shuh, hard work never killed nobody, 'specially when they got nice positions like Rosalie. I been workin' all my life."

"Is that so, Mrs. Huggs?" He seemed astonished. "If you'd asked me, I'd've said you'd always been well taken care of."

Granny's ripple of laughter, neither denying nor confirming, lingered after she had left the room. It sounded like the laughter of a young girl.

Tucker doubled up in laughter of his own as soon as she was gone.

"What's the idea?" Rosie hissed at him. "Comin' here talkin' that way in front of my Granny?"

"I enjoy a little bit of danger," he said, coming over to embrace her. "Don't you?"

Rosie remained resentful, though it was hard to keep from smiling at his foolishness. "You fooled her so easy. It was like you was makin' fun of her."

"I'm sorry." He knelt before her in mock penitence. "Don't you want her to like me?"

She twisted uncomfortably in her chair. "Sure." But she didn't sound sure. She felt they had both betrayed her—Tucker by fooling Granny, and Granny by being fooled. For the first time in her life, she doubted Granny's judgment. Couldn't she see past people's manners to what they were like inside? Or didn't she care, as long as the outside was charming?

"Want to take care of her?" he asked. "Want to give her all those nice things she's been begging and stealing from white folks?"

"Sure," she said again, just as uncertainly.

He bounded to his feet and took one of her hands in both of his. "Then help me build up this business, baby. When I finish, there won't be a thing you can't afford."

Rosie's wish to believe him was augmented by her desire to

believe in Granny. Yes, she decided suddenly, Tucker must be someone she could trust. He'd better be.

She was calm and businesslike. "How much you want, Tucker?"

"Oh," he said ruefully, deploring her crisp tone. "You hurt me, baby, you really hurt me. It's not like that. It's how much do you want to invest?"

"Well, how much should I invest?"

He shrugged in "Who knows?" fashion. "More you give me, the sooner we can get our bank together. The sooner we get our bank, the sooner we can get started. It's as simple as that." He leaned over her from behind her chair. "And the sooner we start," he crooned, "the sooner you'll be turned out in clothes that knock the Avenue dead."

"I hope I won't be livin' around the corner from the Avenue much longer," she said.

"Well," he said, "wherever you are, you'll be wearing silk and satin dresses." His voice at her ear had the caressing touch of the fabrics he was describing. "And you'll have minks and sables to keep you warm." The warmth of his arm around her shoulders made the furs seem already real.

It was hard to be businesslike under the circumstances, but her mind went through rapid calculations. "Two fifty, Tucker?"

He appeared to hesitate.

"Five hundred, then?"

"Tell you what," he said. "I don't want to take all your money. Just give me two fifty now, another two fifty when you can spare it, and so on. That way you won't get caught short." He cleared his throat delicately, then added, "Of course it'll take us a little longer to make our move."

Rosie made a sudden, hard decision. "Here's five hundred," she said.

She tore out the check and handed it to him.

Just as Mom wrenched open the door and lumbered into the apartment.

"Bill collectors on Thursdays?" she inquired.

Rosie did the honors hastily. "Tucker, this is my Mom. Mom, this is Tucker."

"Rosie, how many times I told you, introduce the gentleman first?" Granny was in the room, bristling with as many signals as a railroad crossing. She smiled an apology to Tucker, then put a soothing hand on Mom's arm. "Regina, this is that fine young gentleman Rosie's been tellin' us about. Mr. Tucker's a businessman."

Tucker started to bend over Queenie's stiff, uncompromising hand, then changed his mind and shook it.

"We got something in common, Mr. Tucker." Mom's voice was even deeper and coarser than usual. "I'm a businesswoman myself."

She dismissed him after a quick inspection and looked belligerently around her. "Anything to drink in this house?"

Granny was fluttering like a line of clothes in the breeze. "Mr. Tucker was just appreciatin' my sauterne, Regina. You know, that light white wine you always like so much."

Queenie stared at her mother uncomprehendingly.

"Mrs. Fleming's had a hard day," Tucker intervened. "Maybe she'd like something a little stronger."

"Well, I got some nice red port," Granny said quickly. "Just California wine but it's all right for every day."

"I was thinking of whiskey," Tucker said. "Maybe Mrs. Fleming would let me make her a highball."

"You know where it is, boy?" Queenie asked suspiciously.

"No, of course not. Just thought I could help."

"Well, no help's wanted." Queenie went to the cupboard and emerged with a glass and a bottle. "Ain't nobody got to help me pour no whiskey in no glass. When I get that helpless, I might's well lay down and die."

"I always admire independence in a woman," Tucker said.

"You do, huh?" She eyed him with just a trace of flirtatiousness.

"Yes." He smiled engagingly. "Now I see where Rosie gets all her wonderful qualities. She gets her charm and her good

taste from her grandmother. And from you she gets her independence and, if I may say so, her striking looks."

Queenie drained her glass. She wiped her mouth and stared
at Tucker until he was forced to shift his position uncomfortably.

"Nigger," she said at last, "what you want with my little
girl?"

"Regina!" Granny wailed. "Mr. Tucker," she pleaded, "you
have to excuse my daughter. She ain't been feelin' well lately."

"Sorry to hear that," he said.

"Pay her no mind, she ain't got good sense," Mom said.
"Rosie, you come here and unhook my brassiere. And you, boy,
answer my question."

Moving like a sleepwalker, Rosie crossed the room. She un-
fastened the hooks and felt the straining flesh explode free as
Mom sighed heavily.

"I want to make sure she has a good future," Tucker said
easily.

"You do, huh? That's more'n I'm doin', and I'm her mother."
She looked at Rosie searchingly. "Rosie, you believe him?"

"Sure, Mom. Tucker and me, we're gonna go in business."

"Well, I tell you he's lyin'. Never mind how I know. I know.
You believe me?"

Rosie withdrew sulkily to the far end of the sofa. "Naw. Why
should I? You just—"

Queenie held up her hand for silence. "Okay. It don't matter
what I say. You gonna do what you want anyhow. Ain't no way
I can stop you."

Tucker spoke up before Rosie had a chance to reply. "Glad
you see it that way, Mrs. Fleming. Rosie's a grown-up young
lady now. She has to make her own decisions."

Mom stood up. "She thinks she's grown, you mean. And how
she thinks is how she's gonna act, and ain't nothin' you or I
can do about it. I'm gonna go get me some sleep. When she's
my age she'll wish she done the same." She left the room with
Granny bustling at her heels.

Money, You Got Lots of Friends

"I was just leaving," Tucker said, shrugging into his handsome gabardine topcoat.

He was hurt; Rosie could see it. "Don't pay my Mom no mind, hon," she said. "She's just jealous 'cause I got you."

"There's nothing worse than a houseful of women. Especially colored women," he said with an exaggerated shiver.

Rosie advanced hesitantly toward him. She reached up and pretended to adjust his coat collar. "Tucker—"

"What?" he said gruffly, removing her hands from around his neck.

Now she was hurt by his coldness. "Nothin'. I was just gonna say how nice you look. I like your clothes."

He smiled, but his eyes were opaque. "Clothes make the man, baby. Can't afford to skimp on my appearance. First impressions count, especially with your people. You know how Brazilians are." He struck a Beau Brummell pose, then glanced at his watch. "Say, I got to get to work right now."

"This time of night?" Rosie wanted to know.

"Sure. I'll see a couple hundred customers between now and midnight. All the players with systems. 'Course the dream players won't be around till morning. But even if I didn't get any business, I'd have to be out there looking good for my public." Hand on the doorknob, he turned back. "You know, Rosie, I don't like all these questions. I believe that suspicious mama of yours put some bad ideas in your head. Do you think I'm just taking your money to spend it on clothes? Because if you do, you can have it back right now."

He withdrew Rosie's check from his pocket.

"Here. I can't have a partner who doesn't trust me."

"Oh, no, Tucker," Rosie said, pushing his hand away. "I trust you."

Appeased, he put the check back and patted his pocket. "Don't worry," he said. "You made a good investment."

"Wasn't worryin', Tucker."

"Good." He smiled and rubbed his hands together. "Sweetheart, we're gonna be so rich it'll be a shame. I can hardly wait to get started, there's so much money out here to be made. Did I tell you that old fool woman who raised me came into some property uptown? Had a simple old white woman just eating out of her hand. Rich as the devil. And no heirs."

Rosie nodded. "I know. I been by to see her a couple times."

His charming facade disintegrated instantly. She could not have affected him more violently if she had blown up a bomb in his face. "What the hell you call yourself doing?" he fairly screamed. "Checking up on me?"

Rosie's cheeks stung as if she had been slapped, but all she said was, "We never mentioned you." As he struggled to get back his composure, she added, "What you afraid of? You must be scared your mother's gonna work her roots on you or somethin'."

"I told you before, she's not my mother," he said.

Rosie could not hold back her curiosity. "What is she, then? Your aunt?"

"Yes," he said at last. "But I don't consider her any relation. There's no room in my life for her any more. I don't believe in being sentimental." He brought his hand down on an invisible string. "I've just cut her off—like that."

Like you gonna cut me off someday? Rosie wondered, but did not dare say aloud.

"Now you know all about me," he said lightly as he opened the door. "Satisfied?"

She didn't. She wasn't. And she couldn't help knowing that the cutting-off process had begun then and there. Somehow she had alarmed him into it ahead of time. She flinched when he gave her a farewell chuck under the chin. While she was still working up the courage to say or do something that might restore their intimacy, he walked out.

> *"Rosalie, I love you,*
> *Rosalie, be true . . ."*

trailed softly, mockingly behind him down the stairs.

She had turned on her best smile for him. As she closed the door, it shriveled and fell off in one piece.

Money, You Got Lots of Friends

She stared into the hall mirror. The darkness in the hallway made it a black pool in which her face floated like a dead leaf. Her hair had just been done in a stylish new tousle cut; her dress was a beautifully pleated gold wool. But when she looked past them to her skinny figure, her large teeth, her caved-in cheeks, she knew she was a scarecrow.

She coughed suddenly, a brutal spasm that forced her to seize the mirror and hang on. It felt like a great tree being torn up inside her; the trunk shuddering in her chest, the branches trembling to her fingertips. The roots were stubborn, but finally they gave way. She stumbled to the bathroom and splashed gallons of cold water on her face. Finally the fog cleared. The wet china surface gave her a faint reflection of her slack pink mouth and dull black holes of eyes.

She turned her back on her image and marched into her mother's bedroom with clenched fists.

"What right you got talkin' to my friends like that?"

Mom lay stiffly on her back, staring at the ceiling. "Fine friends you got," she said. "Pockets full of hot air, just like their mouths."

"Sounds like you're talkin' about a friend of yours."

"Yeah, Roscoe's no good," Mom admitted. "But this cat's worse. He's smarter." She turned to look at Rosie. "When I was your age I wouldn't look at no Roscoe Gordons. I had all the fine cats after me, and I could pick and choose." She rolled on her back again and murmured. "Lord, when I remember how good I used to look. . . ."

Rosie said, "You always looked just like you look now."

"Yeah? Well you're gonna look a lot worse a lot sooner. Drinkin' and dissipatin' and runnin' around with racketeers—" Mom rolled over. She propped herself on her elbows and regarded Rosie intently. "If you ask me, you don't look so good right now. You better quit one of those jobs and stay home and get some rest."

Rosie was defiant. "I can't afford to quit. I might end up with nothing, like you."

God Bless the Child

"Never mind me," Mom said. "It's you I'm talkin' about. I heard you hawkin' and hackin' in there a few minutes ago. Sounded like the last stage of consumption. Rosie, you ruin your health now, someday you'll wish you had it back, instead of throwin' it away on fancy clothes and fancy niggers."

This was suddenly too much for Rosie. "You don't understand anything," she said, and began to cry.

"Listen, Rosie," Mom said gravely. "Men like him are sweet. They the sweetest thing in life. Have a good time with 'em. But don't depend on 'em for nothin'. Colored women has to shift for themselves. You know that. You told me all about it one time."

Rosie had no answer except snuffling sounds.

"Men like him are here one day and gone the next," Mom continued. "When you go to lean on 'em, they just ain't there."

Granny, in the doorway, said, "Don't listen to her, Rosalie. Just 'cause the men leave her don't mean you can't find somebody decent."

"You mix up everything I try to teach her!" Mom yelled. "Go mind your own business, old woman!"

Granny, though it pained her, obeyed.

Rosie sprang to Granny's defense. "Leave her alone! Why don't you come right out'n say it? You're mad 'cause I'm investin' a little money for myself instead of lettin' you throw it away on Roscoe Gordon!"

"Investin'!" Mom's laugh was brief and derisive. She looked steadily into her daughter's eyes. "Rosie, I didn't see that check. I don't know if you gave him five dollars or five hundred. What's more I don't care." She closed her eyes and fell back on the bed. "Now go away and let me get some sleep."

Rosie leaned over the bed aggressively. "You lyin' and you know it," she said. But no more response was forthcoming from Mom. Soon a soft, bubbling snore came from the pillow.

She ran to the kitchen, where Granny sat sipping tea.

"There's a nice hot plate in the oven, Rosalie," she said. "Just what you like. Ham and candied sweet potatoes."

"I ain't got time, Granny. I got to be to work in twenty minutes."

Granny set her cup down. "No wonder you're so thin. Child, eat. You got to keep up your strength."

"I'll just have a cup of that tea, Granny."

Granny rose. "If I'd known you wanted some I'd've made a potful," she apologized. "You know how I hate them tea bags. Can't you least wait while I brew a pot?"

"Tea bag's fine, Granny," Rosie said, lighting a cigarette. "Told you I ain't got time."

Granny sighed and poured the boiling water. "That's a nice young man, Rosalie," she said. "Glad to see you takin' up with somebody like him, refined and ambitious and all. 'Course he is a bit dark, but you can't have everything. 'Specially bein' the color you are." She set the teacup before Rosie and smiled slyly. "Just try not to have no children, that's all. Black children has a hard time in this world."

Rosie looked up at Granny in surprise. Then she smiled slowly.

"We'll have to fix it so he can call on you when your mother ain't home," Granny went on. "We can't let her spoil all your chances."

"Tucker 'n me are gonna have a lot of money, Granny," Rosie said suddenly. "More money'n you ever seen. He's started investin' for us already." She raised her chin and looked at Granny fiercely, half asking not to be believed. But the old lady nodded encouragingly. "He's gonna make sure I can take care of you."

Granny smiled. "And you got a couple of nice positions, you can be a big help to him." She patted Rosie's hand. "Help him all you can, child. He's gonna be a big man someday."

Rosie nodded intently, her eyes half closed. "Know what I'm gonna do next, Granny? Gonna buy us a fine house. I mean a *big* house. Big's the one where you work." She jumped up from the table. "Plenty of room for you and me and Mom—"

Granny smiled wisely. "And your young man."

"And everything's gonna be fine, Granny! Fine furniture, fine television, fine drapes at the windows—"

Granny joined in the game. "Pictures on the walls, rugs on the floors . . ."

Rosie nodded. "Every room painted 'n papered."

"Linen tablecloths and good china . . ."

"The best! Everything the best!" Rosie hugged Granny, who responded with unusual warmth. " 'Cause nothin's too good for my Granny." She kissed the tissue-fine cheek which smelled faintly of delicate perfume. "Now I gotta run. You take it easy, hear? Don't let Mom make you do no housework."

"All I plan on doing," Granny said serenely, "is make up a nice cold platter and leave it in the ice box for my grandchild."

Rosie blew her a kiss as she, ran from the room.

14

That night at Benny's was like all the others, and the next day at Schwartz's was like all the others, too, and as the weeks and the months blurred into each other, all the days and nights were the same, except that now Rosie collected small sums of money from her customers at both jobs, and made notations on many little slips of paper, and Miltie Newton came by to pick up the money and the papers, once every noontime at Schwartz's, where she slipped out to meet him on her lunch hour, and once every night at Benny's, where she more or less openly conferred with him in the back booth.

On this particular frigid night in February, forty-seven dollars and forty cents was spread out on the table between them, and, from Miltie's pockets and the hollow of Rosie's brassiere, together they had produced over fifty slips. Rosie spread them out and regarded them wearily.

"I wonder if it's too much to ask," she said. "just when the hell all this is gonna pay off?"

"I thought it was, Rosie," Miltie said innocently. "When I went by the club last night, Tucker was standin' drinks for everybody."

"If I waited for him to buy me a drink I'd die of thirst," she said glumly.

"He said it was his public relations," Miltie said.

"Public relations, my foot," she snapped. "He needs to do some work on his private relations. Excuse me."

She got up and went over to the phone on the wall. Dialing furiously, she calculated that more than six months had gone by in this fashion, with her sending over a thousand dollars to Tucker by mail, and the Lord only knew how much by Miltie, and never seeing a penny of it again. It was time.

"Tucker, I got some questions," she said. "I want some answers."

"Can't it wait, Rosie?" he said sleepily. "I'm busy."

"Busy, hell, what you mean, busy?" she snapped. "I thought I was supposed to be your partner."

There was silence at the other end of the line.

"Kick her out of bed, Tucker," Rosie said wearily. "If you can't do that, at least roll over a minute."

He laughed. "Now, baby, you know better than think that."

"I don't know what to think," she told him. "All I know is it's freezing outside, and I still ain't seen those furs you promised me. I ain't even seen you."

"I've been busy," he repeated lamely.

"Is that all you can think of to say?"

His voice was stronger. "I've been working hard for us."

"Tucker, what the hell is going on?" Rosie screamed at him. "What are you doing with all the money I sent you? When am I gonna see some income out of it?"

"Calm down, baby," he told her. "You're forgetting something. I didn't ask you to go in this business with me. You came to me and asked me. Right?"

"Yes," Rosie admitted.

"Well, you must've trusted me then. Why can't you trust me now?"

Now it was Rosie who was silent.

"Every penny you've sent me is perfectly safe. I've put it away for the business, but you can have it back any time. You want it now?"

"No," she said after hesitating a moment. "Keep it for the business. But what about all them orders Miltie keeps bringin' you?"

"Rosie, we can't afford to hold out any of that yet," he said in a reasonable tone. "I'm still turning it over to the bankers. What little I get back barely pays Miltie's salary, and any time anything's left over I save it for the business. You know all this, Rosie. Why make me talk about it over the phone?"

"I'm sorry," she said, then bit her tongue angrily. "I've been putting out for a long time, that's why. I wanta know when I'm gonna get something back."

"It'll start rolling in as soon as we're ready to make our move," he promised.

"Well, I've been ready a long time. You better be ready soon," she said. And hung up the phone.

"Impatient, aren't you?" a voice said over her shoulder.

Rosie turned around, startled. She hadn't seen Benny standing there by the juke box.

"But then," he went on, "you always were. You were in a big hurry the first time you walked in here. I always wonder why some people are in such a rush. We're all going the same place. It must mean some people are in a hurry to die."

She stared at him, unsmiling, while he shook with soundless laughter.

"It's all right," he finally said. "Not everybody appreciates my sense of humor. Only philosophers like me."

Rosie made no comment. Benny's way of talking in riddles left her no clue as to whether he had really understood her conversation. Furthermore, she didn't care. She tossed her head and went back to Miltie.

But a minute later, as she tallied the last of the slips and shoved them into an envelope, she cared very much indeed. Because The Man was standing behind her.

"You could save yourselves a lot of trouble," he said mildly. Rosie turned and stared at him.

His tone was genial. "Why have your friend run those things all the way across town? They're just going to be brought back here tomorrow."

Miltie was on his feet, looking from one of them to the other, his ears and nostrils quivering like a rabbit's. He pulled out his filthy money-pouch and held it out to Benny.

"No, no," The Man said, pushing it away. "It was just a suggestion. Go on, handle things your usual way."

Miltie was out of there like an arrow.

Benny clucked. "I could have saved him all that trouble. It all comes back to me anyhow."

"I don't believe you," Rosie said sulkily.

"Everything comes back to me," Benny said, spreading his arms to embrace the world. "The big rivers, the little streams, the tiny trickles. They all empty into the great big ocean. Your friend Tucker works for Pockets. Pockets works for me."

"That ain't the way I heard it," Rosie said. "I heard Pockets was independent."

"He's as independent as I let him be," Benny said. "And that's what makes me wonder, Rosie. After Tucker takes his percentage, and Pockets takes his, and I take mine—what are you getting out of it?"

It was an especially touchy question right now. Rosie snapped back, "More'n I ever got from you. You ain't made me no offers at all."

"I thought you were too young," Benny said. "I still think so. And I'll tell you something else I think, Rosie. You're in with bad company. That Tucker's a crook."

"Ain't you?"

"Maybe," Benny conceded. "It depends on the point of view."

"Then don't be calling other people names," she told him.

Benny contained his anger well. "I'm being straight with you right now, Rosie. But Tom Tucker never did anything straight in his life. That boy smiles crooked, talks crooked, even walks crooked. He knows better than try any tricks with me. But a young girl like you ought to worry."

"Well, I'm not worrying," Rosie declared. "Why should I? I don't even believe you."

Benny's mouth worked as if it wanted to say terrible words, but his knotted cheek muscles were holding them back.

"All right," he finally said with a grunt of exasperation. "Come on."

He took her elbow and steered her toward the kitchen, where he took out a key and unlocked a door that she had always thought led to the cellar. He flung it open, and Rosie blinked into a small room lit by one dangling fifty-watt bulb. Her eyes could barely take in the long dusty tables, the adding machines, and the piles of discarded tapes curling like white snakes on the floor. She was too dazzled by the money. Piles and piles of it, like a pirate's cave.

He let her drink it in for five full seconds before he closed the magic door and locked it.

"Excuse the bad housekeeping," he said. "I'm late going over the accounts tonight."

Rosie was about to answer when her head swiveled in sudden alarm. Benny's eyes followed hers to the glass pane of the door that led to the alley. Through it, a cop was clearly visible, pacing up and down.

Benny chuckled. "My private guard. Assigned to me by the Department."

Rosie said, "You can't lose, can you, Benny?"

"Of course not," he said. "I play my role."

"And I don't. Is that what's bugging you?"

"You are a mosquito," he said. "A mosquito can't hurt a lion. It just annoys him when it keeps buzzing under his nose."

"You knew all the time," she said.

"I must say you had nerve," Benny said with a trace of real admiration. "I never thought of taking business out front, myself. Out front is my public. This is my backstage. I never mix them up." His face was suddenly fierce, and suddenly very close to hers. "Of course I knew. Did you really think I couldn't see what you were up to, night after night, right here under my eyes?"

"You let me do it," she said.

"Why not?" Benny said. "You had a good little thing going, so I let you keep it."

"Thanks," Rosie said, "for nothing."

What might have been the beginning of a smile faded suddenly at one corner of Benny's mouth. "Look, I told you why I didn't bring you in on the business, Rosie. You weren't ready. But you went and got yourself mixed up in it anyway, so now I'm just trying to save your silly neck. I don't care who you work for. Like I said, it all comes back to me, like the rivers to the ocean. If you want to go on with Tucker till you get your throat cut, it's all right with me. On the other hand, if you want to talk to Pockets, maybe you and he can work something out between you."

Rosie looked in the direction of the brusque wave of his hand and saw Pockets Robinson leaning against the take-out counter. She started toward him. Benny caught her arm.

"After you wait on that new boothful of customers," he said.

Pockets Robinson was a man who preached the salvation of the race through business. He was also a man who practiced what he preached—having opened his first legitimate business, a real estate office, six months ago.

"Trouble with your people," Pockets said, biting into a new clear Havana and spitting the end away—he always said "your race" or "your people" to his listeners, refusing to be identified with them—"trouble with your people is, they got no ambition. They always got to be mixing pleasure and business."

He dipped into the relish dish and helped himself to a hot

cherry pepper. "Take you young people hangin' out in here. If you was white you'd be goin' to school, preparin' for the future. But all you young Watusis want is 'Rock, Rock, Rock' on the record machine."

Benny, making coffee, kept his back turned to avoid being included in Pockets' audience, who were all young and shabby, yet each managed to create a flashy impression.

"Rather have 'roody oody oo' on the rivet machine," one said, "but the man won't give me a job."

"I don't blame him," Pockets said. He used a toothpick to remove a shred of pepper from the small fiery diamond which was set in the center of one gold tooth. "I tell everybody the same thing. You show me a serious-minded young person with some real ambition, and I'll show you a man who's glad to give him a hand."

Rosie, carrying a tray, slid past Pockets. She raised the hinged section of the counter on which his hand rested and ducked beneath. When she popped up on the other side his hand came down heavily on her head.

"Just because you're Egyptian don't give you no right not to speak, gal."

Rosie shrugged free. "Next time you'll pull back a nub, Pockets," she told him with a murderous look.

"Ain't that just like a Senegalese?" he roared triumphantly to his audience. "I don't mess with these Senegalese women, no, sir. They frighten me."

Rosie ignored him for the time being. With a shrug Pockets returned to his favorite topic.

"All I ever hear from you folks is complaints about hard times. Hard times, hard times. What makes 'em think they'd know what to do with good times? Back when we had Roosevelt, how many of you A–rabs hung onto some of that money? No, you was too busy drivin' big cars and drinkin' good whiskey. But a man with some foresight, now, had him a little WPA job and a little night work on the side, he stashed some money away. Then when times got worse he could get him a little *store*, a little *office*. That's what the white man does, and I don't hate the white man, I respect him. I looked at the white man, and I said, 'Pockets, you can learn somethin' from him.' And that's the story of my life."

Benny, rosy, rotund and unperturbed, came from behind the coffee urn and told Rosie, "Okay. You can take a break now if you want to."

She slanted toward Pockets across the counter. "Mr. Robinson, did I hear you correctly? Did I hear you say you like to help ambitious young people?"

He read the serious purpose behind her teasing look and led the way ponderously, as befitted his dignity and substance, to the back booth.

"Ben*jam*in," he called. "A little refreshment for me and the lady."

"You want beer," Benny said without looking up, "you hafta go in the bar."

"This won't take that long," Rosie said sharply, cutting off Pockets' plans for enjoying the drink, the cigar, and the long-winded discussion—all the pleasurable props of being a businessman. "All I wanta know is, will you let me have a piece of your business?"

Pockets laughed freely, but he stopped when he saw that Rosie was not smiling. "What makes you think I'd do that, little girl?"

"You got more'n you can handle. I hear your customers is complaining they can't get service. 'N your money's all tied up in Real Estate. You can't afford a lot of bankin'."

Pockets chewed the cold cigar; his mind was already made up, she saw, but it was important to show signs of careful deliberation. Suddenly he removed the cigar and pushed his glistening face forward. "You wanta work it and split with me?"

"Naw," Rosie said. "Ain't no percentage in that."

Again there was a long deliberating pause while he snapped a gold Zippo and looked at her over the flame, lifting his lip to let the diamond blaze. "Only one way you can make a bigger percentage, little girl."

"What's that, Pockets?"

He closed the lighter with a sharp report. "Uninsured."

Rosie looked at him doubtfully.

"You don't split with the corporation, you don't split with me, you don't split with nobody. You pay your own expenses, and what you make is one hundred per cent profit."

"Well what happens if I get hit?"

He smiled blandly. "You pay, naturally. That's one of the regular risks of the business."

"Well, suppose I get a *lot* of hits?"

"Aw . . ." Pockets chuckled, amused at her innocence. "You ain't supposed to get no lot of hits. You're the writer, you don't need no luck. Your customers do."

Rosie's eyes blinked rapidly as she calculated. "What's the biggest they ever hit you for, Pockets?"

"No more'n five hundred in one week, baby, and that's the God's truth." A thousand, she thought, looking into his smooth brown Babbitt's face. He means a thousand.

Pockets spread his hands. " 'Course, now, you can always do both. Hold out whatever you're willing to stand back of, and turn the rest over to me."

"Takes money to do that," Rosie said.

"Naw," Pockets said with a knowing chuckle. "All it takes is nerve. A lot of my agents do it."

"Does Tucker?"

"My agents don't tell me everything they're doing, and I don't ask 'em. But hell," Pockets said, gesturing toward the counter, "you can always count on Benny for help. He's the straightest businessman in town." He raised his voice. "The straightest white man I know."

Benny, who had not seemed to be listening, began to whistle tunelessly while he polished the coffee urn to a face-reflecting shine.

Pockets' performance depressed Rosie. She had admired him from afar, but at close range he behaved like Benny's pet monkey. She figured his Uncle Tomming was the reason why Benny had given him a start in the rackets. He had probably helped him into Real Estate the same way, by passing along a few barely profitable crumbs. Given a choice between two crooks, Rosie decided to stick with the one she liked the best. At least for a while.

She rose. "Well, thanks a lot, Pockets. Some other time, maybe."

"See that?" Pockets said. "Is it my fault you young people got no ambition?"

Rosie said, "I already got a deal good as the one you offered me."

"In that case, at least lemme give you some advice," Pockets said. "Watch out for one of my agents, a wine-o named Miltie Newton. He might try and take advantage of a woman."

She grinned. "Everything's under control, Pockets. Miltie's been workin' for me a year."

Pockets recovered his cigar and tenderly brushed the ashes from his creamy flannel jacket, his own design, fitted with a labyrinth of secret pockets for slips. "Never trusted that little sneak anyhow," he rumbled. "Only goes to show you're always better off in a nice respectable business. Take my advice, you'll let me sell you this couple of apartment houses I got over on Fox Street. Five hundred in rents every month, rain or shine. Now that's security, girl. Security for the rest of your life. That's the trouble with your people, they don't think enough about these things. But you—"

Before he could get launched on his lecture, Benny called, "Rosie! Phone!"

Over the off-key saxophones blaring from the juke box she tried to hear what Granny was saying.

". . . over here to the hospital, Rosie. . . ."

"What's the matter, Granny, you sick? What are they doin', lettin' you talk on the phone? Crazy doctors!" She twisted the cord frantically in her hands.

"No, Rosie. It's your mother. It's real bad."

She would never forget how the fear drained out of her like a tubful of cold water, leaving a relieved feeling of lightness.

Her relaxed fingers played idly with the cord. Something about knowing those trashy friends of hers would get her in trouble, now all this worry on account of that man, when he never did mean Queenie any good. . . .

"All right, Granny. I'll be right there."

It took nearly an hour to get the story straight from Granny. It seemed the phone call had interrupted her while she was taking a tray to Miss Emilie—the poor thing hadn't been right since Christmas, she was still laying around in bed most of the day, and poor Miss Helen was ailing too. She didn't know what the world was coming to, all this sickness happening at once. Young people today weren't as strong as *her* generation—here she was, still going right on, while they took sick at the slightest little thing. And such disgraceful carryings on! "Right out there on the street, Rosie! I was so ashamed. . . ."

The tears came down, and Rosie patted the frail shoulders.

"I don't know what I ever did to deserve a bad ungrateful girl like her. If I didn't have a good grandchild I don't know what I'd do."

It went on like that for some time. Finally Rosie understood that Mom had been stabbed in a fight with 'Tena Cartwright over Uncle Roscoe.

Then an elderly doctor appeared to shake his finger at them as if they should be ashamed of themselves. It was a bad case, he said, it had been a ticklish operation; the knife had grazed the heart, and with the high blood pressure, the danger was far from over. There might be the question of a clot . . . and then there might not be the question of a clot. . . .

At last he let them go in.

There was a sweet, sickening ether smell in the room. Mom lay fearfully still beneath the covers, her lips swollen, her face bleached a waxy yellow that blotted out all of her freckles. She dozed while suspended bottles trickled red and white and yellow liquids into her through long rubber tubes.

She did not stir when Granny crossed the room and sat down.

But when Rosie, advancing timidly, reached the edge of the bed a hand closed around her wrist with surprising strength.

"Is that you, Rosie?"

"Yeah, Mom."

Mom's eyelids flickered once, humorously. " 'Bout time you got here."

Rosie sat down on a cold metal hospital stool. "What you tryin' to do, huh? Get yourself all messed up?"

"That Wheatena," Mom chortled weakly. "That Wheatena thought Roscoe was gonna marry her. Ain't that some nerve?"

"You should have her arrested," Granny hissed from the other side of the bed.

"What for?" Mom smiled dreamily. "He ain't gonna marry her. He's gonna marry me." Eyes closed, she bubbled softly, "I had on my new pansy print dress, Rosie, and that big black cartwheel hat you bought me. Roscoe had his arm around me when we walked out the Blue Moon. I guess we looked so good together she couldn't stand it, the poor thing. . . . Jealousy's a terrible thing, Rosie. It just tears you apart."

Mom's voice trailed off into hoarse breathing while the bottles continued to drip, drip, drip into her. Turning her into someone else, Rosie thought in sudden panic. She stood up and started to tiptoe backward when Mom's eyes flew open again, wide as cups of black coffee; before either of them could stop her, she was sitting straight up in bed.

"I see you with that hussy!" she yelled. "Don't you think you can ig *me*, Roscoe Gordon!" Her rapid gasps for breath filled the room. "Go on then," she said in a low, venomous whisper. "When my daughter buys me that shop you'll be sorry."

She plummeted back to the pillow like a bag of laundry.

While Granny pulled frantically on the cord for a nurse Rosie buried her face in the rough hospital sheets, listening for the beat, trying to hear it in rhythm with her own knocking heart. She did not raise her head when the door clicked open behind her. Her arms flung across Mom's waist, she muttered over and over into the sheet, "Mom, please Mom, you're the only Mom I got."

After a time long enough for her to soak the sheet the loud wheezing began again. Rosie kept her face buried, not daring to move except to reach for, and find, a hand to hold.

At last the wheezing was replaced by a gently gurgling snore. Rosie ventured a peek over the mound of her mother's belly.

The warm, encouraging hand she held was Larnie's.

But she was looking into Granny's cold, disapproving eyes.

15

Larnie was at the hospital every day, looking in on Queenie. She seemed to drink in strength just from the sight of him at her bedside. Soon she felt well enough to sit up in bed and talk to him.

"Sure cheers me up to have visitors," she said one afternoon. "Sure is nice of you to come. You spend more time here than Rosie."

"I guess Rosie's busier than I am," he said.

"Rosie's busier than anybody's got a right to be," she told him. "I don't know what's gonna become of that girl. It worries me sick, Larnie. Half the time I don't know where she is or what she's up to."

"She's just working hard. She's ambitious."

"She's crazy, that's what she is. Money-crazy. I don't understand her. When I was her age, I was boy-crazy."

Larnie laughed. "I bet you had plenty of boy friends, too, Mrs. Fleming."

Queenie laughed hard and gave his head a playful swipe with her hand.

He ducked and grinned. "I know why you did that, Mrs. Fleming."

"Why?"

"You wanted to see if my hair is real. Girls' mothers are always doing that to me."

Queenie laughed so hard she became short of breath. Larnie had to ring for the nurse.

A chilly little blonde with a superior air, she came in sniffing as if she suspected them of smoking weed, or fornication, or both. She popped a thermometer in Queenie's mouth and turned to Larnie. "If she insists on abusing her visiting privileges, you shouldn't let her exert herself," she reproved him.

Queenie pulled the thermometer out and said, "My daughter insists on payin' for this private room. I guess I got a right to abuse all the privileges I want."

The nurse coolly replaced the thermometer. Plumping the pillow, she said, "Oh yes, you've got a right to do whatever you please. But if you don't watch out, you won't get discharged Friday." She stood there like an icicle, studying her watch, with chilly fingers on Queenie's wrist. Finally she removed the glass needle. "Ninety-nine," she said grudgingly. "Not so bad. Almost normal."

"I could've told you that," Queenie said. "I'm a normal woman in every respect." She beckoned. "Put your head back over here, Larnie."

He winked and did as he was commanded.

"Mm-hmmm," Queenie said with pleasure as she touched his head.

With a loud exhalation of disgust, the nurse clicked frostily from the room.

Larnie sat up again. Together, he and Queenie roared.

"White folks like her always think colored folks are up to something immoral," Queenie managed between cascades of laughter. "I figure we might as well give 'em some satisfaction."

Then she became serious, trying to solve something that had always puzzled her. "I know why they so scared of us. They scared of sex. But I wonder why that is, Larnie? Somebody should tell 'em sex ain't just screwing. It's eating, it's breathing, it's living. 'Course I guess they're scared of them things too. They're scared of themselves, that's what the pot boils down to."

She liked the way his eyes leveled with hers without a trace of shame or sophistication. "Sex is in everything, huh? I never thought of that before."

"Sure," Queenie said with confidence. This was one thing she knew about. "Now, child, young as you are, I don't get any more thrill out of petting you on the head than I would petting a pretty cocker spaniel puppy. —But I don't get no less, neither."

She joined in his strong young laughter because it made her feel young, too. " 'Course right now," she added, "anything more would kill me."

"You didn't fool me, Mrs. Fleming," he said. "I knew what you wanted."

"You just stirred up my professional curiosity," she said archly. "I had to know what kind of process you could have that looked so good. After all, I'm a hairdresser."

"You're a mother, too."

"Yes," she admitted, because he was on to her game. "If you had good honest kinks I wouldn't have any doubts about you. But I couldn't trust no dude with a fancy process."

"Now you know," he said with a smile. "It's just my Indian grandfather."

Queenie smiled. "Ah, boy, I believe we're gonna be good friends. I'm glad. Rosie needs somebody like you to look out for her. She don't have enough sense to look out for herself."

Larnie said, "You worry about her. So do I, sometimes."

"She gets taken in by flash. You know what I mean?"

He nodded. "I think so."

Queenie struggled to find the right words. "The kind of gold that comes in a paint bottle—that's the flashiest. That's the kind she goes for, every time. Now real gold ain't that shiny. It's kinda dull. Rosie don't know that yet. But I do."

His earnest look met hers and deepened.

"You're pure gold, Larnie," she said, touching his smooth bronze arm. "Nothing plated about you anywhere."

Money, You Got Lots of Friends

He moved away uncomfortably. "You don't know me that well, Mrs. Fleming."

"Yes, I do," Queenie said. "But maybe Rosie don't yet. You'll just have to be patient, Larnie. She ain't finished growing up. She still wants all the wrong things." She sighed and lay back, enmeshed in her problem. "I wish I knew how she got that way. Sometimes I can't believe she's a child of mine."

Finally she turned hopeful eyes back to this boy who was so big and strong nothing could possibly be too much for him. She grabbed his hand. "She needs you, Larnie. She never had a father. And I'm sick, my mother's old, we can't do much for her."

"Well, how do you expect me to do what you can't?"

He said this with such exasperated force, pushing her hand away, that she was startled. Before she could begin to frame an answer, the door opened, and they both turned their eyes toward it. Her mother walked into the room.

"I got here soon as I could," she said with reproach in her voice. "My folks needed me today."

Moving lightly and swiftly under her burden of packages and handbag and stone marten furpiece, she approached the bed without further ceremony. She deployed her bundles on it, then rummaged in one and produced a quart of bottled water.

"I brought you this to drink," she said. "Don't drink no more hospital water. Hospitals are full of germs."

Queenie made a sour face as she watched her mother pour a glassful of the pallid stuff. "If you went to all that trouble, you might at least have brought me some gin," she said. "Alcohol kills germs."

"It'd kill you, too," Lourinda said tartly, handing her the glass. She waited, arms folded, until Queenie downed it all. Then she dove into another bundle. "I brought you a decent bedjacket, too. You oughta be 'shamed, wearing that raggedy thing in the hospital. The underwear you had on when they brought you here made me 'shamed to be your mother."

She proceeded to unpeel Queenie's favorite motheaten pink sweater from her shoulders, completely ignoring Larnie, which

God Bless the Child

was no easy feat, since he was still seated intimately on the edge of the bed. Finally he got up to make way for her.

"There," Lourinda said when her daughter was all arrayed in white lace. "Now you look fit to be havin' company."

"This nice boy's looked in on me every day," Queenie said, motioning Larnie back to her bedside. "He's more faithful than my own child."

Her mother acknowledged Larnie for the first time, with a stiff, ungracious little nod, and said, "Rosie's got other things to do besides sit here all day with you." She gave both of them a suspicious stare that was not unlike the nurse's, and added, "How come he's here so much, anyway? Don't he work?"

"He goes to school," Queenie said, as proudly as if he were her own son. "College."

At her side, a very low voice said, "No, Mrs. Fleming."

Queenie drew back, startled. "Huh?" she said, peering into his face.

It was troubled. "I've been meaning to tell you. I'm not in college any more."

She was suddenly ashamed. "I knew all along you had somethin' on your mind besides Rosie's sick old mother. But I was so wrapped up in my own troubles, I never gave you a chance to tell me. I'm sorry, Larnie."

" 'Bout time you got your mind off yourself," her mother said. "You ain't the only one sick. You don't know what real sickness is. Miss Helen's got three nurses, one for each eight hours of the day." She fished out a tiny linen handkerchief and dabbed at the corner of each eye. "This morning she didn't even know me."

"Now don't you start!" Queenie yelled so loud it echoed back from the hall. "I'll listen to your miseries later. Right now I got to hear this boy. What happened, Larnie?"

He expelled a deep sigh. "I quit school, that's all."

Hands in his pockets, he walked over to the window and looked out silently. With his back turned he said, "I lost my scholarship. I couldn't afford to stay in school without it. That's all."

134

Money, You Got Lots of Friends

He turned and spread his hands in a nervous disparaging gesture. "It's not important. I don't need an education." He laughed sourly. "From all I see of people with B.S.'s, that's all they are anyway. A whole lot of b.s."

Lourinda's sharp shocked intake of breath was clearly audible.

Queenie continued to look at him. "What happened?" she asked again.

Under her steady gaze, it began to pour out of him. "Seemed like I worked so hard to get in college, studying and training and practicing and all, when I finally got there it caught up with me. All of a sudden I had to have some fun."

" 'Course you did," Queenie said. "You're young. That's what you're supposed to do."

Larnie refused to be excused. "No," he said. "I should've kept on being serious. My folks were making sacrifices so I could be in school. But did I think about that? No." He banged a fist on the window frame as if trying to inflict more pain on himself. "No, I stayed up late and went to parties and missed half my classes. I drank and smoked and got out of condition. And I lost interest in serious music."

He moved restlessly around the room. Finally he approached the bed. "I don't know what happened, Mrs. Fleming. I used to love the classics. But all of a sudden they began to seem dead to me. I wanted to play something that felt alive, like I feel."

Queenie smiled up at him. He was so tall, tall like a tree; it took her eyes half a minute to travel up to his. And no one had ever been more alive. Except, in her own way, Rosie. "Nothing wrong in that, son," she said.

He shrugged, clearly unsatisfied. "I started fooling around with jazz instead. Pretty soon I was playing jazz all the time, even when I was supposed to be practicing."

His hands made motions more eloquent than speech. His fingers, as she watched them, seemed to have a life of their own. "I couldn't seem to leave the music alone any more. Couldn't play it the way it was written."

"Maybe you're some kind of genius," Queenie said, hoping

he would not catch sight, just then, of her mother's face. The old lady's mouth was pinched into so many grim wrinkles it resembled a comb.

"I'm some kind of jerk," he said bitterly. He turned and met the terrible look that confirmed it. He looked quickly at Queenie again and continued, "My teacher finally caught me playing jazz when I was supposed to be learning a concerto. Well, I was playing the concerto, all right, but I was jazzing it up some."

"If he was a good teacher, he wouldn't have minded," Queenie said.

"It was a concerto he composed," Larnie said, and added unnecessarily, "He was very proud of it."

This time Queenie could not manage anything beyond, "Oh."

He rattled off the rest rapidly. "So he flunked me. And the Dean wouldn't let me take any courses over. I think he wanted me out of school, anyway, on account of a girl I was going around with."

Queenie intuitively knew what this meant. "A white girl?"

"Yes." His look was troubled, but it had the same level honestly as before. "I don't even think about her any more, Mrs. Fleming. I never stopped thinking about Rosie, though."

Lourinda growled deep in her throat, "Boy, where were you brought up, you don't know better than stay away from white girls?"

Queenie snapped back at her, "What other kind you think they got at that University?"

"The worst thing was I didn't even like her very much," Larnie said. "She just kept following me around till I had to pay attention to her. She acted real brave and bold, you know— but she was really scared. Like they all are, like you said."

Queenie asked gently, "How are your folks taking it?"

"Pop doesn't know. He's upstairs in the men's ward. Heart attack. That's why I'm here so much, Mrs. Fleming," he confessed. "I don't come just to see you. I come to see him. When he can talk, he tells me how proud he is, how glad he is to see me amounting to something before he dies—" His voice broke.

When he resumed it was toneless. "I stay up there as long as I can stand it. Then I come down here."

"Well, you can come here as much as you want. And stay as long as you please."

"My mother's up there all the time," he said. "She lies, Christ how she lies. Tells him I'm gettin' every goddamn honor they got in the goddamn school. And he listens and smiles, and I can't stand it." He shot her a defiant look. "So now you know, Mrs. Fleming."

"I know you're a boy who comes to me because he can't talk to his own mother," she said. "Why is it, I wonder? People can never do anything for their own."

"I don't know," Larnie said. "But it's so."

Queenie had a flash of how things might work out after all. "Maybe it all happened for the best," she said. "Now maybe you can spend more time with Rosie."

"I want to," he said, "if she'll let me."

"Make her let you," Queenie said firmly. She seized his hand with all the strength of her will. "You got to try and talk some sense into her, Larnie. She won't listen to me. She's doin' too much. It worries me. She's not strong, she never was. When she was little I had to nurse her through one disease after the other. And lately she sounds like she's got the pneumonia and the whooping cough both, all over again."

Her mother quickly pooh-poohed this. "She's all right. You worry too much. She just has a tendency to colds."

"How you know so much about her?" Queenie demanded. "I'm her mother, and I don't know nothin'. I don't know half the things she's doin', 'cause she won't tell me. But they're wrong, I know that." She turned her stare back to Larnie. "Find out what she's doin', Larnie. Make her stop. And see if you can't make her quit one of them jobs."

He tried to say something and failed.

"What's the matter now?" she asked him.

He stood up and shrugged. "You're looking at me too hard.

Like you're counting on me too much. I can't stand to have anybody else counting on me. At least not for a while."

"Larnie?" she had to cry after him.

"Yeah?"

"At least promise you'll try."

His broad back shrugged once before it disappeared through
the door. "All right. For what it's worth, I promise."

Queenie fell back on her pillows and prayed to the ceiling.
"Lord, please let her listen to him. She wants all the wrong
things."

"She don't want him," Lourinda stated.

Queenie looked at her mother's angry little black buttons of
eyes. It was impossible to look into them; they glittered but had
no depths. "That's what I meant," she said without expecting
to be understood.

"He's got no future," Lourinda said. "He's just a common
loafer. A bum. It shows all over."

"I thought you'd like him," Queenie said with wasted irony.
"Ain't he your type? Light, pretty, part Indian—"

"I look at more'n a book's cover," Lourinda said serenely. "I
see what's inside."

They sat together for five minutes of hopeless silence, with
nothing they could possibly say to each other, until a clatter in
the hall promised relief: the arrival of dinner trays. As the girl
entered with hers, Queenie shrugged out of the new bedjacket.

"That's right, don't wear it to eat in," her mother said.
"Take care of it. It's real Belgium lace."

Suddenly, furiously, Queenie balled up the frothy thing and
flung it at her.

"Here, take this back where you stole it from!" she cried.
"You wouldn't know somethin' real if it hit you between the
eyes."

16

Larnie had never felt his doom weigh on him so heavily as it did that evening, when he climbed Rosie's dark, creaking stairs. He was keeping his promise to Queenie "for what it was worth." But he did not believe it was worth much. He was simply not the same young man who had gone off, sure of his strength, to prepare to conquer the world. Now, in everything, he was a loser, and he no longer wanted to conquer the world. He only wanted it to leave him alone.

In spite of it all, he climbed on. The door downstairs had been open, as usual. Tonight the apartment door was also unlocked. He walked in.

The living room was littered with a handbag spilling coins and lipsticks and a trail of kicked-off shoes and skirt and stockings and girdle. Larnie followed it to the kitchen, where he found Rosie eating her dinner:

Anchovies out of a can, crackers, a big Jewish pickle, black coffee. And a cigarette, smoking in the ash tray before her.

He wanted to scold her for eating such a miserable meal, but she looked so cute and childlike and foolish, sitting there in her minus-A-cup brassiere, popping the end of a long anchovy into her mouth and sucking it in with a slurp, that he just slid into the chair opposite her and sat there smiling.

"Everybody else dresses for dinner," he said. "You're the only girl I know who strips."

Rosie was annoyed, but she dimpled—how could such skinny cheeks have room for dimples, he wondered?—and said, "If you'd let people know you was coming, they might put some clothes on."

"I don't dig people," he said, running a fingertip over her smooth bare arm. "I don't particularly dig clothes, either. I just dig you."

God Bless the Child

—Really, she dug him too, she decided. She had forgotten that Larnie was so nice. Now, basking in his smile, she forgot the cigarette and let it burn down in the tray. She saw his cheek tremble slightly as he moved in her direction. He just couldn't keep away from her. And she didn't want to keep him away. The pulse of his face, when he slid into the chair beside her, was so pleasant next to hers. His skin was smooth and downy, not sandpapery like Tucker's.

But in spite of him her thoughts drifted back to their usual frantic topic: money. Mom's hospital bill was three hundred for the room, fifty for the medicine, seventy-five for the surgeon. Tomorrow the rent was due: ninety. Tomorrow, Thursday, was also the thirtieth: semi-monthly payday at Schwartz's, a hundred and eighty. And she had thirty in her purse turned back to her by Miltie, proof that her constant nagging of Tucker had finally begun to pay off. Eventually these dribs and drabs from him would be enough to take care of the department stores and everything else. Stores could wait, anyway. Even groceries could wait as long as there were tins of sardines and anchovies on the shelf. But she had to bail Mom out of the hospital Friday, and hospitals were more hard-boiled than gangsters when it came to insisting on payment.

It was too much to figure out in her small head. "You got a pencil?" she asked.

Larnie drew back from his attentive examination of the curls around her right ear. "What for?"

"I just got to figure out how I'm gonna pay all these bills."

He dug down in his pocket without a word and produced a pencil.

"Thanks, hon," she said. "There's so many numbers in my head it hurts me. I got to get 'em out before it splits wide open. Could you hand me a couple of them paper towels?"

He did so, with great docility. While she scribbled on the towels, he moved in behind her and gently rubbed her forehead. It felt nice. And he did not reproach her, only said, "Your Mom asked me to tell you something, Rosie."

"What's that?" she murmured, scrawling vast crooked columns of figures.

"She asked me to tell you not to think so much about money."

"She's got a nerve," Rosie said, and sat up straight, away from his hand. "Laying up there in that private room. Who's she think is payin' for her special trays and her private doctors? The Holy Ghost? God the Father?"

"She feels bad about that," Larnie said. "But after she gets out of the hospital, she wants you to take it easy."

"Seventeen and seven is twenty-four, carry the two," Rosie said. "How'm I gonna take it easy? You see that pile of bills?"

He reached out for them. "Well, let's look at them. Maybe you don't need to buy so many things."

Her small hand came down hard on his giant one. "Get out of there. That's none of your business, Larnie Bell."

"I was only trying to help," he said. He was very still for a minute. Then his fingers touched her hair, so lightly she barely felt them. They slid down gently and began massaging her shoulders. It would have been easy to forget about the bills and relax, be passive. She almost did, for a moment. But then she felt a snap as he unhooked her brassiere. It would have been easy to let that happen too. The easiest, most natural thing in the world. But instead she stiffened.

"Quit that," she said. "Quit gettin' in my business. Quit movin' in on me."

"I'm not moving in on you," he said seriously. "I just want you."

"Same thing," Rosie said. She pulled back and stared at him, crossing her arms on her chest as the ridiculous bra flopped forward from her shoulders.

"What are you scared of, Rosie? Are you a virgin?"

"No," she mumbled. "I don't know." She felt two enormous tears start from her eyes and roll down her cheeks.

"Turn around," he said. She obeyed; she trusted him that much, but only that much. He put the straps back in place and fastened the hooks.

"There," he said, patting her shoulder. "What else can I do to make you trust me?" He got up from the table. "Leave?"

She looked up at him for several seconds, while the tears dried as quickly as they had come.

"No," she finally said.

She led him not to her own hard bed but to Mom's big snowdrift. They tumbled into it without undressing and snuggled like a pair of puppies. She was amazed to find him all patient affection. Not just desire: affection.

"We can just lie here like this if you want. It's all right," he said.

"How can you wait so long?"

"I'd wait a lot longer for you." He punctuated it with little nibbling kisses. "Nothing good ever happens in a hurry."

"This is nice," she said. "This is the nicest thing ever happened."

"It'll be nicer later."

"How can you be so nice and lovey?" She hadn't known anybody could be like him, warm and melting through and through. She had thought everybody was like her, all bumpy and scratchy inside.

"I guess because somebody loved me."

Her face was wet again. "You're lucky. Nobody ever loved me."

"Now somebody does."

She didn't believe it. Not any of it. "Who loved you? Your mother?"

"No. Yours," he murmured surprisingly against her ear. "I'm just passing it along."

"Well, I don't care if Mom loves you. Everybody should. Everybody should have some Larnie."

"Not everybody. Just you."

"No, everybody. Me, and my Mom, and Dolly too if she wants."

"Why Dolly?"

"Oh, Dolly's crazy about you, anybody can see that. And she's my best friend, so I don't mind."

Suddenly, fiercely, she twined around him like a vine. "I changed my mind. I want you all for me."

"That's better."

"The best," she said a long time after that, running restless hands endlessly over the smooth mountain of his back. "You're the best there is, Larnie."

"You mean that, Rosie?"

" 'Course I mean it."

"Then why is it, every time I try to get close to you, you run away?"

"You're talking crazy. I don't know what you mean."

"Oh, yes, you do."

Oh, yes, she did. In a way. She had to run away from the thing she was scared of. She could take somebody like Tucker, somebody who was all hard shiny surfaces, as lightly as he took her. But Larnie was so real, so terribly *true,* he threatened to tease open the doors to her own secret passages. She couldn't let that happen. She couldn't let him see how bad she was. At least not yet.

She had found a way to stave it off; by being superior, by teasing. "I changed my mind. I can't keep you all to myself. You're too sweet."

He frowned at her phoniness, but went along with it. "Really?"

"Sure. You're my candy. My great big lump of sugar."

The lines in his brow became ridges when she jumped up and began whisking into her underwear.

"Do you have to go, Rosie?"

"I love candy, honey. But I can't live on it. I need meat and potatoes."

"I've left school, Rosie," he announced. "I'll get a job soon."

She dropped a kiss on his forehead. "Fine. But don't worry about it now, hon. Just go to sleep. Mom and Granny won't be home tonight, so you can stay here. I'll be back soon. Wait for me."

Things were just as good later, when Rosie got back from her shift at Benny's, and they would have been as good again the next morning when the alarm rang. But she only had half an hour to get to work.

Larnie heard the alarm first. He stretched out one hand to muffle its screaming, and reached for her with the other.

Lord, it was hard to tear herself away from his sleepy morning face; it was even better than his wide-awake look. And, half asleep, he wouldn't notice her faults or her fears.

But she had to leave. "Let me go, baby," she said against his bare shoulder. "I got to get movin'."

"Seems like you just got home half an hour ago," he complained.

"Oh, I had time to get me a few winks," she said.

He chuckled. "And a few other things."

"Oh, Larnie, stop that!" she screamed suddenly. "Stop playing around. You know I got to go to work now."

He released her immediately. He even gave her a little shove out of the bed. "Go on. I won't stop you."

Now she was sorry. She was tempted to hang back a little. But he lay there unmoving. She finally got up, coughing, and shuffled around the room for her slippers. When she lit a cigarette the coughing stopped.

"Just tell me one thing, Rosie," he asked the ceiling. "What are you tryin' to do? Make all the money there is?"

"No," she said around her dangling cigarette. "I'm just tryin' to have some kind of a decent life."

"You call this a decent life? It's not even living. It's just running."

She breathed a sigh of impatience. "You saw my Mom laying up in the hospital, didn't you? Lord knows when she'll be able to work again. You know my Granny's getting old. And that old lady she works for is gonna die any minute, then she'll be out of a job, too. You oughta know I've got to hustle."

"All right, hustle," he said. "But do you have to have two full-time jobs?"

She sat down on the bed to work her nylons up her legs. In the cold light of early March morning, Mom's room was all a shabby gray. "I can't stand the sight of this place much longer," she said. "I was born in this room. I been in this rat trap ever since. Do you think I want to look at it all the rest of my life?"

His hand caressed her hip through the satin slip that clung to it. "You didn't notice it last night, did you?"

"No," she admitted. Then she moved away. "But I notice it now. And I always would, between times."

She lurched to her feet and snatched up her dress from a chair. After she had wriggled into the dress she clung to the chair, coughing.

"Rosie, you sound awful. Come back to bed. You only had three hours' sleep."

"It's enough," she said.

"You make me feel bad for making love to you," he said softly.

"Never feel bad about that, lover," she said. "That's better than sleeping."

"Then stay home with me this morning."

"No." She ran over to the mirror and tore a comb through her hair, lit another cigarette, then collapsed in a new fit of coughing. This one was too much for her. She staggered back to the bed and flung herself on it, pounding the pillow and Larnie indiscriminately with her fists.

He patted her shoulder until the spasms passed. "That store can get along without you for one day," he said.

"I can't get along without my pay check, though," she sobbed.

"Stay home, Rosie," he urged. "You can sleep now. Later on I'll make you some breakfast."

It sounded good for a minute. Go to sleep, forget about the bills, forget about everything, and wake up and be waited on. She burrowed into the pillow.

"That's right," he said. "Go to sleep. Let me take care of you. I love you."

She was up in an instant, looking at him suspiciously through streaming eyes. He had to be lying. How could anybody possibly love her?

"Don't lie, Larnie," she said in a rasping voice. "You don't love me. You just wanta screw me."

She snatched up her satchel and headed for the door. Larnie knew there was nothing more he could say.

He felt an enormous sadness that was not just for Rosie and himself. Like a dried-up ocean bed, his desolation was vast enough to include everyone. Oh, he would try to get Rosie to trust him; oh, patiently, over and over. But each time it would not get easier, it would get harder. He was, after all, a loser, not a lover.

Larnie turned his face to the wall, turned away into sleep, to escape the vision of everybody's failure becoming his failure with Rosie.

17

As Rosie got skinnier and more hollow-eyed and coughed more, she gradually got used to sleeping less. She had the wiry strength of weeds and other undernourished forms of life, the kind that thrives on starvation and toughens on struggle. That and her youth and her driving energy seemed to let her do more than anyone else.

But there were times when she felt a knock in the motor, a warning that she might be climbing too many hills in high gear. Being Rosie, she ignored these episodes as long as she could conceal them. The first time this became impossible was that morning at Schwartz's.

After waiting on six customers, she took a break. She walked past the fitting rooms to the little closet that served as a washroom for the salesgirls and splashed cold water on her face. Since Mr. Schwartz had ordered her out of the stockroom, she had no place to sneak cat naps in the mornings.

"Don't do me no more favors," she muttered to him and the

mirror, which showed her eyes congested with sleep and lashes beaded with sand. She lit a cigarette to wake her up. Her first drag started a bout of coughing that left her eyes flooded with tears.

She turned the water on full force and began to slap her face with it—furious blows that arrested the coughing and awakened her sluggish skin into angry needles of pain. She slapped until she had gotten even with her body for being inadequate to her demands.

Face dry and tingling, she was about to walk out on the floor again when warm moisture touched her upper lip. She looked in the mirror. A red stream was trickling from her nose.

"Goddamn!"

Rosie snatched up a wad of towels, soaked them, pressed them at the bridge of her nose and the back of her neck, then leaned against the wall, head flung back, exhausted.

That was how Betty Perlman found her when she walked into the washroom.

"Gosh, Rosie, you're sick!"

"Just a bad head," Rosie muttered. "Too much party last night." But on Betty's plump, placid face—suddenly wiped clean of expression—she read the truth.

"God, you're sick," Betty repeated helplessly. "What can I do?" Her hands, hovering nervously in the air, were offered to Rosie and withdrawn from her at the same time.

"Light me a cigarette, will you, doll?" Rosie said casually. She made the mistake of raising her head.

"Sure, wait a min— Ooh!" Betty squealed. "I can't stand blood! I'm sorry—I'll get Mr. Schwartz."

"Damn fool, come back here!" Rosie hissed too late. There were sounds of running feet outside. She dabbed frantically with the towels to make herself presentable.

Betty called through the door, "Rosie, you all right in there?"

"Sure." She opened the door for Betty. "Now what you wanta run tell Mr. Schwartz for?" she complained. "You wanta make me lose half a day?"

"Rosie, you look awful," Betty said. She stepped aside. Rosie saw Mr. Schwartz standing behind her and behind him, to one side, Aaron with a little smirk that made his face resemble a Kewpie doll's.

"I'm fine," Rosie lied. Head high, she walked out of the washroom with complete poise. Then the floor rose swiftly to meet her and she felt Aaron's fingers digging into her arm.

"Leggo," she mumbled, shrugging his hand away. "Jus' a little nosebleed. Happens all the time." She turned to Mr. Schwartz. "Let me get to work. Ain't I got customers?"

"Edie's taking care of them."

"Them's her customers. What about my customers?"

"Betty will take care of them."

"Look, it's starting again!" Betty cried. She covered her face with one hand to hide the sight. "Send her home, Mr. Schwartz! Send her home!"

Rosie sniffed, swiped quickly with the back of her hand and elevated her chin to stop the bleeding. She was hurt by Betty's outburst even though she understood it. No matter how much people liked you, they didn't want sickness around.

"I ain't goin' nowhere," she said defiantly.

The expression of concern on Mr. Schwartz's face became more urgent. "I have called a cab, Rosalie," he said, one hand guiding her toward the door. "You must take care of yourself. See a doctor. We need you."

She stopped. "I'm fine, Mr. Schwartz."

"Have you looked at yourself?"

He turned her to face a full-length mirror. A wild-eyed, gray-faced stranger swam into view through a haze of dishwater.

"Like a ghost you are. Trembling like a leaf. This is fine? Ah, no, Rosalie. You are sick."

He put an arm around her shoulders. His voice was warm and sympathetic. "Perhaps you think I keep too busy to notice these little things. But I am interested in every one of my girls. If a girl is sick, if she is tired, she has only to tell me—I want nothing from her but she should rest and get well. I know some men, I will not name names, who drive their girls, make them work like slaves. But I do not have that on my conscience. I give rest rooms, I give full lunch hours. I give rest periods morning and afternoon. So if a girl gets sick, Rosalie, I know is not from working in Schwartz's Store. She is maybe doing too much on the outside, that's all."

Rosie stiffened and pulled away from him. "What I do outside here's my business, Mr. Schwartz. You payin' me to be here eight-thirty to five-thirty. You got no right tellin' me what to do the rest of the time."

"Of course," he agreed with a gracious little shrug. "On that I will give you no arguments. But if you make yourself sick—then you can *not* be here from eight-thirty to five-thirty. Am I wrong?"

Rosie sat on a chair and folded her arms stubbornly. "I ain't goin' nowhere. I'm puttin' in a full day."

Aaron put his less than two cents in. "Uncle Sol says you go home, you go home, Rosalie. Who owns the store, anyhow—him or you?"

Mr. Schwartz shot a quelling glance at his nephew, then continued talking to Rosie in that odd, half-comforting, half-insinuating tone. "All I ask is, you think about what I have said, Rosalie. We need you here. But we need you well." He half-closed his eyes and joined his fingertips. "Somewhere have I read that no one can serve two masters. I think this is a message for all of us, Rosalie, unless we are supermen. And these days, where are the supermen? Only in Germany. Not in Schwartz's Store."

As she jolted forward from the chair he extended his hand to help her to her feet. "The cab is waiting, Rosalie. I will pay for it."

The words forced themselves past her lips. "Keep your money, you damned Jew!"

Even in her helpless anger, Rosie admired the way the old man kept his dignity by pretending not to hear.

"I will pay for the cab," he repeated. "All I ask is you remember what I have said. And get well."

She stared at him with resentment mingled with a new respect, then whirled to spill her fury on the others. "From now on don't do me no more favors, you hear?" she flung at the quivering Betty. "Mind your own business!"

Then she rushed from the store to conceal the nosebleed which had started again.

"You gonna fire her, Uncle Sol?" Aaron whispered.

The old man rubbed his chin thoughtfully, then turned on his nephew.

"When I do, will I be asking your permission?"

Rosie's anger and her nosebleed wore off quickly in the back of the cab. She glanced at her watch. It was eleven-thirty; she wasn't due at Benny's for eight more hours. She thought of going in early but the supper-shift waitresses would resent her premature appearance, and the tips would be slim anyhow.

As the cab passed through streets clotted with children and traffic, she looked nervously for a sign of Miltie. But it was too early; he never came around before afternoon. She had missed him as well as her morning customers. She sighed resentfully. Time lost was money lost.

She would have to find some way to stay awake after this. Some pills or something. She thought of going past Skyros' Drug Store for some, then remembered that since Old Man Skyros was raided last month, he was funny about insisting on prescriptions. Briefly, she considered going to a doctor, then shook her head and laughed. She didn't know any doctors.

Should she go back home to Larnie? Part of her wanted to, but another part pulled back. She couldn't stand so much closeness again so soon. Even if Larnie didn't nag her, or fuss over her, or make love to her, he would not let her *be,* inside the hard shell of herself, where she needed to be for awhile.

She had a sudden, perverse desire to go to Tucker's apartment instead. She could be with him, enjoy him, and still be alone. Larnie told her the truth and made her feel uncomfortable. But Tucker would talk a lot of trash to her, and make her feel good. Pride more than anything else decided her against it. The last time she had dropped in on him unexpectedly—well, she didn't want to be greeted by that look of annoyance again.

150

Money, You Got Lots of Friends

Should she go home and catch some sleep? She could put Larnie out, tell him she was tired. Lord knew it was true. Her skin burned, her muscles ached, and heavy weights were pulling her eyelids down. She could see her bed, her own narrow little single bed, in her darkened room. She sank gratefully toward it, then abruptly rejected it just before her head touched the pillow. Something inside her had exploded singing into bloom.

"Turn around, man," she told the driver. "Turn around 'n take me downtown."

Rosie had bills at nearly every store, but she had just remembered one charge account that had been idle for months. Maybe she couldn't replace the money she had lost that day—but she could spend it, and that was the next best thing.

Spending money was a need more ferocious than sex, more urgent than hunger, which came down on her with predictable regularity—about every two weeks—as well as whenever things went wrong. Buying necessities was no good. Lots of money had to be spent on things she didn't need, and some had to be lavishly wasted before she could breathe again.

When she swept past the doorman at the store's entrance she felt a surge of lust at the glittering counters, the racks hung with shadowy silken mysteries, the hushed alcoves where saleswomen tiptoed and beckoned. All the things were spread out, inviting her to possess them. Her eyes roved restlessly; her mouth tasted hot and salty. She hurried through the store as if pursued because she had so little time in which to touch and see everything.

When she swept out three hours later with two pairs of shoes, a cashmere sweater, a rayon slip for Mom, and a silk dress and a pint of cologne and six lace handkerchiefs for Granny, she felt purged and at peace. She was happy again, and her strength was restored. If necessary, she could now wait tables for six straight shifts at Benny's.

Spending days were rich-lady days. It would spoil the game to ride a trolley. So she hailed another cab, and felt the excited glow spread on her cheeks as the driver arranged the packages around her. Her brusque manner dared him to raise an eyebrow when she told him the address.

God Bless the Child

The driver was discreetly silent, and when she had paid and tipped him she had exactly two dimes left over.

She tossed them in with the tip and ran singing up the stairs.

Once again Granny was in the doorway, shushing up all Rosie's joyfulness with a wagging skinny finger. "Be quiet. Your mother's home from the hospital."

Rosie was surprised; Mom wasn't supposed to be discharged until tomorrow. "Who brought her home?" she wanted to know.

"This young man who says he's a friend of yours," Granny said as Larnie came forward.

For once Rosie showed some impatience with the old lady. "Oh, Granny, stop putting on. You know Larnie. You've met him a gang of times."

She dropped her packages where she stood and went to him swiftly, saying, "If Granny didn't say thanks for getting Mom, here's my thank you." She kissed him and turned back to her grandmother, smiling. "You better get so you recognize Larnie, Granny. You're gonna see a lot of him."

"I can't keep all these miscellaneous people straight, Rosie," the old lady fretted. "You have so many friends, and they all look alike to me. You forget your Granny's getting old."

Rosie was ashamed. She left Larnie's side to console the old lady. "I'm sorry if I was mean," she said, hugging her. "Now don't cry, Duchess. Look at what I brought you."

She bent and rooted through the packages. "This is for you, and this, and this. And this." The last, handed over without hesitation along with the rest, was the cashmere sweater she had meant for herself.

Larnie cleared his throat. "I hope you didn't run up a whole lot of new bills, Rosie."

Normally this remark would have made her bristle, but she was too gay this afternoon. She ran lighthearted fingers through her short curls and tossed her head so they bounced. "What's the dif?" she said. "You know how it is with us rich folks. Easy come, easy go."

"Yeah," he said. "Well, your mother's bill is over four hundred dollars."

"I know all about her bill," she said, staring at him. She had to look away from the honest seriousness in his eyes, so she turned her back and began, with elaborate casualness, to move around the room. She hummed a little tune as she went from one to another of the few small, glowing objects that made the apartment even more dreary by their brilliance.

Picking up a little goblet from the beat-up telephone table, she said, "This here crystal is called Waterford, ain't it, Granny?"

"That's right," the old lady said from the corner, where she was industriously ripping open her packages. "At the house we have service for fifty. Goblets, sherbets and wines."

"Mm-hmm," Rosie said. She set it down, walked over to the coffee table, and picked up a dish that held a few stale crumbs of candy. "And what do you call this? Wildwood?"

"Wedgwood," Granny said. "Careful how you handle that piece, it's rare."

Rosie put it down gently and touched a vase that Mom had made over into a lamp base. "What about this Chinese stuff, Granny?"

"Cloisonné ware," Granny said. "It's part metal, you can't break it. The way you people live around here, I shouldn't bring home anything else. Watch your feet!" she exclaimed as Rosie flopped on the couch and swung up her legs, barely clearing a figurine on the coffee table. "That's German porcelain. It's eighty years old."

Rosie picked up the ivory and pink shepherdess and played with it, mocking its sweet smirking expression. "Don't worry, Granny." Her eyes met Larnie's. "You oughta know I'm used to nice things."

He returned her defiant stare with one of hurt and puzzlement. She quickly looked toward Granny. "Pretty soon you'll have a nicer place to keep them, too."

"Is that a promise?" the old lady asked.

"Promise," Rosie said. "A beautiful new house."

"My, I like this scent, Rosie," she said, spraying herself extravagantly. "I always did."

"Sweets to the sweet," Rosie said, and threw her a kiss. With reluctance she turned her eyes back to where Larnie stood like a statue, helpless, gigantic and patient. "Did you have any trouble about the hospital bill?" she inquired.

"No," he said. "They needed the room, so they had to be nice about it. But it's due right away."

"Don't let it worry you," she said airily. "Is Mom sleeping?"

"I don't think so," Larnie said. "Last time I looked, she was reading a magazine."

"Well why didn't somebody say so?" she said indignantly. She leaped up, knocking the figurine to the floor after all. It wasn't broken, though. She quickly replaced it under Granny's baleful stare. "Jesus Christ. All this time we've been talkin', Mom's been awake in the next room. Come on, lover. Let's go visit her."

"What's the matter?" he said as she grabbed his hand. "You afraid to go see her by yourself?"

She looked at him angrily. He knew too much; he even knew, somehow, that she felt to blame for Mom's sickness. She dropped his hand and flounced away.

"Come or don't come, I don't care," she said, and went into the bedroom without a backward look.

She immediately assumed the rough teasing tone she always used with her mother. "So they finally threw you out, huh? I figured they'd be getting sick of you pretty soon."

Queenie heaved up like a mountain from among lesser mountains of pillows. "Yeah," she said. "The doctor said I looked so healthy, I was makin' all the other patients feel sicker."

"I knew it," Rosie said, though she thought Mom looked terrible—bloated where she should be thin, and sunken where she should be plump, and sallow all over. "What else did the doctor say?"

Larnie had followed her after all. His voice came over her shoulder. "She's supposed to stay in bed two more weeks, and stick to her diet, and take this medicine three times a day."

Money, You Got Lots of Friends

Queenie smiled at him as he poured out two pills and handed them to her with a glass of water. "This boy was wonderful, Rosie. He took care of everything. When I heard they was gonna discharge me ahead of time, I didn't know what to do. I knew my mother wouldn't be no help. She has sickness where she works too, and she gets so mixed up she can't tell me from her white folks. So I called up here. But I knew you wouldn't be home."

"How could I?" Rosie snapped. "I have to work."

"I know, Rosie," Mom said. "That's why I was so glad to hear him answer. He brought my clothes in a suitcase, and called for a cabulance, and got my prescription filled, and everything."

"I would've done the same if I'd been here," Rosie said sullenly.

"Sure, I know that," Mom said, smiling. She fumbled for and found Rosie's hand, and said to Larnie, "This girl always thinks somebody is accusing her of something. I never saw nobody so sensitive. I don't know how she could get that way, livin' with somethin' as tough as me."

"That's just how," Rosie answered her.

Mom swallowed hard, then patted Rosie's hand. "Anyway," she said, "you came home early when you heard I was here. That was nice, Rosie."

Rosie ducked her head quickly to hide the tears that were running down her face. Tears of shame because, while shuffling all the possible ways of spending her free afternoon, she had never once considered going to the hospital. Then she gave up trying to hide anything. She looked up.

"I didn't know you was home. I just left work early, that's all."

"How come?"

"I didn't feel so good," Rosie admitted. She added lightly, "Wasn't nothin' serious, though. I feel fine now."

"Well what was it? Another of them coughing spells?"

Rosie was silent.

"Rosie, answer me!"

But Rosie didn't have to answer. Or, rather, the answer burst from her in a series of tearing coughs that seemed likely to turn

God Bless the Child

her inside out. The more she tried to stifle the coughing in a handerchief, the worse it became. Finally she just had to hang onto the bedpost and let it have its way with her until it subsided.

"Rosie," Mom said, "that cold's hangin' on too long. If it *is* a cold. You got to see a doctor."

"Naw," Rosie said. "I just got to cut down on cigarettes."

Larnie backed Mom up, saying firmly, "Cut down on cigarettes and see a doctor too."

"Ah, leave me alone," Rosie flung at him over her shoulder as she went to a far corner of the room. Defiantly, with trembling hands, she lit a cigarette.

"A doctor wouldn't hurt you, Rosie," he said. "He'd help you."

"What you know about it?" she said, resentfully regarding his broad chest and his arms like fireplace logs. "You big, healthy ox, you never needed a doctor in your life."

"You see what a handful I got when I had this child?" Queenie said. But her smile was a sad one. "I can't handle her when I'm well. You know I can't now, sick as I am. I'm countin' on you to make her take care of herself, Larnie."

Larnie shrugged. "I tried to make her stay home from work this morning, Mrs. Fleming. You see how far I got."

"Well try some more," Queenie said, "till you make her quit some of her foolishness."

Her deep look at him implied a well-understood pact between them. Rosie caught it immediately.

"He can't make me do nothin'," she said. "He ain't my father."

"I wish you did have a father," Mom said. "That's what's wrong with you now."

"Well, is it my fault I don't?"

Queenie's eyes bulged as she tried to answer. Clutching her chest, gasping for air, she suddenly made Rosie think of the pet goldfish she'd once taken out of its bowl, in a childish experiment. Mom looked exactly like a great, gulping, flopping goldfish. The sight horrified Rosie and paralyzed her.

Only Larnie was able to move. He ran quickly to the bed and snatched the pillows away. Soon Queenie was lying flat and breathing easy.

156

"Don't upset her so much," he said to Rosie. "Remember, she's still sick."

"Everybody's sick," Rosie said in disgust. "This house is worse than a damn leper colony. It's a damn House of Usher, that's what it is. Granny!" she called suddenly. "Granny!"

The old lady came in. She had changed to her new dress of rose-colored silk. In the center of the room, she held out the skirt with both hands and curtseyed.

"Rosie, I just had to try this on. It fits perfect." She was so pleased with the dress she even smiled at Larnie. "My grandchild's so good to me."

"Glad you like it," Rosie said. "Granny, looks like you're gonna hafta be in charge around here for a while. Everybody else is too sick to lift a finger."

Smoothing the front of her dress, Granny looked at Rosie uncomprehendingly.

"I mean," Rosie explained, "you'll have to take off a couple weeks from work so you can look after Mom."

"Oh, I couldn't do that, Rosie," Granny said innocently. "My folks need me."

"Ain't we your folks?" Rosie asked sharply, then bit her tongue. She heaved a deep sigh. "Granny, how's Mom gonna get her meals 'n her medicine? She can't get up for two more weeks yet."

"Oh, I spect she'll be up before then," Granny answered. "The doctor sent her home, didn't he?"

"He said she has to stay in bed. She's still sick, Granny." She made a helpless gesture to Larnie for aid.

"A minute ago, she couldn't get her breath," he said.

An irritable harshness replaced the usual lilt of Granny's voice. "Don't talk to me about sickness. That's all I've heard for three months. Nurses and doctors. Needles and medicine. Temperatures and pills." She sat down on the edge of the bed with sudden heaviness. "I been with Miss Helen forty-five years, Rosie, and the last couple weeks, she don't even know me. Not one sign of recognition. But I keep right on doin' for her, 'cause I know she wouldn't want nobody else to do it. Taking her temperature, taking her her trays, feeding her, nursing her around the clock."

God Bless the Child

Her head drooped alarmingly. "It's thankless work, Rosie. It wears me out. I don't feel so strong myself these days."

"I know, Granny." Rosie was full of remorse. "I'm sorry."

"It's a terrible thing, watching somebody you love die, when you been with her all your life, and you know it means your own time's comin' soon."

"Granny, don't say that!" Rosie cried in terror. She touched the old lady's shoulder, whether to console her, or to reassure herself, she could not say. "Please don't say that."

"Oh, it's true," Granny said. "I know it. But I got to try and be of some use while I'm still here."

She got up with sudden briskness. "I got to get back right now. I just had to make sure everything was all right here. Now I know it is." She smiled. "I know my grandchild will take care of everything."

"Sure I will, Granny," Rosie said. "Don't you worry about a thing. Just try and take it easy."

After the old lady left the room, Mom's voice rose from the bed as if from the bottom of a well. "A fifty-dollar dress. What else did you buy her this time?"

Rosie was trembling. "A thirty-dollar sweater. A ten-dollar bottle of cologne. Six one-dollar handkerchiefs. Is that too much to spend on her in the little time she's got left?"

"She'll outlive us both, Rosie," Mom said in the same deep, hollow voice. "All her life she's lived in white folks' houses. Ate their food. Had their comforts. You and me, we've had to take their crumbs."

"Hush," Rosie said. "You shouldn't be talkin' now."

But Mom went on with a grisly catalogue. "Cold water flats. Drafts. Dampness. Chills. Fevers. Bad heat. Bad plumbing. Bad food. Bad air. Rats. Roaches. Pneumonia. Scarlet fever. T.B."

"Cut it out!" Rosie yelled, covering her ears.

Mom rolled over on one side and looked at her. "But that ain't so bad, Rosie. What kills me is seein' you kill yourself for her."

She sat up in spite of Larnie's attempt to restrain her. "Let go of me, boy. It's got to stop now, Rosie. Take your pick. You can keep one of them jobs or the other. You can't have both."

Rosie laughed. "Who'd you say I was killin' myself for? I'd cry if it wasn't so funny. Those things I bought Granny ain't nothin' compared to that hospital bill I got to pay tomorrow." She ignored Larnie's shocked look and added, "Plus them nurses I got to hire to take care of you around the clock."

Mom fell back on her pillows. Her voice was suddenly much lighter, like air leaking out of a tired balloon. "I just wish, while 'Tena was stabbin' me, she had aimed better. She could have saved you the expense."

"Yeah," Rosie said without mercy. "That way I could collect on your insurance, too."

Mom closed her eyes. "Don't worry, Rosie. The way I feel, you won't have to wait long."

Larnie's face was screwed up in pain. He got up and strode quickly from the room.

Rosie followed him to the front room.

Hands shoved deep in his pockets, he stood facing a blank wall. "Don't worry about getting a nurse," he said without turning around. "I'll look after her."

Rosie interposed herself between him and the wall. "What you plan on doing? Moving in?" She looked at him narrowly. "That won't save me no money. I bet you eat enough to feed four hogs."

"Never mind," he said angrily. "Forget it. I just can't stand to hear you talk to her that way." His voice rose. "Dammit, Rosie, she's your mother!"

"If you gonna hang around here, you're gonna have to learn to stand a lot more," she told him. "Face it: my mother ain't to me what yours is to you. She never paid to send me to no school but the School of Hard Knocks."

Suddenly she found a new way to hurt him. She had to use it. "Say, how come you left school, anyhow? Your folks change their minds about payin' for your education?"

He collapsed into a chair.

In an instant she was all on top of him. "Larnie, Larnie, I'm sorry," she said, running her hands over his face. "I should never have said that. It was none of my business."

"It's all right, Rosie."

"No, it's not," she insisted. "You should've slapped me. Why didn't you?" She turned her cheek. "Go on, do it now."

"I could never do that to you."

"You should," she said. "I'm no damn good."

He held her at arm's length. "You're good, you're bad, you're sweet, you're mean, you're all sorts of things. It's all you, Rosie, and I love it all. Don't you understand that?"

"No," she said. "I'm bad through and through. Nobody could ever love somethin' like me."

He said, "I told you last night, somebody does."

She stared bleakly at the wall over his shoulder. "Yes, you said it. But it ain't so. Nobody could love me. Not even my father 'n mother."

"Oh, you're wrong about your mother, Rosie." Pain tightened his face.

"No. Mom don't love me. Or else she'd've made my father stay." There, it was out, though she had to sob it out against his shoulder.

Granny came into the room then, carrying her handbag, with her hard round little hat screwed down on her head. She coughed to make her presence known and said, "Rosie, I forgot to tell you. A person named Miltie was here looking for you."

Rosie looked up but did not move.

Granny came closer. "He wanted to wait for you, but I shooed him out of here. I didn't like the looks of him, Rosie. I didn't like him one bit. You ought to be more careful how you choose your friends."

Rosie lifted her head from Larnie's shoulder. "He's not a friend, Granny."

"Well, whatever he is, he was sure in a hurry to see you." Granny stared at Rosie until, self-consciously, she disentangled herself from Larnie and scrambled out of his lap.

"I'll get in touch with him right away, Granny. Thanks."

The old lady turned and started out of the apartment.

"Don't you want me to call you a taxi?" Rosie called after her.

Granny kept right on walking. "No thank you." The door slammed.

"You buy her fancy clothes, you ride her around in taxis, you promise to buy her a new house," Larnie growled. "What are you trying to do, Rosie? Take the place of her rich white folks?"

"That proves you don't love me. If you did you wouldn't say things like that."

"Lots of people love you, Rosie," he said wearily, like someone who no longer believed in God repeating a grace. "You just don't ever give 'em a chance."

"No," she said, staring at him. "Nobody ever loved me. Nobody except my Granny."

18

The Avenue had layers and layers of classes within its masses of underprivilege. Benny's was broadly democratic, serving everyone from Cadillac riders to Holy Rollers, but the Blue Moon catered to the rock bottom, the permanent relief recipients who had given up believing in any salvation except the bottled kind. Here you went to hear the worst language, watch the goriest fights, and see the most unspeakably dirty linen aired in public. Here you also went to buy the cheapest wine, so naturally Rosie looked here first for Miltie.

She found him at a corner table, slumped so low his chin rested in the puddle left by six or eight sherries. Grabbing the back of his collar, she pulled him up like a puppet on a string.

"What's the idea, comin' by my house and upsettin' my Granny? I thought I told you, never show your face where I live."

"Wha?" he said, looking up vaguely. "Whassa matta, Rosie?"

"I said, what was the idea comin' by my house today?"

He continued to stare at her—or, rather, at a spot just to one side of her—through mists of sherry.

"Wake up, you winehead bum," she said. To aid him she delivered a sharp crack across his face. "Wake up, I said!"

He only blinked, as if used to blows, and shook his head slightly as if wondering what he had done to deserve this one.

"You want another one?" she asked, waving her fist under his eyes. "Where you want it this time, Miltie? In the teeth?"

He blinked again. A large tear rolled down and left a wobbly clean path down the center of one grimy cheek. "What did I do wrong, Rosie? Just tell me."

Rosie dropped her hand and sat down beside him. Her eyes started to fill, too, because she was so ashamed. Suddenly she understood why Mom had been stabbed in here. The atmosphere of the place brought out the worst in everybody.

At the sound of a scream, she jumped up again. A big man was slapping a young girl around at the bar. While the bartender watched with the stone face of all Avenue bartenders, she slid to the floor.

"Get up!" the man hollered. "Get up so I can hit you again."

Rosie growled something unintelligible.

"Don't get excited, Rosie," Miltie said. "They're probably married."

Before he could stop her, Rosie was at the bar, battering the man's arms, chest and head with her giant pocketbook. It was an effective weapon. "You stop that!" she cried between blows. "Stop it now!"

He had stopped it long ago, but Rosie didn't give him a chance to answer or defend himself. While he cringed and nursed his bruised arms she turned her back and told the bartender, "Bring me a draft beer. Bring my friend all the sherry he wants. And see if you can't keep some order in here, so we can have a conversation."

She tossed a five on the bar and went back to the table.

"God, Rosie," Miltie said. "You better not never come in here no more. You better hang onto your money, too. You'll need it."

"What you mean?"

"We got an emergency," he said, and held out a grimy slip of paper.

The message was obscure: "109–1–J. Perkins, M. Crump."

"You owe them people a centipede, Rosie," Miltie said.

"A what?"

"A thousand dollars," he said, incredibly. "Five hundred apiece."

She stared at him. He had to be crazy.

"Where you been all afternoon? One–oh–nine was it."

"Ah, Miltie, I'm tired," she said, suddenly slumping in a position identical with his. "Don't play no games with me today."

"I was never what you would call a religious boy," Miltie said, "but I been sittin' here all this afternoon prayin'. 'Lord,' I prayed, 'please let Rosie have some connections.'"

"Well of course I got connections," she said indignantly. "Tucker."

Miltie shook his head. "I was prayin' for some connections I didn't know about."

She grabbed Miltie's hand. "Come on. Let's go find Tucker."

Miltie didn't move. He looked at her mournfully. "Forget it," he said.

Because she looked so baffled, he got his point across with a list of synonyms mostly not to be found in the dictionary. "He's long gone. Vamoosed. Cut out. Flew the coop. Split the scene. His stool at the club ain't warm no more. His apartment's got a For Rent sign."

She felt her eyes and her brain grow as foggy as Miltie's had been. His voice reached her from a great distance.

"He done you dirty, Rosie. He didn't cover none of your bets. Only his."

She burst into loud absurd sobbing.

"See, that way, he could take his money out and be safe too. I think he was planning on keeping it going a long time. This happened too soon for him. In a way you lucky, Rosie."

She cried louder.

163

Miltie patted her shoulder awkwardly. "I know. Two hits in one day, that's bad luck. If they was any more I'd say a Fix was in. But two, that's just the bad breaks. Lady Luck gettin' mad and favorin' somebody else."

She couldn't take it all in, Tucker's treachery, and her gullibility, and her mounting debts, and what Miltie was saying too. She could only rouse herself to deal with a small unimportant part of it.

"Did you know he was doin' this, Miltie?"

"Yeah, I found out," he admitted. "He paid me not to tell you." He ducked his head, avoiding her steady look, and added rapidly, "I needed the money bad, and I said to myself, you was probably safe anyway, on account of working for Benny. I figured Benny would cover you. Won't he, Rosie?"

"No," she said. "Benny only covers Benny." She closed her pocketbook with a snap. "So whoever they are, Mr. Crump and Mr. Perkins will have to wait."

"They can't wait, Rosie. Listen." He pulled her sleeve as she got up to leave. "It ain't just them. Everybody hates a welcher."

She shrugged. "Let them hate us then."

His voice grew shrill. "Rosie, you don't know what you're sayin'. Everybody on the Avenue is touchy these days. Lots of people gettin' laid off. Mr. Ahmed's been stirrin' 'em up, too. Every day there's a new riot someplace. Today it might be us."

"You mean it might be you," she said. "I didn't take those particular orders. You did."

He slid down in his chair until he seemed about to disappear under the table. "I'll haunt you, Rosie," he said in a thin voice that was already ghostly. "I'll come back and haunt you, I swear I will."

"It'd be better than havin' you haunt me alive," she said. "Your corpse'll smell better."

His voice as she crossed the room grew higher, more piercing and feminine. What it said finally arrested her progress.

"I'll tell 'em it was you! And I'll tell 'em where to find you, Rosie."

She whirled. "Look," she said. "Keep your miserable mouth shut. And keep your miserable stinking self away from my house. Keep away from my Granny, and stay outa my way, too. The mood I'm in, I just might kill you myself." She felt suddenly very old, like a grandmother herself, trying to bring up somebody else's delinquent children.

"Rosie, are you gonna pay off?" Miltie screamed at her.

"I don't know. I'll see what I can do."

"I'll never cross you again, Rosie, I swear it."

"You may never get the chance," she told him. "You better worry about that later, anyway. Right now just think about findin' a better place to hide."

Benny, with his surface as bland and smooth as a stone polished by the sea, was still such a mystery to Rosie that she did not know what to expect when she asked him for money. She was prepared for a refusal, but not for one as abrupt as, "Positively not. I never make loans."

"Can't you break your rule, just this once?" she asked plaintively.

"Rosie, I've told you before, it's not a question of rules. It's a question of roles." He smiled at the agility of his own word-dance. "Other people were born to play The Fool. Not me."

"Everybody's somebody's fool," Rosie muttered.

"So I hear," he said. "So you have learned."

"Yeah," she said. "Maybe someday you will too."

"I doubt it," he answered calmly.

His immunity had never been more of an affront. "Why not?" she growled. "What right you got to be different from everybody else?"

"Divine right," Benny said.

From the depths of her misery she looked up at him with numb incomprehension.

Benny explained with a history lesson. "My family has always been in charge here. My father was the Don, the ruler, in this neighborhood before me, and his father was the Don before him.

Back in the old days, when everybody on the Avenue was just over from Palermo."

He waved a spatula encrusted with red and green peppers. "My role is to rule." He had the nerve to smile again as he pointed the spatula at Rosie's chest. "You have a role too. You're supposed to take orders. If you played your role, your life would be easier."

Rosie took in most, if not all, of this, and she did not like any of it. "I hate you!" she finally screamed.

Benny frowned. "No, no. That's the wrong spirit. I don't hate you, Rosie. I don't hate anybody."

"Naturally not," Rosie said. "You're winning."

"You might as well hate God, Rosie. He made things this way."

"Benny," Rosie moaned, "I don't need no sermons. I need fifteen hundred dollars."

"Look," Benny explained gently, "this is the way I have to look at things. If I got involved in half the things I see every day, I'd go out of my mind or kill myself. I tried to help you. I told you exactly what would happen. To make you listen, I even showed you my backstage."

"Benny, I'm hurting," she whimpered.

"The pain was written into your part," he said.

"I'm hurting for money, not philosophy," she told him.

"Then I can't help you."

A hand brushed Rosie's arm lightly, leaving a trail of goose bumps. "Maybe I can help," a spooky voice said.

Rosie backed away as Shadow pulled a wad of bills from his pocket. She stared at the money and could think only of how it had been earned for him. "I don't want your money, Shadow," she said. "It's dirty."

"All money is dirty," Benny commented.

Shadow said, "Is it the terms you're worried about? Don't worry. I know you'll pay me back." He smiled thinly. "Some day or other, some way or other."

"Benny, get this skunk away from me!" Rosie cried.

The Man make a jerky upward motion with his thumb. Shadow instantly scuttled away into the darkness.

"Benny, I'm hurtin'," Rosie said softly. "You hear me?"

"I told you I can't help you," he said. He seemed to hesitate on the brink of a decision. Finally he waved toward one booth over which a cloud of cigar smoke hung like a canopy. "But maybe Pockets can."

She gave him a sudden look of understanding. Pockets' help was simply Benny's help in disguise. If he preferred to do it this way, through a puppet, so he could maintain his show, it was all right with her.

Rosie ran over to the booth where Pockets sat in solitary splendor, chewing a cigar and sipping V.S.Q.

"I need fifteen hundred, Pockets," she said without any preliminaries, and stuck out her hand.

Pockets turned toward her with slow amazement, like a hippo startled while taking his mud bath. "Not so fast, little girl," he rumbled. "What's my guarantee?"

"Isn't Benny's word good enough?" she asked.

Pockets looked in The Man's direction. After a moment's hesitation it came: the barely perceptible nod.

"Well now, little girl," he said, "don't stand there like that. You make me nervous. Sit down, sit down."

She barely complied, perching on the edge of the seat. "I'm in a hurry, Pockets."

"You young people always are. That's the trouble with you, you never stop to think things over. And then you get in difficulties. Right?"

She nodded miserably.

"You're lucky there are a few older people around who take their time and consider, so they can bail you out of your mistakes."

This time she had to endure his lecture and his cigar smoke in her face. She shut her eyes and tried to breathe through her mouth, but failed. She began coughing.

"Well, little girl, I think I can help you," he finally said. "But times are tight. A thousand is all I can spare."

It was the first concession; Rosie knew there would be more. "It'll do," she said.

"And we'll have to have us an agreement."

"What's that, Pockets?"

"Pretty much like I splained to you before. Just one difference. You bring me everything. You don't hold out one penny. —'Course I know you wouldn't, after the way you just been burned."

"That's true, Pockets," she agreed. So it was all over town, at least the underworld part of town. She couldn't even be a fool in private.

"And one thing more." He waved the cigar dangerously close to her face. "You don't make nothin'. No percentage till your bill is paid."

Rosie hesitated on the verge of anger, held back by desperation. Pockets said, "You got a better offer? Go. Take it. You're free."

He had her by the scruff hairs, and he knew it.

"No, I'll take yours, Pockets," she said wearily, inwardly raging at Tucker for putting her in bondage to this fat fool.

His meaty hand gripped hers. "Good." Then he had the nerve to wink. "Just because you're so young and pretty, I'll try and help you keep Miltie in line."

"Do that," she said. She counted up the money that had suddenly appeared on the table. It was all there, but none of it was hers. She sighed and pushed it back to him. "You can start right now. Find him and make sure he delivers this where it belongs."

He rose with clumsy courtliness. "I'll be glad to. I know it makes a woman feel good to have a man take care of these things. A man has more experience."

"Yeah," Rosie said ironically, thinking of Tucker, thinking ahead to the sweet moment when she would get her hands on him.

"I'll see this gets delivered on time," her fat new knight said, patting one of his myriad pockets. "You can count on me. And I know I can count on you, Rosie."

Rosie stared into empty space. "Do I have any choice, Pockets?"

But, privately, she was already making other plans.

19

"Credit I can give you, Rosalie," Mr. Schwartz said. "Credit here on clothes, credit at Maury's on furniture, credit at Gilbein's on furs. Rugs, appliances, a car, anything you want, I can get you credit. But cash? No."

He stared glumly at the papers that littered his desk in the hot little office next to the stockroom. "Cash I haven't seen in so many years, if you tell me it is now red or blue instead of green, I don't know to argue." He pointed to a pile of papers. "By this time you ought to know how this business is run, Rosalie. Like the world is run. On credit.

"Here are the invoices. Already, on them, the manufacturers got credit. That's their problem and the factors', I don't worry. And here—" he pulled out a card-file drawer "—is our file of charge accounts."

He picked up a few cards and riffled through them. "It is the business of Second National Bank to collect from these and pay those. Me, I sit here in the middle, and no cash enters my hands. Only problems and pieces paper." He spread his hands expressively, letting the cards fall back in the drawer. "You ask then how I live? Credit cards." He opened his wallet, and a waterfall of them descended. "This one is for our vacation trips to Miami. This, for my suits at the tailor's. And this one, the health credit card, for my wife's operations." He smiled. "Somewhere I even got a credit card for credit cards."

"You been in business forty years, Mr. Schwartz," Rosie persisted. "You mean to tell me you ain't got no little nest egg of cash somewhere?"

"Ah, no. Now you're not talking cash, Rosie. You're talking capital. And capital is not mine to spend." He counted on his fingers. "First, is the stockbroker's. Second, my wife's. Third, it belongs to my kids, for whom it is invested in trust. Never, never is it mine. All I own is these cards." He shrugged. "You see me here, a poor man." He wagged his index finger at her. "But don't feel sorry for me."

"No danger," she said dryly.

"By me it's a fine way to run the world, on credit. Money is the root of all evil. So now we are delivered from evil." He rose. "Besides, for what do I need money? What do I care, as long as my people are happy?"

He could barely reach her shoulders, yet he managed to put an arm around them. "You are one of my people, Rosalie. You know that. Say what you need—I will see that you get it."

"I need money!" she fairly screamed. "That's what I've been tellin' you."

"But money is for something," he said stubbornly, "and that something I can maybe get you, on credit, cheaper than you can for cash. What is it, Rosalicha? A new dress for a party?"

As close as they were, the gulf between them stayed as wide as the ocean between the U.S. and Africa. If this was all he thought she wanted out of life— She looked at him angrily. "No. A new house."

"Ah," he said, and took his arm away. "It is difficult. For such a small girl, you have large wishes. But let me see. I have an old friend, Edelman, Vice-President of a Savings and Loan. He will maybe help with the mortgage. But naturally you have first to have the down payment."

"Naturally," she repeated with an edge of sarcasm that was wasted. "But that's just what I ain't got, Mr. Schwartz."

His brows drew together at her sharp tone. She softened it and said, "I had it, but I had to use it for a couple emergencies. You know my Mom was in the hospital."

"I didn't know." He looked concerned. "She is better now, I hope?"

"No." She didn't want to give him any comfort. Besides, it was true.

"My condolences," he said, and sighed. "Troubles, sickness, age, bills, more sickness. This is life. With my wife it is female complaints. I never knew with one woman so many things could go wrong. Cysts, tubes, bad inner tubes, weak sidewalls, she is like a patched-up jalopy. She runs, but that's all. Last time, I think it was the spark plugs they took out. And charged me four thousand dollars."

"I only need half that much, Mr. Schwartz," she pleaded. "I got to get that house. If I don't get outa this neighborhood soon, I'll die."

"How impatient is youth. Over disappointments, it always expects to die. You sound like my daughter. 'Dad,' she said, 'I will die if I do not get a chinchilla neckpiece.' But I am old, I know better, I was not frightened by her announcement. She did not get it, and she lived. —You too will live, Rosalie."

"If you call it livin'," she said gloomily, staring at the floor. It was a superb act; she'd already saved up most of the down payment. She simply hoped for enough from Mr. Schwartz to get Pockets off her back. Deliberately she raised her hand to her nose and snuffled.

"Do not cry, Rosalie," Mr. Schwartz said, patting her shoulder. "You and me, we will think of something."

She looked at him with sudden hope.

"Perhaps, for you, my friend Edelman will arrange a very special mortgage. Maybe, instead of the down payment, he will take money in escrow. And maybe, instead of money, my note. It is difficult, but I have heard of such things. I will ask him."

It was not what Rosie wanted, but how could she show her disappointment when he offered her so much? "You good to me, Mr. Schwartz," she said. On impulse, she leaned over and kissed the old man on the cheek.

He backed away hastily. "Please, Rosalie, no demonstrations. With all the troubles I got already, suppose my nephew should walk in here. My wife is not a well woman, and he is a bearer of tales."

"Sometimes I think you afraid of that little cream puff," she said.

The old man sighed heavily. "Can I deny it? I have hugged a snake to my bosom. An asp, like Cleopatra. Me he makes nervous, my employees he upsets, my family he terrifies. With all the troubles I got already, I need a house detective? Always he watches. Behind every door, he sees assassins. When he sees nothing, he invents." He sat down suddenly. "Worst is knowing he watches me too. For signs of dying."

"He'll have to wait a long time before he sees any," Rosie reassured him.

"Don't be so sure, Rosalie." Mr. Schwartz put a hand on his chest. "Sometimes, the pump here, I feel leaking. And sometimes a roaring like the sea. Especially when I look at him, and consider he is my own flesh and blood. Aaaaah!" He looked up. "But of my troubles, enough already. We were speaking of your little problem. Have we solved it?"

Rosie's tongue came out and wet her lips. "Not exactly, Mr. Schwartz." She spoke rapidly. "Oh, I appreciate you helpin' me with the mortgage and the furniture and all. I'll take you up on it, don't worry. But I still need cash."

Mr. Schwartz gave her a deep look. His eyes held hers at the same time they took in her every detail, the nervous bravado, the long ash on her cigarette, the shaking hands with long chipped ruby nails. He shook his head sadly. "Rosalie, I fear to say it, yet I feel it. You have not been altogether honest with me. —I ask you, what is the problem? A house, you say. Very well, I say, a house we will get you. But, you say, that does not solve the problem. Therefore I must ask. Forgive me, but are you in some kind of trouble?"

"Of course not, Mr. Schwartz," she said too quickly.

"Oh?" He raised his eyebrows. "Very well. I am old, I grow stupid. Please explain to me patiently. I am waiting."

"I told you!" she screamed. She took a deep breath, shut her eyes, and added in a low voice, "I mean I told you all I can."

"So," Mr. Schwartz said. "And I have told you all I can do. I think, Rosalie, this closes our discussion. Until you are ready to open it again."

With a sharp nod of dismissal, he turned his back on her and began shuffling through the snowdrift of papers on his desk. Rosie groped for the door through tears that were now genuine. Before she reached it, it opened on a blurred tableau of people.

"Oh, there you are, Rosie!" Betty Perlman cried. "I've been looking all over the store for you. Five of your customers were in already. —Her customers are really loyal, Mr. Schwartz," she babbled in her breathless thoughtless voice. "They won't let anybody else wait on them."

"I'm on my way to take care of 'em now," Rosie grumbled, "if you'll just let me pass."

"Oh, they all left but one, Rosie," Betty said. "She's right here. But the others said they'd be back later. And they all left notes for you." She advanced toward Rosie with several folded slips of paper.

Rosie made a move to snatch them, but it was not quick enough. Aaron came forward, and his hand came down hard on her wrist. "I think Uncle Sol might be interested in those, Rosie."

Sullenly she let him pry her fingers open. She noticed how apt the old man's comparison was. Aaron's sliding walk, his ratty little eyes, his stolid face all resembled a house detective's. Now, as he ravished the notes, his expression changed from excitement to dull bewilderment. She felt a momentary triumph.

"I can't make head or tail out of these, Uncle Sol," he admitted. "The way the stock's been disappearing, I thought she was running a stolen-goods ring. But I guess I was wrong."

"If you must watch somebody," the old man said without turning around, "don't watch the help. From now on, watch the strangers, the customers."

"I guess you're right," Aaron said. "These slips don't have nothing on them but a lot of phone numbers." Reluctantly he started to hand them over to Rosie.

Her relief lasted less than a second. It was replaced by a sickening feeling that told her it was all over. She saw the exact moment when the light clicked on in Aaron's brain; a small, dim, fifteen-watt bulb, but sufficiently illuminating nevertheless.

"Numbers!" he cried gleefully. "That's it, Uncle Sol. She's been writing numbers. All the time, right here under our noses."

173

Mr. Schwartz swiveled in his chair to face them and held out his hand silently for the papers. But he did not look at them. Only at Rosie.

"Can you tell me he is wrong? If so, please say it."

She knew how much depended on his question. She could not bluff that look, nor could she hide from it.

"I am waiting for you to speak, Rosalie. Can you call him a liar?"

"No," she said.

The third member of the group of visitors to Mr. Schwartz's office had stayed dimly in the background. Now she rushed forward.

"Oh, Rosie! It's not true!"

"Dolly!" Rosie exclaimed. "What the hell are you doin' here?"

Her friend stepped back from embracing her. "I'm home from school. I came to see you."

"Well, you see me," Rosie said dryly.

"Yes," Dolly said. "Oh, Rosie, this is awful! I don't understand." She began to cry.

"Nothin' about it you could understand," Rosie said. "I don't expect you to."

This only started a fresh gushing from Dolly's eyes. Suddenly Rosie found herself bawling too. "Oh, hell," she said, and snatched two tissues from the handy box on Mr. Schwartz's desk. "Here, stop that fool crying."

"Rosalie?" Mr. Schwartz questioned softly.

"Yes, Mr. Schwartz?"

He spoke with immense, ancient sorrow. "I think this morning has already been more than I can bear."

"I'm sorry."

"So am I. Now you will please help me to bring it to an end, by leaving quietly."

Puzzled, she looked from him to Aaron and back again.

Mr. Schwartz made a helpless gesture. "Whatever we owe you, we will send through the mail."

Rosie gasped, although she had no right to be surprised.

Aaron's face wore a tight little smile of triumph. "He means you're fired. You're lucky. If it was up to me, I'd report you to the police."

Dolly shrieked and caught one of Rosie's hands. Betty pressed the other one, mumbled something, then darted out of the office in obvious terror.

Rosie ignored them both. She was watching Mr. Schwartz's shoulders. They heaved suspiciously, and sagged in a way that reminded her suddenly of the back of a very old man. In that moment she realized how thoroughly she had failed him. Not only had she shown that she was not legitimate; she had proved that Aaron was.

She wanted to comfort him somehow, say it wasn't necessarily so, but Dolly had an arm around her, guiding her to the door.

"Come on, Rosie," she urged softly.

"You look like a nice, sensible girl," Mr. Schwartz said in a strained, moist voice. "Why don't you try talking sense to her? She had a nice future here. Now all she has is a past. Talk to her. Make her see that everything she does is ruin."

"I'll try," Dolly told him. "I promise."

At that, Rosie broke away from her arm. It felt too warm and too restricting. "Doll, come by and see me at the house tomorrow morning. I ain't got time to talk to you now. I got to take care of some business."

She made her getaway quickly, on high heels that clicked a message of independence across the floor. Once outside, she might have found peace in the anonymous bustle and glare of the Avenue. But Aaron's final comment still stung her ears.

"Yeah," he had said. *"Funny* business."

20

Tucker's phone rang twelve times without an answer, and so did his doorbell. The super who lived in the basement of his apartment house knew nothing. But then he was the type with whom knowing nothing and everything was a stock in trade: a slim slippery Negro with a scraggly goatee and liquid eyes and a sly grin that proclaimed a secret joke. The joke was that everybody had a hustle, including you.

He gave Rosie an elaborate, unconvincing performance of innocence. "Baby, I don't know if the gentleman's moved away, or what. If you his old lady, you better get in touch with him yourself."

"Oh, has he got a wife?" Rosie asked, forgetting that a direct question would never elicit a direct answer from this type of hippie.

He laughed with a droll shrug. "Ain't everybody got a wife somewhere or other? Sure. Everybody has a wife except me. I'm just a poor, lonesome young bachelor."

"Well, how long since you saw him last?" Rosie asked impatiently.

"How you expect me to know?" the hippie screeched. "Baby, I got five floors and six tenants on each. Long as they wrap their garbage and pay their rent, I don't ask no questions."

He stepped back and gave her a slow once-over that made her warm all over. "What you want to see him so bad for, anyway? He don't treat you like he should, a fine young thing like you." He flung the door to his apartment wide; cool piano music drifted out. "Now, I'd like a chance to treat you right, baby. Why don't you come in and rest yourself awhile? Listen to some sounds."

"Later," Rosie said. But she deliberately gave him a slight smile.

"Well, how much later, baby? I can't wait forever."

"Couple hours," she lied blandly.

He put his hand to his mouth. "Step in here just a second, then."

She followed him across his threshold and waited while he pulled the door partly shut behind them.

He said in a stage whisper, "I think that cat's up there right now. He left town in a hurry the other night. He was movin' so fast I never expected to see him again. But an hour ago he came back for his things. His car's parked in the alley out back, and I seen him move some suits out to it already. It's a fine short, too, a fine new Caddie. You'd better hurry if you wanta catch him, though. He's one fast-moving cat."

Rosie handed the super a five and said, "Buy some Scotch to go with the sounds."

"You know I will, baby," he whispered, letting her out again. "For you I'll get Chivas Regal. Hurry back, now."

She wouldn't, and he knew it, but he didn't have any serious objections. He willingly pressed the buzzer to let her into the hall.

There were no signs of life at Tucker's door, and a pile of rolled newspapers proclaimed that the tenant had indeed vacated the premises. The keyhole revealed nothing to her eye. But when she put her ear to it she heard the rapid gush of water.

She banged on the door with both hands and called his name. "Let me in! I know you're in there."

Finally the water shut off. A second later the door suddenly gave on the apartment. He stood there, wet and slippery as a black seal except for the rakish accent of a white towel worn apron fashion around his waist.

"I bet I'm the last person you wanta see," she said. "But that ain't stoppin' me."

He looked painfully embarrassed, but he bowed graciously and backed into the room. "Hand me that bathrobe behind the door," he said stiffly.

She found it: a deplorable rag of drab gray wool. Wrinkling her nose, she held it out to him with reluctant fingertips. He crossed the lapels beneath his chin and knotted the belt firmly around his waist.

This tickled Rosie. "You funny," she said, and giggled. "Wrappin' up in that funky bathrobe like some old lady. You ashamed to let me see you naked when I got clothes on?"

He turned and strode quickly to the bathroom, his dignity marred by the sound of his big wet feet slapping the floor. Her answer was a slammed door followed by the sound of running water turned on full to drown all other sounds.

Rosie giggled again. When he finally came out, shining clean and sharp in gray slacks and sweater, she had rummaged in a desk and found a bottle of dubious whiskey.

She waved the bottle at him. "Your hospitality ain't so hot, Tucker. I had to help myself."

With an expressionless face he went back to the bathroom and returned with a water glass into which he poured a drink for her, keeping the bottle. He motioned her to the least broken-down of his two chairs and took the opposite one, with only the blown-out shreds of a cane bottom, himself.

"Now, what did you want to see me about, Rosie?"

His bland expression infuriated Rosie. She refused to sit. She stood, tapping her toe meaningfully and letting her cigarette ashes drift down and disappear into the threadbare carpet. "What you think? My money."

Tucker raised his arms and let them fall to his sides despairingly. "Baby, I'm sorry. You caught me at a bad time." He pulled out his wallet and inspected it ruefully. "Will twenty do?"

"Not unless you mean twenty hundred."

He made the gesture again, slapping his knees. "I can't do it, Rosie. I don't have that money. It's all tied up in assets."

"Ass-what? You mean you spent it on women?"

"No, expenses. Clothes. Bills. My car."

"I'll take your car then," she said promptly. "Gimme the keys. And leave your clothes in it, I'll take them too."

"Little materialist," Tucker said. He lunged toward her suddenly and pinioned her wrists. "You're the greatest, Rosie. Know why? You know what you want, and you won't quit till you get it. Don't care how you get it. Almost tough as me. But not quite." He twisted the skin on her wrists cruelly. "Not quite, huh? Not quite."

This attempt to work on her with a combination of charm and strength showed Rosie he would use anything to get out of the spot where she had him squirming. But it also showed her that she had him there. With a swift well-placed movement of her knee she was free.

He yelped and looked up at her in pain and astonishment and, for the first time, something like respect. She folded her arms stubbornly. "You better pay me now, unless you want some more. Next time I might put you out of commission permanent."

"But I told you, Rosie, I can't pay you." He spread his arms to show his helplessness. "I don't care how determined you are, you can't get blood out of a turnip. You'll just have to wait till I get on my feet again. Then I can pay you back with interest. Everything I owe you, plus an extra thousand."

Rosie wasn't buying. She made an abrupt gesture. "If you gonna be able to do that, how come this place looks like Tobacco Road? I look around here, I don't see no lamps, I don't see no television, I don't see no decent chairs. I couldn't even find no decent whiskey. So you best come on quick with a good story." She produced her other find, a shriveled tangerine which she peeled as she talked. It and a dried-up rind of cheese had been the only items in his refrigerator.

"I'm waiting," she said, and popped a section into her mouth.

"The way you see me living now is just temporary, Rosie."

"Yeah? And what about our partnership? Was that temporary too?" In spite of her conscious advantage, she lost her "cool" and began to rage at him. "Tucker, did you really think I was such a fool you could run out on me and get away with it? Disappear with my money and leave me with two big hits and nothin' to pay 'em off with?"

"Oh, baby," he said, eyes widening like innocent lamps, "you hurt me if you really think I'd do a thing like that."

"Think, hell. You done it. Last Thursday."

He was all amazement. "I had to go out of town on an emergency. I didn't know you got hit, Rosie. Believe me."

She sighed at her own momentary willingness to do just that. "Tucker, you're twisty and tricky as a monkey maze. I don't believe nothing you tell me."

"Is it my fault you don't trust me?"

God Bless the Child

"I'd rather trust the Devil. At least I know what he's after."

"Look, I'm really sorry. I'll give you a note for all of it."

She cried, "What good is a note with your name on it? It don't mean nothin'. It ain't even your right name."

"I've been waiting for that," he said quietly. "All these years. I always knew you'd throw it up to me someday."

"You wanta do something for me? I'll tell you what you can do. You can tell your mother to knock two thousand off the price of the house."

"For once and for all, she is not my mother," he said, his face working strangely.

"What relation is she, then?" Rosie demanded.

Tucker sighed. "All right. I don't know why I should expect you to give me any peace about it. You never give me any peace about anything else. You push and push people till they have to push back, Rosie. But it doesn't make any difference now. I might as well tell you. You know what a State child is?"

Rosie nodded. "An orphan."

"A bastard," he corrected her, bitterly.

"And the State pays people money to raise them."

"That's right, and it doesn't care how they raise them. Well, from the time I was eight, I was Esther's State child. She and her old man were getting those checks nice and regular, but that didn't stop them from reminding me, twenty times a day, if it weren't for them I wouldn't have a home. As it was I didn't have a name. They just called me Boy."

Rosie looked at him with new gentleness, remembering that day in second grade, how lost he'd been. "They kept you out of school, too."

"Yes. I didn't learn how to read till I was twelve. I slept in their cellar and ate their leftovers and did all their dirty work—"

"You mean the scrubbing and cleaning?" she interrupted.

"Yes, I did that too. But mostly I did the dirty work for Esther's seances. When she had her phony shows, I'd sit under the table and be the ghost, throw my voice around the room. I'd turn off the lights and howl in the dark. I wore tennis shoes

180

so they couldn't hear me move around. Sometimes I grabbed people. You should have heard some of those old sisters scream when I touched them."

Rosie couldn't help laughing. "I bet you did a good job. She should've paid you for it."

He didn't return her smile. "She hated me for it. Every time she looked at me, she had to know she wasn't some kind of a supernatural saint, she was just an evil old crook. Like every other phony on this earth, she wanted to believe she was real."

"Everybody's part phony and part real," she said softly.

"Yeah," was his thoughtful reply.

"Now Esther's got money, maybe she'll help you out of the hole," Rosie said hopefully. "Tell her to cut down the price of the house, and we'll be square."

"Rosie," he told her, "I learned one thing from that evil old woman. People shit on you, and then they say, 'Go away, you smell bad.' "

Rosie felt herself stirring with sympathy and, in spite of everything, a revival of the old attraction. She moved closer to him and said gently, "Well, you don't need her now. You got me."

He held her at arm's length. "I don't want your pity. I'm the last man on earth you should feel sorry for, Rosie."

She frowned, trying to understand why they were suddenly being so decent to each other. Then she gave it up with a sigh for the complexity of all people. "I'm sorry to push you, Tucker, but I've tried everyplace else, and I need the money bad. Mom's been sick."

"Sorry to hear it," he said.

"And I lost my job at the store on account of this mess."

He bowed his head as if it were all too much for him. "God, Rosie." She tossed him a lifeline to snatch, even if it would mean drowning them both. Her lashes fluttered; her voice dropped to a husky whisper. "And I'm gonna have a lot of expenses, buyin' furniture and fixin' up the house to get it ready for you."

She waited anxiously for the smile, the word, the sign that would be enough to make her say, "Forget about the money."

He was visibly jolted, but only for a moment. When his face was recomposed he said, "Don't include me in any more of your plans, Rosie."

"What you mean, Tucker?" she asked tremulously.

He was angry. "Rosie, tough as you act, you're much too nice. You came to me once and practically begged to be taken. Now here you are doing it again. No one should be so nice, Rosie. It's not a nice world."

He got up quickly, went to a closet, and returned with a battered briefcase. After opening it and rummaging through rumpled shirts and balled socks he withdrew a bundle of money and U.S. Savings Bonds bound with rubber bands. He riffled the stack once and handed it over to her.

"Here, Rosie." He spoke very rapidly, without looking her in the eye. "Rosie, you know you're lots of fun, I like to see you now and then, old times' sake and all that, you're a grand girl and you're great kicks, but as for anything else, you know it doesn't make sense. It just doesn't make sense at all."

She stared at him.

"Well, aren't you going to count it? It's what you came for."

She said, "I know too much about you now. Is that it, Tucker?"

"No," he said. "I may have been nobody once, but I'm going to be somebody very soon. My past can't hurt me any more. It's buried. I killed it long ago."

"You ain't killed it, Tucker," she said softly. "It's killin' you." But she rose submissively when he stood up and led the way to the door. Once there he said, "That's all the money I have right now. I think, when you count it, you'll find we're square. But if we're not, just let me know. I'll settle the balance right away. Goodbye, Rosie."

The door closed on his blandly smiling image. But it hung before her, just out of reach, all the way home. Oh, he was a rat, there was no doubt about it. Being decent only made him a rat all the more.

182

She remained meekly silent until the cab reached its destination. When the driver handed her change over she slapped his hand, knocking it forward and scattering the coins on the floor.

He turned, startled, to see a streaked, twisted face that screamed at him,

"You can keep the money, fool!"

21

"Why don't I gain weight?" Rosie demanded when Dolly walked into her bedroom. "Will you please tell me?" She thrust a scrawny arm from under the covers. "Just look at that arm. Chicken bone!"

"Rosie," Dolly said, "you've been asking me that same question for years. I'm still giving you the same answer."

"Damn shame," Rosie muttered, reaching for the fifth of V.O. that rested on her night table. "They oughta use me to stick sandwiches together." She settled down in the covers again and looked at Dolly obliquely. "So tell me," she said.

"Rosie," Dolly said hesitantly, a little frightened by the way her friend's hands trembled at this hour of the morning," you can count two pounds for that TV set in the front room. Maybe four for the fur coat you just bought. Two for that watch you just gave your Mom—"

"Sometimes," Rosie said, frowning, "you're so damn smart you give me a pain. I'm supposed to let Mom's birthday go by without getting her a present?"

"No, Rosie, of course not. But that watch?"

Rosie tossed off a whiskey, blinked, and poured herself another. "I should of got her something cheap, you mean? A nice bottle of toilet water, maybe?"

"No, Rosie. But a gold cocktail watch with diamonds—let's face it, your mother sits around the house all day, she never goes any place, what does she need a watch like that for?"

God Bless the Child

Rosie glared at Dolly. "That's just why she oughta have it, you jerk! She oughta have all the damn diamonds in the store, you hear me, and if she asks for 'em, she will have 'em!"

Dolly decided it was time to change the subject. "How is your mother now?"

"Why don't you run in the next room'n see for yourself?" Rosie answered. "She always wants to see you. She asks for you all the time."

"Okay, I will," Dolly said.

"Wait, Doll." Rosie leaped out of bed and caught her arm. "Don't say nothin' about how much weight she's put on."

Dolly looked at her questioningly.

"See, the doctor made her quit drinkin' on account of her heart," Rosie whispered hoarsely. "She gets nervous without a little taste now and then, so she eats instead. She's kind of embarrassed about it, you dig? Wait." She scrabbled under the bed and fished out a pair of battered moccasins into which she thrust her toes. "I better come with you."

"Here's Doll, Mom," Rosie announced, her moccasins flopping behind her. "Doll, don't Mom look terrific?"

"Wonderful," Dolly agreed.

Rosie's mother, wrapped in a scarlet robe and seated in a sunflooded chair by the window, was a beautiful but disturbing sight. Queenie must have gained over fifty pounds. She had that look of extreme ripeness, the last stage before death in voluptuous persons, which Dolly had seen in certain Renoirs. The contours of her features were blurred and softened almost to dissolution, and in the riotous reds and golds of her face Dolly could almost see the flowers that would bloom on her grave.

A hearty breakfast tray lay across Queenie's lap, and the table at her side was heaped with fruit and candy. "Well, if it ain't the little schoolteacher," she said, wiping the last crumbs of a coffee cake from her mouth. "You've put on weight."

The obvious answer, *So have you,* died in Dolly's throat and left her grinning foolishly. Dolly was a good thirty pounds overweight; it spoiled her loveliness, but she was good-natured about it. The reason was that all through her strict childhood she had

184

coveted the riches of poverty. Though ragged and ill-fed, children like Rosie had always seemed able to produce a few pennies for licorice braids and B-B Bats and Mary Janes and the other sticky delights that made up, as far as she could tell, the bulk of their diet. Over the years of deprivation she had built up a terrible hunger for these forbidden sweets, and now her chief gesture of adult independence was to buy and gobble candy bars, even the ones that tasted awful, three and four times a day.

"Looks good on you, though," Queenie conceded as she reached for another coffee cake and plastered it with butter. "You married yet?"

"No," Dolly admitted.

"What's the matter? Ain't you got a boy friend?"

Embarrassed, Dolly glanced sidewise at Rosie's impassive face. She instinctively kept the details of her private life from Rosie, if only because they were so dull in comparison to hers. "—Yes, sort of," she said finally.

"Well, that's better'n nothin'." Queenie scrutinized Dolly intently while her hand dipped into a box of chocolates and blindly, shrewdly selected a large cherry center. "You like it?"

"Like what?" Dolly asked innocently.

Queenie bit into the candy and grinned lewdly, revealing a wide gap framed by two small teeth stained with chocolate. "You know what I mean. Marriage life."

"But I told you, Mrs. Fleming," Dolly said patiently. "I'm not married."

"Who says you got to be married?" Queenie chucked Dolly familiarly on the arm and roared with delight. "Lord, when I was your age, what I wouldn't do."

So far gluttony was the only form of sensuality Dolly permitted herself. Now Queenie was tempting her with others. "Well," Dolly said with self-conscious lightness, determined to humor the sick woman, "a few kisses never hurt anybody."

"Kisses?" Queenie snorted with contempt. "I tell you, when you're really in a hurry, you ain't got no time for that foolishness. Hell, it only takes a few minutes anyway."

Dolly was getting angry. There was something revolting about this mammoth middle-aged invalid titillating herself with sexy talk. Then Rosie said, "Doll, I hope you don't mind Mom's teasin'. Sometimes she gets pretty rough," and Dolly realized what had been going on. Rosie had accused her before of having no sense of humor. Suddenly it excited her to imagine what it might be like to have Queenie for a mother, instead of the thin, stringy-haired woman who had called her name this morning when she was on her way out of the house.

"Dolores! You've been in my dresser things again, haven't you?"

Dolly's mother had been sitting at the vanity, powdering her lined face a ghastly white. She had set the puff down when Dolly came in, and pointed indignantly to the never-used collection of china-backed toilet articles—comb, brush, hand mirror, shoe horn, button hook (button hook!), file—that were always aligned, perfectly parallel, at a thirty-degree angle to the edge of her dresser.

Following the trembling finger with her eye, Dolly had seen that the shoe horn was a fraction of a degree out of line. To her shame she then felt a wrench of fear, the echo of childhood terrors. She made a firm denial.

"I wish you would tell the truth, Dolores. If you must meddle with my things, at least put them back where you find them. I can't stand *slov*enly, *mes*sy—"

Her mother had slammed the vanity drawers violently, symbolically closing them on Dolly's fingers, and Dolly had walked out containing her pain, because there were no places for crying in her mother's uncomfortable house. It was scrubbed, every day, with a vengeance against the gods that had made them colored, as if Mrs. Diaz hoped eventually to scrub her family white. Even the bathroom was as spotless as a plumber's showroom display. The gleaming tiles, the precisely folded towels, the waste basket that never held so much as a scrap of tissue, all seemed to say: "Superior beings live here: they are not really dirty." Or, more accurately: "They are not really Negroes."

As a matter of fact, Dolly thought, looking enviously at the lavish disorder of Queenie's bedroom, Rosie and her mother were probably cleaner than either Dolly or hers. Dolly had refrained many times from bathing simply because it was impossible to clean and polish the tub afterward to her mother's shining standards. There always seemed to be a streak of cleanser left, or a stray hair, and that was enough to desecrate the temple and bring down torrents of recrimination on her head. Dolly had learned very young that it was easier just to go dirty.

Dolly gave a sigh. Perhaps all mothers and daughters were doomed to fight blind helpless battles, she thought, hearing Rosie speak coldly to Queenie.

"I just paid out three hundred dollars for them new teeth of yours. How come you ain't wearin' 'em?"

Rosie's mother clapped a guilty hand to her mouth. "Lord, I forgot, Rosie," she said through muffling fingers. "I had 'em on this morning, but they hurt me so bad I took 'em out again." Watery-eyed, she ducked her head in Dolly's direction. "Excuse me, please. I'm sorry."

"You oughta be," Rosie said grimly. "Sittin' there gummin' your breakfast when there's company in the room." She took Dolly's hand and yanked her to the door, then yelled from the hall, "Don't expect me to bring you no more company! My friends'll think I can't afford to buy you no teeth."

Back in the doorway of Rosie's room, a small, abject, earth-colored creature awaited them with downcast eyes. It was mainly male, Dolly decided, though it was surely partly female; and somewhere under its layers of grime, it might be white, but was probably colored.

An animal growl escaped Rosie's throat when she saw her visitor. She pushed him into the room quickly and shut the door.

"Dammit, Miltie," she whispered hoarsely. "I thought I told you to stay away from where I live."

He said piteously, through a shapeless blubbery mouth, "But you didn't meet me at the store today, Rosie."

She gave a sigh of penitence. "I'm sorry. I don't work there no more. I forgot all about you this morning. All I could think about was sleeping."

God Bless the Child

"Well I hung out around there, and I saw all your customers for you."

Dolly could not imagine who this creature might be or what part he played in her friend's life. Rosie was like a small, nimble spider spinning strange, far-reaching webs out into the world.

Clearing up the mystery, Miltie produced a greasy drawstring bag. "This is the collection. You want me to take it to Pockets?"

Rosie snatched it from him. "Hell no. Don't take him nothin'."

Miltie looked startled.

"From now on, bring me everything. Understand?"

"But I thought—" he began.

"Am I payin' you to think? Don't worry about Pockets. Him and me will be straight."

"Rosie," he pleaded, "ain't you even gonna look at the slips? They's some big ones in there. Maybe you better get yourself covered."

"Maybe you better let me make the decisions," Rosie told him.

Dolly had backed off to a corner after getting a whiff of sour wine in her face. Now Rosie also wrinkled her nose. "The nerve. Comin' in here smellin' like a wine vat. Did Mom or Granny see you?"

"I don't think so, Rosie. The door was open, and I sneaked in."

"Well you just sneak yourself out the same way," Rosie ordered. "Now." She gave him a little shove toward the door. But she was not fast enough.

Granny came in, a dry little insect, crackling as she walked in her precise black shoes. Her eyebrows lifted a fraction when she noticed the stranger who stood there reeking, but she did not dignify him with a greeting, only gave him a wide berth, as he deserved, and turned critical eyes on Rosie.

"You shouldn't be receivin' callers in your bedroom. You should be up and dressed by now."

"He's just a delivery boy, Granny," Rosie lied.

Money, You Got Lots of Friends

Whatever Miltie's age, and it was not easy to determine, he was not a boy. Dolly doubted if he had ever been one.

But Granny neither questioned Rosie's statement nor asked what he had come to deliver. "Let him get his business over with, then," she said.

Rosie told him, "We won't need no more orders from the drug store today."

With a mumbled "Yes ma'am" and a tug at the forepart of his cap, Miltie disappeared.

Rosie said, "Did you notice, Doll? He had so much wine on his breath he stunk. Some stores don't care who they got workin' for 'em."

Dolly, though she did not really care to cooperate in this conspiracy, said with a straight face, "Oh, it's terrible."

The old lady smiled, satisfied, and began rustling about the room, emptying Rosie's overflowing ash trays and picking up the scattered underthings that waved like pennants from every piece of furniture. She moved with great speed and lightness and, watching her, seeing the quick nervous intelligence dart from those terribly sunken eyes, Dolly could see where Rosie got her restless energy.

"Rosalie, I told you that was inferior fabric in these curtains," Granny said now at the window, her voice a queer broken echo of some grand dame in some vanished Victorian household. "They're comin' apart already. Next time, mind you ask for genuine hand-made Irish lace."

"It's hard to find, Granny," Rosie apologized.

"I know." The old lady sighed. "Nowadays they make everything on machines. You young folks think that's fine," she said with a tiny concession in Dolly's direction, "but I never will understand what all the rush is for. Nothing holds up like it used to. You never see quality work like they used to do in the old days."

"Whew!" Rosie whistled when Granny finally finished her grumbling and fussing and left the transformed room. "That was close, Doll. I'd sure hate for her to know about Miltie."

God Bless the Child

"Rosie, I thought after what happened yesterday you'd give up this—" She didn't know what to call it. "This madness."

"Give it up? Hell no, Doll. I'm just getting started. I can always get another job."

"Haven't you still got your job at Benny's?"

"Sure. I meant another day job," Rosie said.

Dolly had to keep trying. "Rosie, you're wearing yourself out. You're just doing too much."

"But I makes loot," Rosie said, rolling her eyes in comic minstrel-show style. "Lord, yes, I makes loot. Dolly, did I show you them fine slippers I just brought home for Granny?"

From beneath her bed she pulled a glossy white package printed with the gold monogram of a good downtown store. She ripped it open. Nestled inside were a pair of mules made entirely of black Persian lamb, curled against each other like two living animals. Only Granny's feet, tiny as a child's or the bound feet of an Oriental woman, deserved to be so extravagantly shod.

"Thirty-nine fifty," Rosie announced. She waved her hand impatiently. "Oh, I know, I know. But do you think she'll like 'em?" Her face, turned anxiously toward Dolly, was like a hungry child's.

"She'll love them," Dolly said, giving up. Rosie returned the rich little things to their nest of tissue paper, then was suddenly gripped by a fit of coughing.

"All right," she said with a weak laugh when it had passed over. "Die young, have lotsa friends at your funeral."

An insane flame of gaiety leaped up in her eyes. "Say, Doll, let's plan my funeral. Right now! You're in charge, see. I want you to get six cases of Scotch, and fry up forty chickens, and hire a hall and invite three hundred cats!" She squirmed excitedly, clutching Karmie, the big purple plush teddy bear that shared her bed with a dozen other fabric animals. "You hear, Karmie? Mama's gonna have the craziest funeral in history! And you're gonna be there, and we'll have a five-piece combo, and lots of chicken salad, and much, much gin!"

Money, You Got Lots of Friends

"How about the preacher?" Dolly asked, laughing in spite of herself.

"Aw, shuh, girl." Rosie poked her mouth out in a rosebud pout. "Who would preach a funeral over somethin' like me? Ain't you got no sense?"

"It's not a funeral without a preacher," Dolly insisted. Her imagination always lumbered along clumsily at least two steps behind Rosie's.

"All right, I'll ask Karmie," Rosie said, snatching up the toy and hugging it to her bony chest. The thing had one of those evil buck-toothed Walt Disney faces; it leered at Dolly over Rosie's shoulder.

"Should we have a preacher at my funeral, Karmie?"

The head shook violently.

"Karmie says no. No preacher."

"No preacher, no funeral," Dolly pronounced.

"Shoot!" Rosie brought her hand down hard on the bed. "You ain't gonna be in charge after all. Not at my funeral. Put you in charge, it'd really be a wake. You always spoil everything." She lit a cigarette. "How come you always mess up? What is it? What ails you, anyway?"

"I guess I take things too seriously," Dolly said.

"You guess you do? You guess you do? Now get this, Karmie," Rosie said, putting her arm around the bear. "There's this big jerk of a girl here, see, got the nerve to call herself a hipster, too, and I ask her why I don't gain weight, you dig, and guess what the damn fool does? She tells me! Now, what the hell do you say to that?" She shook the bear's head again. "Karmie says all he can do is just shake his head."

Dolly was silent.

Rosie looked her up and down slyly. Suddenly she pointed her finger at Dolly's nose. "You know what ails you, gal? You ain't got no better sense than to hang around with a nut like me! That's all." She hugged the bear tightly. "Grown gal twenty-one years old still playin' with teddy bears. If that ain't a damn fool, I don't know what is. That's all right though, Karmie.

Mama loves you just the same." She crooned to the bear, rocking back and forth, until a dry ripping cough burst from her, forcing her to drop the toy and stifle her spasms in the bedclothes.

Granny returned then. "Is Madam Queen planning to get up today, or does she want breakfast in bed?" She fixed Dolly with tiny black eyes in enormous sockets finely fretted with wrinkles.

Rosie's head popped from under the covers, tousled and with streaming eyes from the coughing, but meek, all the brashness gone, meek and rabbity and a little scared. Their eyes caught and held. Rosie hesitated a moment, then spoke with infinite gentleness. "No, Granny, I'll get up. I don't want you doin' that for me."

The old lady's eyes lingered on Rosie's face. "I ain't got nobody else to do it for," she said simply.

Rosie expelled a violent sigh. "All right. You can bring me a cup of black coffee."

"You don't eat enough to keep a bird alive," Granny complained.

"All *right*, Granny, a piece of toast," Rosie said, her voice picking up some of its normal sharpness. Granny nodded, with a slight curtseying dip in Dolly's direction, and hobbled swiftly out of the room.

"God damn it," Rosie spat the moment Granny was gone. "God damn it, Dolly, you see how she always wants to wait on me? She misses waiting on those white folks, that's why. That rich woman she worked for finally died, Dolly, and she didn't leave Granny a thing. I told her when she quit, 'Granny, you'll never have to wait on nobody no more.' "

"She wants to do it for you," Dolly said. "That's different."

"She's too good to wait on anybody," Rosie said fiercely. "Least of all me. But I go on letting her do it. What am I, lazy or something? —Don't answer that," she said, turning laughing eyes on Dolly. Her face went soft. "You know," she said, "she's a real lady. Like they used to be, in olden times. She's more of a lady than that old bitch she worked for. When I see her picking up and cleaning after me and the rest of the bums I have around here, I get so mad I want to—"

Money, You Got Lots of Friends

She broke off as Granny tiptoed into the room with a tray. On it were a cup of black coffee, a piece of toast, two soft-boiled eggs, a fruit cup topped with sherbet, and a rose in a glass vase.

"Eggs," Rosie said in disgust, and immediately put the plate on the floor. "Here." She gave Dolly the fruit cup and a spoon.

Dolly held them gingerly, feeling guilty under the old lady's searching eye.

"Rosalie," Granny said in a dignified, reproachful voice, "that's made the way Miss Helen used to like it. With sherbet and burgundy wine."

Rosie gave Dolly a meaningful look. "In that case, Granny, I'll try it." She took it back on her tray and said offhandedly, "There's some junk I brought home on the table. You can have 'em if you like 'em."

Granny advanced on the table. She picked up the box and delicately extracted the fabulous fur mules. Squinting against the light, she examined them slowly and critically, picking at the little seams where the soles joined the uppers, poking at the lining with her fingernails, sniffing the leather of the soles and, finally, rubbing her fingers over the surface of the fur.

"Real Persian," she said at last. "Real well made, too. For these days."

"Ah." Rosie's face was transfigured. "You like them."

"Very nice," Granny said, carefully replacing the tissue. "Kind of fancy for an old lady like me."

Rosie put her hands on her hips and sat straight up in bed. "I ask you," she said indignantly. "Is that an old lady standin' there?"

"If you ask me, she's about twenty-eight," Dolly said.

"Well, maybe thirty," Rosie corrected her.

"Go on, both of you," Granny chirped, and left the room with the box borne high in both hands.

"That's my heart, girl," Rosie said, looking after her. "I'm tellin' you, that's my heart. If anything ever happened to her—"

She shivered as if an icy wind had suddenly entered the apartment which was always overheated to keep Granny comfortable.

Her eyes, enormous in her fine-boned face, opened wide on fear. "You know," she said, reaching out for Dolly's hand, "sometimes I just lie awake at night and shake, I'm so scared. Scared of somethin' happenin' to her, I mean. I just know I wouldn't want to go on livin' if she was gone. And she's so old, Dolly, God she's so old, it makes me sick to think of somebody bein' so old. She's almost seventy. God!"

She was clutching Dolly's hand, digging into it with her long sharp nails.

"She'll live to be a hundred," Dolly said reassuringly.

Rosie's grip relaxed. She lolled back in the bedclothes. "I know I won't live to be fifty. God! Who the hell wants to?" She lit another cigarette and puffed dreamily.

"Rosie?" Dolly asked softly.

"Huh?" She was absorbed in the cloud of smoke she was making.

"Do you remember, in school, the story of Shylock—"

Rosie nodded, eyes suddenly bright. She loved a story.

"—how he wanted a pound of flesh from someone who owed him money? That's what you're doing, Rosie. Every time you buy Granny a present, you pay for it with a pound of your own flesh. And you can't spare it. She's right. You don't eat enough."

"You still talkin' about that? God, you're gettin' to be a real drag. I *mean*."

"Well, look at you. I bet you don't even weigh a hundred pounds. How long do you plan to keep up this foolishness, working around the clock, sleeping four hours a night? I don't understand it, Rosie. I need eight hours' sleep every night or I'm dead. How long do you think you can go on like this?"

"Now you sound like Mom," Rosie said wearily.

"Mom cares about you. So do I." She grabbed Rosie's hand. "Rosie, be glad you got fired from the store. It's your chance to get some rest. Don't look for another job."

Rosie sat up, nervously alert. "Listen, Doll. Listen hard now, 'cause this is the last time I explain it to you. I got a home to maintain. I got a family. Granny's never gonna work again, and Mom probably ain't either. I've got to make a home for them, a good home, 'n keep it up if it kills me. You know what it is to struggle? You know what it's like to fight rats 'n bedbugs every day of your life?"

Dolly shook her head.

"You're lucky," Rosie said. "People like me, we gotta struggle. I don't mind. It's worth it to get the things I want."

"I feel bad about you, Rosie," Dolly said heavily, weighed down by her own failure. "I know you're heading for trouble, and I can't do anything to stop it." She looked at her friend painfully. "I guess I don't try hard enough. Something always holds me back."

Rosie returned her look casually, but with a hard glint in her eyes. "What's that, Doll?"

"The way you are. I don't know anybody else like you. I know you're doing crazy things, and breaking the law, and running down your health, but—" Dolly groped; sighed; finally settled for the approximate words. "The way you live is so exciting. So glamorous."

Rosie stared at her a moment longer, then threw back her head and laughed raucously. "You simple ass. Hell, this ain't glamour. This is just poverty."

She leaped out of bed then with sudden brisk purpose. Dolly tried not to look at her as she peeled off her pajamas and stuck one leg into her jeans; she was so unbearably scrawny, with toothpick arms and sharp bones jutting where her hips should be. "Come on, Doll," she urged, already at the head of the stairs. "I got to show you something."

As they clattered downstairs they met Larnie coming up.

"Hi, Doll," he said with his quick surprised wonderful smile. "You graduate yet?"

"Next month," she told him. "You?"

The light went out of his face as quickly as it had come on. He shrugged. "Aah, I gave it up. Who needs a B.S.? Most of the people I know are too full of b.s. anyway."

God Bless the Child

"Maybe that was funny the first time you said it," Rosie snapped, "but nobody's smilin' any more. Ain't you noticed?"

Dolly said softly, "But you wanted college, Larnie. You wanted it so badly."

Ignoring them both, he whistled a little tune. "Where you girls going, dressed up so fine?" he said with a dig at Rosie's jeans.

"None of your business," Rosie said promptly.

"She has a surprise to show me," Dolly explained.

"Oh, she must be taking you to see the madness. Her latest piece of insanity. Fleming's Folly, they call it."

"Hush," Rosie said. "It's a surprise."

"Oh, I wouldn't dream of spoiling it." He winked grotesquely. "You're in for a real treat, Doll."

Rubbing his hands, he went into a carnival barker's routine. "Step right up, folks!" he called, his hands a megaphone. "See the Biggest Freak of All—The Poor Girl Who Thinks She's a Millionaire! Barnum's Most Amazing Exhibit—the Little Black Girl Who Was Born Eating a Silver Spoon! Watch her magic act! See her make money disappear! See her turn everything else into shit! Can she keep up this three-ring circus? Can this little girl from the slums find happiness living like an aristocrat? Just pay your dime, folks, step right up and see!"

He ended his amazing, insulting performance with a rough burst of laughter, then abruptly pushed his way past them and vaulted up the stairs.

Dolly stared after him, stunned by so much talent, shocked at its waste.

"Come on, Doll," Rosie said tightly, on the verge of tears. "Don't pay no mind to him and his fool clowning."

But Dolly hung back, watching his broad back disappear with false jauntiness around the landing. Its swagger, and the sadness it disguised, were new and disturbing. Either this was a totally different Larnie, or she had never really known Larnie at all.

Dolly was beginning to wonder if she had ever really known anything.

THREE

Them That's Not Shall Lose

22

After what must have been the longest single-fare bus ride in the city, Rosie and Dolly descended into a neighborhood that resembled a battlefield. It teemed with police, pickets, yelling teenagers, scowling white troops and grim black ones. The battle lines were unclear; in less than a minute Dolly spotted one mixed skirmish and two monochromatic ones.

More frightening, to her, were the spectators—a great blob of surly jelly held back by police lines. This mass howled and surged occasionally, but mostly it was silent. Still. Waiting.

Rosie led the way through it boldly, pushing past the police who lined the block with their eyes and guns trained on a besieged house on the corner.

"Hurry up, Doll," she urged. She poked her friend with the tip of her umbrella to push her across the street. "God, you are the slowest thing, I swear! Look out for that car, now!"

She burst out laughing. The police car, turning short, had just missed them.

"You drag your feet like a knock-kneed, bowlegged cow. Don't know why I ever asked you to come," Rosie scolded.

Her hand caught Dolly's and squeezed it to sign that she was joking. "Don't mind me, girl, you know I'm half crazy. I swear, when I stay away three hours I'm scared it'll be gone when I come back."

Her big cowhide shoulder bag, studded with brass nails, bumped rhythmically against Dolly as they moved along. "Girl, you know me and my big mouth, I just had to tell somebody. Mom ain't got nothin' to say about it, so I ain't about to tell her. And I'm surprisin' Granny with it for her birthday. Did I tell you? She's gonna be seventy."

Dolly was breathing hard, trying to take it all in and keep up with Rosie too. "But Rosie," she puffed, painfully conscious of how much she needed to lose weight, "I still don't know what you're taking me to see."

Rosie stopped in the middle of a step, arms akimbo, astonished. "Damn, Doll, I thought I told you. My new house."

Dolly stared as a parade of hymn-singers swayed toward them and a wave of police rushed out to intercept several bands of teenagers who were approaching with rocks at the ready. It looked, from a distance, like a complicated, exquisitely precise ballet. "Some housewarming," she said dryly.

"I was supposed to be the first colored on the block," Rosie said with some annoyance. "Them people on the corner jumped the gun on me. I don't care, though. Let them catch all the hell. When it's over, I'll move in."

Dolly had suddenly remembered that she knew this proud neighborhood. Long ago, during the worst summer of the depression, the summer of the year teachers' salaries had been cut to the bone and law offices had been dusty with disuse, she had come on the bus with her mother to deliver the piles of ironing to Madison Drive.

Her mother did the clothes at home, working late at night in the kitchen where nobody could see her, and packing them carefully in a shiny suitcase that deceived no one. At the first house the maid had sent them to the back door, and Dolly's mother had rung the front bell again to demand her money . . . then, when there was no answer, had sent Dolly to the back door alone because she was too proud to let the woman see the tears of humiliation making deep channels in her ivory face powder.

Dolly sighed and looked around at the landscape. It had not altered from her childhood memory. In spite of the temporary disorder surrounding them, the tall houses retained their aloof dignity, like queens holding back their skirts as a vulgar crowd passed. They were still picture-book castles, and their trees still cast cool lakes of shadow on endless pastures of lawn. Whatever the enormity of her mother's pride, she thought, it was nothing beside Rosie's. Her mother had only asked to be admitted at these front doors. Rosie was moving in.

Them That's Not Shall Lose

A permanent crowd had formed in this street since the first colored family broke the pattern of the block. The police were out in full force to prevent more riots. Dolly shrank from moving into the circle of their attention, but it only heightened Rosie's swagger. As they stepped out into the street, one of the policemen grabbed Rosie roughly by the arm.

"Hold it, sister," he said. "Where do you think you're going?"

"I ain't your sister, Mister," she told him. "Let go of me." Her free arm described a grand sweeping arc and came to rest, pointing. "Home, that's where I'm going. That's my house over there."

The policeman peered into Rosie's face. His stern expression wavered, probably at the expression he saw there, and he released her. They gained the opposite sidewalk.

No one was allowed to approach the barricaded corner house, but next door, the N.A.A.C.P. lady had set up her card table, right beside the soapbox occupied by Mr. Ahmed's disciple, and was doing a brisk competitive business.

Dolly decided to keep it going. She fished out the only bill in her wallet.

"Honey," the N.A.A.C.P. lady said to the disciple, "could you let me have change for a five?"

He silently dug into his pocket and produced five ones.

"Thanks," the N.A.A.C.P. lady said. She looked him over and added, "Say, honey, don't I recognize you? Ain't you Laura Morgan's child?"

He nodded.

"Didn't you used to go to Mount Pisgah Sunday School?"

His grim expression softened a bit. "Yes," he admitted.

She smiled. "I thought so. —Here you are," she told Dolly, handing over the change and a membership card. "Thanks for joining our fight for freedom. Now help out this nice young man, too. Buy one of his magazines."

Charmed, Dolly complied. Then they each held out an eager handful of literature to Rosie.

"No thank you," she told them both. "I don't need no leaders." She turned to Dolly and announced in a loud clear voice, "I oughta chase all these damn people off my property. I got a right, you know. —I wish you hadn't given 'em nothin', Doll. They got a nerve, turnin' my neighborhood into a circus."

She marched up the steps and took out her key, oblivious to the hostile eyes that now stared out at her from faces of every complexion.

The electricity had been turned off. The house was musty and damp. But it was cool as a cave, and refreshingly silent after the hot howls of the street.

"Damn! It's black as me in here!" Rosie exclaimed. Her giggles bounced off an echoing high ceiling. Then she bumped into a fireplace and her groping hands found a candle.

She struck a match which she also used to light a cigarette. "Don't be scared, girl. It's haunted, but the ghosts won't get you. Come on."

And she led Dolly at a breathless pace through the house, which was awesome with its high ceilings, and panels of rich dark wood, and great, foggy mirrors in heavy gilt frames. With ease they slipped from the angry clutching hands of the present and stepped, like two Alices, into the dream of a leisurely, eccentric past. It was a strange past to Dolly, but somehow Rosie had made it her own.

She postured before the mirror in the master bedroom, saying, "Here is where Miss Birdie Rice dressed up for company."

"And here," she said, running into the adjoining sitting room, "is where she received lady callers."

Sitting on the edge of the enormous claw-footed tub in the bathroom, Rosie told Dolly how Miss Birdie Rice had been the richest and grandest lady of Granny's neighborhood.

"She was like a queen or something, no lie," she said, mouthing the words around a dangling cigarette, squinting against the smoke. "Miss Helen Livesey, the lady Granny worked for, was one of her best friends. But when Miss Helen came to call, she had to send up her card and wait downstairs just like everybody else. Miss Birdie was rich, rich, *rich*. She had a title or something from England. And *clothes*—"

Them That's Not Shall Lose

Rosie leaped up and flung open one of the cavernous closets. An odor of dust mingled with lavender issued from its depths, where a solitary metal hanger swung crazily to and fro. "Granny says Miss Helen's clothes couldn't even compare with Miss Birdie's. They were all made in Paris by dressmakers. By *hand*."

She laughed and hugged herself in ecstasy. "All her life Miss Helen was jealous of this house. And now it's Granny's."

Dolly wanted to hear more. Somehow, Rosie had managed to make her curious about this rivalry between two women who lived long ago in a remote world. "I'm surprised you don't want Miss Helen's old house," she said. "Isn't it around here somewhere?"

Apparently this was a breach of tact. Rosie jumped up abruptly and handed Dolly the candle. Vaulting one leg over the banister rail, she whooped and slid down to the well of darkness below. There was a cry.

"Rosie?" Dolly called fearfully, looking down. "You all right down there?"

A minute of terrifying silence was finally broken by the inevitable giggle, which erupted into a raucous laugh.

"Come on down, stupid," Rosie yelled. "I can't find my matches."

Dolly descended, only half reassured, to find Rosie intact at the foot of the stairs.

"Hit my can on that damn statue," Rosie complained, pointing to a bronze boy David who stood at the foot of the stair rail, triumphant and tall in the light of Dolly's guttering candle. "I sure wish I had some meat back there like you." She rubbed her flat backside ruefully. Then Dolly was the one who laughed.

"I been dyin' to slide down that thing ever since I first saw it. But I forgot about that statue," Rosie grumbled. "That never would have happened if I could see in front of my face in here. —Doll," she said suddenly, "run out and ask that damn cop to lend me a flashlight."

Dolly looked at her in amazement.

203

"Well, what are you waiting for? Go on. I pay taxes, don't I? I got a right to ask him."

Dolly continued to stare until Rosie exploded into merciful mirth. She poked Dolly in the ribs and grabbed her arm.

"Don't let me scare you, cuddy. You're all right. Kinda stupid, but all right. Let's get out of here."

But for a moment Dolly could have sworn that Rosie was serious. If her bubbling sense of humor had not overcome her, she would have demanded the loan of the flashlight from the policeman, and what was more, she would have gotten it. She had never known what in Rosie's skinny frame and scarecrow looks gave her the supreme assurance to defy all authority. But she had had it ever since second grade.

It took Rosie five minutes of fumbling with the unfamiliar keys to secure the vestibule door with its panels of pink- and amber-tinted glass and the outer door of massive oak. They stood on the porch, hand in hand, blinking at the brawling scene below like two children come out of the enchanted forest. Rosie adjusted first; her curses quickly found new objects with scarcely a break in their flow.

"We shall not," sang a stolid group circling on the sidewalk, "we sha-all not be moved."

"Like hell you won't be moved!" Rosie shrieked at them. "You better be off my sidewalk before I count to ten!"

They stopped, and stood blinking up at Rosie with mild startled eyes like black velvet. Finally, hesitantly, their leader detached himself from the circle and approached the porch.

"One," Rosie sang out. "Two! Three! —Oh, Reverend Colby," she said in sudden contrite recognition. "I didn't know it was you. I'm sorry."

But before she could accept his offered handshake another, more arresting figure lurched toward her, that of a beggar in a World War I Army overcoat with a huge burlap sack slung over one shoulder. The sack bulged with a shape of the size and apparent weight of a small child. This he opened and held out to her.

Them That's Not Shall Lose

The simple gesture of begging seemed to release all the demons from the nightmare-box of Rosie's childhood; Dolly truly believed her, in that moment, insane.

"Now look what you've dragged up here with you!" she raged at the angels. "Bo Ditley!"

Like some terrible witch in a play, she leaned over the balcony, waving snakelike hands and hurling curses dipped in lizards' blood. "Get away from here, now! All of you! Get away! Get away!"

The angels dispersed in ragged confusion. They were halfway up the block before they reassembled, smoothed their ruffled wings, and discreetly resumed chanting out of Rosie's earshot.

"You fight everybody who tries to help you, Rosie," Dolly said.

"I can't stand church folks, anyhow," Rosie answered. "While they're fillin' your ears with prayers, their hands are in your pockets. The only time they love you is when they bury you."

"But—"

Rosie interrupted with an imperious gesture. "But nothin'. If they really wanta help me, let 'em clear out." She shuddered. "Bo Ditley up here already. My God! —I don't need nobody to help me mess up this neighborhood, Doll. I'm the only one's gonna live here. Except for Mom and Granny, 'n I can't bring them here anyway till this mess is over."

"In other words, this is a one-woman move-in movement."

"That's right," Rosie said, with a wink. "And if you know me, you oughta know it ain't necessarily non-violent."

"Rosie," Dolly said thoughtfully into space, "in your own crazy way, I think you may be a great woman."

But her friend, who would not have understood this anyway, was no longer there to hear it. She was running around the corner in pursuit of a large lightning bug.

"Rosie, wait," Dolly panted, catching up to her. "We can take the bus."

The suggestion gave Rosie strength for a last spurt. She raced out into traffic and opened the door. "Don't be a jerk, Doll, I know where you live. I'll drop you off on my way."

Resigned, Dolly climbed into the taxi.

Beside her, Rosie's voice climbed to a new level of meaning. "Ha ha. I just thought of somethin' funny, Doll. I ain't never seen your house."

"It's nothing to see," Dolly said. "It's just a house, Rosie."

"Naw, I bet it's fine," Rosie said. "Tell the truth, Doll."

Dolly, picturing the hysterical order that prevailed throughout her mother's house, decided sadly that, no, it had no mystery, no romance, certainly none of the slapdash color and bravado that Rosie loved. She would hardly term it "fine."

Rosie chuckled then. "Don't worry," she said. "I ain't gonna ask you how come you never asked me."

Dolly's heart contracted guiltily. "I never thought you'd want to come."

"Don't lie, Doll," Rosie said huskily. "You never could lie worth a damn. I know your folks wouldn't like me." She hunched forward, fists to her cheeks, for a minute of fierce silence.

Finally, stubbornly, she said, "Your house is fine, though, ain't it, Doll?"

Her house? Dolly never even called it that. It bore the imprint of no personality except her mother's. Her father was nowhere in evidence; he had been banished long ago to his downtown law office and the nook in the attic where he kept his "nasty" pipes. The husband henpecked about his smoking: it was the great American joke, the one nobody took seriously. Dolly hated her mother's need to shun the casualness which Negroes were supposed to have, the need which turned her husband into a walking cartoon and sent her daughter running to people like Rosie for reassurance that she was alive.

"My house is all right," she said, without enthusiasm.

"Is it fine as mine?" Rosie persisted.

Dolly told her, then, what she wanted to hear. For once it was the truth. "Rosie, that house of yours is the most magnificent place I've ever seen."

Them That's Not Shall Lose

Rosie darted a quick, suspicious look at her friend. Satisfied, apparently, by what she saw, she exhaled deeply.

"You take a lot of cabs, don't you?"

"Yeah, girl." Rosie lit a cigarette. "Them buses don't make it. They stop for too many miscellaneous people. Cab goes where I go 'n nowhere else."

"I don't understand—" Dolly checked herself, then proceeded firmly. "I just don't understand how you can afford it, Rosie. Where are you getting the money to buy that enormous house?"

"Aw, child," Rosie said, "you know the jobs I work are just for contacts and spendin' change. I got so many other deals goin' I can't decide which one to concentrate on."

Dolly knew what this meant. She was not impressed. "Why do you need such a big place, anyway? Are you thinking about getting married?"

"Could be," Rosie said mysteriously.

"Is it Larnie?" She touched Rosie's hand impulsively. "I'm glad, Rosie. I was glad to see you and him back together."

Rosie sounded disgusted. "Doll, you *are* stupid, I swear. Sure we're together. But I ain't about to get tied up with nothin' like that."

"You should," Dolly said quietly. "He's a great guy."

"You want him? You can have him," Rosie said. When Dolly ducked away from her brazen look she smiled, rolled the window down and flipped out her cigarette. "Doll, I don't wanta be tied down to him or to nothin' else that'll hold me back. You just watch my dust from here on in. The way things are goin', I'll probably end up a millionaire. Pretty soon I'll just sit home and let the loot roll in. Can't you see me? I got on this fine negligee, and I'm sittin' there on my chaise lounge eatin' caramels. . . ."

Suddenly Dolly wished for a sharp, cruel knife to cut through the insidiously spreading web of fantasy in which Rosie was caught. It was all the more dangerous because she was able to make it shimmer for others.

"Why don't you stop kidding yourself, Rosie? There aren't any colored millionaires. There never will be."

Rosie's face hardened. She said no more, just looked away until the cab reached Dolly's door. Then she murmured a cold, abstracted "See you, Doll." Her eyes were as remote and brilliant as black diamonds.

23

"Witch! Tormentor!" Mr. Schwartz cried. "Six months now, and not a word, not a sign. All night long in nightmares I see you, Rosalie. Starving, walking the streets maybe, in jail maybe I see you. Then shaking I wake up and ask myself, "Why? Why this lovely young girl, tender like a rose, bright like a dollar, should get in trouble? It must be this awful place, I say, this terrible Avenue. And you, Solomon Schwartz, are you a god, to judge? A judge, to punish? What kind man anyway, that this girl could never talk to you, and the one time she asked for help, you could not listen? After that, sleep again I cannot. —So my nights are spent, Rosalie. Now am I to have no peace at all? Will you now haunt my waking hours too?"

Beaten back by this tirade, Rosie retreated hastily to the door.

"Vell?" the old man asked impatiently, with an abrupt wave of his hand. "Why then are you here, if not to haunt me?"

Then, incredibly, beatifically, he smiled. "But you are here now, so stay." He beckoned. "Come. Sit down."

She drew up a shaky chair to the familiar corner desk, smothered with papers, from which Mr. Schwartz daily made war on his three enemies. Creditors. Competition. Chaos.

"How's business, Mr. Schwartz?" she asked him.

He said casually, "Oh, the store, it runs. Always it runs, Rosalie."

Then he threw up his hands and let them fall to his lap.

"Aaah! Why lie? It runs, yes, but like a train with the engine missing, and me behind, pushing. I cannot let up for one minute the pressure, or it will die. Once, with one eye closed behind me I could, but now— Now, old I am. Old."

His beatific smile came on again. "But only from looking at you I am young again, Rosalie. What brings this visit?"

Rosie fought back her sudden timidity. "I would've come before, Mr. Schwartz, only I was half afraid to after what happened. Then I remembered you said you might could help me get some furniture. I'm in my new house now, and I thought maybe—"

He raised a hand for silence. "Say no more. What kind of furniture you want? Is no problem."

Rosie warmed to her wondrous inner visions, an exotic mixture of Granny's descriptions, carefully remembered, and magazine pages, carefully saved, and all the cocktail lounges she'd ever been in and all the movies she'd ever seen. "I don't want just any old furniture, Mr. Schwartz. I want somethin' fabulous."

"What you want, I know without you saying. You want what my nephew Aaron—with his nasty mouth, he should only get cancer—what he calls Jewish Renaissance." Mr. Schwartz made a suitable face, like someone eating persimmons.

After a moment of embarrassment at the reference, Rosie burst into free relaxed laughter, in which he joined her. "It's all your fault, Mr. Schwartz," she said. "I worked for you so long I'm half Jew myself."

He nodded sagely. "Of course. This is why you are so smart." He wagged a finger at her. "But only half smart, Rosalie, or here you would still be."

She breathed deeply.

"Forgive me," he said quickly. "I did not mean anything."

" 'Sall right," she said. She was puzzled about something. "I didn't see Aaron around when I came in, Mr. Schwartz. Ain't he here no more?"

The old man put a hand on his heart. "Don't ask. It hurts me here just to think of that *schmendrick* with his lying and his

God Bless the Child

conniving. —You know, Rosalie, ever since you are gone, the store suffers. The customers are complaining, the records are confusion, the orders are coming in wrong or not at all. And from him, always some lie, always some fancy explanation. But this is no ordinary cover-up artist, Rosalie. This is the great Max Factor, in person. Would you believe it? It got so, every time he knocked on that door, I felt my heart knock twice in answer. Every time his shadow fell on me, I felt the Angel of Death pass over, the great Malach Hamorvess himself. My ruin he was plotting, my grave he had prepared. Already he was in mourning for me, I saw it. Then I knew was him or me, Rosalie."

The old man paused, breathing so heavily Rosie was frightened for him. "—About Aaron, don't ask. He's somewhere in Jersey destroying my brother-in-law's shoe business. More I don't know. More I don't want to know."

He made the motion of spitting, which Rosie thought must be the Jewish counterpart of crossing oneself. "Aah! Just to talk of him leaves in my mouth such a taste. Like ashes. —Let us talk instead of your new house, Rosalie. How many rooms?"

Deep in calculation, she watched her fingers swim rapidly through the air. Finally she looked up and said, "Ten. Not countin' the top floor I'm shuttin' off."

The old man looked startled. "A house, did you say, Rosalie, or a hotel?" His expression took on a sudden shyness; it was odd, like a delicate flower blooming on a gnarled old tree. "Are you still running the—the policy book?"

He interrupted himself quickly with his hand. "No, no, no, don't answer. I don't want to know. Even to ask was bad manners."

He swiveled in his chair and beamed at her. "I have a cousin, a decorator, a genius, will give you everything stunning, Rosalie," His eloquent hands furnished a lavish suite of rooms in that stuffy little box of an office. "French Provincial he will get you, modern Chinese, anything you want. Custom sectionals, any size, any shape—S's, L's, X's, Z's. Beds round, oval, square, even triangular, if you happen to sleep triangular. Wall to wall

210

draperies, and lamps like the Museum Modern Art, only better. And little doodads—" He kissed his hand to her. "Everything stunning, Rosalie, I promise. And all for a very nice price."

Crazy little electric trains were careening up Rosie's spine, her shoulders, her scalp. "When can I see him, Mr. Schwartz?"

"Oh, any time, Rosalie. Now, if you wish. I will take you." He leaned toward her suddenly. "Is only one condition. You come back to work for me."

Rosie stared at her pointed patent-leather toe describing jerky semicircles in the air. She stammered out. "As—as a salesgirl?"

"No," he said decisively. "As my right hand. Assistant manager, assistant picker up of pins, assistant giver of smelling salts. Assistant in charge of everything. Six hundred a month I will pay to start, Rosalie. You are worth more, but is all I can afford now. Later—" he shrugged "—who knows?"

She stared at him, baffled. Here it was again, the one thing she couldn't cope with. Love, undeserved, unexplained.

"And Rosalie," he said with an intent look, "no more questions from me. Your life outside, only keep it outside, and I don't care. Understand?"

"I don't know what to say, Mr. Schwartz."

"Say one word only. Yes." He put his hand on top of hers for a moment. It was a beautiful study in worn pastels: reddened fingers with taut pink knuckles, brown age-spots superimposed on raised blue veins. Nowhere was it really white. "I am old now, Rosalie, I need you. Is a good thing to be needed, don't forget. I think, the best thing in the world."

The furniture began to arrive that afternoon, in vans and wagons and on the shoulders of endless jovial slow-moving hourly wage Santa Clauses.

Rosie was everywhere at once: hovering over the deliverymen, urging them simultaneously to move faster and to be more careful; darting from room to room to test and retest the reality of things she did not yet dare believe in.

"You a regular itch, Rosie," Queenie said from her new throne, a white whale of a plastic lounge chair that could be cranked into any of twenty-three "heart-saving" positions. "Those men know their business. Why can't you leave 'em alone? Sit still a minute."

Rosie tried, then said, "I can't, I'm too excited." She jumped up to change, for the fourth time, her arrangement of brilliant ruby and emerald ceramic ash trays.

"There's one thing you forgot, though," her mother said.

"What's that?" Rosie asked absently, stepping back to study the symmetry of the giant ceramic cats, one red, one green, with glowing rhinestone eyes, who had just taken up guard at either side of a noble fireplace. "You know what this room really needs?" she said. "A live dog. A collie, or a red setter, or a spotted Dalmatian, to lie in front of that fireplace, like you see all the time in magazines." She sighed. "But I ain't got time to train no dog to lie still like that."

Mom said, "You forgot to get a little iron colored jockey for the front yard. —'Course I'd like a white one better," she went on without flinching under Rosie's suddenly glaring look. "Blond, with blue eyes, so there wouldn't be no mistake about who lived here."

"Shut up," Rosie said.

On moving day and ever since, Mom had been her biggest problem. She had squatted in the old apartment like a malignant mushroom that refused to be uprooted from its rotting bed, glowering silently while crates and furniture flowed around her in two directions, the larger eddy bound for the Salvation Army, the smaller for the new house. Only once had she called Rosie aside to say brokenly, "You know, Rosie, it hurts me to see you leave so much behind. Like you're in a hurry to get rid of everything that reminds you of where you come from. Has it really been that bad?"

"Yes."

After that Mom locked herself into a stillness so immobile Rosie thought they would finally have to take a crane and swing her, bed and all, out the window and onto the flat bed of a truck. But at the very last minute she came to life and stumped downstairs, still in her old red kimono, leaning on Larnie's arm.

In the car, Rosie hadn't helped any by accusing Mom of deliberately prolonging her illness to make life rougher on everybody else. "You don't take your medicine, or stick to your diet, or do anything the doctor tells you," she said. "Sometimes I think you just ain't trying."

"I'm trying to do what you want, Rosie," her mother answered. "Die. So you can collect my insurance money. You're gonna need it to help you keep up that mortgage."

She twisted the knife after driving it home. "You don't have to worry 'bout no fancy funeral for me, neither. Just bury me in the cellar, along with all the other worn-out stuff you don't want no more."

Granny stepped in and saved Rosie, who was choking. "Now, Regina, if you can't say anything nice, just keep quiet for a change. Lately your mouth is always full of vinegar. If there's one thing I hate to see, it's women turning sour when they get old."

"Old? Old?" had been Queenie's last shocked words for a long time. While Larnie drove in stony silence, she sat beside him, staring straight ahead as if she, too, had to keep her eyes on the road. Rosie and Granny were left to toss the pingpong ball of excitement back and forth between them in the back seat, with only an occasional false bounce.

"Where you plan to have the dining room, Rosalie?"

"I hadn't planned on a dining room, Granny. I'm gonna put a breakfast nook in the kitchen."

"Breakfast nooks," Granny stated, "are for breakfast."

"All right then, Granny, where do you want the dining room? The big room next to the kitchen, or the little one next to that?"

"Well, the big room gets more sunshine, it's light and airy."

"All right, Granny, the big one it is. You can have the little one for your sewing."

"I'll make some tie-back curtains. Dotted swiss or organdy."

"I saw a fabulous limed oak dining suite the other day, at one of the showrooms."

"Just remember one thing, Rosalie. Good taste don't cost no more than bad."

Through all this discussion, throughout the long, long drive that was farther than she had ever traveled in all her life, Queenie remained quiet. She did not speak until they reached the cool green fish-tank atmosphere of their new street and saw, swimming through it, four pickets like stately swans. Then she leaned forward and spoke to herself.

"Is this what they fightin' for?" she asked softly. "So we can be fools?"

She had made it plain ever since that this was her firm attitude. Rosie fought it when she had the strength, though it was like fighting a bronze statue, and ignored it the rest of the time, since her mother was, after all, an invalid, and statues were, after all, easy to ignore. Larnie's mournful looks and headshakings were more difficult to evade, though she could always shut him up by snapping, "It's none of your business."

But they were all behaving like ungrateful children. Even Granny's voice, ever since they had moved into the new house, had taken on a more imperious tone, as if she had added the previous mistress's prerogatives to her own.

"Rosalie," she demanded now in the doorway, "will you please tell me just what those men are doing in the cellar?"

"What men, Granny?" Rosie asked innocently, though the sound of hammering was beginning to shake the house.

"They came bargin' in without even askin', and they been hammerin' and sawin' down there till my ears are ready to split open. I want you to go right down there and stop them."

That tone again. In the past Rosie had always obeyed it without question, but today she remonstrated gently. "Maybe I asked them to come, Granny."

"You didn't ask them to come," the old lady declared. "Oh no, you didn't. You couldn't. They been trackin' dust all over my clean floors and tearin' up the cellar and I don't know what all. You go down there and stop them. Right now, Rosalie."

Rosie flew past her to the stairs. Downstairs was the still-unused rumpus room in which she had installed Philippine mahogany paneling and a black tile floor.

She called up, "It's the bar I ordered, Granny. Custom made. Come see."

Granny came down the stairs cautiously. She moved toward the bar as though she expected it to come to life and bite her.

Of glass bricks with gleaming brass trim and mirrored shelves, it ran the length of one wall. Now one of the workmen threw a switch: Rosie's initials, in pink neon, lit up the center while, at the edges, lights melted from violet to green to orange. A continuous built-in rainbow.

"Ain't it fabulous, Granny?" Rosie said proudly.

Granny was silent as the two workmen, their job finished, turned their backs on the marvel they had wrought and clumped up the stairs.

Lord, the harder she tried to please Granny, the less she was satisfied. Rosie's face glowed, reflecting pink neon, but her voice was sick with anxiety. "Don't you like it, Granny?"

"Mighty gay," the old lady grumbled. "This ain't a taproom, you know. This is a home." She touched one of the luminous panels and instantly drew back her finger as if it had been burned. "Might not be so bad if you turned them lights off," she said.

Rosie stamped her feet and howled, "It's no good without the lights, Granny! You don't understand. I want it to look expensive!" Raking lightly at the front of Granny's dress with her nails, she repeated, "It's got to look expensive!"

Granny sat down suddenly on a bar stool upholstered in zebra-striped plastic. She looked like a sober gray dodo bird who had inadvertently perched on a TV antenna.

"Go on, go on," she said, waving a hand weakly. "Don't mind me. Don't let me spoil your young pleasures."

Rosie knelt contritely and put her head in her grandmother's lap. "If you don't like it I don't want it, Granny," she sobbed against the smooth gray nunlike cloth. "It's all for you, don't you know that?"

God Bless the Child

At a stiffening beneath her cheek, she quickly put her voice in a brighter key. "Sure! Don't you know why I fixed up this room? I'm gonna throw a party for my Granny!"

"Ah, stop all that foolish talk," Granny said.

But when Rosie looked up, she was smiling.

"Why not?" Rosie demanded. "I wanta show everybody how my Granny can cut a rug."

Jumping up, she caught Granny's hands. She danced her once around the cellar, then up the stairs, hands on her waist from behind, Conga style.

"Rosie, go on with your foolishness," Granny said. "Stop that! Stop!"

But Rosie could tell she was pleased. She began to be entranced with her idea.

"Tonight, Granny! We're gonna have your party tonight, before you get a chance to change your mind! It's gonna be a real proper party, too. Like a church social. A church-folks party!"

Back in the living room, she minced over to a table and picked up an imaginary teapot. "May I pour for you, Mrs. Frisbee? How many lumps? Lemon or cream?"

"If I know your friends," Queenie said, "they don't want nothin' but gin and whiskey."

"Everybody ain't like you," Rosie said. "Some of *my* friends are nice. —We'll need about two hundred of them little cream cheese sandwiches, too, Granny. We better get busy! You know we can't have a proper social without little cream cheese sandwiches!"

She whirled: Mom was trying to keep from smiling, and Granny was beaming, so she began to tiptoe around the room, making plans.

"Two rows of chairs, see. All the men sit on one side. All the ladies sit on the other side. And no loud talkin' or rowdiness. If they do, you get to bop 'em on the mouth!"

"I'm glad to hear you plan to keep the noise down, since there's a sick woman in the house," Mom said.

Treating her like a statue, Rosie went on, "We're gonna listen to nice slow classical records, 'n when the dancin' starts, I'll walk around with this." She waved a ruler that had been left by one of the workmen. "Make sure there's at least ten inches between 'em. 'N every man's gotta dance with my Granny."

She tapped her head with the ruler. "Now, what else? Let me think. Oh yeah, renditions. We can't have a proper party without renditions. I'll get Larnie to play the piano, and I'll ask my friend Dolly to come on with some poetry. You remember Dolly, Granny, you like her. She's real proper!"

"I ain't seen the back yard yet," Queenie said, "but there sure must be a money tree growin' out there."

"God, you're mean. Mean, mean, mean!" burst from Rosie. "I never knew anybody could be so mean. You don't want me to have any fun at all. You just want me to be as old and sick and miserable as you are. Well I'm not, you hear? I'm young, and I'm alive, and I can't stand it!"

Rosie only stopped when she saw her mother's eyes grow as wet as hers. There was a long silence.

Finally Granny piped, "Rosalie, are you going to ask that nice young man?"

"What young man is that, Granny?" Rosie asked innocently.

"That nice Mr. Tucker. Who else would I mean?" Granny took her by the hand. "Now, Rosalie, you haven't gone and stopped being nice to him, have you? I haven't seen him in such a long time. And here I was hoping I'd live long enough to see your wedding."

"I'm still nice to him, Granny," Rosie said uncomfortably. "He's just very busy these days. You know how it is when you're in business." She gave herself airs with a feather duster, waving it like a fan.

The old lady was silent.

Rosie patted her frail hand. "I'll ask him. Sure, Granny. When he hears you're lookin' for him, he's bound to come."

She broke free of the old lady's radiant smile and ran toward the hall.

"Now let me get on the phone and invite everybody. It's three o'clock already. I gotta give 'em plenty of time to get proper!"

24

Rosie's cream cheese sandwiches were magnificent and inedible. They were tinted pastel pink and green and arranged on a three-tiered crystal tray in patterns that were obviously not meant to be disturbed. After they had been passed and refused, the bar that silently churned its rainbows into the room was used for the serving of pale pink lemonade and bright green Kool-Aid.

As each couple arrived, Rosie led them to Granny's chair for elaborate introductions, then separated them into the seating arrangement she had designed. Soon an uncomfortable row of girls sat facing an uneasy row of men.

Rosie darted restlessly from background to foreground, harvesting invisible bits of litter from the floor, feeding the hi-fi a steady diet of Nelson Eddy and Jeanette Mac Donald, and urging liquids and sandwiches on her underworld friends, who all strove heroically to balance cut-glass cups and plates and lacy napkins on their knees with grace. The only topics permitted for general discussion were the state of your health and the weather. Men were also allowed to exchange low comments about sports with their neighbors, and women might engage, if they wished, in whispered discussions of clothes. Both sexes were supposed to cough discreetly, at regular intervals, into elegant handkerchiefs.

The three old ladies who surrounded Granny, sipping daintily and sighing and rustling their fans, were the only ones who seemed to be enjoying themselves. Everyone else seemed afflicted by a terrible itch. They looked about desperately, but no opportunities for scratching were in sight. As the minutes creaked along, the old ladies' fans flew more and more furiously, whipping up the air like egg white until it was stiff with discomfort. The little smile on Granny's face grew broader and broader. Twenty people crossed and uncrossed their legs thirty times.

Of all the young people, only Dolly seemed comfortable within the constraints Rosie had imposed. She sat with the calm propriety of a nun, hands resting quietly in her lap. On her right Ginger and Amber tugged nervously at identical tight satin dresses which kept doing exactly what they had been designed to do, ride high above the knee. On her left Bettina, the shapely stripper from The Cotton Club, suddenly ashamed of the endowment that earned her salary, seemed to be trying to wriggle down lower into her low-cut dress.

"Aw, don't hide it, honey," rumbled Pockets Robinson from across the room. "It looks good."

While everyone else looked shocked, the old ladies calmly took command and healed the breach of deportment.

"I went to see Miss Jenny Hankins laid out today," said Mrs. Olive Fussell, the oldest of the three. "Sad."

"Mmm, yes," agreed Miss Bessie Harris, "but wasn't she a lovely co'pse?"

"Mmm, yes," Miss Olive replied. "She looked so sweet. Like she was just lyin' there dreamin' and would wake up by and by."

"Sad," said Miss Mary Scott. "Did you stay for the wedding?"

"No," Miss Olive replied with regret.

"Oh, that's too bad," Miss Mary said. "It was Lucia Luby's child. She made a lovely bride."

"I was there," Miss Bessie said. "Mmm yes, I was there. I was glad they had the viewing first. I always like to get there early and see everything. It sho' was a lovely ceremony."

"Mmm yes," said Mrs. Lourinda Huggs, who had lately taken up church and embroidery to fill the gaps left in her life by her white folks, "that it was."

Except for a cough from Miltie Newton in the corner, the rest of the room was painfully silent. Bettina, wriggling and tugging miserably, pulled out a cigarette and asked Dolly if she had a match. Dolly shook her head, and the unhappy dancer, after a quick look around, stowed the contraband cylinder down her splendid bosom. She was not unobserved.

"Mm-hmm *yes*," Miss Mary emphasized with a decisive downward flourish of her fan.

Silence. Deadly oppressive silence, like a vacuum; all the air seemed to have been sucked out of the room.

Suffocating, poolroom owner Bud Lewis fished a sphere from his cup and said, with nervous humor, "First cherry I had all year."

There was scattered laughter until Rosie's baleful glance searched the room and found it out. Another hush fell.

Pockets Robinson leaned forward with a courteous cough and said to Granny, "I think he meant they ain't been in season, ma'am."

This only drew forth a more widespread ripple of laughter. Rosie, seeing that the thin bubble of her party's propriety was ready to burst, gave an imperious signal to Larnie.

Gravely, with only a slight held-in dance in his walk to betray his drunken amusement, he got up and went over to the piano in one corner. The group quickened slightly. Any distraction was preferable to what had gone before.

But Larnie chose to give them the most well-tempered, orderly Bach he could think of, unsullied by ornaments or dynamics. On and on it went, in monotonous machinelike progressions, while faces looked at each other in dull, baffled anger, and feet that had been poised for tapping drooped limply. At the end there was applause, but only from the old ladies.

Larnie did not wait until their genteel clapping was over. He plunged immediately, with drunken assurance, into the "Chromatic Fantasy and Fugue," and this time he held even the most sluggish attentions. The first runs seemed to fling open the ceiling to the sky. Notes flew overhead like swallows over city roofs, flock after flock, only to be scattered into gray clouds homing toward the south by rapid changes of key. Then the miracle happened.

The theme twisted, turned inside out, shed its solemn skin and was transformed into something quite different. A nimble arrangement of notes like bursting pinwheels above, and underneath a rhythm which was compellingly familiar, like blues, like gospel, like an amplification of the human heart. As it pulled in and out, back and forth, hands began to clap softly, and feet began to shuffle. Even Queenie, who had planned to stay aloof from the proceedings, found this music irresistible. She perched on the top step, eyes closed, swaying dreamily.

Larnie went on chasing star-trails until they were breathless from keeping up with him. Finally he took pity and, with chords hewn of solid stone, brought the thing to its ponderous climax. It still swung majestically in the after-echoes, like a rock balancing on the edge of a chasm.

Dolly forgot herself and cried, "Wonderful!" in the ensuing cave of silence.

Larnie stood up, smiling, glassy-eyed, pleased, acknowledging waves of applause and cries of "More. man! More!"

"Now, lemme give you the lowdown on this cat Bach," he said with a confidential wink at his audience. They sank into expectant silence as he sat down and launched into a skipping Gigue from one of the *English Suites.*

"Now Mister Bach was church folks and all that, you understand, but he had his lighter moments too. Wasn't nothin' he liked better than jammin' awhile." Larnie sneaked a subtle syncopation into the rhythm, then let it disappear. There were appreciative chuckles.

" 'Course, now, when the Deacon or the Archbishop was in church, Bach played it real dignified." Larnie put his nose in the air and curled his fingers with dandified precision. "But when they cut out, man, that church started jumpin'."

The Gigue became a boogie, fast and driving, with a tickling antiphonal movement high in the treble. "Now one day Bach was jivin' around like this, compin' with his left hand and soloin' with his right, when the Bishop sneaked in the back way. But Bach dug him soon's the door opened. He got right back on that righteous kick."

God Bless the Child

The music was solemn again. "The Bishop digs it, and he nods real pious, and says, 'Fine, fine, Brother Johann, just what I like to hear.' And he goes out of church again, so naturally Bach gets back in the groove right away . . . till he hears some of the congregation filin' in."

Larnie closed the jazz improvisation with the traditional figure and chord. Still in his role, he half rose from the piano bench, smiled, and bowed. "The congregation applauded. And Bach stood up and took a bow, just as proper as you please." Intoxicated with his own acting, Larnie dragged a finger down the keyboard. "Bach just knew he was slick, see. He just knew he had 'em all fooled."

He paused significantly.

"—and then, somebody in the congregation yelled out, 'Crazy!' "

A great roar of laughter went up from every throat, and a cannonade of applause followed. B.J., the gambler, got up to clap Larnie on the shoulder.

"Man," he said, "I'd sure like to get you a drink, if this wasn't such a lame, dry party."

Only one small tinkling note of condemnation sounded in the swell of praise. But Granny's "Disgraceful!" was sweeping enough to include both B.J.'s remark and Larnie's performance.

She suddenly rose, and her three companions rose with her.

It was eleven o'clock, they explained sweetly: their bedtime. They conveyed the guilty impression that it was the bedtime of all decent Christians, but there was also, in their worn voices, a sighing admission that young people will be young. Rosie tried to stop their swift exodus and her mother's, but other urgencies were demanding her attention. Long before the cellar door had closed behind the last pair of sensible heels, her guests were clamoring around the bar.

She produced fifteen bottles, four of bourbon, four rye, and seven of White Horse Scotch. "Everybody get on the Horse!" she shouted. "Let's ride!"

A minute later, riding high on the nips she had already sneaked into her lemonade, she screamed triumphantly, "Bang! One dead soldier!" as she tipped the first empty bottle on its side.

The lights were turned off; only the bar glowed balefully from one wall. The real music was started and couples flowed onto the floor like dark liquid poured from a single bottle. Chairs were kicked over; here and there a girl shrieked; now and again Rosie's strident voice was heard proclaiming, "Six dead soldiers!" or urging "Get on the Horse!" But soon it was swallowed up in the general roar.

Dolly, stumbling without her glasses along one wall, skirted the crouched figures engrossed in a crap game by the bar; it was led by B.J., a professional gambler who would surely part all the others from their pay checks. "Put your money where your mouth is," he chanted, shaking his fist above his head. "Shake that thing and make me sing, roll and satisfy my soul."

A great roar went up at the other end of the room. Bettina, having ridden the Horse a good distance, was going into her specialty, eyes tightly closed to preserve the illusion of privacy that was necessary before she could take off her clothes.

In the darkest corner a lone hulking figure sat, chin gripped in one hand, like God brooding over His world gone wrong.

Dolly almost cried; she was so glad to see Larnie. LIFE, to her, meant a magazine, and something else, something fiery and explosive, that only happened to two-fisted men and brazen women. It never happened to genteel people like herself except when they entered the orbit of an intensely combusting person like Rosie who could turn them into moons. Dolly had been eager for the excitement promised by Rosie's party; she had been longing to see how Rosie would fill her old house with new LIFE. But she had felt painfully out of place all evening, except for that almost holy interval when Larnie played the piano.

She ran up to him eagerly, as to an ally. He was the only other person there who was not a member of the underworld. She wanted to throw adoring arms around him, tell him how thrilled she had been by his talent, but all she could do was peer at him in her nearsighted way and extend a formal hand.

God Bless the Child

He took it and held on like a drowning man. "I'm all alone, Dolly. Sit down and talk to me." He put a clumsy arm around her waist and pulled her suddenly onto his lap. "Lovely lady, sit down'n keep a lonely man company."

His tie was askew and there was a large damp stain, the remnant of a spilled drink, on his shirt front. Dolly saw the film over his eyes, smelled the reek of his breath.

"My God, Larnie," she exclaimed. And slipping from his startled embrace with ease, she stood over him and scolded like the schoolmarm she was.

His eyes cleared, then darkened with shame. "Sorry, Dolly. That wasn't me talkin'. That was I.W. Harper."

"But you never used to drink at all," she reproached him.

"Lots of water gone under the bridge now, Dolly. Won't hurt to throw a little whiskey down there, too."

Lord, Larnie too, sinking into the swamp of Rosie's underworld. "Larnie," Dolly asked angrily, "what's happened to you?"

"I know what you're thinking," he answered. "You think it's all Rosie's fault. But it ain't, Dolly. I had to quit college. I got in some trouble up there."

"What kind of trouble?" She was unable to imagine that the gentle Larnie she knew was capable of making trouble.

"Oh, I was laying some stupid little white chick, and she went and sounded on me," he boasted in a wholly uncharacteristic way. He even talked differently now, Dolly noticed. She was less shocked by what Larnie had said than by the way he said it. Once he had spoken in clear correct sentences, but now, probably to please Rosie, he splashed his speech with the blurred vivid colors of slang. "Was your family upset about it?" she asked him.

"Pop died," he said with chilling simplicity.

He banged his palm with his fist. "He died thinking I was still in school. Have you any idea how mad that makes me? —No, you couldn't," he answered himself. "Mom lied, right up to the end. She said it would kill Pop to know I quit school. I said it would kill him workin' to keep me there, too, so what was the difference?"

Her heart constricted at the matter-of-fact way he said it.

"I told Mom from now on she's gotta take me the way I am, B.S. or no b.s." He squared his shoulders belligerently. "Way I look at it, everybody's gotta take me like I am."

She returned his look steadily. "Sure, Larnie. Why shouldn't they?"

He stared at her in suspicious silence.

"Don't you realize that what you did with that Bach tonight was something original, something that's never been done before?"

"So what?" he said with an angry disparaging movement. "Look, Dolly, I had my chance to become a musician, learn the classics, get an education. And I goofed it, fooling around with jazz, wasting my time. I'm a failure."

"Oh, no," Dolly breathed. "You're a genius."

He smiled at her, sweetly, mockingly. It was worse than an argument, because she could sense the stubbornness that lay behind that sweet smile. But she went on with stubborn courage of her own, "You said playing jazz was a waste of time. Well, I think it's a waste of time for you to play anything else. Why play other people's music when you can do something that wonderful all by yourself? I took piano lessons once myself, Larnie, and I know if I took them all my life I'd never be able to play like that. —Oh, sure, you should practice scales, learn harmony, get the basics, but don't stop creating. Never stop creating."

Suddenly she realized that she was clasping one of his hands tightly in both of hers while she looked deeply into his eyes. She let his hand go and finished lamely, "You're creative, and I think it's wonderful. But maybe that's because I know I can never be."

"Yeah," he said. "It all depends on the point of view." He resumed staring glumly at the floor in the pose in which she had found him.

She tried another tack. "Larnie," she asked softly, "suppose your father were still alive. Don't you think he would be even prouder if you created something all your own?"

"No," he said. "My folks are just like yours, Dolly." Under his breath, he sang,

> *"I got the bourgeois blues,*
> *Gonna spread the ne-ews around."*

He broke off to look up, with a grimace, at the heaving crowd on the dance floor. It spewed forth a laughing couple who stumbled over them and staggered on without apologizing.

"Rosie won't even talk to me any more, Dolly. I don't know what's going on in that crazy little head of hers. Killing herself, working night and day for this. Things she don't need. People who don't even care about her." He looked up at her with sudden eagerness. "Maybe you could talk to her, Dolly."

Now it was he who made her hand disappear in his two paws. "She won't listen to me. But maybe you can make her see before it's too late."

"Make her see what?" Dolly asked with sudden hardness. "That she's destroying herself and you too?" She wanted to cry out against the sin of such waste.

"Aaah, maybe it's too late already." Larnie shrugged. "Forget it, Dolly. I don't even know why I asked you."

The hi-fi wailed something about its not wanting him, somebody else could have him.

"What are you doing here, anyway, Dolly?" he asked abruptly. "I mean, you got nice parents, you've finished school, you got a profession, you probably got nice friends—why do you keep on coming around here?"

She thought about it awhile, then said simply, "I love her."

"That's it," he said, engrossed in the floor. "There's no getting away from it, is there?"

There seemed to be no fight left in him; he would give up everything he wanted, now, without a struggle or a murmur. She wanted to hit him or yell at him to shock him out of his dumb submissiveness, but instead, after a moment, she patted his shoulder and went off to try.

Rosie leaned against the bar, her hair in damp disheveled ringlets, her eyes great circles of fire in the dark.

" 'Lo, Doll," she crowed. "You havin' a good time?"

"Rosie, what's the matter with you?" Dolly asked foolishly.

Rosie pointed. "Look up there, Doll. Look up there and tell me how many dead soldiers."

"Rosie, can't you see?"

"Tell me, I said! How many?"

Dolly counted the empty bottles. "Nine—ten."

"Just ten?" Rosie tried to grope her way along the bar, but her fingers slipped on its slick surface. She huddled into a ball and began to cough steadily into her hand. "Get on the Horse!" she roared. "Everybody ride!"

Dolly's mouth was dry. She had heard of people being blind drunk, but Rosie looked worse, much worse than any drunk she had ever seen. "Let me help you, Rosie," she said. "You ought to lie down."

Rosie's eyes were burning slits. "You ain't havin' a good time, Doll. I can tell. What's wrong? Ain't you had nothin' to drink?" She waved a fifth of liquor. "Here! Get yourself in the mood."

"I don't want any, thank you," Dolly said primly.

Rosie made her voice deep and booming. "Who you think you are, gal? When Rosie parties, everybody parties!"

"Rosie," Dolly said again, reaching out a hand to support her friend, "please let me help you."

"Don't need no help." Rosie sat down suddenly on the floor. "I'm fine."

"Look at you, you can't even stand up!" Dolly wailed. "I'm going to get Larnie."

Rosie's low voice was a tiger's growl of warning. "Doll, don't you do that. I'm waitin' for somebody."

"Who?"

Rosie went on as if she had not heard the question. "Child, let me tell you about Granny. You should've seen her tonight, before you came. Cute? Eyes bright as buttons! She's just crazy about him. She didn't even wanta go to bed till I promised to wake her up when he got here."

"Rosie," Dolly persisted, "nobody else is coming at this hour."

Rosie's eyes snapped open; they were dangerously bright. "What you know about it, Doll?"

"I know it's half-past two in the morning," Dolly said, "and you're half dead."

"I'm all dead." Rosie slipped down blissfully in one slow flowing movement until her head touched the floor. Dolly bent over her, preparing to harangue her some more, but it was useless. Rosie's eyes were tightly closed, her mouth was open, and she was fast asleep.

"You can't do anything for her," a voice said. "But you could do a lot for me."

Dolly stood up quickly, pulling at her lapels, even though she recognized the eyes that were staring down the V of her dress. They belonged to an interesting new person in her life who seemed to be a male counterpart of Rosie.

"Easy there," he chuckled. "We're old friends. Oh, I know, you don't remember me from school. But I remember you. You were the pretty little bonbon, all wrapped up in frilly paper, that I wasn't allowed to touch. Only someday, maybe, if I got to be rich and famous."

Well, he was not yet rich, and he was infamous, but Dolly found him fascinating even though she didn't know whether she liked him or not.

She was not surprised to see him here at Rosie's gathering of thieves. Sometimes, fretting against her mother's petty restraints, Dolly longed to break the stern unmentionable laws, to commit a real crime. She did not have the courage to act on her wish, but she was secure in knowing that anything important she did was all right with her family. Even going around with an outlaw was all right, as long as he was polite and well-dressed. As long as she kept the bathroom spotless and her toilet articles impeccably arranged.

"Let me take you home. There's nothing more you can do here," he repeated at her elbow.

Dolly gave a last look around: at Rosie, snoring softly; at Larnie, slumped in the corner where she had left him; at the demented crowd that had forgotten them both.

"I guess you're right, Tom," she said.

It was just a minute later, Rosie thought, when she awoke suddenly and looked around to find Dolly gone. She sat up. The party had thinned out considerably. While the last record in the stack started again, two couples dragged listlessly around the floor with closed eyes, using each other's shoulders as pillows. The pink curve of the "R" had developed a nervous tic; soon her entire initial would be blanked out. The crap game had broken up, and thirteen fatally wounded bottles lay on their sides. Rosie flicked the little catch that opened the jeweled case of her cocktail watch. A quarter to four.

She leaped up and tugged at Watty Myers, who sat playing solitaire on the bar, laying out his cards beside the fallen warriors. "Any messages for me, Watty?" she asked urgently. "Any phone calls?"

Long-faced, orange-skinned Watty turned, blinked pale sleepy eyes, and recoiled. "Gawd, Rosie. You look like one of my customers." Watty made a good living managing his mother's funeral home and selling life insurance and cemetery lots. He wore perpetual mourning on his face.

"You sure nobody asked for me?" she persisted.

He seemed to hesitate. "There was one person."

"Who?"

"I was that person," he told her stiffly, with an injured air. "I looked all over for you." He pointed to the corner where Rosie had slept with a little flutter of distaste. "I found you. Then I sat down here to wait till you woke up."

Rosie folded her arms. "Well, I'm awake."

"So I see. Welcome back to the land of the living." He grinned, showing just the edges of his upper teeth. "To get to the point, dear, I had the pleasure of meeting your grandmother for the first time tonight, and I know if I were fortunate enough to have a wonderful grandmother like that, I'd do everything I could for her."

"Ain't she somethin'?" Rosie grinned. "Do you know she fixed all that punch and sandwiches all by herself?"

"No!" He was properly incredulous. "She certainly deserves the best you can give her. Peace of mind, ah—, security, ah—"

Liquor had delayed Rosie's reactions, but now her lip curled slightly. "What you sellin', Watty? Insurance?"

He smiled his cautious tooth-edge smile again. "You might call it that. Some of my friends call it subterranean real estate. Ha ha."

Before she could absorb his meaning he had whipped out a colorful folder and was spreading it on the bar. "Now, you'll notice that Rolling Hills covers seven beautiful acres, and that there is a minimum distance of five feet between plots. We're trying to develop this new section here, and that's why I'm able to do you a favor. Right now you can buy a single plot for twenty per cent less, a double plot for a third less, and a family plot for half off the regular price. That includes perpetual care and plantings and—"

"Get out of here, Watty."

"But Rosie. I want to do you a favor!"

"Larnie!" she called. "Larnie! Will you come throw this faggot out of here?"

"I'm leaving," Watty said, rising with injured dignity. As the tall, well-muscled form approached he sidled along the wall, then scurried up the stairs like a large orange crab.

"Somebody messin' with you, Rosie? Where is he?"

"Larnie." She swayed against him. "Larnie. I think I'm gonna be sick."

She managed to walk up the first flight of stairs alone, but he carried her up the second. His hands supported her over the basin, washed her face with clean cool water afterward, and scrubbed up the mess from the bathroom floor. His arms carried her, following her brief whispered directions, to the back bedroom and put her on the bed.

When he looked she had the sheet pulled to the bridge of her nose. Two mischievous eyes, eyes that ten minutes ago had been black holes of fear, peered out at him.

"You think Rosie's awful," she said weakly. "You won't ever wanta come near Rosie again."

"You know better than that," he said, sinking his hands in her masses of new-crisped curls.

"Do somethin' for me?" she whispered.

"Anything."

"Go downstairs 'n chase all them niggers home."

He was already at the door when she called out, "That ain't all!"

He stopped obediently and turned.

A delighted shiver passed through her as she saw only herself in his eyes.

"After that, come back up here 'n undress me."

25

But when he came upstairs again she was having a dream, of floating on a raft in mid-ocean, surrounded by silence except for squeaking distant birds, and their cries and the massaging of the waves were all mixed up with his voice and his hands unbuttoning, soothing, exploring. She slapped one of them away as she might a mosquito.

" 'M sleepy. Go 'way. Leave me 'lone."

Anchored and drifting at the shadow line dividing sleep and waking, she thought faintly, What a nice guy he is, and why do I always have to be such a mean stingy little bitch? But she was too sleepy to feel her guilt as painful. When his delicate disinterested touches were replaced by purposeful ones, she stayed limp, with no intention of responding. He withdrew for a minute, then again began to run light therapeutic fingers down her back.

Thus reassured, she was really asleep when the shock came. He had found her after all.

An indignant scream caught in her throat and was released as a long hissing sigh. Lord, women were vulnerable; once opened to a man, they were never safe from him. Tenderness and anger fought within her in retreating and advancing waves. She wanted, successively, to escape with a violent hurting movement, and to turn and fold him in a great greedy embrace. Because she could do neither, anger won when finally he bruised her neck with his teeth, and sighed her name, and immediately fell asleep, leaving her to stare into the blank darkness with hot wakeful eyes.

But finally she slept too, and in the morning there were kisses multiplied by her vague remorse, and she thought, He tastes so good because he's so young; young men have cleaner mouths because they haven't spent so many years smoking and swearing and drinking. Though lately Larnie had taken up all three, as a certain softness around his middle was beginning to testify.

But everywhere else he was hard as granite, and she was too bony herself to be much good at cushioning things.

"I'd hate to be married to you," she said when his seemingly endless pleasure abated. "I'd hafta go around on crutches."

And taking this as a compliment (this was another track event: the 400-meter, the two-mile relay), he smiled and said, "You're not the first to complain."

In that moment, she clearly hated him.

But in the next, for some unclear reason, she grabbed his ears and pulled them toward her. He laughed and sought her mouth, which she gave with a strange sweet resignation. After that kiss she said, "You live here from now on, Larnie." It was not an invitation, it was a statement.

His eyebrows arched in surprise.

"Why not?" she said with an airy gesture. "There's plenty room."

Why not, indeed? Back on the Avenue there had been many

stranger living arrangements than mere couples who were not married. Married women who kept their maiden names, single women with several married names and men to match, husbands who mysteriously disappeared while children just as mysteriously appeared, all accepted as matter-of-factly as the sun's rolling around the sky. Life had only one secret, and Rosie had learned it, back in that great stewpot in which light particles bubbled while those burdened with too many morals sank. People would accept anything, once you dared to do it. The hardest part was just to dare.

He finally gave a grunt of assent that was more of a groan, and used his last strength to move down half a foot and drop his head, like a large wilted sunflower, on her shoulder. For a long time she stroked his incredibly soft brown hair, as light and insubstantial as a cloud.

But that sweet mood dissipated, too, as she continued to study him, twice as tall extended, and suddenly grown twice as heavy. No longer maternal, or, if still so, in the way of a tired middle-aged mother of a disappointing grown son, who had to repeat endlessly, "Get up, you great big lazy nogood; get up, get out, get a job, bring me things, bring me money," she freed herself with a gentle determined shove. Just in time, too, for his eyes were open again, intensely golden again, and questioning.

"People have to do other things too," she said. She added plaintively, "Don't they?"

"No," he said. "This is really all there is."

"Not for me," she said stubbornly.

"Why not?" he asked, mockingly echoing her husky tone; beginning, dangerously, to stroke her arm.

"Because." Because she was suddenly tired of that disordered bed; suddenly hungry for clean crisp sheets to be stretched taut on it, and for herself to be in a full bubbling tub, and for a table somewhere to be set with china cups thinner than paper and fragrant coffee. It was up to her to make all this happen immediately.

"Because I say so," she repeated firmly, and got up with a

wrench that took all her strength, strength she might need later to fight some critical illness. Let him lie there in his stupor, dreaming of her.

He stared at the ceiling through cigarette smoke. "Say, Fox says music is really conversation, did you know that? Saxophones are old men, he says. Trumpets are young guys, pianos and clarinets are women. All talking. Isn't that fascinating? It's part of his jazz theory."

Damn Fox, she thought. Damn him to hell with all his theories, and all men too, the way they roll over and roll right back into the world. Suddenly regretting her invitation, she took it back halfway.

"You can have the little room across the hall," she said. She started a roaring tub to drown out any further comments.

Larnie took the hint and went, with a step that was still sure, to the pleasant maple-and-red-gingham room across the hall. Through two hours of her singing and swearing and splashing he wondered, What in hell can she be doing in there? But he waited patiently until he heard her return to the bedroom, and fuss around some more, and finally subside into silence. Then he tiptoed back the way he had come.

Yes, she was asleep. At the sight of her small spreadeagled form, complex emotions stirred in him—tenderness, pity, resentment. He went into the bathroom. Clouds of scent suffocated him. Something soft and wet brushed against his face. Larnie looked up, in amazement, at what appeared to be a swarm of snakes dangling from the ceiling.

Finally the steam cleared and he recognized her tangled stockings—tan, brown, rust, gray, green (green!), black—all alive, writhing and dripping. He also recognized a slip, and something else he thought was a brassiere. But what were those other strange slimy beasts that menaced him with sharp hooks and eyes, predatory claws and teeth?

"I knew there was a trap here somewhere," Larnie said aloud. He laughed at the sound of his own voice, partly to keep alive his own sense of himself, for he felt like a swimmer dangerously out of his depth among these complicated submarine creatures. When he turned to look in the mirror, a garment like an octopus swatted him across the forehead with two of its cold metal tentacles. Rubbing his bruises with vague foreboding, he wondered whether he would ever find his way out again, whole and alive, as simply as he had entered with his simple need.

Still sunk in thought, Larnie bathed hastily; dressed; went downstairs; flung himself on the great scarlet S-curve of Rosie's new sofa. But its serpentine form was never intended to accommodate his long straight one, and with a groan he got up again.

There was the door; he had only to walk through it to regain his independence. But instead he turned his back on it and contemplated his surroundings. So this was to be his home.

—Only temporarily, Larnie quickly promised himself. Only until he got a job, any job, and could afford a place of his own.

Like a newly caged lion, he paced Rosie's brittle jungle of hot-colored ceramics and African masks and gleaming tables, and tried not to think of how little time she would need to tame him.

Madison Drive had already begun to change subtly from Dolly's awesome first memory of it. By the time Rosie and Granny and Mom moved in, the trees that had lined the street were already thinning out, and the last embattled white families were holding out against the steady swarms of Negroes who were cheerfully settling in on all sides with their flocks of children, their beat-up furniture, their audacious music, their aromatic cooking and their big shiny cars. On every visit Dolly counted fewer trees and more Chryslers, Cadillacs and Lincolns, and wondered. The tall houses were still formal, but they were somehow more approachable; life was moving into all the available spaces, and its attendant threat of chaos hung over everything.

One sign of chaos was the door of Rosie's house swinging open, probably left that way by the party guests who had drifted in and out until morning. Dolly let herself into the long dark hall that must have once been an impressive gallery of embalmed portraits and, passing the arch that led to the front room, caught a glimpse of Larnie on the couch. He was leaning back against folded arms, eyes abstracted to the ceiling. Something proprietary in his pose suggested that he was now a part of this household, though it seemed strained and awkward, as if he were still unsure of his role in it. It would have been better, Dolly thought, if he were barefoot and arrogantly picking his teeth.

All this was a flashing impression, lasting less than two seconds, before he noticed her and smiled in a grimacing way. He jerked an ironic thumb upward to indicate that Rosie was still in bed.

At that moment Rosie's grandmother suddenly appeared from some shadowy recess of the house, broom in hand, her head shrouded in a quaint lace dusting cap.

"I guess that lazy girl is still sleeping," she grumbled. "You can go on up, though. It's time she was awake."

Granny led the way up the dark curving staircase. "This here is the original wood," she said. "Over fifty years old. You feel these stair treads? Solid. Not a creak anywhere."

It would take Dolly many more years of knowing Rosie to understand all the reasons why she had wanted to own this particular house, but now, hearing the pride in the old lady's voice, she knew the main one. Granny would never have lived as mistress in Miss Helen's house . . . but she was convinced this one was even better. It was the perfect compromise, satisfying both her urge to grandeur and her deeply ingrained sense of place.

Granny revered Miss Helen Livesey's house. She had shown it to Dolly on walks through the neighborhood, with bitter disapproval for the "field niggers" who were its tenants now. "Look at 'em," she would say, pointing to an innocent-looking cluster of children on the porch, "makin' finger marks all over Miss Helen's piazza." And she would scream at them until they scattered in sullen groups. She had taken Dolly down the streets of this neighborhood and made her cry real tears for the bygone splendor of those tall brooding mansions that now teemed with too many Negroes. Whenever Dolly walked with her she felt herself slipping, bit by bit, into the invisible past, until its orderly patterns became more real than the chaotic present that flowed around them.

"Here we are," Granny said now, and grandly flung open a door as if exposing some rare work of art to view for the first time. But instead there was only the sunlight streaming across Rosie, nude, curled up in the middle of the wide pink bed like the little dry nut in the center of the giant bonbon.

Granny walked over and shook her energetically by the shoulder. "Wake up, girl. Wake up and cover yourself. You got a visitor."

Rosie sat up shamelessly, yawning, scratching her matted curls. "Oh, Doll. You still here? Party's over." Then she groaned as if remembering all she had been through in the past twelve hours. "Somebody shut them damn window blinds. The light makes so much noise I can't hear myself think."

"—That's better, Granny. Thanks," she said as the old lady snapped the cords rapidly, like machine-gun shots. She regarded Dolly through slitted sandy eyes. "What time is it?"

"Three o'clock."

"In the afternoon?"

"Yes."

Rosie sighed and stretched voluptuously. "Oh, hell, you might's well stick around then. Next party starts in six hours." Then she seemed to have an alarming thought. "But what day is it, Dolly?"

"Sunday."

"Oh, thank God," Rosie said in a husky fervent voice. She dropped back on the bed. "Thank God. I thought by now it might be Monday. I'm supposed to start back at Schwartz's tomorrow. I thought I was six hours late my first day back on the job." Coughing mingled with her laughter, drowned it. At last she got it under control.

"I came by to see how you were feeling, Rosie," Dolly said

when she was quiet. "I was worried. You were awfully sick last night."

Rosie looked at her hard. "Fool, I wasn't sick. I was just drunk. Don't you know the difference?"

"What do you want for breakfast, Rosalie?" Granny interrupted sweetly. "How about some Canada bacon and a nice omelet?"

"Oh, Granny, don't mention food to me." Rosie rolled her eyes eloquently. "Not the way my stomach feels."

"You haven't had anything to eat, that's what's wrong with you now."

"No, Granny. Please. If you say another word about food, I'll be sick, I know it. Just go away. Please. Go away."

The old lady made a phantom disappearance that was too quick for Rosie's remorseful, "Oh, Granny, I'm sorry. Come back. I'm sorry."

"Oh, Doll, I'm so mean," she wailed, beating the bed with her fists. "You hear how I talk to her? What makes me so mean?"

"You're only mean to yourself, Rosie."

Again that glaring, suspicious stare Dolly knew so well. "What you talkin' about?"

"I'm talking about you. Going back to work at that store when you ought to be in a hospital."

Rosie's eyes narrowed with sudden determination. She bounded purposefully from the bed, ran over to her fantastically cluttered dressing table and returned with a nearly full bottle of perfume which she thrust into Dolly's hands with one hand while buttoning a mammoth mannish shirt with the other.

"Present," she said. "Girl, if you thank me I'll kill you. I'm sick to death of the stuff."

Dolly took it; she had no choice. Refusing a present from Rosie was as impossible as refusing the love of a child. She gave freely, asking nothing in return but the opportunity to give more. It was like a disease, as if she were trying to bleed herself of the miserable germ of poverty that had lodged early in her blood. It was also a way of getting around Dolly. Whenever she presumed too much on their friendship by offering advice, Rosie teasingly threatened her with a present.

—God, the presents Rosie had thrust on her, Dolly thought angrily—the presents, all tinged with blackmail and cunningly disguised as hand-me-downs to make refusal impossible. Clothes. Jewelry. A wrist watch. A radio—

"Rosie," Granny said, so close behind Dolly she started in the midst of her troubled thoughts.

She had come into the room as swiftly and silently as she had left it, without so much as ruffling the air with her tiny presence.

"That person named Miltie was here again. He left this for you." With distaste, she dropped a foul sack of clinking coins on the bed. "I took it from him, Rosie, but I've told you before, I don't like him coming around here. If you have to see him on business, do it someplace else."

So that was Granny's attitude, too: "I don't care what you do, as long as you keep it out of the house. Break the law, get in trouble, kill yourself even, it's all right as long as I don't know. As long as you don't make a mess on my rugs." With sudden repugnance Dolly looked at the old lady's hooded cobra eyes and thought they veiled sinister threats.

"I will from now on, Granny," Rosie said meekly. "I promise. I'm sorry if he bothered you."

"All right, Rosie. That's all I ask. I don't think it's too much."

"*Yes*, Granny."

"And Rosie, Larnie's downstairs." She shot a sudden piercing glance at her granddaughter. "Rosie, did he spend the night here?"

Rosie tossed her head with transparent nonchalance. "Oh, Granny, how do I know? This place is too big for me to keep track of everybody who stays in it."

"Well, he wants to use the car. I told him—"

"Never mind, Granny," Rosie said, leaping up, revealing thighs like brittle twigs beneath the tentlike shirt. "Just tell him I'll be right down."

As she stepped into Army-chino shorts and zipped up their fly and raked a comb through her three-inch ringlets Dolly tried to imagine Rosie leading a normal woman's life with Larnie or any other man, and could not. Impossible that those narrow hips would ever bear a child, or that this slender patience could ever carry the responsibility for another life.

A slash of bright red lipstick, and Rosie was dressed for the day.

"Come on," she said, suddenly all energy. "Let's go see what my lazy lover wants now."

He was still sprawled on the living room sofa, handsome and sullen, a little overweight now, but with skin tawny all over like caramel candy and great golden eyes like a cat's and the movements of a lazy spoiled cat and the same kind of casual underlying strength.

"Sun's high in the sky," Rosie said to him. "Thought you was goin' out to look for a job today."

"I changed my mind," he said sulkily.

"Well you can just change it again," she said. "We don't need no loafers around here."

He looked at her steadily. "What'd you hide the car keys for? You knew I had to go see about a job."

She took the keys from the pocket of her shorts and twirled them around her finger. "What's the matter, you too great to walk or something?"

"Ah, shoot," he said, turning his face to the wall. "Rosie, I told you that job was way out in West Chester. I was supposed to be there at nine this morning."

She crossed the room and stood over him, twirling the keys. When she spoke her voice crackled over him like electricity.

"If you wanted that job bad enough you would of got up at six this morning 'n hitch-hiked out there. Walked. Crawled. You didn't need no car keys from me. Your feet could of got you there. But here you are, still stretched out on my sofa, 'cause you're nothin' but a lazy bum."

He turned to face her angrily. "I wanted that job, all right. I wanted it bad enough to go see the man on a Sunday. It's your fault I didn't get there."

"Don't fault me 'cause you fouled yourself," she said pertly.

"Give me the keys," he said, his face screwed up in determination.

"Ask me nice." She cocked her head to one side and hid the keys behind her.

"Bitch," he growled. "Give me them keys."

"Make me."

One deft arm whipped out like a snake and pinned her to the couch. He scrambled around until she was trapped, giggling and squirming, beneath him. "Shut up that laughing," he said, and pressed his fingers over her mouth while his other hand worked the keys out of her clenched fist. But as soon as he released her Rosie began to giggle again.

"I said shut up that laughing," he said, looking down at her. "What's so goddamn funny?"

"Nothin', baby," she said, choking. "Just—you don't need that job anyway. You know you got me to take care of you now."

He slapped her, a hard stinging blow that made her eyes bulge wide and fill with tears.

"Larnie. Larnie baby," she said, holding her face in her hands. "I'm sorry."

He touched her head gently. "Yeah," he said, "I'm sorry too. But it don't make things any different."

She sighed. "I just didn't want you to take that job, lover. That's why I kept the keys."

She turned to Dolly for support. "Unloadin' crates at a warehouse, Dolly, it'd tear up his hands in a week. I already got him a better job, at Benny's, playin' piano. But he's so damn stubborn—" She clucked her tongue. "He wants to find his own job, no matter what kind."

"You can't understand that, can you?" he said angrily.

"No," she said, staring at him. "No, I can't. I never could understand mules. I think they're the dumbest animals in the world. Why don't you go see Benny? He pays good money, and he wants a piano player. And that's what you are."

Dolly saw the exact moment when he gave up the battle, his

shoulders caving in as he looked down at Rosie and shrugged. "All right. I'll talk to him."

"Well, thank God," Rosie said. "Thank God."

He left the room with a slouching purposelessness in his walk, all the tension gone from his magnificent frame.

"Pour me a drink, Dolly," Rosie said from her incredible scroll-shaped couch. "Make yourself one too."

Dolly brought the drinks and sat down beside her. The tears were not dry on Rosie's cheeks, but the determined set had already returned to her fierce little face.

"Rosie," Dolly said softly, "when are you going to quit knocking yourself out? When are you going to slow down long enough for him to marry you?"

Rosie tossed her drink down in one gulp. "I can't marry him, Doll. He's no good."

"He's too good," Dolly said. "He'd do anything for you."

Rosie looked at her sharply.

"He wants to work. He wants to take care of you."

Rosie turned the glass in her hands, which were trembling. "He ain't big enough to take care of me. Nobody is." She caught Dolly's hand. "Doll, you remember what it was like when we used to live downtown? Our house was so small the rats came out of the walls in the apartment. They were too crowded in the cellar." She gave a raucous laugh. "Mom was out workin' all day. My father didn't take care of her. He was gone when I was four years old. Granny was ironin' clothes when she should've been on a pension. Her white folks didn't take care of her. So I made up my mind I was gonna take care of myself."

She leaped up and flicked the switch on the record player. "And I am takin' care of myself, cuddy, don't you worry. Never worry 'bout this mule." The record spun crazily on the machine, wobbling as it went round and round. Rosie spun and spun about the room. She was a very good dancer.

"Rosie," Dolly said, "what are you going to do?"

"Do?" Rosie laughed, stopped dancing and shut off the music at the switch so that the sound died in a moan. "I'm gonna go up'n see Granny, that's what I'm gonna do. Gonna show her the new things I bought for my hope chest. Wanta come along?"

And, skipping, she led Dolly up the stairs.

Granny's bedroom was a fantastic jumble of precious bric-a-brac and cheap furnishings, the souvenirs of her long dual life. They sat together—the old lady erect on a French chair fragile as a dream, and Rosie at her feet on a fat plastic hassock—like two hens clucking over pieces of grain, inspecting the new lingerie and linens for Rosie's "hope chest." Granny was sewing, as usual; her hands were always fussing with some piece of exquisite and utterly useless work. Today she was etching a fine square of flowers on a satin cushion that no one would ever dare use. At Rosie's insistence, she laid it aside and held a nightgown up to the light so that the delicate stitching showed through.

"That's a real fine piece of handwork there," she said in her voice like the music of flutes. "Not quite as nice as Miss Helen's linens, though."

She took up her embroidery again and began to ramble, the old pictures falling into place in her mind like the fragments of color in a kaleidoscope.

"I remember Miss Emilie's weddin', Rosalie," she chanted. "They wouldn't let nobody make them little sandwiches and pastries but me, and nobody else could serve 'em, neither. And I dipped the champagne punch out of a real solid crystal bowl that were in Miss Helen's family ever since Lincoln was President. It had carved trimmin's all over," she said, moving her old fingers as though they could still feel the relief beneath them. "I was the only one they could trust to handle it. It must have weighed pret'near thirty pounds, but I always polished it and put it away by myself. I was strong in those days." She made a silvery little chuckle. "I almost got to thinkin' that bowl belonged to me, 'cause I was the only one took care of it. You could look in it and see rainbows. I used to hold it up to the light and see 'em all the time. I always called it my Rainbow Bowl."

Rosie was breathless. "What happened? Did it get broken?"

"Oh, no, child. 'Course not. Told you nobody took care of

treasures like that but me. Let me think now, what did happen to my bowl?"

She concentrated, eyes closed, head lifted to catch the thread of memory wound in the complex web of her brain. Then her eyes opened, and they were bright and young. She snapped her fingers. As she talked the light in her eyes slowly died. "I remember now. Yes, I remember. It was sold along with all the other things when we moved. All the pretty things in that house sold and gone. Lord, that was a terrible day. A terrible, terrible day." She moaned softly as she rocked back and forth. "Rosalie, that house was a palace. A real palace for kings and queens."

"Granny, how much you think a bowl like that would cost? Today, I mean?" Rosie asked urgently.

"Lord, child, I don't know. Hundreds of dollars, I guess. It was a mighty rich piece of work."

"Dolly!" Rosie called from across the room. "Bring me that pile of magazines over there."

"I guess I ought to be going," Dolly said, rising.

"Don't be an ass," Rosie said sharply. Granny clucked, and Rosie's hand flew to her mouth. Then laughter welled up and she stifled it in her sleeve. "Just bring the magazines, for God's sake."

Dolly lifted the heavy stack of *Harper's Bazaar*s, *House Beautiful*s and *Town and Country*s, magazines in which Rosie read not one word of editorial print, but which she bought because, as she had told Dolly, "I like to look at the ads."

Rosie scrabbled furiously through the pages, flipping through one magazine in a few moments to toss it aside and grab another, while Granny sat and rocked and sewed patiently, a little abstract smile on her withered face. Finally Rosie found what she was looking for. She thrust a full-color advertisement under Granny's eyes.

"Is that it, Granny?" Her voice was soft but urgent. "Is that your bowl?"

"Yes," the old lady breathed after a profound silence. "Yes." Her eyes suddenly glistened with tears. "It was just like that. Every way."

"That's all I wanted to know, Granny." Rosie scrambled to her feet and tossed the magazine across the room.

"Child," Granny said, taking one of Rosie's hands in both of hers, "you ain't goin' to run out and buy that thing for me?"

Rosie hesitated, then said, "Well, we'll see." She patted the old lady's bun of fuzzy white hair.

"I don't want you to do that, Rosie," Granny said, shaking her head slowly. "I know that thing must cost pret'near a hundred dollars. You shouldn't be spending that kind of money on foolishness."

Rosie plucked playfully at her grandmother's cheek. "How many times I told you not to worry 'bout money 'n things like that? It's time for your nap, anyway."

"Rosalie, I don't want you to—" the old lady murmured feebly. But when Rosie was gone a smile of pure childish anticipation illuminated her face.

She picked up one of the petticoats Rosie had bought. "We'll save this one for her wedding," she confided to Dolly. "She'll have a real fine wedding like Miss Emilie's. —She ain't gonna marry that musician trash neither," she mumbled as she took up her embroidery again. "She's gonna get herself a nice professional man."

Before Dolly left Granny's room she walked over and picked up the magazine from the floor where Rosie had flung it carelessly. It was still open at the page she had shown Granny, one of those gorgeous full-color Crystal-Craft ads. The object it pictured was the most elegant thing Dolly had ever seen. Beneath it, in chaste slender letters, was printed:

"The Presentation Punch Bowl
Sculptor: Paul Roberts, Commissioned by Crystal-Craft
One Thousand Seven Hundred and Fifty Dollars"

She was still repeating the price under her breath when she walked downstairs again. Rosie crossed the living room swiftly and snatched the magazine from her hands.

"Nosy, ain't you?" she said with a trace of nastiness. "Who said you could look at that?"

"Rosie," Dolly said, "excuse me for asking, but you're not really planning to buy this thing, are you?"

"You're excused," Rosie said. "Maybe I am and maybe I ain't, but in any case it's none of your goddamn business."

"Rosie," Dolly pleaded, "your grandmother's a very old lady. Her memory isn't what it used to be. When she sees a picture in a magazine, maybe she thinks it's something she remembers, but —oh, hell, Rosie, sometimes I think you're just plain crazy."

Rosie flung herself on her stomach on the sofa. Her face contorted, she kicked her legs in the air and pounded her fist into the cushions.

"What I buy is my business, not yours, not nobody else's! I buy it with my money, not with nobody else's money. And nobody's got a right to interfere. Nobody, you hear, Miss Nosy? Oh, why can't people just leave me alone?"

Dolly, on the edge of the sofa, touched her heaving shoulders. "Because they love you, Rosie."

Rosie expelled a violent breath and sat up. "My old fur coat's hangin' in the hall closet. I'm sick 'n tired of it," she said in a voice that was very small and cool and dignified. "I want you to take it."

"And don't let me see you around here again," she screamed as Dolly ran from the room, "unless you got it on!"

26

"Well," Mom said calmly a few weeks later, "that's what God put you on this earth for. Just don't go bringin' it in the world and then expect me to take care of it."

Rosie walked swiftly to the other side of the room. She turned her back and tried to stare at the wallpaper, but it swirled like the ocean before her eyes. "You ain't fit to take care of nothin'," she muttered.

"Yeah, that's what I get for all I went through to bring you up. Nothin' but sass and trouble. I might of known this was comin'. You was a fresh little hussy when you was six years old."

Rosie turned; her mother's blurred, swollen face swam into view. "I didn't learn it at school," she said in a low voice.

"Well, never say you learned it from me," Queenie said. "You never would listen to nothin' I said. You always was stubborn and strong-headed as a mule, even when you was a baby. You used to spit out the bottle fast as I put it in your mouth. 'Course you'd take it from her. Yeah, you'd take anything from her," she repeated with odd satisfaction, "but it's me you come runnin' to first time you get in a little trouble." The rocking chair creaked under Mom's weight as she stirred and settled in a new position.

"I don't know what for," Rosie cried. "I don't know what ever made me think I'd get any help from you."

"Yeah, it was always her," Mom went on, "her you ran to, not me. You'd cut yourself and keep it hid from me all week, lettin' it get all festered and angry, so's she could bandage it when she came home. Then she'd say, 'Queenie, why don't you look after your child?' Hah!" Mom laughed shortly. "You always would spite yourself to spite me. From the day you was born, you was the meanest, spitefullest little baby I ever seen."

"Is that why you always hated me?"

Mom's head jerked back sharply. Her eyes widened and darkened, staring at Rosie as if they had never seen her before. At last she spoke softly. "You was born in a bad year. Maybe you reminded me of too many wrong things."

Mom's fingers tied themselves in a knot in her lap. "I won't lie. I didn't want you, Rosie. You came along just when I was beginning to live my life. But if it hadn't been you it would've been somethin' else, I guess." All her bulk rose and fell in a sigh. She leaned forward tensely. "Look at me, girl. Look at me hard. Can you remember what I used to look like?"

Rosie stared. The stiff, scarred fingers groping toward her filled her with an aching sickness.

247

"I don't remember you ever lookin' any way but the way you look now," she said harshly.

Mom's eyes bulged, but she said nothing for a long time. "Your father lived with us till you was four," she said finally. "You must remember him, Rosie. He used to ride you around on his shoulders. You would hide behind the door every night, and the minute he walked in you'd jump out and holler, 'Get on the horse!'"

Larnie was the big strong man with the jolly face and the comforting ways that she had lost a long time ago and given up hope of ever finding again. But Larnie was forever wanting to be alone, to go out, to work; forever withdrawing into one of his sullen moods, and she was forever fighting because now, after waiting so long, she had a right to all his attention and time. It was Mom's fault that the big jolly man had gone away, leaving Rosie to grow up wild while her mother turned inward to a mirror reflecting the myth of her vanished beauty. Rosie shook her head violently. "Naw. I don't remember nothin' 'bout him."

"Poor little orphan child," Mom said gently. "We was happy then. We could of gone on bein' happy, too, if it hadn't been for her."

Her face became hard and spiteful. "She made out Clevie just married me on account of you bein' on the way. Fact was, he would've married me anyhow. I knew it, but she kept talkin', and it worked on my mind till it wouldn't leave me no peace. Then while I was tied down to home with you she tried to make out he had another woman on the side. All lies."

Mom had lifted the lid of the garbage pail of the past. Rosie did not want to see what was inside. "How you know?" she demanded. "Maybe it was true."

Queenie shook her head stubbornly. "She was out to break us up from the beginning. He didn't suit her high-and-mighty ideas." She chuckled. "She named me 'Queen Victoria Regina' out of some magazine. With a name like that, I had to marry a king. Grover Cleveland Fleming wasn't good enough. He was just named for a President."

Her sigh contained twenty years. "He stuck around a long time though, Rosie. When he couldn't take it no more, he cut out for California. I couldn't blame him."

Rosie's old, passionate, shameful wish came to the fore. "Why didn't you go with him? I could've stayed behind with Granny."

"I asked myself that question many a time. I'll tell you why. I was too soft. I couldn't stand to think what might happen to you."

Her hand caught Rosie's in a sandpaper grip. "When I saw you wasn't gonna be good-lookin', I knew you had to be tough. Maybe I done wrong, but it's too late to change now. She made it harder for me, spoilin' you all the time, till I had to be twice as rough on you. Sometimes I had to act tough just to keep from spillin' love all over you." She wiped her eyes. "When you gave me back sharp answers it hurt me bad, Rosie, but I was glad inside. It meant you could take anything and throw it back, too. Now you got to tell me, baby. Tell me if I done wrong." Mom was choking; it was the hardest thing she'd ever had to say.

Rosie could not make it any easier. The comforting words backed up in her and became a dry cough that bent her in two.

"Baby? You sick?" Queenie drew the quaking shoulders against her knees, trying to quiet them. Rosie shook her head. But the coughing made her a liar.

Finally she was able to say, "It shouldn't surprise you I don't wanna get married. You're the one taught me to be independent."

Queenie sighed. "I know, I know."

"And what my father did ain't my fault. It ain't my fault Roscoe left you, neither."

To her surprise, her mother laughed. Roared. "You still think I hold that against you?"

"Yes." Rosie stared at her gravely. "And you know what else I think? I think you're jealous now 'cause you got nobody, and I got Larnie."

"Well, you're wrong," her mother said. "You couldn't be more wrong, Rosie. I don't even think about Roscoe no more. Getting married to him was just a crazy notion I had. I knew it even while I was talkin' about it. A man like that laughs at marriage, whether he goes through with it or not."

She stroked Rosie's hair. "Larnie's different though, thank God. And I'm not jealous one bit, Rosie. Just glad, 'cause I know he'll be good to you."

"For a while, you mean."

"No. Forever. I could die in peace if I saw you married to him."

Rosie, on her knees, was coughing again. And crying, too.

"Go on and marry him, child," her mother's voice said from far above her. "He'll take good care of you."

Rosie pulled her face back and gave Mom one of her stubborn looks.

"I should've kept my mouth shut," Queenie said immediately. "I should've known, whatever I said, you'd do the opposite."

"It ain't that—" Rosie began.

"It's her, ain't it? She don't think he's good enough. Well, she'll be dead soon. What's she gonna do for you then? You ain't good enough for her neither, ain't you found that out yet? You ain't gonna be good enough till you turn white."

"Shut up!" Rosie howled.

Mom went on more quietly, "Rosie, listen, forget it's your Mom talkin' to you, just listen to what I say. You're sick. You ain't in no condition to cross Nature. You got to marry him and stay home and take it easy."

Rosie jumped to her feet and stared at her mother. "You been talkin' a long time. You still ain't said nothin'."

Mom's broad face was wrinkled in perplexity like a bulldog's. "Rosie, what's happened to you won't hurt you, it's what a woman's made for. But you try and cross it up, sick as you are, you'll wish you had the trouble you got now."

"I'll ask you one more time," Rosie said. "You plan on helpin' me or not?"

"I swear, I never hoped to help a child of mine that way."

Queenie heaved herself up from the chair and was supported briefly on her hands before she sank. The chair rocked vigorously in rhythm with her panting breaths. "I'm scared, Rosie. Look."

Her outstretched hands were blurred by tremors. Rosie's unwilling eyes, slanting past them, caught the amber gleam of a bottle beneath her mother's shawl. "Baby, I can't help you. —Baby! Ain't you gonna say nothin'?"

At the door, Rosie hesitated, then said, "You tried."

Holding her wrist to keep it steady, she dialed the number, heard the clicks like balls dropping into place on a pool table. Finally a sultry movie-star voice came on with, "Hello, there."

"Let me speak to Shadow," she said.

She got Granny out to a church supper, then went to work on Larnie. She found him in the little room on the third floor where he retreated most afternoons to his hi-fi and his hundreds of records. Rosie recognized the one who was with him, a little goateed drummer, called Machine for his precision and his tirelessness, who was mad like all drummers, his mind driven to fever pitch by the incessant rhythms he heard even in silence. She had seen Machine often on the sidewalk, rapt eyes rolling to heaven as he caressed his long elegant conga drum, surrounded like a black Pied Piper by crowds of children and youths. As they swayed, arched their young backs, rolled their pelvises, shuffled their feet to his hypnotic rhythms, you began to believe that this man could make all Africa rise again, right there on the Avenue. If he played long enough, they would cast off their civilization like their badly fitting clothes from Schwartz's, seize spears and descend, in howling naked hordes, on the white usurpers of their power.

But why Larnie chose to spend his days with music, when he had to spend his nights producing it at Benny's, was an infuriating mystery which Rosie took as a personal affront. Her own obsession, money, was no help in understanding someone else's passion—particularly for something as frivolous as music, particularly when it was preferred to her company. There he sat, eyes closed, playing on an imaginary keyboard, while Machine thumped soft dub-dubs to accompany Miles Davis's moaning trumpet. As they swayed gently in unison, she recognized and resented a primitive male ritual that shut her out. To drive a wedge into it, she gave her voice the sarcastic cutting edge of an axe.

"I hate to interrupt you music lovers. But have you ordered your tux yet, Larnie? You know you got to take me to the Blues' Promenade this Saturday."

Larnie looked up with a grimace; he hated formals and stiff high-society functions. "Aw, Rosie, do I have to?"

Now that she had his attention, she teased, "I got me a sharp black dress 'n a sharp yellow escort. I can't disappoint my public."

He made the mistake of giving in a little. "There's still plenty of time, hon. I can rent one the same day."

"Not to go with Rosie you can't!" she screeched. "I don't want you in no rented tux. It's got to be made to order." She put her hands on his shoulders from behind and rubbed up against him. Briefly, reluctantly, he was hers again.

"You think I'd let you put these shoulders in ready-mades?" she said. She pressed some money into his hand.

He pushed it away, scowling. "I'd rather not go, Rosie."

"I know!" she screamed. "You'd rather stay home 'n listen to records." She ran over to her enemy, the phonograph. "You can't even turn this thing off when I'm talkin' to you. Well, I'm gonna put a stop to that. Right now!"

She snatched up Miles Davis and hurled him to the floor. He shattered satisfyingly. "That's only the first one!" she proclaimed. "You're gonna take me to that dance if I have to smash every record in this room."

Machine ducked and cringed as another platter bounced off the wall above his head. Shrapnel splattered down on him.

"Man," he said drolly, making for the door, his precious drum wrapped in his overcoat, "you should've told me your pad had fallout."

"Rosie, what's wrong with you?" Larnie asked. "Have you gone crazy, or what?"

She was infuriated by his mildness. "Nothing, you big dumb ape! I just want you to pay me some attention for a change."

"I'll pay you some attention all right," he said grimly. He grabbed her arm as it reached for one of his rare Art Tatum records.

"Careful, man," warned Machine from the doorway. "I do believe that woman is radioactive. —Look out!" he yelped, for Rosie was free again. "Body and Soul" spun up to the ceiling like a rifle target. A second later it lay in slivers around her triumphant feet.

With a muttered, "So long, man. I got to find me a shelter *now*," Machine disappeared.

"Boy, this feels good," Rosie said, panting happily. "I might take up music as a hobby." She looked around her wildly. "Now, lemme see. What else can I smash?"

Larnie simply said then, "You win," and took the money from her hand.

"You better hurry," she told him. "The tailor closes early tonight. —And make sure he gets all your measurements right the first time!"

She closed the door behind him; locked it; leaned against it, breathing heavily, for several seconds; then ran to tell her mother that they were alone.

Shadow was punctual, as she had known he would be, arriving on the dot of seven.

"You a doctor?" Queenie asked suspiciously. "You don't look like no doctor to me."

"Please, Mom," Rosie begged. "Just help him. He knows what he's doin'."

He bent over her. A river of ice started wherever he touched her. "If you'd worked for me this'd never happened," he told her. "I take good care of my girls."

He was hurting her, but she managed to laugh. "Then how come you learned 'bout this stuff, Shadow?"

"I'd prefer it," he said softly, "if you'd refer to me as Mister Jones. You understand. In situations like this, some things are always beyond our control."

His prickly whispering shot needles of fear through her, but she laughed again. "Okay. Get it over with, Shadow."

"How long?" Mom asked fearfully.

He looked at his watch. "It will take about two hours, I should say. You," he told her, "must hold her down and keep her quiet."

He took off his dark glasses. Rosie squeezed her lids together to avoid glimpsing his unnatural eyes. All the tremors were gone from Mom's hands when they gripped her shoulders; the strong fingers seemed to have thoughts of their own, like Larnie's.

She fought it, stiffening and even laughing when she could, until it became a hopeless muddle of her own pain and someone else's cries. The worst was the clear moment when he approached her with a wad of cotton soaked in chloroform and she looked up at last into his blank colorless eyes and knew who he was and was glad to see him coming.

27

Here he came again, busting in the house like a cannonball. Slamming doors and stomping like a two-ton truck on wheels. He stumbled over a scatter rug in the hall and nearly upset one of the twin gilt twigs of chairs that had flanked Miss Helen's sitting room doors.

You'd think he never had no home, Lourinda thought. Great big overgrown mule of a boy. You'd think he was raised in the woods somewhere.

He skidded to a stop at the foot of the stairs and leaned an elbow on the post to strike a match. He was wearing another of those vivid corduroy sports shirts that Rosie bought him; this one was wine-red, and opened to the hollow of his chest. When she moved toward him he looked up suddenly. With surprise coloring his cheeks, he was showy as a sunset.

"Didn't know you was here," he said.

"This is my house. Where else would I be?" she demanded, silently disposing of him, along with all other gaudy things, with a single word: "common." But her voice had betrayed her nervousness over how close he'd come to smashing her precious things. She looked around furiously for a change of subject; found it in the flat parcel draped casually over his arm.

"Them my granddaughter's dresses you draggin' all over the floor?"

The brown paper rattled a warning as he jerked it away from her. "Not hers or yours neither," he said rudely.

He made as if to start upstairs, then turned back suddenly and held the package out to her, ripping it open with his thumb. "It's my new made-to-order tux. Go on, Granny. You know you wanta see it."

I'm no relation of yours, she thought, bristling. Never will be, neither. But her fingers groped, then greedily ravished the irresistible powdery down of cashmere. They tore at the paper, and what showed through was dully blue.

"You plan on wearin' a blue suit to take my granddaughter to the ball?"

"Midnight blue, Granny. The latest and greatest. Cuts black any day." He did a tap step that landed him, with a shattering crash, four treads further up her hardwood stairs. "Practical, too, Granny. After tonight, it'll look good up on the bandstand."

Laughing, he charged up the stairs, crackling paper as he went, a common loud-mouthed tavern musician who was, if anything, even more vulgar in her presence.

Lourinda heard him stomp into Rosie's bedroom. "Hey, skinny mama, you dressed yet? Look what I got to wear to our wedding!" There were delighted squeals and a great rustling of paper. Then the door was closed.

From the hall table Mrs. Lourinda Baxter Huggs picked up a square inch of carved crystal, one of her antique butter chips defiled by his ashes. She gazed down her long dim hall until it became that other hall, long ago, where she had supervised endless processions of ignorant little milk-faced maids in the polishing of silver and the waxing of floors. And they had all called her "ma'am"; they had better if they knew what was good for them.

"He's just too big," she finally exploded. "He's too big to fit in any place but a stable. This," she told the respectful silence, "is a home."

Upstairs, Queenie was saying, "I ain't gonna let her go. Look at her. I never knew somethin' that black could be that pale."

Rosie, as if to contradict her, dug into the rouge jar and rubbed her cheeks more orange.

Queenie snatched the jar from her. "You gonna get back in that bed? Or do I have to pick you up, sick as I am, and throw you in?"

Larnie, sensing that this was the first of their quarrels that concerned him, hung on the outskirts more uneasily than usual. The two women were not absorbed in each other and so did not exclude him. Rosie, in her floor-length slip, stared into the mirror. Mom, in her housecoat, glared at the wall. He was expected to do something. But his mind, dulled by the habit of deafness to their regular arguments, was unable to decide what it might be.

Now Rosie's eyes leveled with his in the mirror. "Hand me my hairbrush, Larnie."

He sprang to obey.

"Give me that." Queenie snatched the brush from him and advanced on her daughter as though she intended to use it upside down. But instead, reaching up awkwardly so that he realized for the first time that Rosie was taller than her mother, she began brushing out the tiny curls at the nape of the thin neck, taking gentle pains to fluff each one. "That Cecil don't know how to curl you," she complained softly. "You got fine little baby hairs back here."

Again the eyes in the mirror slid to his. "Larnie, look on the dresser, you'll see my wave clips, bring 'em here."

"Sit still, boy," Queenie ordered before he could get moving. "She's got enough waves for two heads now."

He sat, listening nervously to the rhythmic crackling of the brush.

Queenie started up again after a short silence. "You can go to all the dances you want next month. Just keep your hips home tonight. You ain't had but four, five days to get over it."

He rose then, reluctantly, letting one hand cling to the chair for security. "Get over what, Mom? What are you talkin' about?"

His words underscored his status as interloper in this family. Queenie was not his Mom, Rosie was not his wife, and at any time either of them could tell him she was none of his business. Most of his behavior in the house was calculated to avoid getting told.

"I had a little stomach upset the other night," Rosie said lightly, ducking her head into the brush to stop it in the middle of a stroke. "Mom, what you tryin' to do, make me bald? —Hey, clown, I thought I told you to bring me them wave clips."

Queenie stood with her hand, holding the brush, surprised in mid-air. "You promised me you'd rest and you lied. Now you stay home, or I'm gonna tell him."

The eyes in the mirror flew to him like trapped birds. "What you standin' there for? Go put your tux on."

"You been sick again, Rosie?" He took a step toward her. "How come you didn't tell me?"

Her laugh sounded false. "Will you go get dressed, fool?"

"I think you oughta tell him, Rosie," Mom said doggedly. "Right now."

He had a sudden hollow feeling that it was too late anyway. For too long he had ignored all the warnings; now the horror, whatever it was, was upon them. He looked from his beloved's bony features, burnt cinnamon dusted to mat brown, eyes spangled and mascaraed to distract attention from the deep hollows beneath them, to Queenie, her harvest moon face sagging and shining with sweat, and saw for the first time a strong resemblance.

"You broke your promise," Rosie said so coldly a knife turned in him, until he realized that she was talking to her mother.

"You broke yours," Queenie said.

He faced Rosie and caught her naked shoulders in his hands.

257

He was shocked, as always, by the delicacy of the bones. "Tell me or I'll shake it out of you."

Her eyes rolled drolly, teasing him, and her tongue flicked its bait between her teeth. "Don't believe her, lover. She's just jealous 'cause she ain't goin'. She—" A tiny "chee" came from her, a bird's surprised cry of pain. She hugged herself, doubled up on her folded arms and skittered into the bathroom. The door was locked before either of them could reach it.

"Let me in, baby!" Queenie screamed, banging on the door. It did not yield; neither did the solid silence behind it. She turned and beat on Larnie instead. "Get that door open, fool! She's havin' a hemorrhage in there."

He prisoned her flabby arms in his fingers. "You let her kill my baby?"

She seemed to be coming apart; it was like seeing a mountain shake in a storm. She tore free with massive strength; struck him again and again until he sank to his knees; continued flailing his head with both her hands.

"Aah," she cried in hoarse tearing sobs, "aah. Fuck your baby. I've killed my baby."

Larnie took his turn banging at the blank door, using his hands like clubs. When he had dreamed of becoming a concert pianist he had massaged them every night with vaseline. Now he wished he had spent his life splitting rocks, so his hands might be hard enough to make a dent in that door. They could not, of course, but he kept hammering for the satisfaction of seeing them become torn and raw. When he gave up, the silence on the other side was dense.

There would be no more help from Queenie—she had retreated, like a great wounded cat, into some dark cave of animal woe, and was giving out deep hissing sobs and moans. He slumped against the wall and waited—waiting was all you ever did in the really important moments—waited, with dull resignation, for the final horror to appear, faceless and with hair like snakes.

But when the door suddenly opened it was only Rosie, with a calm scrubbed face that was, if anything, less pale.

He stared at its empty composure and thought that perhaps this was the final horror after all. That women could carry life and death inside them, curled against each other like the yang and the yin, as casually as they carried their pocketbooks, and make the choice as lightly as they chose a white purse or a black one.

"Why, Rosie?" he asked her hoarsely. "Why?"

Her eyes opened wide on blank innocence. "A baby, lover?" she asked gravely. "What would I do with a baby?"

He sagged to the bed, cold, yet sweating. "I don't know," he admitted. "You're a baby yourself."

She was already busy again at the mirror, reapplying the mask of glamour—false color, false eyelashes, false everything—industriously decorating an abyss.

"You could at least have told me, Rosie," he said.

She turned. The effect, even though he had watched her create it, would be enchanting if he could forget what she was, a murderess.

Running her little finger daintily along the edge of her lip, she answered, "Why? Wasn't nothing you could do about it."

He had been swimming in an ocean of horror all evening, but now he touched its bottom and felt unspeakable things crawl and slither beneath his feet. You trusted women. You believed they had been given so much power because they were in touch with some mysterious source of knowledge that made things come out all right. Yes. But suppose you trusted them and then, in the critical moments, they turned out to be the same fools you saw every day in restaurants, chattering like parakeets, and in stores, fighting over ribbons and costume jewelry? With reeling but relentless logic he realized that this outcome was far more likely than the fantastic notion that these featherbrains were engaged in some mystical communion with Truth. Larnie wondered how the world had kept going so long. How much longer it could keep going. Watching her dispose of her powder puff with the same nonchalance that she had disposed of his child, he wondered about everything he had always taken for granted.

God Bless the Child

"I shouldn't have had to do anything," he growled. "I should've been able to trust you. But I won't any more. Wash that mess off your face and get in bed. You're not going anywhere tonight."

She turned back to him, frightened by the sudden authority in his voice. She said, with sudden guilty eagerness to please, "Sure, Larnie, if you want me to. Sure."

Now she was sorry. Now. Oh Lord.

Even Queenie was roused from her primitive stupor long enough to stare at him and say, "Boy, why couldn't you ever talk to her like that before?"

He could not answer. As he stood there, mute, his rage at Rosie emptied out of him and left a sour residue of shame, shame at his own endless duckings and dodgings and delays, his fatal postponing of the business of being a man. He looked at the girl who was waiting obediently for him to tell her what to do, and she was no longer Medusa but Rosie. Their eyes met across the room in a brief flicker of recognition, like stars sending faint messages across outer space.

"Never mind," he said. "What difference does it make now? It's like lockin' an empty barn." He patted her shoulder with awkward sadness to soften that unnecessary cruelty. "Go ahead and get dressed, hon. So will I. Maybe we'll even have a good time."

With the help of a tumblerful of gin, he got through his own preparations, coming out of his alcoholic fog only when it was necessary to subdue the silly bow tie, then returned to Rosie's room to watch the women at their deadly serious rites of frivolity.

Granny brought in the dress, a mountain of black froth fresh from the ironing board, and helped Rosie into it with elaborate cluckings. Rosie preened and posed for her benefit; Queenie, the wreck of her sunk in a chair, paid no attention. She seemed deflated to a heap of bones, as though all her bulk had been a mere puffiness of air. She made no further protest while Rosie chattered and finished dressing, and when her daughter backed toward her she reached up obediently and did the hooks with terrible robotlike efficiency.

At last came the moment when Rosie turned to face him with

a model's assurance and Granny's crystal beads flashing fire around her neck. Her mouth made a sly curve, and her eyes slid toward him hungrily. But as if in a dream, when he reached out to her, she took a floating step toward the old lady, and he knew that none of her seductiveness was meant for him.

Somehow they found their way to the hall where colored society's most exclusive male club, the True Blues, was holding its famous annual pre-Christmas dance. Without exchanging a word, they headed straight for the bar. They kept up with each other in grim silence, downing Martini after Martini with workmanlike efficiency, while around them flowed a laughing crowd of Negroes in formal dress, the men dapper in tuxedos, the women dazzling in silks and furs and gems. So assured was this crowd in its elegance that an ignorant alien might well believe the United States to be populated with exotic black millionaires and drab white peasants.

What a wonderful dream, Larnie thought, temporarily beguiled; what a wonderfully different country it would be. Expanding in the first warm glow of the gin, he constructed a brief fantasy in which the jazz pianist Erroll Garner was elected President, and, having appointed a Cabinet of striking sports and entertainment figures, decreed that all political speeches would henceforth be scored instead of written. Applause. . . .

But in the morning, these gorgeous costumes would turn to rags. It was all a mirage, a cruel fake, but Rosie, God help her, believed in it. It exhilarated her, and now she wanted to dance.

Dolly, who was already in the ballroom, in white hoop-skirted lace like a Southern belle, her glasses tucked in her white satin evening bag, a bracelet of white orchids on her wrist, also found herself being drawn onto the floor. Counting time, and concentrating on managing her enormous skirts gracefully, she missed the orchestra's sudden plunge into a swift swing tempo. Her partner, who never jitterbugged, stopped dancing immediately and shifted her protectively behind him, out of the line of fire.

And there she was face to face with Rosie. A blurred, beautiful

Rosie, kicking up a storm of black net and satin, swinging out
in a bold arc at the end of someone's taut arm. At the height
of her swing, a split second ahead of the beat, she ducked her
head to sip from a Martini glass and came up flower-faced and
laughing. She took a little skip toward her partner, shrieked,
dropped his hand, whirled and flung her arms around Dolly,
enveloping her in waves of gin and perfume. She was having one
hell of a time. She hoped Dolly was too. She drew back from the
embrace, wiped her eyes, hiccupped and started scolding.

"Child, where you been? I shouldn't even speak to you. I ain't
heard from you since the last time I invited you over. You got to
have special invitations? Who the hell you think you are? Damn,
you look good, girl. What you been up to? Whatever it is, you
look good!"

Her cigarette in its ebony holder bobbed dangerously beneath
Dolly's nose. "You havin' a good time? You look too serious. Ha
ha, you can't see, that's why. Where's your glasses? —Girl, don't
mind me, it's Mr. Seagram talkin'. Here, meet my friend Mr.
Seagram!"

Dolly obediently swallowed the concoction Rosie forced between her lips.

"Come on, Doll, stop keepin' secrets. Tell me what you been
doin'!"

No one, no one would ever be as glamorous as Rosie. Dolly
felt as if all her life had been preparation for this one moment.
Trembling and ecstatic as when she had offered herself for her
first kiss, she advanced her hand with its winking diamond.

"Damn! You tryin' to blind me?" Rosie mocked. "Why didn't
somebody tell me they was wearin' ice cubes these days? Girl,
I oughta kill you. You went and got engaged without even tellin'
me!"

The sudden dizzying blow of the gin to Dolly's brain mixed
with the happiness bubbling on her lips. "It's all on account of
you, Rosie. —I mean, naturally, you're the first to know."

"Well, I'm waitin'! How about an introduction? Who is he?"

Them That's Not Shall Lose

Now she would hear it, the long-awaited praise. Good old Doll! I never knew you had it in you!

But instead Rosie's glowing face became glazed; her eyes dilated, and for a moment her mouth trembled like a slapped child's.

But for a moment only.

Then she was shaking both their hands in both of hers and stepping back, head cocked on one side like a parakeet's, to survey them as a pair.

"You gonna have five kids," she told them, lifting her glass in a toast, " 'n four of them gonna be light 'n bright like their mama. You can give 'em all them fine movie star names like Lana 'n Rhonda 'n Gary 'n Rory. But watch out for Number Five!" She tipped the empty glass and ran her tongue around inside it. "Li'l Number Five's gonna be dark with nappy hair, and she's the one you gotta name after me."

"Come on over here, Larnie," she called, seizing him by the cuff. "I'm gonna be a godmother! Come toast my godchild. Ain't they sweet, hon? Two of the greatest people I know! Go on, kiss the bride!"

Larnie smiled appropriately and, with Tucker's stiff nod of permission, bent and dabbed at Dolly's cheek. Rosie's perfume, Dolly noticed absently, wondering what had gone wrong, was all over him.

"Now I gotta kiss the groom," Rosie announced. "It may not be Emily Post but it's Rosalie Fleming."

Clowning like a blonde movie star, she pursed her mouth, lifted her skirt and sashayed forward to plant a noisy salute beneath Tucker's nose.

He received it with bad grace. Shrinking from the circle of attention Rosie's antics had attracted and wiping his mouth with an unconsciously fastidious hand, he took a step backward.

"You didn't use to mind the taste of my lipstick," Rosie told him. "What's the matter, you scared to act natural in front of your future wife? I know what to do about that!"

Seizing his arm with one hand and Dolly's with the other, she propelled them toward a table. "Do the honors, Larnie," she ordered. "Doubles all around!"

Before Dolly could refuse, a glass was thrust into her hand.

"Down the hatch, now," Rosie said. "Drink hearty and stay with the party."

Dolly shut her eyes and swallowed recklessly. Then she opened them, blinking with surprise. She did not feel any different.

"Atta girl," Rosie encouraged. "Come on, you gotta catch up with me."

This time Dolly had more courage. "Cheers," she said before refilling her glass, as she had seen an actress do in a movie. In a moment she was looking at Rosie through its clear bottom, seeing her eyes magnified like wavering pools.

"Go, girl!" Rosie crowed. "I believe you can stay with the party long as me!"

There was a strange heaviness in Dolly's head, but she boldly held out her glass for more of Rosie's praise.

"Tucker's in the public relations business now, Rosie," she chattered. "Isn't that wonderful?"

"Well, well," Rosie said. "Legitimate at last."

While Dolly giggled, and Tucker glowered, Rosie went on, "Girl, you're all right. Dolly's real regular, that's what I tell everybody. Nothin' hincty about her just 'cause she's light and she's bright and she's been to college. You a swell gal, Doll, and you deserve everything you get."

"You deserve the best, too, Rosie," Dolly said, feeling very sentimental. "Larnie's a wonderful guy."

"My consolation prize, huh?" Rosie gave Larnie a careless hug. "Yeah, he'll do."

"No, Rosie, he's wonderful! You just don't appreciate him!" Borne to exhilarating heights on a wave of liquor, Dolly began to chatter recklessly. "I just hate these phony formal affairs, don't you? I'm so glad you were here, Rosie. You and your kind of folks are real, you know what I mean?"

"Well, good. You can come slummin' over my house any time you want."

Their eyes met and, for that moment, within the area of that look, they were both sober. All the wires in Dolly's head were still crossed, but now one of them connected imperfectly, and she remembered something Rosie had confided to her years ago, while they were still in high school. Until now she had not connected that boy with this man who sat at her side.

He had seemed to appear, wicked and well-dressed and worldly, from nowhere the night her father had brought him home unannounced after a Blues smoker. He'd chatted agreeably with Dolly's parents for an hour without once taking his eyes from her, while she kept expecting him to disappear in a puff of smoke.

"Interesting young fellow," her father said afterward. "Ambitious, too. He should go far."

"Yes, but who knows where he comes from?" her mother queried. "I don't know any Tuckers in this city. Does he have people in Washington? Richmond? Baltimore?"

"I doubt if it's even his real name," her father answered. "He wanted me to put him up for membership. But something about him didn't ring true to me."

"Well," Dolly's mother reflected, "at least he has lovely manners. And beautiful clothes."

And that settled it. Dolly was permitted to go out with him. She never told her parents that he turned out to have a background in the rackets and a number of shady friends; they would hardly have appreciated that side of his charm.

"—Yeah, you all right, Doll," Rosie was saying. "You reg'lar. You ain't too good to get drunk with your old friends. I don't hold nothin' against you. No hard feelin's. You a better wife for him anyway."

Tucker stood up then and tried to force Dolly's coat around her shoulders. "I've had about enough of this," he said. "Let's go."

Dolly fought him. "I'm not ready."

He pulled her roughly to her feet.

"Now, wait a minute, daddy," Rosie intervened, swaying up

from her chair. "Treat her nice. If you bruise it, you can't use it."

He brushed her hand from his sleeve as if it were a small, disgusting insect. It was a light gesture, but as effective as hitting her. She stumbled backward, lost her balance and slipped to the floor.

"Tom, help her!" Dolly exclaimed. "Can't you see she's sick?"

"She's drunk," he said coldly. "This is what you have to expect from the lower classes. But I never expected you to get down on their level."

"I'm sorry, Rosie," Dolly said tearfully. "I'm sorry." She broke away from Tucker's restraining grip on her elbow and, in that instant, also freed herself from his fascinating hold over her. It had been gradually loosening, anyway, as their whirlwind courtship slowed down and he grew less amusing and more serious. He had seemed to offer her an escape, which she eagerly accepted, from the tiny, terribly claustrophobic world of Negro society; but why had he brought her here tonight, if not to show her off for its approval?

Wondering this, and clinging to his arm too tightly, she had watched the pompous Grand Promenade. First the guests of honor, a singer and a statesman who had been dragged here for the sake of charity. Next the famous-notorious—artists and athletes, columnists and cabaret owners, baritones and racketeers. Finally the businessmen and professionals, doctors and lawyers, preachers and politicians who were members of the True Blues. They were all short, dark, bald men with gigantic, glittering, golden wives. As they passed in review, Tucker's slate-colored hand had covered her pale one eagerly, and she had glanced down and not been reassured. Her dashing young outlaw, her romantic Robin Hood, now that he had turned businessman, merely wanted to use her as a wedge to enter the world of respectability. If she married him, she would be more suffocatingly imprisoned than any minister's or dentist's wife.

All this came to her clearly as she heard herself screaming, "Look at him, Rosie! Isn't he the poorest excuse for a man you've ever seen? Look at him! He's not even human!"

266

Them That's Not Shall Lose

Even with her head on a level with Dolly's knee, Rosie managed to keep more of her dignity. "Whatever he is, he's yours," she answered, covering her disintegrating face with her hands. To Larnie, who was kneeling at her side, she said, "I just got a headache, lover. Must be the strain of all this high society. I think you better take me on home."

Then, because he moved too slowly and had not yet enclosed her within the protective circle of his arm, she jerked out her jaw in an angry convulsion. "Didn't you hear me? I said, 'Take me home!' "

In the car, she huddled over her folded arms, convoluted and secretive as a crab. He drove the big new convertible with absent-minded skill, though keeping his eyes on the traffic. "Were you really partners with him, Rosie? What kind of partners? Partners in crime?"

"None of your business, you big dumb ape," she snapped.

"One of these days," he told her calmly, "you're going to call me an ape once too often. Why do you think I take so much stuff off you, anyhow? Just to get in that dried-up skinny little space of yours?"

Her hand darted out as if to slap him, but instead it raked at his face with sharp pointed claws.

"No," he answered himself, "that's not why. You just don't have sense enough to stay alive without somebody like me around." As his cheek caught fire he saw the dangerous brilliance of her eyes in the mirror. "You remind me of a little white girl," he said thoughtfully. "A frantic little white girl I used to know in college."

"I ain't interested in your girls. Just drive the car," she said, and settled back into her shell.

It was another of those times when Larnie wondered why he was drawn to this urchin who preferred pajamas to nightgowns and preferred nothing to either, who thought being a woman meant loading yourself with all the clanking jewelry you could carry, and was just as easily taken off or put on. But then there were the times when she emerged slippery and wriggling from the shower, with her mouth swollen into a pout and her hair thickened and tangled with steam and her breasts nodding their small black faces, and he was unable to imagine a life without her.

At his side, she was forcibly ejected from her shell of silence by a bout of coughing. When he tried to stroke her shoulders, she shrugged his hand away.

"Aw Rosie," he pleaded, "quit pretending. You know you need me."

"I don't need nobody," she managed between coughs. She began to curse mechanically, under her breath, and he knew her other trouble had returned. Though she allowed him to lift her from the car and carry her weightlessness up the steps, she was as remote as a duchess being helped across a ditch on her land by a peasant.

Then her eyes angled past him. He followed them, and saw the thing that was pinned to the door. A scab of sickly leaves and mauve satin.

Instantly she summoned the strength to scramble from his arms. He let her go; he saw in her face that she would claw him again if he tried to restrain her. She flew to the door and wrenched it open.

"Granny!" she cried out. "Oh my God, Granny! Where are you?"

The tiny gray figure seemed to materialize, in that instant, out of air. It dominated the doorway and cast a long shadow backward into the hall.

"She's gone, child," she said. "Her heart give out right after you was gone."

With a wordless cry Rosie darted into the hall, ran back and forth uncertainly, hovered, then flew up the stairs.

"No use to run up them steps," Granny called. "She ain't up there. Wasn't no way to reach you at that affair. The undertaker's been here with his basket and gone."

Larnie started to follow Rosie, but the way was barred by the old lady, who lifted a warning hand like a stone guardian of the grave.

Them That's Not Shall Lose

"I never said nothin' before," she intoned. "She never asked me, and I figured it was her business who she brought in the house and who she didn't. I'm just an old-fashion grandmother, but I don't believe in interferin' with young folks. Now I'm gonna speak my piece and be done. It don't look right for you to be stayin' here now her Ma's passed on."

From deep inside the house came a shriek. Then silence. Then a low siren's wail that would go on and on forever.

Granny's delicate features lifted, listening, then tightened into a knot of wrinkles. "You hear, boy?" The hollow voice breathed a damp chill over him. "You can't help her none goin' in there now. She won't want you. She'll just want to be here with me."

He heard. He nodded, respectfully, in dumb obedience. Every night he had watched the old lady go from room to room locking doors and windows. Now the tall house stood sealed and fortressed against him. Even as he listened, the latch clicked twice, and a chain scraped across the door. He resisted an urge to smash it with his fists; he knew, by now, how impotent they were against the clever barriers erected by females. He turned away as the light footsteps receded and a voice caroled, "Granny's coming, Rosalie. Don't be getting your eyes all red, now. That's my sweet grandchild."

28

Larnie paused at the door and listened to the music that issued from Benny's. Los Cubanos, Machine's group, now going into their frantic sign-off theme, were a maracas-and-bongos outfit who had immigrated from not quite south of the border: Alabama. Larnie filled in on piano between their sets. The job, lousy as it was, had turned out to be the one remaining thing that propped up his pride. Quitting school, moving in with Rosie, not being allowed to help her with the bills or influence her wrongheaded decisions, had all been milestones on his rapid slide downhill. It had been pleasantly cool back in October when he had reluctantly taken the job, but the nights were cold and raw now. He shivered and ducked inside.

The one advantage of working nights at Benny's was that it made Rosie want to quit. She had said often that she couldn't keep her mind on her work with him in the next room, and that she couldn't stand seeing "all them pretty women hangin' on my pretty man." Larnie had been dubious, though. Getting Rosie on anything like a normal schedule could only be temporary. Sure enough, she was still on the job, putting off quitting from one week till the next. On her rest periods, she would be queening it in the back booth of the restaurant section, handling her real work, which she vaguely referred to as "insurance policies," and keeping an eye on him without being seen.

Larnie walked down the polished length of the bar, nodding to the scattered regulars who always came early, then ducked suddenly behind the bar and poured himself a shot of Scotch. Benny gave him a funny look without saying anything, then went back to wiping the bar with deliberate little circular sweeps of his rag. Benny never really said anything. He just gave you one of those funny accusing looks. Larnie decided he was going to have to get him told about that soon. His hands felt sensitive and powerful as he walked over to the little red piano.

"Yo Larnie! Don't take all night! Get to work." A heckler in the place already.

"Leave the man alone. I heard he was a good piano tuner once."

The taunts affected Larnie strangely, making him obstinate. He had planned to be obliging, he was going to give them some "Red Bank Boogie," fast and loud, the way they liked it, but instead he got up from the piano and walked over to the bar again.

"Beer, Benny," he said. Benny smiled and handed it over. He was only funny about whiskey.

But then he leaned over the bar and said in a low voice, his phony, chummy, confidential voice, "Look, Larnie, it's after ten already. Get busy and give 'em something they like. You know."

Larnie nodded. He knew, all right. And Benny should know by now that his soft I'm-depending-on-you routine didn't cut any ice with Larnie. But a fast rock 'n roll number, which was what the crowd wanted, was all they really deserved anyway. All they knew or could ever know.

He shuffled back, took a long cool teasing swallow of beer, and set the bottle on top of the piano. Then he sat down and stretched his fingers twice. Curving them ever so gently, he waltzed into the opening bars of "Red Bank Boogie" with the casual, thoughtful detachment that always annoyed the crowd, though they seldom knew they were annoyed and never knew why. Larnie knew. The music drew them helplessly into its rhythms, but he remained aloof. He tore savagely into the riff in the bass, crashed down into another key, then took it up into the treble, high, quivering, backed up by an insistent bass.

He could hear them all around him, clapping hands mechanically, beating their feet and shouting. The trill grew stronger, the bass speeded up and reached a climax, and then a plummeting glissando down to C below the staff set the whole thing off again.

"Ow!" they screamed in chorus. Fast and loud they wanted it, and fast and loud they got it, with subtle chord substitutions that were wasted on them; but always, also, with the strong beat they demanded. Finally, smiling, knowing that he had tricked them just a little, Larnie let the thing die down and ended it on a dissonant minor seventh. It was a hollow victory. The whistles and applause were unbelievably loud.

He stood up and turned around, facing them, forcing a smile. One of the boys called out, "You're workin', man."

Larnie smiled and played the game. "Pay my salary, daddy." This meant a free drink. He moved over to the bar, gulped it down and nodded his thanks. People like that needed a chance to be sports, to patronize, and he didn't mind giving it to them. He went back to the little piano satisfied, knowing it had been

271

an even exchange. The drink was important to him, too. After the third one he could play what he damn well felt like playing, and if nobody liked it he wouldn't care. Benny might turn on the juke box at top volume and drown him out, though.

That had been only the second drink, and he was still a little wary. He tried a compromise number, "Bop at the Waldorf." It was on the fast kick that the public (Benny's word) liked, but it had some changes that he could do interesting things with.

More people were straggling into the already crowded bar. Halfway through "Bop at the Waldorf," Larnie felt a heavy hand applied to his shoulder and was overpowered by whiskey-breath on his face. It was Clint again, of course. Clint was the character who dragged in, already loaded, every weekend night, hoping to coax a chance to bellow into the mike.

Seeing him, Larnie laughed. Everyone got a chance to perform sooner or later around here. Benny was philosophical about it. If it got too raw, he just switched on the juke box.

"Play me a little 'Stardust,' Larnie," Clint said, his gold-capped teeth glinting in the red and blue neon from the window.

Larnie groaned quietly. Clint was more the "Rockin' at Midnight" type, if anything.

"How 'bout it, Larnie? 'Stardust' for an old pal who sings like an angel. My angel singin' and your angel playin'—man, that's the greatest."

Clint's smile was so broad it bisected his face. Larnie gave in. "Sure. But buy me a drink first."

Clint pointed to the Scotch, indicated a double with his fingers and pointed to Larnie.

Larnie swallowed the drink fast, hoping it would help him slide past Clint's off notes without hearing them too clearly. The long narrow room was beginning to tilt just a little, first on the side where the booths were, then back toward the bar. Not enough to make the people fall out of their seats. Just enough to spill the drinks, he thought, each word articulating itself in his brain so clearly he knew he must still be sober. Just-enough-to-spill-the-drinks.

He slid into the cool blue opening notes of "Stardust" as Clint bent eagerly over the small mike at the bar. The raucous voice came in before the beat, but Larnie caught up and lapsed patiently into the mechanical accompaniment. Slurred and Southern, Clint's voice slid lazily from note to note, hovering with hoarse uncertainty between tonality and speech register. When it was over he got a big hand, bigger than the one they'd given Larnie.

Clint bent over him again. "Let's try 'Laura,' daddy."

Larnie was angry. He liked that number. "Look, Clint, we can't have any encores tonight. Weekend. Crowded. No encores. Get it?" He put his hand on the little man's arm and gently pushed him away.

"Okay, Larnie," Clint said, still smiling. "I won't forget you when I'm famous. My ol' friend Larnie Bell gave me my first chance, that's what I'll say."

"Thanks," Larnie said, thinking, Damn it, he probably will. He rubbed his stinging eyes and looked around. The narrow room was dense with smoke, a webbed one-piece screen like a curtain, veiling the moving shapes and colors behind it. The place was well filled. There were dozens of people imprisoned behind the latticework of smoke, desperately guzzling Benny's liquor and giving their money in return.

Now Benny beckoned, holding the receiver of the bar telephone in one hand.

Larnie wondered dazedly what errand he would have to perform for Granny this time. Probably the old lady just woke up with a taste for champagne. Then, his head clearing slightly, he remembered joyfully that she had put him out of her house last week. He was no longer her errand boy. He could hardly wait to tell her so. He snatched the phone from Benny eagerly and crouched behind the bar, which acted as a baffle for the noise.

"No, I can't guess who this is," he said moments later. Then he exclaimed "What?" so loud that Benny started and turned his dark expressionless eyes in Larnie's direction.

"How did you find me?" Larnie asked next. "Oh. I see. You called my mother."

He held the phone dumbly for two more minutes, no longer

really listening, his mind working fast. "All right, baby," he said after the lateness of the hour and the difficulty of finding the place and the dangers of the neighborhood had failed to discourage her imperturbable innocence. "I'll look for you in half an hour. What are you wearing?"

After he hung up he went to the other end of the bar and buttonholed Benny. "Say, man. You know that phone call I got?"

Benny grunted noncommittally.

"It was a chick I know. An underage chick, man."

"So?"

"She's comin' down here to see me."

Benny shrugged. "Long as she sees you on your time, it's no skin off mine." He turned his bulky enigmatic back and began rinsing glasses in the bar sink.

"Benny," Larnie said in a low voice, "maybe I'm not making myself clear. This chick is white."

Benny swung about slowly and faced him with an expressionless mask. "Far as I know it's legal, sonny. You want me to pass a law?"

Larnie wet his lips and tried to frame an apology that would get past this man's strange armor of pride. "You still don't get me, Benny. I know you try to run a straight place, but this chick is trouble. Wherever she goes, The Law is right behind."

"Oh," Benny said, drying his hands briskly on a towel. "What is she, jail bait?"

Larnie swallowed. "Yeah. If she gets in here and decides to stick around, anything could happen. You could lose your license."

"I doubt that," Benny said. But he seemed more interested. "What does she look like?"

"Cute," Larnie said. "Real little and cute. She looks so innocent you wouldn't think she knew her way from here to the corner, but don't let it fool you. She'll be wearing a red dress tonight, and she's dark, she looks Italian, but she isn't. Naturally. You'd never catch a nice Italian girl pulling tricks like that."

"Naturally," Benny echoed, his mouth pulled down in a grimace. "It's only the white ones."

"Yeah," Larnie said nervously, confused, not getting it. "Look, she'll be here any minute. I'm not sticking around, Benny. I'll make up the time later."

"All right, I'll get rid of her for a favor," Benny said. "I only wish I knew what was in your mind, sonny. Then maybe I'd know why I'm doing this."

"Look, Benny, I wouldn't wish this chick on my own worst enemy. That's the only reason why I'm telling you."

As he ducked out the door he heard Benny's strange stifled laugh, and knew that he was pleased. Larnie did not regret what he was letting his ex-girl friend in for tonight. The thought of her following him down here, into the very bowels of the black ghetto, just as she had pursued him all over the campus, made him furious. Suppose Rosie should see her? He shuddered. How far did he have to run, anyway, to escape her? Not that she was the tramp he had described to Benny; far from it. No, she was a nice, high-minded little girl; well-meaning, burning with ideals, innocent of the things that were always working underneath when people thought they acted from noble motives. Her innocent eagerness was what had ruined him. Alone, he might have continued to plod along safely in his shell, untouched and unmoved, for another three years. But with his color standing out in high relief against hers on the campus, and his nerves exposed to a constant rain of vague hostilities, he had known he would never graduate, and he had quit trying.

Now, blithe and innocent and supremely secure as always, she was waltzing back into his ruined life. He watched from the shadows of the side entrance as she came in, looked around her uncertainly, and headed for the bar.

"I'll have rye whiskey and ginger ale," she said to Benny.

"Sorry," Benny told her. "We don't have it."

"Beer, then."

"Fresh out."

"What have you got?" she asked crossly.

"Not a thing."

She gestured helplessly. "What are all those other people drinking?"

He pointed to the sign, *Positively No Minors Served.*

"But I'm not a minor!" she protested, opening her purse on the bar. "Here, I can prove it."

Benny's sad face got longer and sadder. He picked up her purse, closed it and handed it back to her.

"You aren't interested, is that it? Your mind's already made up." She turned indignantly to the nearest members of the crowd. "Are you going to let him treat me like this? Won't somebody help me find Lonnie?"

Larnie chuckled softly. He was less than twenty yards away from her, yet he was as safe as if he were on the other side of the world. With Benny on his side, there was no need to worry about the others. No Negro would ever reveal another's whereabouts to a white stranger.

Machine's band had wound up its number in a crash of chords and percussion. Its members began to leave the stand raggedly.

"Won't somebody please help me?" she asked again. "I'm looking for Lonnie, Lonnie Bell. He's a musician. He plays the piano here. You know him, don't you?"

The nearest men ducked their heads and shifted their positions so they were all looking away from the girl, but around the room, eyes that had appraised her warmly strayed to her again with suspicion and hostility. They had closed ranks in the baffling, impenetrable solidarity Larnie understood. Any white person who made inquiries in here was assumed to be a representative of some menacing force like The Law.

Finally a grotesque figure detached itself from the far wall and limped toward the girl. He was thin, tattered, scarred like an alley cat; his hair was stiff with rancid oil, and a high shine coated his pure African features. Clint stopped in front of her and swayed gently.

"Any friend of Larnie's is a friend of mine, baby," he said. "Jus' tell me where you live. I'll take you home."

"Don't touch me!" the girl shrieked, though he had not moved, and backed away from him. Larnie observed the moment when her horizons contracted sharply and permanently, shutting out adventure, beckoning her to safety and home.

Still chuckling to himself, he slipped in the side entrance, the Ladies' Entrance, after he saw her leave. He went over to the little piano, shook his head to clear it of the cottony feeling that always came at about this time, and began to pick out the delicate opening bars of "Ramona," his own song. He played it with the melancholy ardor that was right for the chords, not bothering to add the touches that might make it go over with the crowd. The audience was silent and expectant throughout the number, and Larnie sensed that something important was happening between him and them. Encouraged and excited, he plunged into the "Goldberg Variations." There were places in the eighth and fifteenth measures where he usually took off on a jazz tangent, but tonight he passed them and went on, unwilling to tamper with Bach's perfection, the clusters of notes coming too fast for him to rearrange them. The crowd was with him all the way.

Until Benny pulled one of his tricks; he switched on the juke box and Fats Domino came out loud, fast and horrible.

The thread between Larnie and his audience was broken. He found himself back in the disorganized noise of the club, sickening with smoke and the delayed effect of the liquor he had drunk. He stumbled over feet in the aisle. Friendly extended hands caught and supported him.

"Get back to work," Benny told him as he passed. "You got fifteen more minutes."

"Didn't you hear?" Larnie shouted over the noise. "I quit!"

He barely made it to the men's room. He hadn't realized how drunk he was. He washed his face, wondering at the bags that appeared below his reddened eyes. He'd look pretty sick in the two-twenty low hurdles these days. Then he took a second look and froze, staring at the angry stranger who faced him in the mirror. Eyes blazing, forehead knotted with wrinkles, jaw thrust forward at an angle that was an open invitation to battle. Larnie knew that his once easy, gentle nature was slowly being reshaped into something black and mean, but he had not realized that he was also becoming ugly.

Good, he thought with a short happy laugh. Good. If he was less attractive, women would no longer want to ruin him. He congratulated himself on having the courage to quit his job without knowing where his next meal would be coming from. Perhaps, paradoxically, that was what gave him the courage. If he could still count on Granny's rich biscuits and sausages in the mornings, and on long afternoons sunken in the luxury of Rosie's satin cushions, he would be afraid to give up his last hold on independence. But now Larnie seemed to feel his independence firmly in his hand.

Cold sober now, he rinsed out his mouth and went back into the din of the club. Clint and two other amateurs were whooping it up at the piano. Benny, wearing that funny smile that was not a smile, was allowing them a short period of grace, but his omnipotent hand hovered near the switch.

Larnie raised a hand to him in mock salute.

"Come back any time, sonny," Benny called. "I'll teach you to be a bartender."

The hell of it was, Larnie thought as he went out into a cold gust of wind and turned his footsteps toward the marginal warmth of his bare little furnished room, the hell of it was that he probably would.

29

Rosie had not known her mother had so many friends. She was pleased by the first shy visitors: the little crippled newsboy who had also been Mom's numbers writer—Mom had been independent to the last; Lottie Mae who had worked with Mom at the beauty shop; Mrs. Peoples, the simple-minded old woman who lived next door to them downtown and always gave them Sunday morning rolls from her ample fragrant Saturday baking. Their mumbled words of consolation trailed off quickly; they wrung Rosie's hands, gazed speechlessly into her eyes, and left her touched by their honest sorrow.

But the second tide brought with it a wave of professional mourners. Fat officious bustling church ladies who strutted like pigeons in white Altar Guild uniforms, filling the house with pious chatter and the refrigerator with potato salad and fried chicken. Drowning in a flood of cards and messages, phone calls and visits, food and flowers, Rosie grew resentful. She began to suspect Granny's efficient hand behind the scenes, producing it all. She wondered why, if all these people had loved Mom so, they had not come around while she was alive.

On the third day after her mother's death she stalked into the dining room and found it full of strangers writing death announcements and thank-you notes, licking and sealing envelopes like a flock of industrious vultures. Her ears were assaulted by their honeyed reminiscences of a woman they had scarcely known.

"Always smiling. Always a ray of sunshine."

Like necrophilic cannibals, they licked their lips over the words.

"So sweet and kind."

"So good, so generous."

Lies, automatic lies, even if the words were somehow true. "She was not !" Rosie cried out suddenly. "My mother was tough and stingy. She was mean."

"Poor child," they clucked, and two of them led her away, stifling her shocking outcries against strange stiff bosoms that were supposed to be comforting.

Even if they could listen, Rosie could not explain how her harsh corrective words had been meant with love. Let Granny supervise the funeral, since she gloried in fussy details and bustling preparations. It was Rosie's business to mourn, and she trusted nobody else to do it for her.

But it was not long before she had to submit to being patted and pinned into a new black dress and swathed in smoky veiling. Then Watty Myers arrived with his long mournful russet face like a female hound's to help her into the first black car of a long mournful caravan.

Nothing that had been said about her mother at the house could compare to the violence that was done her at the church, a grim building Rosie had never entered before and hoped never to enter again. The minister's sermon, the eulogy, the testimony of the saints to Queenie's saintliness were all bland poisonous sirups poured over the truth of what her mother had been, a homely dish of tart apples. The answering "Yes, Lords" and "Amens" were like the twitchings and sighs of an ecstatic body of which only Rosie, like a paralyzed finger, remained unresponsive. She stared straight ahead, numbed by dull pain, trying to keep her eyes away from the elaborately coifed and painted effigy in the coffin. But they kept straying back for just one more outrage. No! she cried silently for the tenth time. No! Her mother would never have chosen that horrible pink lace dress. If it were up to Rosie, she would have been buried in her ragged comfortable old bathrobe.

Voice after voice droned on endlessly. Rosie did not notice that the last one was silent until a cold hand touched her elbow. A croaking voice said, "Will you cover her for the last time?" Watty Myers, the proud author of all these indignities.

Rosie got up stiffly with closed eyes and let him guide her blind halting steps to the altar. But once there her unwilling eyes flew open. Fearfully, then in surprised recognition, she gazed down at the strong resolute line of her mother's jaw and the clear curve of her ironic smile, still asserting her character even in the face of death, even beneath the frivolous mask of paint.

With a quick glad gesture Rosie pulled up the satin blanket, to keep that indomitable memory intact for herself before anyone could destroy it. And though she felt like giving a triumphant shout, she began to cry for the first time.

At that same moment notes fell around her like the first drops of a sympathetic rain.

Mom's favorite hymn, "Just a Closer Walk with Thee," sweet but irresistibly, almost mischievously rhythmic. Around the church, voices joined in, at first humble and scattered, then swelling.

Back in her seat, Rosie looked up with moist relieved eyes to the organ loft and recognized the sturdy outline of the angel who was playing. Larnie. Of course.

The hymn ended, he slid imperceptibly into a strange elegant melody, angelic but unsentimental. She did not know its name, Bach's "Arioso," but she would always remember this music, so ruggedly loving, so sad and spare and perfect. It was the only true thing that had been said about her mother that day. Her recessional. Yes.

Satisfied, Rosie decided to end this funeral, all by herself, right now. She rose, ignoring Watty's frantic signals, and trudged up the aisle to take up her post at the door of the church. Granny quickly joined her. Soon hundreds of faces were passing, pausing, peering into theirs, mumbling and moving on. Miltie. Lottie Mae and Miss Sophie, two blurs of navy blue. Mr. Schwartz, a trembling white blob in a sea of chocolate. Another face only faintly darker beneath a sweeping brim; a cool glove that held her hand briefly, then hurried on. Dolly. Rosie recognized only these few, but she was able to smile at all of them, with clear loving eyes, because she was no longer angry with her mother. Having made her peace with Mom, she no longer needed to be angry with anyone else.

Once home from the cemetery, Rosie locked herself into the front parlor that had been shut off all week from company because she had refused Granny's repeated requests to clean it. She cherished its sharp pine scent as relief from the sickening flower odors that hung in all the other rooms. The tallest, proudest Christmas tree in the neighborhood had dominated her living room with a splendor of silver rainbows. Now with each of her steps it spattered more brown tears on the neglected display of presents.

She shuffled over and knelt beneath the lowest of the dry branches, quickly pushing aside the pile of unopened presents her mother would never see. Here were her own things: a sweetly smocked blouse, from Larnie, that would never be at home with the starkly tailored things in Rosie's closet; from Mom, a flannel robe, soft and warm as a nursery blanket. From Granny there was a yellow Florentine leather jewel box, dented and scuffed, but tooled in gold, with a faded maroon velvet lining. The key was missing, but it did not matter; Rosie had no jewels to keep in it, anyway. She had praised it more than any of her other presents.

She brushed the needles from the black sealskin coat she had given Granny and draped it carefully over the back of a chair. Then she removed her other gifts to Granny from their boxes and folded them tenderly. The postman rang while she was smoothing the wrinkles from a pale gray housecoat that had cost sixty dollars.

The first letter she opened read:

"Dear M i s s F l e m i n g:

"We appreciate your patronage.

"Won't you please settle your account immediately so that we may continue to serve you?"

It was the usual Second Letter: a mild reminder. Third Letters were more firm, and Fourth Letters came from lawyers and were downright threatening. Rosie almost always paid at least part of a bill after a Fourth Letter, since Fifth Letters usually mentioned the date for repossession.

Kneeling on the floor, she tore all the envelopes open, spread their contents around her and arranged them in descending order with Fourth and Fifth Letters on top. Next their moves became as intricate as chess. Leffler's was dropped to a low position because they were an easygoing store; even their Fourth Letters were friendly. Golden's was a mean store, quick to repossess;

they moved up into the vacated spot. Dunmore's Department Store called her attention to a figure outstanding since August; they moved up two notches, only to be nudged lower by Rovner's Furniture, with the largest bill. The bottom place fell to Schwartz's, because Mr. Schwartz would continue to trust Rosie as long as she continued to work for him.

—But that might not be for too much longer, she reflected soberly. Her new habit of oversleeping, plus the greater distance she had to travel, made her late almost every day; and once arrived at the store, she dawdled endlessly over duties she would once have dispatched with one stroke like the crack of a whip. On some days she felt wonderful, even blissful; on others, doped and lethargic. But always she moved through her chores like a sleepwalker through dreams.

"I think I was mistaken about you, Rosalie," Mr. Schwartz had said recently. "You were not meant for the life of business. Nor, I think, for marriage." With a picturesque fluttering of hands and eyebrows, he had concluded, "You were meant to be a butterfly."

Mom had put it differently on one of Rosie's late mornings. "That Mister Schwartz forgot the most important rule when he took you back, Rosie. Never be too nice to colored people. They can't stand it."

Anyway, he had yet to fire her for the second time, and she decided, dreamily studying the bills spread around her, to appease the top row with partial payments and scatter a few postdated checks among the second ranks. In this way her Christmas debts would be settled sometime or other. She yawned. Probably by next September.

The phone rang as she was reaching for her checkbook. It was Miltie. He sounded nervous and sober.

"You remember them orders I brought you this morning, on number Three-Oh-Four?"

"Yeah?" she said suspiciously. She had not even looked at the slips.

"Well, there's twelve of 'em gotta be delivered tonight."

Suddenly wide awake, Rosie sucked her breath in sharply. Her

283

eyes were closed; her lips moved in unaccustomed prayer. In witless haste that morning, distracted by the funeral, she had ignored Miltie's warning, "Heavy betting on one number. You better let me turn this batch over to Pockets, Rosie. You better just back the leads."

"Leads, hell," she'd snapped, without taking time to look at the notations. "I'll back everything I'm big enough to back. Hand it over. I need every cent to pay my bills."

"But all on one number, Rosie," he'd pleaded. "Looks bad. Smells like a Fix to me."

"You're drunk, you got the D.T.'s, you're seein' ghosts," she'd snarled. "Even when you're sober you're scared of your own shadow. Fix, my foot. Somebody's house number was in the papers, that's all."

But she should have listened to Miltie. Ever since his one defection he had been as loyal and trustworthy as an eager puppy. She sighed—the Lord knew she'd brought this on herself —and said, "Call me back in an hour."

"They won't wait that long," he told her. "I'm in a phone booth down to Benny's, and three of 'em are sittin' here starin' down my throat. You better get movin' 'fore I'm forced to tell 'em where to find you. I ain't lyin', Rosie. It don't feel safe out here."

"I said call me back," she said sharply. "And listen: see if you can stay off that wine."

Her nails dug furiously at an imaginary rash on her thigh as she called a few competitors. B.J. was hurting to the tune of five thousand dollars. Pockets Robinson complained that all nineteen of his pockets were empty. Rosie calculated swiftly, swore, decided she would have to try to arrange a second mortgage.

On the way to the bank she checked in at Benny's and found no sign of Miltie. Somewhere he had pulled a fog of wine around him and was lying inside it trembling. In the restaurant section no one was being served; workmen were shouting over the whine of saws and scrambling through snowdrifts of fallen plaster. She stared as a large palm tree walked past her on blue denim legs into the bar.

There business as usual was going on more briskly than usual, with a dozen sports standing drinks for a noisy crowd. Renovations, a new crowd of big spenders—it looked as if Benny's were Under New Management. But Rosie knew how to read the signs. They spelled instead that Benny was on the right side, the white side, the only winning side of the deal.

"Tough, kid," he said as soon as he saw her.

"Is that all you can say?" she demanded.

He shrugged helplessly. "What else can I say? Look, I told you a long time ago you were heading for trouble. But you wouldn't listen to me. You refused to play your role." He leaned toward her awkwardly, trying to soften the blow. "Look, Rosie, I'm sorry. I didn't make this lousy set-up. I just run it."

It was like God's saying, "I didn't make this lousy world. I just run it." And when God says that, Rosie thought dizzily, where do you turn?

"I had nothing to do with it, Rosie, believe me. I didn't even know it was scheduled to happen. The Machine made the decision."

"What's The Machine?" she asked, picturing a crane like a great blind dinosaur, dipping its giant scoop-shovel snout to pick up her tiny figure and deposit it on the rubbish heap. It was an accurate picture.

"I don't really know," Benny admitted. "I'm just a cog in The Machine. It never bothers me as long as I keep it oiled."

Benny was just another small, stocky, perspiring man in rumpled clothes as he explained, "The Machine is big money, Rosie. White money. Not Italian, pure Anglo-Saxon lily white. Banks and investment houses. They invest in policy just like they invest in corn and cotton. When they decide that little independent people are draining off too much of the profits, they fix you."

"You mean they can fix the race-track numbers in the papers?"

God Bless the Child

"The Machine can do anything it wants, Rosie. Start wars if it wants. Elect Presidents."

"But who are they?" she insisted on knowing.

"They're the ones with the Power."

That crazy old rhyming riddle, the one about The Man with the Power, teased and tore at Rosie's mind, which was already stretched beyond its own power to understand.

"They're such high and mighty people I sometimes stop believing in them. But every time I do, something like this happens to remind me they're real." Benny smiled apologetically for having stepped out of the grand role he was supposed to play for her into the small one he played for these others.

At last Rosie understood his concept of people as tiny dolls wound up by a giant hand and set down to perform in a play for the amusement of the gods. Right now they must be roaring like thunder up there. No use asking for help from another poor performer as helpless as she.

"Tough, kid," Benny repeated as she turned and stumbled out of the door.

Worst was knowing that the invisible Powers who had tipped off those bets and arranged those fatal numbers in this afternoon's paper had nothing against her personally. If she could keep body and soul together for a few more weeks, she might even find herself working for them.

Meanwhile Miltie was alone in the streets with the ones who had not dared to hope for this hour in forty years of betting pennies on dreams. They had names and faces as well as fists and weapons, and they would not be patient.

Keeping a narrow eye out for him as she hurried on to the bank, she missed most of the other sights and sounds that eddied around her. Suddenly she came up against a solid shape that bulked large and immovable across her path.

It was Bo Ditley, the beggar, looking exactly as he had when Granny had threatened her with his visits a lifetime ago. ("He kidnaps little girls and carries them off in that bag. I don't know what he does with 'em. Eats 'em, maybe. If you don't wanta find out, you better start behavin' yourself.")

Bo Ditley's Army overcoat was cinched by a wide leather belt that made its skirts flare out and separate in front. Beneath it Rosie counted three pairs of trousers, denim over khaki over flannel. The upper part of him was bulged out like a woman's with layers of sweaters, and a knit sailor's cap of navy wool was pulled over his ears and topped by a high felt hat. These were the clothes he wore all year round. Like a snail, carrying his house on his back, he slept in whatever alley or vacant lot was last on each day's scavenger route.

Rosie noted all these details mechanically, in abstract terror. Then his bleary yellow eyes caught sight of her. He revealed his toothless black cave of a mouth and held out the opened bag.

Then she was flying, a hand to her mouth, back down the Avenue as fast as she could run. Her heels pounded the sidewalk; the street was crawling with monsters and shadows, all the ogres of childhood come back to get her.

Until she heard her mother's voice, tough and comforting: "What you afraid for? Don't nothin' want you." Mercifully, urgency lifted its whip from her shoulders; gratefully, she realized that all the banks were closed now. She slowed her steps to a serene walk toward safety. There was nothing more she could do until tomorrow.

30

By the time Rosie reached her door her breathing was almost normal. She hurried inside and ran upstairs to find Granny. She wanted to tell her what was wrong; she needed to sob out the whole fantastic story against a broad bosom or into a capacious lap.

But there were no comfortable places on Granny's reedy little figure. And she had other things on her mind. Unwrapping the new pastel sheets Rosie had brought home a week ago, she touched one with a shrinking finger and said, "You know I don't

God Bless the Child

like muslin, child. I never sleep on nothing but percale." She dealt the cruelest blow as an afterthought. "Plain white's perfectly all right with me, too. I don't need a lot of gay colors I can't see in the dark. I just like to feel good percale next to my skin."

Ordinarily Rosie would not have been discouraged by this; it would only have spurred her on to greater heights in pleasing Granny. But now she was silent. Granny must have sensed that something was wrong, because she decided to let it go. Instead she offered Rosie the only kind of comfort she had ever been able to give.

"Rosalie, take a minute and run upstairs and look on top of my chiffonier. There might be something there for you."

"Oh, Granny, not a present!" Rosie tried to sound reproachful, but the old childish excitement spilled over in her voice.

"Just a little something I brought home." Granny chuckled. "Go on, hurry up, now, before it runs away."

Rosie ran breathlessly up both flights of stairs. Two minutes later she descended slowly with a wad of yellowed tissue paper.

"That's the last thing I have of Miss Helen's, Rosalie," Granny told her. "When I was leavin', Miss Emilie sneaked it in my hand. She said she didn't want me to think they'd ever forget me."

"I'll treasure it, Granny," Rosie promised without much conviction. It was an old cameo in a tarnished setting, probably brass. She turned it over in her hand. The clasp on the back was broken. She wanted badly to believe that it was priceless treasure, but she could not prevent her knowing eyes from assessing it as worthless, cast-off junk.

To conceal her crying, Rosie hugged the old lady tightly, until she felt a stiffening and sensed that Granny was repelled by so much display of emotion. A horribly humorous thought crossed her mind then. Probably all the things Granny had ever brought home were junk.

"How stupid can you get?" she asked the room, standing up, laughing at herself through tears.

288

Them That's Not Shall Lose

"What a jerk," she declared, pressing both hands to her chest, disguising her terrible ripping coughs as laughter. "I oughta go stand in a corner."

Laughing, coughing and crying all at once, she tottered into the living room and fell into a chair. She had been lethargic of late, and subject to more prolonged fits of coughing, but never before had her knees betrayed her by folding beneath her without warning. Since Shadow's visit great tunnels had been hollowed out beneath the surface of her strength, though, and cave-ins were always imminent. She had disparaged the buried treasure of her femininity to keep its value concealed from his reflecting eyes, but he had not been deceived; he had stolen it from her anyway.

She wished with all her heart for Larnie; he was the only one who could put it back again. Since his departure from the house he had paid Rosie an absurdly polite visit every day; he always remained standing, kept his coat on, and stayed no longer than ten minutes. He no longer borrowed the car, and he would not accept food or drink or anything else she offered. Now, as if in answer to her need, the door rattled, footsteps shook the house, and he walked in.

Seeing his square, handsome figure fill the doorway, she was flooded with her old unreasonable resentment. He had no right to be so big and strong while she felt so brittle and small. She must make him as weak as she was or send him away.

Her voice prickled with wire barbs. "Now you got somebody else, it's nice she can spare me a little of your time. Tell her I said thanks a lot."

"You know where you stand with me, Rosie."

"Yeah, on the street corner," she snapped. "Your tail don't stick around here long enough for the dust to settle on it. Well, you don't have to bother comin' no more."

He did not answer.

"I might have sent you a Christmas card," she went on glumly, "but I don't even know where you live these days. You stayin' at home with your mother?"

"No."

"Well where then? How come you got so many secrets all of a sudden?"

"You have secrets from me," he told her. "I guess I can have secrets, too."

That put her off balance. "Everybody's got secrets," she replied uneasily. "Nobody knows everything about nobody."

"Everybody has to trust somebody. Why can't you trust me?"

"I trust you," she said weakly.

A sob tore at his voice and roughened it. "Aah, Rosie, how can I find out what's in that hard little head of yours? I can't stand hangin' around here not knowin'."

"I said I trust you," she mumbled sullenly.

"When was the last time you went to see a doctor?" he demanded.

She was stubbornly silent.

"You see? I'm no use to you. I was gettin' so I wasn't any use to myself. That's why I started staying away, Rosie. I was beating myself to death tryin' to get through that stone wall." He kicked one of Granny's slim golden chairs and glared at its refusal to fall.

She was half scornful, half tearful. "When you leave, you sure leave good. You know you ain't spent the night with me in more'n a month?"

"Rosie, I swear, it kills me as much as you." Though his back was turned, she knew he meant it. "But the next night I spend with you will be our wedding night."

Rosie's entire life until this moment had been dictated on her own terms. It was unsettling to find the situation reversed. She tested her new feelings cautiously. "You wanta know what's on my mind? That's easy." She laughed. "I got to figure out how to get rid of that nasty old Christmas tree."

He moved with swift purpose. In less than twenty minutes the tree, sawed and broken into neat sections, was stuffed into the fireplace and the room was filling with sensuous smoke. He dusted the last of the needles from his hands and turned to look at her, the burning tree spilling its last glory on his face.

Rosie had to shield her eyes from the dazzle of Larnie by firelight. She took a deep draft of the pungent smoke into her lungs and was instantly drunk. "Well," she said recklessly, "there's all them Christmas bills."

He stalked about the room, gathering up armfuls of fancy boxes and loose finery.

"What you gonna do, Larnie Bell?"

"What you think? Return all this stuff."

Rosie was deeply shocked. Never in her life had she considered returning any purchase to any store. "Put 'em back!" she yelled. "Put every one of 'em back, you hear?"

"They aren't paid for, are they?"

She shook her head.

"Then they don't belong to you."

He stooped to take her face in his hand and spoke with maddening gentleness, spelling out a primer lesson for a five-year-old. "Hon, there's something you've got to learn. You can't spend money you haven't got."

She flew at him, hissing and clawing. "Them's Mom's things you got there, fool!"

He fended her off easily. His face was grim. "I guess you're lucky she died."

She retreated to her chair and sulked there, fist to her mouth, staring at him as if he were Frankenstein's monster.

"She can't use these things now," he said more gently. "You know she wouldn't want you killing yourself to pay for 'em."

Two large tears started down her cheeks. Before they could reach her chin she was drying them on his shirt.

"What else is there, hon?" he asked softly.

"Nothin' you can help me with, Larnie, I swear."

"You don't know that unless you try me and see."

But she was not up to it yet. She took refuge in more tears and in teasing. "I just can't let you in on every little thing, Larnie sweetheart," she said, winding snakelike arms around his neck. "There's some little things a woman just can't tell a man."

Sighing, he extricated himself and stepped back, leaving her small and tearstained and alone. "What you mean," he said, "is you'll wait and tell me when it's too late. You did that once too often already, baby."

"Larnie?" she said uncertainly. "You ain't gonna run out on me now?"

He appeared to be unmoved.

She stretched dramatic arms toward him. "Don't leave me, lover. Please. I need you."

It was half of what he wanted, but Larnie was through with settling for halves. "Marry me then," he told her. "Soon."

The curtain between the living and dining rooms fluttered ever so slightly.

"You can come out," he called. "I was just leaving."

There was a delicate pause of decision before the old lady emerged, her face corrugated by hatred, and adjusted her expression for Rosie's benefit a fraction of a second too late. Then Larnie was gone, carrying Christmas out of the house as abruptly as he had brought the New Year in.

Rosie stared open-mouthed at the space he had left. Perhaps it was because he was so large that it seemed so empty. She looked once more at Granny, then dashed out of the house, calling his name in a weak voice. It splashed softly in the air. "Larnie! Larnie!" Mercifully he had not gone far.

She found him right outside, bending over what looked like a heap of somebody else's Christmas trash in her gutter.

"The nerve of those neighbors," she said. "Leave that stuff, Larnie. Come back inside."

But he did not move, only said in a strange sick voice, "Don't come any closer, Rosie."

"Larnie?" she questioned softly, suddenly afraid, yet disobeying him.

He moved abruptly, spreading his arms to hide whatever lay at his feet. "Don't look, Rosie. Go back in the house."

"What is it? Let me see." Then she no longer needed to ask.

Such a tiny heap of dried leaves, already bruised and pounded into mulch, to be all that was left of Miltie. Nothing recognizable but a soft slack mouth, a flapping doll-like hand. Larnie stepped back and his burden slipped to the gutter noiselessly, like leaves, like rubbish.

"I heard this funny bubbling sound . . . I looked . . . he was calling your name, Rosie. And then he stopped . . . just stopped. Do you know him?"

"Yes." Now the chill that would never leave her again settled into her bones and fanned outward. Too much death in one day. Too much. An icy wind stippled her flesh with goosebumps. A thick black sky like a cape of mourning was folding down silently over the tall roof of her house, bringing a cold tomorrow closer.

"He was comin' to warn me," she said through chattering teeth. "He didn't rat on me, Larnie. If he had they'd of come after me instead." The tears were turning to crystals on her cheeks.

"You're cold." Larnie's arm was around her firmly, turning her away from the pitiful thing in the gutter. "Come on inside."

The call to Watty Myers took only a few seconds. By now the undertaker knew the way very well. He was becoming a commuter to Rosie's house.

Behind the locked door of Rosie's bedroom Larnie listened with ever more dull and hopeless eyes to her chilling childlike recital of financial misfortunes that would stagger a Rockefeller. Passionlessly she described her revolving charge accounts; her impounded savings accounts; her debts, consolidated, squeezed, expanded like accordions. Credit stretched beyond its limit; checks written on air.

On and on she talked, like an innocent abroad in the world, babbling a foreign language of first mortgages, second mortgages, attachments, back taxes, judgments, sheriffs' fees, until his head ached and reeled. Her life was a monstrous Gothic cathedral of credit built on water, no more real than its reflection. Finally the abyss of the Fix that had opened suddenly at her feet to be filled with money, and had swallowed poor Miltie instead.

He had been a fool to imagine he could slay this monster with a rude direct action, the way he had attacked her Christmas expenditures. Now he realized what a hollow pitiful gesture that had been, cutting off the ear of the dragon only. He could not wade into the forest to confront this beast; it was appallingly real, but it existed only on paper and in her small troubled head. All he could do was reach for her.

But that was enough. She had told him everything now; there were no secrets left, no barriers. With a sudden weary, beautiful movement she turned to him, opening like a small golden flower, opening lips, arms, everything everywhere at once. The touches of her suddenly gifted hands were all over him; when his hands responded they were moistened by her tears. He groaned; she arched; her small rippling vibrations stirred to match his violent ones. They fell apart, staring at each other.

"Oh, no," she said then in a hoarse new voice. "I don't wanta love you, Larnie. I need a man who can do me some good."

"I tried to tell you, Rosie," he said sadly, "but you couldn't understand. This is all the good there is."

Her piercing poignant cry showed that she understood now. Yes, this was the good thing a man was supposed to do, the only good; smooth away the rough scars, heal the angry sore places, so she could feel, finally, soft and lovable from the inside out. But why should it happen now? Better never than now, when she was ruined, sick, a mess, nothing but trouble to him, to anyone. Coughing horribly, she did not hide her face, hoping the sight would drive him away.

But he only wrapped her in the covers, like a doll. And wrapped the bundle in his arms.

"How can I let you go away again, Larnie?"

"You couldn't make me leave you now."

Her last lunge toward escape only locked them more firmly together.

Hours later, in the night, an insect sting pricked Rosie's bare shoulder. She shrugged it off, but its fretful voice kept buzzing in her ear. She awoke to find Granny bending over them.

"Rosalie," she whispered, "is that boy coming to live here again?"

Rosie drew a deep breath. "Yes, Granny. I guess he is."

The old lady stiffened and pulled back. "Well, I always got another home." In the dark, in her new silver robe, with her features softened by shadow and her long white hair let down her back, she looked like an elfin child.

Rosie's voice was calm. "I'm gonna marry him, Granny."

"Well, you don't have to worry," Granny said after a pause. "I got another place I can go."

"You know I don't want you to leave, Granny."

"You ain't gonna listen to nothing I say if I stay."

Rosie shut her eyes, but said what was necessary. "Not if you say anything against Larnie."

With a sudden movement she turned on the light that mercilessly exposed shriveled skin and watery eyes, turning the child into a hag.

Terror crossed Granny's face, the terror of stricken vanity at the thought of being discovered in that light by the sleeping Larnie. Her hand darted out quickly, but it faltered before it managed to extinguish the lamp. Rosie saw it tremble, and knew that in that moment her grandmother had begun to die.

But she had begun to want to live.

31

"Come on over, cuddy," Rosie's thin, shrill voice raged at Dolly over the phone. "Where the hell you been? I'm havin' a few friends over tonight. You'll never guess. Larnie and I just got married."

God Bless the Child

"Okay," Dolly said, surprised and pleased in spite of her misgivings. She wanted to see Rosie. It had been a long time.

Rosie met her at the door. She was bonier than ever, and great dark circles ringed her eyes. She was high, too, and on something besides liquor; her pupils were mere specks floating aimlessly in wide brown seas.

" 'Bout time you got your hips over here, girl," she scolded. "Where's your friend?"

Dolly needed to unload her guilt right there in the vestibule along with her rubbers and her umbrella. "Rosie, there's something I have to tell you. I had forgotten all about you and Tucker. I never even connected him with you. Please believe me."

"Bygones all gone bye-bye, Doll. Where is the old buzzard, anyway?"

"I don't know. The last I heard, he was in New York."

Rosie posed indignant hands on her hips. "What you mean, 'the last you heard?' "

"It was over three months ago, Rosie."

Rosie's lips were parted, but no sound came. Fumbling with the fasteners on her galoshes kept Dolly from having to look at her. "That night, Rosie—that awful night—I hated him for what he did to you. It felt like he was doing it to me. I—I gave him back his ring, Rosie." She kicked her galoshes into the corner and straightened slowly. "I don't think I'll ever hear from him again."

She had a lot to thank him for. That night, while she recoiled from the revelation of how deeply he despised people like Rosie, she had also been forced to realize how wildly she herself romanticized them; how far, in trying to correct her mother's snobbery, she had fallen in the opposite direction. And she had been faced with the unpleasant truth that both attitudes were equally false; that at bottom they were identical. It followed that everything important Dolly had ever done had been for Rosie— either as a gesture of appeasement (to Rosie who was despised instead of Dolly), or as an offering of worship (to Rosie who was bold where Dolly was timid). If she could do one last thing for a girl who was neither, who was merely her friend, she might begin living for herself.

She had done it. She had broken with him, in spite of the intense fascination he had for her. She had acted; she alone was responsible. It was a new feeling, neither good nor bad; merely a part of life, which Dolly was learning to spell lower case. It all seemed so long ago now that a feeling of unreality came over her, as if he had never existed.

"Rosie," she asked in a dreamlike state, "who was he? I mean, who was he really? I never even knew his real name."

Rosie laughed. "I don't know. Maybe that old geechee fortune teller conjured him up with one of them spells of hers."

"He said he was nobody. He said a Negro is always just a symbol, not a man."

Rosie chuckled. "He was a man all right. But I guess you don't need me to tell you."

Dolly shook her head. "I was a symbol to him, too. He never really needed me as a woman, Rosie. I don't think he ever needed anybody."

With a sudden, compassionate movement Rosie drew Dolly inside. "Then let's pretend he wasn't nobody, Doll. Let's pretend we just made him up out of our heads." Laughter conquered her coughing. "Lord, we sure did one hell of a job, didn't we? Who would believe it?"

Six men and four girls were sprawled around the living room, drinking Rosie's expensive liquor, helping themselves to food from the glass lazy-Susan cocktail table in front of the sofa. As Dolly walked in she was nearly blinded by the dazzling reflection of light from a shiny object on top of the television set.

"First let me show you the wedding presents, Doll," Rosie said, her eyes brilliant with moisture and excitement. "A toaster 'n four lamps 'n luggage 'n three tablecloths 'n a silver platter 'n a carving set 'n. . . ."

"And a partridge in a pear tree?" Dolly asked, smiling. For that was what Rosie really wanted, that and the swans and the golden rings and the rest of the fairy loot; nothing less would ever satisfy her.

Rosie pouted. "You got no right makin' fun, Dolly Diaz. Even if I did buy some of 'em myself." She whirled and attacked the phonograph, on which the members of a cool jazz combo were having a private conversation.

"Larnie, them cool sounds give me a headache. Don't be playin' no funeral marches at my wedding!"

She put a mambo on the machine instead and began a solo dance, her angular hips cutting the air like knives.

"Come on over here and sit down, gal," Larnie said. "You're supposed to rest." He was stretched out on the floor by the fireplace, thoroughly drunk. One of the girls tittered.

Rosie pretended to be angry. "Oh shucks, Larnie. I thought you was gonna dance with me." But her voice had a meekness Dolly had never heard in it before except when she spoke to Granny, and she obeyed, swaying a little with drunkenness, tripping over the cocktail table. His arm, raised to catch her, spilled a tray of cheese and crackers which landed, cheese-side-down, on the thick white rug.

As if by signal, Granny immediately came quietly as a shadow into the room. She did not say a word. She merely stared at Larnie. He met her gaze with drunken arrogance. Then she bent her old legs and began picking up the mess from the floor.

"Don't do that, Granny," Rosie pleaded.

The old lady, oblivious, continued picking up the crackers.

"Granny!" Rosie stamped her foot. "Didn't you hear me? Stop that!"

Granny, who was kneeling, went on gathering crumbs into her apron.

"Granny, please," Rosie whimpered. "I won't have you doin' this."

The old lady, mumbling "Excuse me," crawled on her hands and knees between one of the girls' legs to retrieve a cracker that had rolled under the couch. Rosie was reduced to hysterical tears by the time Granny finished clearing away the debris and left the room holding out a skirt full of crumbs.

"Go home!" she screamed to her guests. "Go home!"

"Now wait a minute," Larnie said, getting clumsily to his feet. A cracker Granny had missed had crumbled beneath him; bits of it were stuck to his pants. "My friends aren't leaving till they've had some punch to toast the bride and groom."

He walked over to the TV set and picked up the flashing object. Holding it at arm's length, he carried it to the cocktail table.

With a shock Dolly recognized the magnificent bowl from the magazine.

"I can mix up some great punch," Larnie said. "I'm a great bartender. I used to be a musician, but I quit that job. I'd rather mix good drinks than play bad music any day."

He began opening bottles and emptying them into the bowl while Rosie watched, stiff with anger. "This here thing is real pretty, hon," he said. "But it's never been used. I say, what's the sense in havin' nice things around if they ain't ever used?"

He emptied two bottles of champagne into the bowl and began to stir. "You know what this thing cost?" he asked. "More money'n I ever made in my life. You know how she paid for it?" Looking at Dolly, he put his thumb into the mixture, licked it, nodded, and reached for the sugar bowl. "You know how she paid for it, Dolly? Working sixteen hours a day and running a racket on the side and borrowing from everybody who was fool enough to lend to her. —That is, if it is paid for, which I doubt. Nothing else around here is."

Larnie raised his voice. "Look around you, folks. Take a good look. The walls, the furniture—it all looks real, doesn't it?" He laughed. "Well, it's not. Everything in this room is just a figment of her imagination. Thass all. A figment of her imagination."

"Stop it, Larnie," Dolly heard herself say hoarsely. "You knew what she was like before you married her. She's always been this way. Did you think you could change her?"

Without answering, he dipped a spoon into the bowl, tasted, added some lemon juice, and recommenced stirring. "But that's all right," he said mildly. "She did it all for Granny. It's nice for a girl to love her dear old Granny. —For years I been hangin' around here waitin' for her to die." He looked at Dolly hopelessly. "You got an education, maybe you can tell me. Why don't she die?"

He arranged a dozen cups on the table. "All right, everybody, here comes the punch."

Raising the bowl high, he began to pour. It slipped from his hands, as he had known it would, and went splashing and crashing from the table to the floor, where it landed with a hollow *bong* and lay intact, gleaming wetly in the pool of liquid like an evil eye.

Then Rosie, like a mother with an injured child, was picking up the bowl, crooning to it, wiping it with her skirt. When it was dry she held it out. "Look right here, Dolly. You can see the rainbows. Just like Granny said."

"All right, everybody," Larnie said. "The punch is gone. Sorry, but the party's over. You can all go home."

Rosie stamped her foot. "I don't want them to go home!" she cried perversely. But at a look from Larnie she subsided. The crowd left willingly enough; they knew and wanted no part of Granny's wrath.

Then Rosie announced, "I want Dolly to stay."

Larnie looked at her. "Dolly, you want to stay?"

"On your wedding night?" Dolly said incredulously. "No, kids. I'm on my way."

"Oh, stay, Doll," Rosie pleaded. "Please stay. I'm going to bed soon. You stay and keep Larnie company." She was sitting crosslegged on the floor, clutching Karmie's stuffed purple body in her arms, refusing to grow up. She would rather keep her guests all night tonight, or throw her husband and her best friend together, than admit that she was now a married woman, and responsible. Dolly saw Rosie clearly for the first time, without the distortion of her own needs, and she was not a marvelous, glamorous creature after all; she was just a child. She started sadly for the door.

Larnie saw her to the vestibule. They shook hands.

"Congratulations," she said to him. "I'm glad you finally did it."

He shut the door carefully behind them, then whispered, "Don't mind anything she said tonight, Dolly. She's not herself now. The doctor's got her loaded up on drugs."

In answer to her gasp and her unspoken question he explained quickly, getting it over with, "There's nothing else he can do for her. He doesn't know how she's kept going this long. Her lungs are like—like rags, Dolly."

Rosie's voice floated out from the living room; they both started guiltily, wondering if she had heard his choking explanation.

"Show Dolly the wedding pictures, Larnie."

Dolly said, with numb automatic interest, "What pictures? Let me see."

"Oh, nothing," he said. "Just a joke. She's tired, I got to get her to bed."

Then he gave up the lie, threw up despairing hands. His face under the porch lantern reflected strain, horror. "Can you beat that, Dolly? She wanted me to show you her X-rays."

Dolly's hands reached out to him then in an effort at comfort. It was a gesture that sprang from compassion, but it ended as something more, if only a mutual huddling for warmth. They parted finally and, stepping back, recognized each other for the first time. Though she was the first to say, "No," he quickly echoed it, and closed the door.

32

Granny said, "Did you tell her?"

Larnie said, "No. No sense in that now."

"It's a mercy," Granny said. "Long as she don't know, it don't seem true."

"It's true all right," Larnie said. "We gonna lose this house and everything in it, and even then we won't be finished payin' all she owes."

Granny said, "Hush, boy, she might hear you. She won't never let it happen."

Larnie said, "She can't not let anything happen, not now. Time to stop believing in fairy tales."

Granny sounded like she was going to cry. She sounded like that a lot of times, but she never did. "No use talkin' to a crude person like you. You've no idea what a refined person has to go through."

Larnie sounded like he was going to cry, too. "Don't you ever hear nothing? That's the trouble with you and her both, you never listen with nothin' besides your ears. Didn't you hear the doc either? When he said she's been livin' on nothin' but nerve for years?"

Granny began to hum a little tune.

"He said if she has absolute rest, there's a chance. But she doesn't dare even move. If she catches cold and it turns to pneumonia—"

"Doctors don't know everything," Granny said. "Neither do you."

Larnie was crying now. "You're no help at all. I might as well go talk to myself. You never hear anything I say."

He was going.

"Sometimes I think nobody ever does."

He was gone.

Granny's voice was so close Rosie felt her fierce breath on her face. "You too good for him. You come from something and you're somebody!" Then she was gone too.

Rosie smiled because Granny didn't know it, but she was becoming nobody fast. The doctor had jabbed her arm with something that helped her to disappear, and she was already almost invisible. She liked being invisible because she could sneak in so many places.

Right now she was in a fabulous garden. It belonged to some

rich white people, but they couldn't see her to chase her away. The garden had bridges of marble running over bubbly rivers of champagne and many beautiful marble statues. The air was perfumed with orange blossoms, and there were long silver Lincoln Continentals gliding down the paths between the trees. If you got tired of walking, you just stepped into one and said, "Take me where I'm going." The garden had fruits and flowers of all kinds, and every kind of bird and butterfly.

When she saw the giant butterfly with transparent rainbow-striped wings fluttering on the path just ahead of her, she gave chase through hedge mazes, under kneeling willow trees, across a small pink marble bridge. Each time it seemed that she was going to catch it, it fluttered just beyond her reach. But she went on pursuing it, up and down hills, until it entered the deep black woods.

"Tired," Rosie mumbled, breaking the surface of sleep. "So tired." She was about to give up when her fingers closed around the fragile wings, and she woke up.

She could still feel the quivering of insect life inside her clenched hand. She sat up, staring, and slowly opened her fingers.

The roach darted away as soon as she freed him. He ran in crazy circles on the blanket until she thought he surely must have worn himself out. Finally he stopped at the headboard, crawled up the bedpost to the very top and teetered there. Rosie froze.

The roach started down the bedpost again, then stopped, as if suspicious because he had met no opposition. Suddenly he flung himself outward and landed right side up on the bed-clothes that covered Rosie's breast. He scurried in one more small, perfect circle before he finally came to rest and took possession.

Screaming for her mother, Rosie flung back the covers. Then she remembered and called instead, "Larnie! Larnie!"

But there was no answer.

She turned back and contemplated her old friend. "You sure

followed me a long way," she remarked as he skittered into a crack in the baseboard. "How come you like colored people so much, anyway?"

She added, with increased emphasis, "Well, maybe you like me, but I sure don't like you." Rosie crouched and carefully explored the crack with her fingers. "There better not be no more," she mumbled.

There weren't any more roaches. But there was something worse: the dry empty husk of an egg. And her shuddering hand came away with a coating of fine brown powder.

"Termites!"

Rosie flew downstairs to check the rest of her house for signs of decay, and found them everywhere she looked. Streaks on the walls, scars on the furniture, a long crack down the face of the marble mantel that resembled the west coast of Africa.

The question was: were they new, or had they been there all the time? Had her living room shrunk overnight to its present crowded proportions, or had it always been less grand than her magnifying imagination made it seem? One thing was clear: she had fought and clawed her way to the place where she wanted to be, only to see it crumble into the same ruins she had left behind.

Rosie threw back her head to laugh at the joke, but what came out was a sob.

She ran into the dining room. On the floor, in the corners, more brown powder mingled with droppings of white plaster. Rosie looked up at the stained, scabby ceiling until it spun and seemed to sag dangerously toward her.

The question was: had she bought a palace . . . or just an old, drafty, run-down, rotting house?

The kitchen was the room she most dreaded inspecting. Rosie cheated a little before she entered it, turning on the light and pausing to give them time.

Was it her imagination, or had there been hundreds of little scurrying movements at the corners of her eyes?

Rosie flung open a cabinet and began to pull out dishes, not caring that Granny's precious flowered china crashed to the floor along with the glass salad plates from the dime store. She was more interested in the little black dots that moved. There. And there. And there.

And everywhere.

She ran from wall to wall, banging, smashing, squashing with both hands, eyes blurred with tears and rage, not knowing how many she killed. But there were too many for her; they danced in front of her eyes like black rain.

At last she turned out the light and limped into the hall. As she moved back through the rooms, Rosie thought about her life, and it had been like hurrying through a series of doors leading to a party, hearing the gay music and the tinkling laughter always receding, always one room away. But when you got to the next room, it was dark and empty, too.

The question was: was the party still up there ahead somewhere . . . or was there really no party at all? Had it existed only in her imagination—this gay, glamorous world inhabited by beautiful, perfect people—or was it still out there, shimmering just beyond her reach?

Rosie only knew, suddenly, how cold she was, and how alone, and how badly she needed to be back in bed.

On the first stair-tread, she remembered what had been in her bed before she left it.

The question was: *Did rich white people have roaches too?*

As her mind admitted the possibility for the first time, Rosie really did laugh, from the top of her voice to the bottom, a full free laugh that echoed through all the rooms. Yes, maybe they did have roaches, and termites, too, and dandruff, and tooth decay, and falling hair. Granny had never mentioned such things, of course, but they still might be.

Rosie sat down weakly on the steps, undone at last by her own cosmic laughter. The joke was on her.

"Oh Lord," she whimpered, "please don't let me see another one tonight."

But when she opened her eyes he was there, as she had known

he would be, moving slowly up the baluster with all the dignity of advanced years. A patriarch cockroach, enormous and real. As old as the house, as old as Time.

Rosie jerked the closet door open on its rickety hinges, threw a mink-collared Persian lamb jacket around her shoulders, and ran out into the night, not feeling the wet cement beneath her bare feet, not knowing that cold rain soaked her fine night-gown and dissolved her face into little brown rivers running down into the great black lake of fear.

Shadow, in the front booth, was the first to see her. He laughed, a humorless hissing sound like a snake, and said hoarsely, "What a get-up. You're a real comedian, Rosie."

Observing her tremors, he added, "Stop shaking. What you scared of? The way you look, don't nothin' want you. Your personal appearance rating is down, baby, way down."

She smiled then because, briefly, he had sounded like Mom.

Then he said harshly, "Christ, go back home. You're a mess, Rosie."

The crowd in Benny's was startled to see something small and dark and swift dart through it then like a demented arrow. It was a thin girl in a soaked nightgown; apparently drunk, for she was screaming and gesturing wildly. She seemed to be de-manding service at the bar. Refused, she began to smash things, knocking a dozen glasses to the floor with one sweep of her hand.

It was all over in a few seconds. The crowd watched indif-ferently as the bartender, a large caramel-colored man whose jowls gave him a sullen middle-aged appearance, lifted the girl easily and carried her out into the night. Her hair was a mass of wet tangled snakes, but her face was now peaceful as a sleep-ing child's.

Dolly trudged along in her sensible oxfords, carrying her chino raincoat over one arm and her briefcase full of third graders' papers under the other. She was thinner now and, because she held herself more erect, taller. She had not meant to walk so far after school, but the first softening of spring was in the air, and one block led to another. Soon she was turning into the street she had meant to avoid, approaching the tall haunted house which she had always felt wanted to fill itself with death in order to die.

Granny was sitting alone on the porch, her hands strangely idle in her lap. She looked at Dolly but did not recognize her. She seemed to have passed at last over that invisible boundary which separates enduring old age from old age that merely imitates life by breathing. Her eyes, no longer focused brightly on a vividly remembered past, seemed to see only some misty unknowable future.

Larnie came out, kicking the front door open. He slammed it shut and kicked it again for good measure.

"That door was made before you were born, boy," Granny reproved him. He did not answer.

Dolly hesitated, then walked on. The flutelike voice was borne to her ear by the wind.

"Now mind, I want nothing but lilies and carnations for this funeral. Don't be ordering none of them cheap little roses."

APPENDIX:
SELECTED REVIEWS

From *The Christian Science Monitor*, September 10, 1964

Keen, sharp, even brilliant novels by Negro writers have become a commonplace. In the last twenty-five years, Richard Wright, Ann Petry, James Baldwin, Willard Motley, Ralph Ellison, John Killens, Paule Marshall—and these are only a few—have written with awesome power of a world twisted by the paradoxes imposed upon it. If the white reader continues unhearing, unseeing, it is not because that paradoxical world has been withheld from him.

Kristin Hunter in "God Bless the Child" has added a little more depth to the picture, a few more fresh details. She has the gift of words and of insights. She has taken a ferociously alive little Negro girl, Rosie Fleming, who lives in the Negro ghetto of a northern city. This world bounded by schools, beautyshops, bars and moldering tenements has an indomitable will but lives a life of enforced separation from everything that would insure a homogeneous society. Somewhere, on the other side of that invisible boundary, are nice houses, a choice of jobs, hopes fulfilled.

● ● ●

Rosie is the youngest of three generations of Fleming women, and all three women are bitingly alive. Grandma has an iron conviction that she can transfer the gentility of her white "folks," for whom she has worked forty years, to her daughter and granddaughter by dressing them in her employer's old clothes. Queenie, her daughter, is too vulgarly honest, too rawly experienced, to be caught in this trap. But Rosie, all mother-wit, tension, rebellion, lives half-caught, half-free, manipulating, maneuvering, allowing her grandmother's dreamlike respectability to breed hot fast dreams in herself.

● ● ●

Rosie is a born career woman. By the time she is eighteen she is on her way, twisting, snaking, through the jungle in which she lives. All she wants is to make her own money and plenty of it, buy her independence, get grandma back where she belongs with her own family, fight lewd, blowzy Queenie into being a brisk, well-corseted member of Rosie's society, manage every detail so that no loose ends can act as a whiplash.

Appendix

Her plans are poignant and appalling. She knows all the temptations and thinks up all the answers. She is so wiry and skinny she does not need sleep or food; she can work eighteen hours beating the system.

She never quite understands what system it is that is beating her.

In the Negro ghetto there are not enough jobs to go around, yet in time Rosie holds three. Even so they do not pay for the gifts with which to buy Grandma, or for Queenie's private hospital room and nurse, or for the house which Rosie must have as her own status symbol.

In the Negro ghetto there is also not enough hope to go around. Decent relationships disintegrate almost before they get started. Larnie, Rosie's boyfriend, wins a scholarship but he cannot make the grade in college. The gifted few who escaped have blazed no trail for the others.

• • •

This sounds like a social tract. It is not. "God Bless the Child" is a lively sharp, swarming story of people. But they are people who have had the doors slammed on them once too often, who have been hobbled by the moral deformities of a fabricated society. The life they lead is like an immense, macabre charade which acts out conditions of privilege and security. When the unreality becomes too great then the police arrive, the bottles fly, the nightsticks crack, and the rest of the world watches from the safe side of the invisible boundary.

Miss Hunter does not miss a sight or a sound of humor, pain, or vulgarity. Her eye is sharp, her ear true. The novel is, I think, too long, the pace too frantic, but the explosive vitality does not obscure its humanity, nor lessen Miss Hunter's cool and relentless irony.

Henrietta Buckmaster

From *Book Week*, September 13, 1964

Though white characters barely enter the pages or the territory— the Negro section of an unnamed Northern city in Kristin Hunter's first novel—they are forever there in spiritual presence dominating the life of Rosie Fleming. They are the Furies that incessantly whip Rosie, all "skin and bones and energy," to get something better from life than what her loose-living mother, a hairdresser, has been able to provide. Rosie wants a world like the one forever described by her snobbish grandmother, a servant to rich white people. It is an impossible, beautiful, perfect world where little girls never worry that some of their Rice Krispies are roach eggs.

To get to that never-never land, Rosie sacrifices herself completely. Before she is out of her teens, she is working days in a dress shop and waiting on tables nights in a rough saloon and pushing her way into the money end of the numbers racket. And somewhere near the end of the struggle, Rosie suddenly asks: "Did rich white people have roaches, too? . . . Yes, maybe they did have roaches, and termites, too, and dandruff, and tooth decay. . . ."

Though Rosie's story could have easily taken on overtones of soap opera, Kristin Hunter never lets it wander near the maudlin. The only nagging doubt is why one doesn't bleed for Rosie Fleming. I'm afraid the answer is that one doesn't believe her every inch of the way. Her involvement in the numbers racket is on the shadowy side and therefore so is her success—if unpaid bills can constitute success. Furthermore, one can only be with Rosie in a social-worker sense. She is a "case" we follow with interest and sympathy. Empathy, the tear duct of the mind, is withheld possibly because the nature of Rosie's personality and drives keeps the reader from being one with her.

Though Rosie's story is dominated by her grandmother's white dreams, Miss Hunter has not, in any way, attempted to inject sermons on race relations into her novel. She has defined herself as a storyteller and to that end has crammed a large canvas with all the sights, sounds and smells of an overcrowded ghetto festering with life.

Haskel Frankel

Reprinted from *The Chicago Sun Times.*

From *Library Journal*, September 15, 1964

A Negro girl brought up in a city slum resolves that she will have all the pretty things her grandmother has seen in years of waiting on "white folks." The quickest way to money seems the best as she works at two jobs, becomes involved with the numbers racket and overextends her credit. As she moves toward destruction in search of the glittery and false, she is unable to see the value of real virtue, such as the honest, steadfast devotion shown to her by her lover. The lure of the flashy is an interesting and timely theme for a psychological study. In this first novel, Miss Hunter displays insight into the secondary characters, as well as the heroine, so that the work is convincing and

Appendix

sometimes moving. The problem is a literary style too hackneyed for a penetrating study. The novel has some of the appeal of John Williams's *Night Song* and *Sissy*, though it is not so polished. Recommended as an aid to interracial understanding.

Mary E. Kelley

Reprinted from *Library Journal*, September 15, 1964. Published by R.R. Bowker, a division of Reed Publishing, U.S.A. Copyright ©, by Reed Publishing, U.S.A., a division of Reed Holdings, Inc.

From the *New York Times Book Review*, September 20, 1964

"I want things," says Rosie Fleming, the Negro heroine of "God Bless the Child," a first novel by Kristin Hunter. "I want things so bad I'd kill myself to get 'em." And Rosie does kill herself, riding a toboggan of work and whisky in a long, fast slide to extinction.

In the daytime, small fierce, bright Rosie is head clerk in Schwartz's department store in the large Eastern city where she lives. At night she works as waitress in Benny's Bar, a hangout "on the Avenue" for the dissolute. Before and after and in between, she's a bustling merchant in the numbers racket.

What made Rosie run? Not having things is one reason. Another is the roach-infested tenement she shares with her grandmother and her mother. But the real impetus comes from the opposing values she learns from the two older women. She's forced to choose between the frank, amoral, earthy world of her hairdresser mother, Queenie, and the aped gentility of her grandmother, who for nearly half a century has been a maid to a rich white family. Granny is a snob who has adopted the most rigid values of her white employers: "For 40 years she's supported Hoover and hated Roosevelt; refused Heinz and insisted on S. S. Pierce; snubbed the Italian help and bobbed her head to the English ones."

But Rosie adores her. The material for daydreams springs from Granny's stories of the rich white and the high life, of her occasional return home in a chauffeur-driven limousine, sometimes laden with cast-off toys, clothes, even leftover food. As she grows to womanhood, Rosie concentrates her ferocious energy on getting money and buying things that will turn her wretched life into luxury.

Miss Hunter, a Negro writer from Philadelphia who is also a teacher and a journalist, views her material at close range. In her hands, Rosie's story assumes tragic proportions. Rosie succeeds in getting things— from a red party dress to a $1,700 crystal bowl; she even manages to